MOR...
BLESS ...

"*Bless Me, Father* is written in the venerable tradition of the urban bust-out tale of young men and women trying to escape the stultifying embrace of 'the neighborhood' without destroying themselves in the process. Immediate comparisons that come to mind are Sidney Kingsley's *Dead End* in theater, Martin Scorsese's *Mean Streets* in film and Vince Patrick's *The Pope of Greenwich Village* in fiction. There are moments in this book, about boxing, about the nature of masculine fear, that are quite unlike anything I've ever read or seen or heard. A solid premiere for Mark Kriegel."
—Richard Price

"Displays a thrilling knowledge of the finer points of fighting, and skillfully conveys the sense of a faded past embedded in the present."
—*The New Yorker*

"Has the power of *Mean Streets* or any of the dark, originating novels of film noir. It explores the world Martin Scorsese has captured on film . . . Kriegel's voice is uniquely his . . . As de-sentimentalized, deglamorized but mesmerizing portrait of the Lower East Side as you will find. It's the turf well south of Don Corleone, and Kriegel, an exceptionally gifted writer, captures it in the urgency of well-handled present tense and in dialogue that simply sounds real . . . Original and unexpected . . . We have been on these particular mean streets often before in film and fiction, but never with quite the same sad and unsparing clarity of vision."
—*Los Angeles Times*

"Kriegel makes a tightly written, fast-paced debut with this novel about a mob lieutenant who witnesses the effects of betrayal and retribution on himself and his sons. Kriegel weaves a tangled web of drama and intrigue, complete with a surprise ending that packs a nice punch. The author also scores heavily with the gritty authenticity of his setting and his well-drawn cast. Mob novels may be a dime a dozen, but this one, heralding the arriving of an unusually talented author, is well worth its full cover price."
—*Publishers Weekly*

Continued . . .

"Kriegel pulls it off . . . impressive."   —*Kirkus Reviews*

"Compelling . . . A remarkable piece of work . . . The situations and characters reek with the flavor and odors of the streets. The story unfolds as if you are peeling an onion. The rhythm and meter of the prose sometimes approach the poetic."
        —*San Antonio Express-News*

"Gritty and absorbing . . . Kriegel displays a keen understanding of what boxing represents. Kriegel knows the streets of New York well, and he masterfully uses the city as a backdrop for a coming-of-age story filled with violent action and plot twists. Still, *Bless Me, Father* is primarily a psychological novel, and in that sense, it reveals as much about boxing as it does about its characters."   —*Ring Magazine*

"*Bless Me, Father* is so satisfyingly written, its descriptions of New York City's Greenwich Village so rich and its characters so engaging, the *Daily News* hardly seems the proper forum for Kriegel's skills. Kriegel maintains his gift for detail, which at times nudges toward genius . . . It's a pity that Kriegel spends so much time and so many words on the Giants and Jets, and not enough with the worlds that await his creation."
        —*The Fan*

"An impressive debut."   —*Forward*

BLESS ME, FATHER

Mark Kriegel

BERKLEY BOOKS, NEW YORK

This novel is a work of fiction. Any references to real people, events, establishments, organizations, or locales are intended only to give the fiction a sense of reality and authenticity. Other names, characters, and incidents are either the product of the author's imagination or are used fictitiously, as are those fictionalized events and incidents that involve real persons and did not occur.

BLESS ME, FATHER

A Berkley Book / published by arrangement with
Doubleday, a division of Bantam Doubleday Dell
Publishing Group, Inc.

PRINTING HISTORY
Doubleday edition / March 1995
Berkley edition / December 1996

All rights reserved.
Copyright © 1995 by Mark Kriegel.
Book design by Casey Hampton.
This book may not be reproduced in whole or in part,
by mimeograph or any other means, without permission.
For information address: Doubleday,
a division of Bantam Doubleday Dell, Inc.,
1540 Broadway, New York, New York 10036.

The Putnam Berkley World Wide Web site address is
http://www.berkley.com/berkley

ISBN: 0-425-15574-9

BERKLEY®
Berkley Books are published by The Berkley Publishing Group,
200 Madison Avenue, New York, New York 10016.
BERKLEY and the "B" design
are trademarks belonging to Berkley Publishing Corporation.

PRINTED IN THE UNITED STATES OF AMERICA

10 9 8 7 6 5 4 3 2 1

For Harriet and Leonard Kriegel—
lovers, parents, myth-cripplers

and in memory of Nicky Sommer and John Cotter

BLESS ME,
FATHER

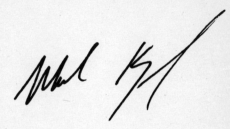

CHAPTER

1

December 1965.

PADDY BLOOD RUNS through the layers of tape and gauze with surgical scissors, splitting the rings with a single, surly slash. He won't even look at the guy, loosening the laces with a quick dip of the fingertips, as if a foul steam were rising from the gloves. Something the old man does not want to touch.

Usually, after a fight, Paddy Blood removes the gloves in a slow, proper ceremony: cutting through the tape, liberating the fingers, allowing the fighter to rediscover his hands. By habit, he will clasp the fighter's hands in his own warm, callused paws. What passes between the fighter and the trainer is almost a caress. Paddy Blood does this for all his guys, win or lose.

But not this one. Not tonight.

This one was never his guy, just another bully with big plans for himself. This one is so vain. He cherishes rituals. His eyes beg for Paddy Blood to do it the right way.

But the trainer refuses to return the fighter's gaze, and leaves without a word. Paddy Blood is ashamed of himself. He should have known better.

FRANK BATTAGLIA watches him go, his face florid, his body stooped. He understands he will never see Paddy Blood again.

Only in his dreams.

He is alone now, in a dressing room on the Fiftieth Street side of the Garden, sitting slumped on the rubbing table. No rubdown tonight. Another privileged ritual he has been denied. He hears voices from the corridor and wants to know what they are saying, what they are saying about him. He wonders if anyone will ever again call Frank Battaglia a tough guy.

The dim light of a bare bulb comes off the pale green walls, casting Frank in a ghastly pallor as he considers himself in the full-length mirror.

He has suffered no outward damage—no bruises, no blood, nothing. It would be much better, Frank thinks, if there were some blood. He presses his knuckles to the soft part of his nose. He considers crushing his own nose. Wonders if he could. If he could get away with it. Nah, they would know. They saw.

They all saw.

He remembers his cousin, Phil Testa, explaining why this fight would be such a great score: "It's gonna be in the Garden. The Garden, Frank. You'll destroy the guy, kill 'im. This yom can't hit for shit. We checked him out. Everybody's gonna be there. The whole neighborhood. Even the Fatman. The Fatman wants to see you fight."

The Fatman.

Frank Battaglia is not even tired, which is strange considering the exhaustion that overcame him in the ring, a gasping, panicked fatigue he had never before known. His greasy duck's ass haircut remains in place. He wonders if he is handsome, if he can ever be. Frank Battaglia thinks of the kids who come to the Village with their long hair. Jerkoffs.

He examines his hands. And wonders why the nigger didn't go down.

Frank Battaglia begins to heave with sobs.

It wasn't supposed to have been like this, his night at the Garden. He had envisioned this evening for so long, pictured it so well, his night, in fantastic, greedy dreams.

Looking through his reflection, Frank Battaglia remembers it now as he will forever:

Everything began properly, exactly as he had imagined. It seems that only a moment ago he was grunting and snorting in front of this very same mirror, working up a good sweat, admiring himself, enjoying the attention.

The dressing room was packed with well-wishers, mostly guys from the neighborhood, guys who wanted to get on his good side. After all, Frank was going places.

Even the Fatman came by, saying he wanted to check on his investment.

"I'm not like most of these people," he had said. "I'm not big on the fights. But you're from the neighborhood. And they tell me you're good, that you got balls. That you got a future."

Frank was very impressed. The Fatman wore a charcoal Chesterfield and gold cuff links. "So I came to see for myself," he said.

"Appreciate it," said Frank. "All you done for me."

Everything was going fine.

Frank was led from the dressing room through a dark corridor, with Paddy Blood walking a pace ahead. The cutman kept his hands on Frank's waist, guiding him toward the ring. The cutman was a wino. Frank could smell the guy, the sweat, cheap booze on his breath.

They reached the arena, momentarily blinded by the bank of overhead lights. It felt as if they were emerging from a deep cave. Cheech DeFranco, Frank's pal from Morton Street, was there to greet them. Cheech was jumping around yelling, "Here comes the next champeen." Cheech was like that, always carrying on like a retard.

Frank looked up, focusing through the glare, taking pleasure in the pungent fog that snaked around the steel girders and hung stagnant over the ring. The translucent vapor smelled of Nedick's hot dogs and Luckies and Garcia y Vega stogies and arnica and sweat.

The wino pushed him through the ropes, and Paddy Blood began to mumble curses under his breath. Frank didn't understand why Paddy had to act so fucking gloomy all the time. He was ruining the occasion. Shit,

Frank Battaglia was part of something big now. That's what he thought looking out from his corner.

Frank could make some of the faces. Politicians. Wiseguys. Reporters. Sure, he was gonna be in the papers. He saw the broads that came with these men. Only classy broads sat ringside. Most of them had blond beehive hairdos. Frank wondered if they had blond pussies, too.

And hey, wasn't that Rocky Graziano?

The Fatman was ringside. So was Cheech, still carrying on like a retard. Cheech sat with Philly Testa. Looking down from his corner, Frank thought Philly must have been very jealous of him. Frank's father was there, too. His old man wore a nubby plaid jacket and a worn tweed cap. Frank was embarrassed to have him sitting in the same row as the Fatman.

Rapid, yelping voices came from the balcony. Spanish. The PR's were taking bets. Frank looked up and saw a dark man in a pale guayabera shirt and white broadbrimmed hat. He was hollering in staccato time, like an auctioneer, flashing the fan of bills in his hand.

"Just you worry about what you gotta do," squawked Paddy Blood. "Combinations." The guy worried so much. Paddy Blood had more fucked-up rules than a priest.

Frank wondered if there was a lot of action on him. He could've kicked himself. He should have put money down. They all do it, bet themselves. All the big guys.

At the Garden, before everyone he had ever known, anyone who mattered, Frank Battaglia was announced as "The Pride of Greenwich Village."

Big hand for Frank.

Then he saw the nigger.

They came together for the referee's instructions. The wino was still breathing in his ear as Frank gave the nigger his hardest look. The nigger looked like he was just waking up. The guy wasn't so big. Or built. Journeyman. Fattened-up light heavy. From Philly. Or Newark. Somewheres where they grow a lot of nigger fighters. Frank Battaglia didn't care. Frank was a tough guy. He'd taken out a lot of niggers before. He'd taken out a lot of guys. Most of the time, he used garbage can lids. Or garrison belts. Or baseball bats.

The neighborhood guys, the wiseguys from the club, the Ninth Ward Rod and Reel on Bedford Street, used to call Frank a crazy kid. Then they got to thinking that he could make a prizefighter. Neighborhood guys are like that. You're a terror in the street, hey, they think you're a natural.

So they went to the Fatman, told him that's what they had—a natural. They told the Fatman about this Paddy Blood; the guy knew what he was doing, knew how to make fighters. The only thing was, Paddy Blood didn't like to play ball, didn't take many kids from the neighborhood, not those kind of kids, anyway. He was a cranky old bastard. But the neighborhood guys explained that if they could just use Fatman's name, then this Paddy Blood would understand.

Frank Battaglia took a last glance at the Fatman. Watched him shift in his seat. Check his watch. Like he was late for something. Frank hoped he would watch him closely. Frank had trained hard. Hadn't fucked any broads in a month. Not even Theresa, which was fine by him because her belly was already out to here, and the thought of fucking her made him a little queasy. He hoped it would be a boy, though. Frank Battaglia wanted to have a kid with his name. A junior.

Dropping to a knee, Frank crossed himself, making a little ceremony.

He could hear the wino's ratchety voice, talking to Paddy Blood: "Someone oughta tell these guys. God ain't got nuthin' ta do with it."

The bell rang. Frank and the nigger began to feel each other out.

The first moments passed like his dreams. Frank felt so strong, and the nigger cooperated. He wasn't so slick. Matter of fact, he walked right into it, Frank's best punch.

Just a looping overhand right. Paddy Blood wasn't wild about it. He said Frank loaded up like a bar bouncer.

Called the punch "primitive." That's the word he used. Paddy was crazy about combinations. More of his rules. But Frank Battaglia threw the big right with rage and power. Cheech, who watched too much rassling on TV, called it "the sleeper," because it put guys to sleep. Nobody ever stood up to that punch.

Frank Battaglia defined himself, his worth, with that right hand.

He hit the nigger good. He could feel it, catching the chin flush. The angle, the leverage—perfect. Through his glove Frank could sense something glorious and gruesome: resistance at the base of the mandible, then, breaking through, a crunch and a pop, releasing gristle from bone. He was sure of what he felt. He was sure.

He broke the nigger's jaw.

Paddy could bitch at him later about the combinations. Fuck that. Cranky old prick.

Funny thing was, after the punch he could hear Paddy yelling, frantic. Screaming out the numbers.

Paddy Blood had this system, identifying the punches and their targets by numbers. Frank was supposed to know the combinations cold, have them memorized like some sort of numerical catechism. But he would forget, get confused. Didn't matter. Frank got in trouble, he always had the big right hand.

But there he was, in the ring, with Paddy screaming: "Seven-seven-two"—double jab, straight right—"Seven-two-one"—jab, straight right, hook.

The numbers meant nothing to him.

The nigger was still coming. A broken jaw and he was still coming.

Frank searched his opponent's face, looking for signs of damage left by the big right hand. But there was nothing. The nigger looked the same as when they started.

He began to hiss at Frank with jabs.

The punches did not hurt so much as they distorted Frank's sense of space and time. A couple of jabs and he felt dizzy. Frank reached back again for this big punch, only to get smacked with another slick jab.

Finally, Frank got off the right. The nigger weaved under and in, doubling up on the hooks, body and head.

Paddy Blood was still yelling numbers, but Frank could no longer hear him. All he could hear was the buzzing murmur of his own fright.

Frank lunged like one of Cheech's rasslers from TV. He held on to the opponent with an awkward bear hug. The fight had just started and Frank Battaglia was more tired than he had ever been.

A scatter of boos ran through the arena. But Frank didn't hear that either. Not until later.

His arms were wrapped around the nigger's trunks, the black guy's arms in a "what, me?" gesture, as the ref approached to separate them. Frank didn't want to let go. He was working on instinct now. He tried to bite the nigger's stomach.

The boos grew louder. A hail of paper popcorn boxes flew into the ring.

Off the break, Frank threw an uppercut, a punch of vicious intention. But not even close.

The nigger began to work him over good, hooks and right hands. Philly Testa was right; all things considered, he couldn't hit much. But that, too, didn't matter. That wasn't the point anymore. Frank could barely breathe. He was paralyzed with panic. The humming in his ears grew louder.

He offered his hands like a punk schoolboy, turning his head from the blows.

Even the ref was confused. He had to order Frank to fight.

More boos. More popcorn. Cigar butts. A beer bottle landed harmlessly in the ring.

Frank Battaglia was gasping. He had no idea three minutes could run into forever.

He went down slowly, almost carefully, limb by limb, like a foal. It was easier that way.

Paddy was still shouting numbers.

The ref began to count. Frank Battaglia looked at him in the way that a boy who has made a mess looks at his mother.

His senses rushed back quickly. The nigger looked in his eyes, mouthing numbers of his own: "eight-nine-ten."

Frank wished he had his boys. And a baseball bat.

HE IS DABBING at his tears when his father walks into the dressing room. Nick Battaglia rushes to embrace his son. "Sshhh," he whispers. The father speaks softly in Italian, telling Frank that everything would be all right, then grabs his son with both hands, by the back of the neck, and pulls him close. "Sshhh."

The father smells like salami. Why did the old man always have to embarrass Frank? He's twenty-one years old. Too old for this. Frank thinks of Paddy Blood yelling out those numbers. That's what messed him up. Got him all confused. Those fucking numbers. Frank couldn't hear himself think.

"C'mon, Dad. Please," he says, shrugging off his father. "Someone could walk in."

Frank hears the voices from the corridor again. Fragments of conversation:

". . . the colored kid kicked his ass."

"Yeah?"

"Sucked his heart out. Kid got enough dog in him to start a kennel."

Frank knows the voice. It's the cutman. Paddy Blood's guy. The fucking wino.

The roar of the main event fills the room as Nick Battaglia opens the door to leave.

Cheech comes in next, all smiles. He's been drinking Southern Comfort. "What happened?" he asks. "I thought you had that yom. Thought you had 'im with the sleeper."

Frank shrugs.

"You miss the count or something?"

"That fucking Paddy Blood," says Frank. "He's yelling all those numbers. I couldn't hear the fucking count, the way he was hollering. Got me all confused."

Now comes Philly Testa. Philly's not smiling from Southern Comfort. He's smiling because he enjoyed it, watching Frank go down. "Fuck it. It's over. Bad night is all," says Philly. "Now let's get laid." Philly produces a roll of bills as his thin smile opens into a big, broad grin.

Frank's eyes narrow as he watches his cousin making a show, rubbing the roll like it warms his hands. It occurs to him now that his cousin might have bet against him. Philly could do shit like that, the cocksucker.

He dresses without a shower, then leaves with Philly and Cheech. The cop in the corridor looks down as Frank approaches. Somebody calls after Frank, "Ya bum. I lost money on ya, ya bum." Frank pretends not to hear. Cheech pretends not to hear. Philly smirks.

"*Maron*, lookada tits on that one," says Cheech, trying to lighten Frank's mood. "Big bazoombas."

They walk through the main lobby, past the statue of Joe Gans, who was a champion about a million years ago, past the Neutral Corner. Tony Janiro tended bar in there.

The way Frank had always imagined this evening's conclusion, Tony Janiro would come from behind the bar, wiping his hands apologetically with a dishrag. "Frank Battaglia," he would say, "yeah, everybody's been talking 'bout you, kid." Frank would shake Janiro's hand and explain that he could only stop in for a quick pop, that he had to be at Toots Shor's, that some newspaper guy wanted to speak with him.

Yeah, Frank had everything figured out.

But now he knows better. He'll never be back at the Garden.

There's all this talk about how they're gonna tear this old place down and build a new one, a new Garden. Modern. Frank can't imagine that. It wouldn't be the same. It wouldn't be as it was supposed to be. What would a new, modern Garden smell like? The inside of a new car?

On the street, Frank looks back one last time. He sees an approximation of his name in strong black letters on the bottom of the marquee. "Frank Bats NY Debut."

Usually undercard fighters don't get their names on the marquee. But this was something different. This was a favor to a friend to a friend, all of it, the entire series of favors, set into motion, underwritten and granted in the good name of the Fatman.

And there he is, sitting in the backseat of his limo, which Frank recognizes as a Lincoln because the doors open ass backward. The Fatman hunches over the seat with his legs dangling into the gutter, his cuff links glittering under the street lamp.

The Fatman crooks a finger and reels Frank in like a fish that died on the line.

"Drop by the place Monday," he croaks. "I got a job for you, piece a work that'll suit you just fine."

CHAPTER

2

May 1977.

FRANK BATTAGLIA WALKS up Carmine Street with his sons. The firstborn, now twelve years old, races ahead, dribbling a basketball into the sunlit Sunday morning. The younger one reaches for his father's hand. He is seven.

Frank does not quite know what to make of him, Nicky, the boy tugging at his arm.

But Nicky will always remember this morning. His father has been away for a long time, on vacation. Nicky knows what the vacation is called—"labor racketeering"—but not what it means.

Nicky pulls the hand close and considers the things that identify his father: the heavy whiff of Aqua Velva, the saint's medallion hanging from his neck, the chest hair protruding from the V in his T-shirt, the big muscles.

"Built," as his father likes to say, "for hooking and clinches." Nicky knows that hooking and clinches have to do with fighting. His father is good at fighting. Nicky decides that his father could beat up all the cops on TV: Baretta, McCloud, Starsky and Hutch together. His father has bigger arms.

"Make a muscle," says Nicky.

The Christ head tattoo on Frank's right bicep is old and

inky and blurred, a watercolor running in shades of purple and black. When Frank makes a muscle, Jesus looks like Bluto from the cartoon. That's how Nicky sees it.

Frank Battaglia walks on, like a barrel with limbs: chest out, arms swinging in cadence with his own insolent march. Like he owns the street. And the people in it.

Alphonse the pork store man rushes out to greet Frank with two big brown grocery bags. The bags are stocked with peaches and plums and plump, red tomatoes and wet mozzarella in cellophane and two bottles of olive oil, one the color of algae, the other Nicky approximates as pale as his morning pee. There are hunks of provolone and prosciutto, coils of sausage, wrinkled logs of soppressata, roasted peppers, a half-gallon container of slippery, fragrant olives. Alphonse, who wears an apron stained with blood, embraces Frank Battaglia, delivers a kiss for both cheeks and another on the lips.

Nicky wonders why some men can kiss and no one will call them fags. He knows what a fag is. His brother told him.

"Good to see you, Frank," says the pork man. "Good to have you back in the neighborhood."

"Good to be back, Al. Good to eat real food. None a that rat shit they serve the niggers. I was about to tell 'em I'm a, whattayoucall, a fucking Muslim. You know what I'm saying, Al? I'm about to tell the guards my name is Frankie X, for chrissakes. Least I coulda ate kosher. Least I coulda ate like half a Jew. Joey Gallo, rest in peace, he goes away makes friends with the yoms. Comes out like some kind of movie star. Like he's some kind of fucking civil rights leader, you know what I'm sayin'? Me? I just wanna eat like a human bein'. *Maron*, you know what I give for a dish of macaroni and sauce? A little fuckin' dish?" He puts his thumb and forefinger close together. "A fuckin' shot-glass full."

"You're home now, Frank. That's what matters. With your family."

"Yeah. I'm home. I got my little one here." The father

smiles, gets into a mock crouch, and throws a playful jab that tousles his Nicky's hair. "I got the other kid here, too," says Frank. "Somewheres."

He hollers ahead to his oldest son. But the boy pretends not to hear; he's busy with his basketball, trying to put it behind his back like Clyde Frazier.

"Hey, stop that silly shit and get your ass over here."

Frank has to holler twice more before the older son eventually ambles over, still trying to dribble the ball behind his back. The boy greets his father blankly, staring through him, locking his gaze on the dead albino rabbits that hang upside down in the window of the butcher store.

"Say hello to the pork man," says Frank.

"Hi."

"This is my son," says Frank. "This is Frank Junior."

"Buddy," says the boy.

"Yeah, we call 'im Buddy."

Frank glares at his namesake. "And this is the baby boy. Nicholas." Still glaring. "We call him Nicky."

"Beautiful boy," says the pork man. "Looks just like his father."

Buddy smirks at his brother, not mean, but funny. Like, what a goof, like Buddy already knows all about this fawning guinea bullshit. At some level, both children must know. Nicky looks nothing like his father. Buddy does. But Nicky? Nicky looks like his mother: dark and slender. His father calls him pretty and it bothers him. He knows that somewhere, somehow, his father interprets these features as an insult. Not correct for a son. Not Frank Battaglia's son, anyway. But when the pork man says he looks like his old man, Nicky beams.

"Pick up the bags," says Frank. "Both a youse."

The boys do as they are told. But Buddy moves grudgingly.

Frank inspects his bags of tribute. "What, no fucking bread?"

Alphonse is back in a moment, falling all over himself, with about a half-dozen fresh loaves, the crusty ones with sesame seeds on top, and as many packs of baseball cards. "For your sons," says the shopkeeper, his eye on Frank as he presses them into the children's hands. "For your sons."

Nicky stuffs the sweet, sugar-dusted gum in his mouth as he shuffles through the cards. He doesn't recognize any of the players' names.

Buddy winks at his kid brother.

"Whatja get?" Nicky asks.

Buddy holds up the card. "Reggie," he says.

Reggie Jackson is Buddy's absolute, all-time, most favorite baseball player.

"I'll trade you," says Nicky.

Buddy shakes his head.

"You can have all my packs," says Nicky. "For one Reggie."

"Nope."

"I'll give you the rest of my gum."

"Uh-uh." Buddy is smiling now.

Frank chimes in: "Lemme see that."

"Buddy got Reggie Jackson."

The father makes a face.

"Smart ass spade," says Frank. "Knocked out a hundred guys like him."

Frank gestures for the boys to put down the groceries, to come closer. He speaks in a conspiratorial whisper. Even his tender moments are illicit collusions.

"I been away for a while," he says. "One day you'll understand. But lemme tell you something. A guy like that, Al the pork man, a neighborhood guy, he remembers." The father made an arc with his forefinger. "They all remember. You know why?"

Nicky shakes his head, a very serious boy. Even at his age, he understands the protocol of deference. Buddy is different, though, unimpressed. Buddy has heard this all before. His thoughts remain with the dead rabbits in the window.

"I'll tell you," says Frank. "'Cause I got respect. That's something you earn. Respect. They remember. All of them. C'mere. I wanna show you something."

Nicky and his father lean together, secret collaborators. The boy now feels part of something big and glorious, a marvelous fraternity, something connected to his father. He feels loved.

Frank pulls a snapshot from his wallet. The photograph is frayed and old, faded to shades of purple and brown.

Buddy has seen the picture before. There is no reason to check it out again. He stands off to the side, wondering if the dead rabbits are born with red eyes, those frozen scarlet splotches, or if that happens at the moment of death.

Nicky is enthralled. The photograph is creased with lines that look like cracks running through a mirror, but Nicky can make out a young man with a big straight nose posing dukes up. His stomach is almost flat, his hair slicked in a long, greasy duck's ass style. Nicky can detect nothing delicate about the man in the picture.

"Who's that?" asks Frank Battaglia.

Now Buddy is trying to say something to his brother, to silently mouth the correct answer. But Nicky doesn't understand what his brother is trying to tell him. He hesitates before answering. "Uncle Philly?" he says finally. Buddy rolls his eyes, and Nicky wants to take it back. He knows he said something wrong.

Frank's expression curls quickly into a snarl. He gives the kid a few smacks. Not too hard, after all, Nicky was just a kid. But hard enough for the kid to know he had made a mistake. About something important.

Nicky cowers before his father. He puts up his hands and looks away, his reflex to soften the blows. One of the grocery bags falls over. Tomatoes roll into the gutter.

"Uncle Philly carried my water. You hear what I'm sayin', Nicky? Phil couldn't fight for shit. Could never. It was me who did the fighting. Always. Just like it's me in this picture."

Nicky feels bad about his mistake, embarrassed, frightened of his father's quick rage, but also a bit guilty, too. He tries not to whimper as Buddy gathers the tomatoes and puts the bag back in order. Buddy hands him the bag, and the card, too, pressing Reggie Jackson into his palm. "I was trying to tell you," Buddy whispers.

The boys follow their father home. Frank Battaglia softens quickly. By the time they got to the tenement on Bedford Street, his voice is gentle again. He is talking to Nicky, but he might as well be speaking to himself: "That's me in the picture, me. I was a kid. Frankie Batts of Bedford Street. The Bedford Brawler.

"Now c'mere and gimme a kiss."

Nicky does as he is told.

CHAPTER

3

June 1986.

OUR LADY OF the Most Precious Blood.

The altar is awash in a high tide of floral arrangements, the best money can buy. The organ hums a dirge as a priest keeps time with the soft, ordinary melody by shaking the urn. Frankincense vapor wafts through the sanctuary, that sickly sweet bouquet moving like a ghost, until the air is choking thick.

Until Nicky Battaglia thinks he will vomit.

His brother is dead. His big brother. Frank Battaglia, Jr., known as Buddy, dove off the roof. Nicky didn't see it. He was told.

His father told him.

"I know this is hard," his father had said. "But it's better this way. Your brother wasn't right. Hadn't been right for a long time, really. There's reasons for everything, Nicky. And now there's a reason for you to be strong."

Nicky knew what his father was trying to say. He was sixteen, old enough to understand.

The holy smoke curls through the church to the slow sound of the organ. Nicky feels it crawl up his spine like a spider.

A tremor runs through his blood. Fear. Fear so great it awakens him from the grief.

Nicky loved his brother more than anyone in the world. Even if he wasn't right.

Who would protect him now?

A terrible shrill voice echoes through the church, interrupting the funeral mass: "Take me. Take me, God. Take me instead." His mother. "Not my baby," she wails. "Take me. Jesus. God. Please, God, kill me."

Nicky prays for Jesus Christ to come down off his cross, to come to life right here in Our Lady of the Most Precious Blood on Carmine Street, where he had been an altar boy, where his mother sent him to confession, and where, usually during weddings, he acquired uncontrollably persistent hard-ons while daydreaming of the centerfold girls who lived under his mattress.

He looks up at the white marble statue above the pulpit, more enormous than ever: Jesus Christ poised like a wounded condor, tilted forward, arms splayed. Nicky waits for Christ's head to snap to attention, for him to come down and save his mother. But Christ does nothing. And neither does this Irish priest.

His mother's howl grows louder, crazier, more frightening. She rushes the casket, which, in deference to all, remains closed. She wants to dive in. A half-dozen guys from Philly Testa's crew form a barrier at the pulpit, preventing her. The task requires unaccustomed care and tact. The gangsters are tense and awkward, except for Tommy Sick. Nicky watches him, Tommy Sick like a bug-eyed sentry up there, like he thinks he's doing the right thing. Nicky hates him. Wishes it were Tommy Sick's funeral.

Philly Testa tries to cradle his cousin Frank's wife. "My baby," she sobs. "Poor baby, my baby."

And the priest keeps on like it's nothing, another civil servant in robes. *Spirito Santi*, and all that, like he's taking money at a toll.

"In the name of the father . . ."

Nicky moves his lips in sync with the priest.

". . . and the son . . ."

As if the lines are from his deepest sleep.

". . . and of the holy ghost. . . ."

He wishes Vinny Ruggiero were saying the mass

instead of this priest, this stranger. His father said they had to take whatever priest they got, that he had to pull enough strings just to have a mass for Buddy in the church, said that he didn't want to hear another word about the Fatman's nephew, goddamn Vinny Ruggiero.

Still, Nicky thinks Vinny should do the mass. That's how it should be. That's how Buddy would have wanted it. Nicky is sure of that. Vinny was Buddy's best friend.

He was a few years older than Buddy, but they hung out anyways. Vinny was a good guy, nice, maybe a little strange. He went to college, but he still hung out. Buddy got a kick out of Vinny. Then, after Buddy got jammed up, the first time, the bad time, Vinny split. Went to the seminary. Nicky thought that was a little wacky, you couldn't fuck girls and all. But that was Vinny, real serious. That was what, more than four years ago now, spring of '82? All the hard-core neighborhood guys called Vinny a hippie priest and half a fag and a social worker. They didn't care for him much after that, especially Nicky's father. His old man couldn't stand Vinny, despised him with a passion, priest or no priest.

His father. Where is his father?

Nicky rises from the pew to look around, tears welling up in his eyes. Then he runs. He runs from the sanctuary, back down the aisle, searching.

Nicky finds his father hiding in the bathroom.

"Ma's crying," he says.

Theresa Battaglia's obscenely painful bawl invades the toilet stall. There is no safe place. Her call is a curse, and both of them, father and son, understand that.

Frank Battaglia rocks back and forth on the toilet seat. In time—and to Nicky it seems a long, long time—he looks up, ashen with grief, but also with fear. His knuckles are bloody. He's gnawed through the skin.

Nicky wants his father to hold him. He wants his embrace, his strength, his arrogant, confident, violent assurance. But it's not there. Not for Nicky. Frank Battaglia looks through the boy, the son who has discovered his fear. And for this moment, this moment alone, they will never forgive each other.

CHAPTER

4

A WEEK LATER, Alphonse Garguilo, the pork man, arrives at the Ninth Ward Rod and Reel for his regularly scheduled delivery. He stands at the door in his blood-stained apron, holding two bags of groceries. Frank and Philly don't look like they want to be disturbed. They're having a talk, back and forth over the bare card table, their voices muted by scratchy melodies from the transistor radio, set to the "Perry Como Station," as Frank calls it. The pork man waits until Philly puts on a smile and waves him in.

"Howya doin'?"

The pork man nods, his eyes darting furtively as he goes to stock the refrigerator behind the bar. Frank calls after him.

"You got good veal this time? I was thinking Cheech could cook up some veal Oscar."

The pork man nods again.

"What the fuck," Frank mumbles. Guy's a nervous wreck.

"How's the restaurant coming?" asks Philly.

"Good," says the pork man. "Good, good. Almost done."

Besides his pork store and his butcher shop, Alphonse

Garguilo also owns a red sauce joint on Thompson Street. Frank and Philly have been going there for years. But the pork man closed it a while back, said it needed "remodeling," said he needed new customers to pay the bills. The pork man went to Frank for a loan. Frank was only too happy to help.

"What's it gonna look like?" asks Philly. "The inside, I mean."

"Nice," says the pork man. "Upscale."

"Upscale. That sounds good," says Frank. "Only don't get no fag waiters. Not like these other places."

The pork man stocks the refrigerator and the cupboards in silence, then waits to be excused.

"Thanks, Al," says Philly. "Tell me when your joint is ready. We'll give it the old taste test."

"Yes," says the pork man, hurrying out. "Yes. Good."

When he is gone, Philly says, "What's the matter with him?"

"Whatta you think?" says Frank. "His kid."

"His kid?"

"Johnny Bump. From Cornelia Street."

"That was his kid? That fucking Johnny Bump from Cornelia Street?"

"What, there's an echo in here? That's what I said. Johnny Bump from Cornelia Street."

"Jesus," Philly said quietly. "I didn't know. I mean, I must not a been thinking about it like that."

"Of course," says Frank. "You got important things to worry about."

"Christ. What's the world coming to?"

"Whattaya mean, what's the world coming to? You gave the order."

"It wasn't me," says Philly. "It was Fatman."

"Well, what the fuck are we here talking about?"

"I told you," Philly says firmly. "I don't wanna get into that. Too hot . . . Jesus, Frank. That's too fucking bad. Johnny Bump from Cornelia Street. No wonder the old guy's upset."

"I don't like how he looks at us. Beady eyes."

"You think he knows?"

"What can he know? He knows what the whole fucking neighborhood knows. Johnny Bump was a wannabe, another junkie drug addict got busted." Frank looks over at the radio, making sure the volume on the Perry Como station is sufficiently loud. "Thing was, I'll tell you what, he wasn't a bad earner. Two baskets of fruit, *capisce*? Feds had a undercover, the whole fucking bit. And those whattayoucallit, they got those mandatory minimums. They tell Johnny Bump he's going away with Leroy for the rest of his life, Johnny Bump folds right up like the junkie he is. They put him back on the street to be a rat. No character, that kid. That's what the old man knows. Same as everybody."

"Tell me about the, you know, the arrangements."

"*Ming*, this is weeks, more'n a fucking month ago, Philly. Now you're asking?"

"I told you, I forgot. I just wanna be straight with the details. In case it ever comes up."

"What, with Fatman?"

"With whoever."

Frank shrugs. "I used that crazy one. You know who I'm talking about. One a those crazy Irish kids. From the West Side."

"We been using them a lot."

"Sure. You said so yourself. There's a lot of things you don't want to get close to. Too hot, remember? These kids do a job. All the unions: the carpenters, the dockworkers, plumbers, painters, you name it. You got these greasy Irish kids, you just let 'em loose when the time's right. And you got no connection. It's like having a whole pack of wolves at your disposal. And this one, this one is like the head wolf. He likes it. This crazy fuck enjoys it, hurting people."

"Yeah, well, how come you know him so good?"

"From the gym, over at Costello's. He ain't a fighter, he just works out, likes to stay in shape. That's what he says. You gotta see him in the ring. A vicious fuck. Dirty as shit."

"He the one with the eye?" asks Philly.

"That's him," says Frank. "You see him?"

"I think."

"Guy got a tattoo right over his eye. A knife, right, like a dagger, you know, the handle over his eye and the blade below, then he got like drops of blood coming off the point of the blade. Looks like he's crying. One time I ask him why he got that. He says 'cause he only uses a knife, like, remember those stilettos, from when we was kids?"

"Right."

"That's what he uses."

"No shit."

"Says he likes to get close."

"Is the guy, blond hair, real blond, like almost white?"

"That's him."

"He the one they tell that story about?"

"From when he was in Attica?"

"Yeah."

"That's all true. One a the yoms in the yard calls him a white devil or some shit. So they get going. And this crazy fuck, he bites the nigger's ear off."

"He is a white devil."

"Then he makes Leroy suck his dick," says Frank. "Right there in the yard." Frank loves telling the story.

"Fucking maniac."

"You're telling me. Guy gives me the creeps. I go see him, to tell him about the job. I meet him in this bar on the West Side. Dingy fucking place. I'm talking to him, telling him what he gotta do, with Johnny Bump I mean. He says, 'No problem,' then he takes out a Black Beauty, right, taps it out in his beer, drinks it. A fucking lunatic."

"And you trust these guys? You trust him?"

"I'll tell you what, Philly, they all wanna be tough guys. Like they all walked out of the same movie. They all wanna prove something to us. But one thing about these crazy Irish kids, they're loyal. I told you. Like dogs."

"I hate dogs," says Philly.

"Well, they like you. Guy says to me. 'When can I meet the boss?'"

"What you tell him?"

"I told him, 'What, I ain't good enough? First, I gotta see how you work.'"

"So he did the Johnny Bump with a knife."

"Sure. I tell him, just leave it somewhere's I can find it. So's I can see your work. So this crazy maniac leaves Johnny Bump in a meat locker. Guy's frozen stiff. A Popsicle."

"This is more than I wanna know, Frank."

"Well, speak to your pal Fatman about that. He's the one costing us money. That fat cocksucker."

"He deserved better."

"Johnny Bump? The kid was a rat for all we know."

"No, the pork man, the father. He deserved better."

"We all do."

"You're right. I'm sorry. I guess I'm like blocking things out again. How you holding up?"

"I told you, I'm all right. I don't mean to be cold-hearted or nothing, but things happen for a reason, Philly. I'll be honest, my kid's dead. Buddy's dead. It grieves me. But really, you ain't blocking it out and neither am I. If you think about it, I lost Buddy a long time ago."

Frank's face has gone pale. He remembers one time, when Buddy went on one of his lunatic episodes, how he told Frank he had special scissors to cut out his eyes. "He wasn't right, Phil. Buddy was what you call a problem kid."

"I know. I'm sorry."

"Wasn't your fault."

"Guess all you can do now is be there for Nicky. He doing okay?"

"You know him. He keeps everything inside."

"It's gotta be tough, Frank."

"Yeah, but the kid gotta be tougher. I been thinking about taking him over to Costello's. Maybe put him in the Gloves."

"Why you gonna do that, Frank? The kid, he ain't a fighter."

"You telling me how to raise my kids?"

"Nah, Frank. I just wish I had one a my own."

"Look, this ain't what I came here to talk about."

Now Cheech DeFranco walks in the club. "Look what I got," he says, holding framed movie posters, one in each hand, showing them off like trophies.

Right hand: *Scarface*, 1932, Paul Muni and George Raft.

Left hand: *Public Enemy*, 1931. Cagney.

"Nice, huh?"

Frank and Philly share a look, vaguely amused. Retard, they think. All these years, guy still acts like a retard.

Cheech points at the wall, toward Richard Widmark in *Kiss of Death."*

"I been thinking," he says. "The poor bastard needs company."

None of them—Frank, Philly, or Cheech—are old enough to remember much of 1947, the year *Kiss of Death* made its first run in the theaters. But they have seized upon the picture and its villain, Tommy Udo, as nostalgia: a sign of better, simpler times, like a ballplayer or a crooner they had heard older guys memorialize on the corner. Each of them had well-rehearsed, gut-busting renditions of Richard Widmark playing Tommy Udo, throwing that old lady in the wheelchair down a flight of steps.

Richard Widmark has been up on the wall nearly twenty years, since Frank and Philly took over the Rod and Reel, made it their place. They thought Richard Widmark added a little class to the joint. A little color.

Other than that, the Ninth Ward Rod and Reel Club— the name being apropos of nothing but an affectation, both comic and long-ago—looks much as it always has. A 1952 photograph of Rocky Marciano knocking out Jersey Joe Walcott remained in the bathroom. Every time Frank takes a piss he finds himself studying Marciano's gloved fist against Walcott's jaw, pressing the mouth into some sort of sinister fruit. As he pulls the chain to flush, Frank can always hear Philly busting his chops, telling him, "That's the last time an Italian knocked out a nigger."

A dim, dusty capsule, the Rod and Reel seems untouched by time: imitation-walnut paneling, folding chairs, and a card table for games of pinochle and scoop. Most of the conspiracies are hatched with Frank and Philly at the card table and the old transistor tuned to the Perry Como station. A tin-framed portrait of Jimmy Roselli hangs on the wall opposite Richard Widmark. There's a felt forty-eight-state flag over the espresso bar and a bottle of Johnnie Walker Black off to the side. That's about as colorful as it gets.

Until now. Cheech is redecorating, deciding whether it's George Raft or Cagney who should get the honor of spending eternity as Richard Wimark's "right-hand man." He looks through his hands as if they form a lens: arms outstretched, palms out, shutting one eye, then the other.

"Can I turn the radio down?" he asks. "I can't hear myself think."

"Cheech," Frank says softly. "What's the matter with you? We're talking."

Irritated, Frank returns to the conversation. His conversation.

"So anyways," he says, "I gotta be honest. That's how I feel about it."

Philly smiles, his eyes distant, watching Cheech redecorate. "That's how you feel about it, huh?"

They have been through this before. Many times. The only difference now is Frank's sense of urgency. Like there's a rush all of a sudden.

Frank wants to make a move on the Fatman. He has his reasons, born of infected ambition, his scheme of the world, and how things should have been. Some of the reasons seem ancient now, unclear even to himself. But Frank doesn't get into all that. Presenting his argument to Philly, he uses only the expedient justifications, summarized with the fingers of his right hand.

Pinky: "He's a greedy cocksucker. Selfish."

Philly is unimpressed. Greedy cocksucker could apply to anyone they know.

Ring finger: "Guy puts on airs. Like he's some kind of gentleman, and everybody else is shit. He lives on Central Park West. What is that?"

"I like to live there myself," says Philly. "I'd like to have a doorman."

"Bullshit. Fatman wants to get out of the neighborhood, good for him. Only why can't he go someplace normal. Howard Beach, Staten Island, Jersey for chrissakes?"

Philly just smiles. He plays all the angles. It's times like this that make Frank wonder if Philly wants to be just like the Fatman. After all, Fatman made Philly boss of the neighborhood.

And left Frank holding his dick to the wind.

Fuckfinger: "Every time one a these young kids gets jammed up with a basket of fruit"—a kilo of cocaine— "Fatman makes like you gotta dispose a the poor bastard."

"That's the way he is," says Philly. "Old-fashioned. Says we got enough cowboys already."

"No drugs," says Frank. "Like his words, they should be carved in stone."

"He's old," Philly shrugs, smiling. Like it's funny. Like it's a goof to get Frank all worked up.

"Who the fuck is he? The Pope? You want to kill drug dealers, fine, start with all these niggers in the street dealing that crazy shit. Whatta they call it, crack? Crack of my ass crack. I see these little fuckin' vials on my stoop in the morning. I ask my kid, I ask Nicky, 'What is that?' 'Crack,' he says. He says even these white kids smoke it."

"Let it go, Frank."

Frank should know better. He's been saying things even the Perry Como music cannot disguise. But Frank has to push, to test. "Is that a good way to haveta run things?" He jerks his thumb in Cheech's direction. "Have to send him out to do your own guys?"

"Leave it alone, Frank."

But he can't. "Bad enough we hadda get the crazy Irish kid to do Johnny Bump. Next thing you know, you'll be sending Cheech out to do Tommy Sick. You wanna do that? You want that on your conscience? *Ming.* I sure as hell don't. Tommy Sick and those kids are good earners."

The smile leaves Philly's face as his eyes narrow.

"You're grieving, Frank," he says. "You're still sick over Buddy."

"Nah. It ain't that. You know it ain't that."

Philly watches Cheech hanging the pictures. The grin returns to his face.

Good, Frank thinks. Let him. Let him smile. He can tell it won't take much to get Philly to go along. Do the Fatman and Philly becomes the boss. Boss of the whole city.

Philly says, "You're gonna love what I gotta tell you."

"What?"

"Fatman got a girl, he wants you to give her an apartment."

"What? He got a girl? He don't even have a dick . . . You heard that?"

"I heard that, and maybe he don't have a dick. But he got a girl."

"White girl?" asks Frank.

Philly nods, in approval as much as agreement.

"Why me?"

"Why you? How the fuck do I know why you? He said she wants to live in the Village. She's a young girl, she wants to live in the Village. Apartments are hard to find. I guess he knows you got a place open. I guess that's why. He says to me, he says, 'Tell your guy, tell that Frank to get her a place.' Said she needs it right away."

"This ain't right," says Frank, watching Cheech banging a nail into the wall. Scarface will be Tommy Udo's right-hand man. "She needs it right away? The greedy cocksucker can't axe me to my face?"

Philly just smiles.

"Fatman's fucking her?"

"Why don't you ask him to his face?" says Philly.

Look at him, Frank thinks: smiling at me like I'm an innkeeper for the Fatman's hoowas. Shit, the old bastard's dick don't even work.

The table, the transistor radio, the bottle of Johnnie Walker Black, the Jimmy Roselli picture, all of it shakes as Cheech drives nails into the wall.

"What are you, a fucking retard?" Frank screams. "Can't you keep it down."

Philly excuses himself. "I'll see youse later."

Frank does not acknowledge him. He's too busy thinking, getting himself worked up.

He would have to give this girl, the Fatman's girl, the old Doyle apartment. That is the only way. But that don't make it right. It bothers him. The principle of it bothers him. The apartment is his. The whole fucking building is his.

Supposed to be anyway.

Frank Battaglia and his sons have lived their entire lives in the building on Bedford Street: a railroad flat built of rough red brick, rusted iron fire escapes, forgotten dumbwaiter cavities. The tenement is an inheritance for immigrant generations and their children: the Battaglias and the Giovanellis and the Cardinales of Sicily, the Doyles of Dublin, all in one way or another, scions of steerage classes. *Ming*, Frank can remember when Italians didn't even count as white people.

Now all that's left of the old country, wherever that may be, are the widows, women with crooked fingers and lined faces, spending the dwindling balance of their lives in sweaters, oblivious to the heat, sitting in folding chairs by the stoop, feeding the pigeons. The old ladies were dying off fast.

But Frank is good to them. That makes him proud. That's how it's supposed to be, he figures, especially for a guy in his position. He takes care of their bills, has Cheech drive them to St. Vincent's when they get sick, and back to the block the ones who hang on. Those who don't, Frank pays for their funerals, even for Mrs. Doyle, who came from a family of Irish pickpocket gypsies. Tinkers, they're called. Frank can't stand them. Fucking Irish. They boil steaks, Jews do the same thing. But at least Jews *understand* they can't cook. At least Jews go to restaurants.

Mrs. Doyle died in Apartment 1A. Just let go in the steamy bogs of her sleep. Her apartment now belongs to Frank. That is the rule. After they die, the set of rooms where they raised their American children becomes his. That should give Frank four of the eight apartments in the building. The two on the top floor, the fourth, are for him and his family. After his parents died, he knocked down the walls and gave the rooms to the kids. Nicky and Buddy.

When Buddy got sick, he put him in the old Cardinale apartment on the second floor. He tried with the kid. He really tried. But Buddy just kept getting worse. It got so that Frank didn't want to see him around. Like he wasn't even his son anymore. There was no telling what the kid might do. The sickness and all. That dead look in his eyes put the fear of God into Frank.

Frank wasn't bullshitting when he told Philly that he had come to terms with what happened to Buddy. It didn't make him coldhearted. His kid went wacko. Buddy just couldn't hack it anymore. And the truth is, neither could Frank. Shit, there was reasons for everything. Besides, Frank told himself, how would it look?

That whole thing with Buddy, what a goddamn mess. Frank had to tip everybody, the cop from the precinct, the clerk from the medical examiner's office, the guy from the funeral home, the fucking Irish priest. In a way, it was just like everything else: you had to keep up appearances. Had to do what was right. Keep it quiet. Try to make things like they ought to be. Something like that.

What the fuck.

Frank did what he had to do.

What he could justify as right.

He thinks again about the Fatman and this girl. The Fatman telling him, through Philly, to give up what's his.

That's the justification Frank Battaglia wants, needs. It's the right thing, he tells himself.

"Cheech, kill the Perry Como music."

CHAPTER

5

FRITZY, THE FATMAN'S driver, gets out first. Walks around the Mercedes limo to open the door.

Frank can't see her yet. He's sitting on the stoop, his stoop, sucking a toothpick, giving his best I-could-give-a-shit look. Like he's been sitting on this stoop for twenty years. Like nothing has ever changed. Fritzy walks toward him wearing a black suit.

Fucking chauffeur. Errand boy. That's what Frank thinks as he rolls the toothpick in his mouth.

Frank waits until he is covered in Fritzy's shadow, then looks up, fixing his eyes on Fritzy's. Telling Fritzy to speak.

"Where you gonna put her?" he asks. Fritzy has armfuls of this girl's shit.

Frank works the toothpick. "You like what you're doin'?"

Fritzy makes a face: C'mon, gimme a break. Not here. Don't embarrass me.

"Who made you the errand boy?"

A hint of capitulation works its way across Fritzy's sweaty brow. "What am I gonna do, Frank?" he asks. "What the fuck am I gonna do?"

Real good, Frank thinks. He can sense the weakness.

"Where you gonna put her, Frank?"

"One-A," he says, looking past Fritzy. "First one in the door."

He can see her now.

The girl is walking toward him.

And she makes up his mind. Right then. For good. For real. Of all his reasons, she seems the best, the most immediate. He sees the girl and figures he might even do the selfish prick himself.

Fritzy helps her with her things. She doesn't have that much. Clothes, crates of books, canvas paintings stretched over wood frames.

Frank flexes as she passes.

He tries not to look. Doesn't want to seem interested. But he is.

She's wearing washed-out jeans that are too big for her skinny little ass, no tits—Cheech would get a laugh at that—no makeup, at least none that he can see, red cowboy boots, a faded Häagen-Dazs T-shirt. Rum Raisin.

I like to get in her rum raisin, he says to himself.

He can't believe the greedy, selfish, no-dick Fatman is fucking this broad—and telling Frank to get her a place. Giving her what's his. What should be his.

The notion fills him with a murderous rage.

He wants to bang this girl. In the worst way.

Frank is brooding on the stoop when he feels a tap at his shoulder.

"I just want to thank you," she says, holding a milk crate stuffed with books. "I mean, when Sal told me . . . well, it's just really nice of you."

"No problem." Frank winks at her, but does not get off the stoop.

She smiles at him and walks back to the limo. She likes him, he thinks. Girls like that liked guys like him. You know, opposites attract. They want something they can't get where they're from. Girls like that, come off like Polly Purebred, really wanted you to fuck them in the ass. Sure.

He sizes her up: good-looking, blonde, well sort of. Whatever, it's a natural color. Frank tries to remember if he ever screwed a natural blonde. He must have. But just can't think of one.

He's got this *goumare*, Tina, Tina what the fuck was her name. She was an unnatural blonde. She can fuck. But so what? It gives him no sense of achievement.

And his wife. How did he ever get mixed up with her? He remembers when she told him she was pregnant. What, was that the night of the fight? He can't even remember anymore. But he remembers her crying. Crying, crying. Like he didn't know. She was already fat in the belly. Theresa. She was no good. Not anymore.

He's watching the girl now.

And so is Nicky, who ambles over, bouncing a basketball.

"Where you been?"

"Playing ball," he says. "Over by Thirteen Street."

Frank makes a face. He doesn't like all this basketball shit. He hears his kid's supposed to be a good ballplayer. But he doesn't like it.

Frank wants his kid to be a fighter. He wants him to fight in the Golden Gloves next April at the Garden. Frank has never seen Nicky in a fight, but can already imagine a headline in the paper: CHIP OFF THE OLD BLOCK.

That would be something, huh?

"Basketball. Later for that. You just be ready for tomorrow."

"I been waiting to talk to you about that."

"What's to talk about?"

Frank thinks about his son in the ring, how he'll do. Nicky's a good athlete. But the kid's a pussy. And it bothers Frank to think that of his son. He knows the kid is in some pain, what with Buddy and all. But hey, that's just how it is. Nicky was gonna have to grow up. It was time. Things were about to change.

Frank watches his skinny son watching the girl, bouncing the ball all absent-minded, starting to walk toward her as if he's alone in a dream. Look at him; the kid doesn't have a clue.

But already, Nicky sees this girl better than his father ever will, discerning the faint rusty hue in her hair, the spray of tiny, tobacco-colored flecks across her cheeks. The interplay of flesh and bone, lissome but never lush: the delicate slope of her neck, a clavicle that seems as fragile as the stem of a teacup, and breasts the shape of a small shark's snout.

Nicky approaches without knowing what to say. He just wants to get close enough to pick up her scent.

"I'm Sam," she says.

"Sam?"

"Samantha."

"Samantha."

Nicky picks up the whiff of warm sugar. Like a bakery, he thinks.

She giggles as he introduces himself.

He's just staring at her.

"Hey, what are you?" Frank yells from the stoop. "Some kinda animal?"

CHAPTER

6

ALMOST DUSK AND the day's heat is gone, the cooling tar on the roof like a mat under his feet, muffling his steps. Nicky walks to the ledge, props his arms against the glazed terra-cotta molding, and leans over the side. His gaze begins with secret deposits of pigeon shit on the catwalk of the fire escape and ends at the brownstone across the alley. He can see through the great frame windows into the splendid ground-floor apartment: high walls lined with bookshelves, fireplace, quilted chairs with little wooden legs, a large, framed red poster splashed with a big French word, and plunging from the ceiling, a lamp, its Tiffany shade made from bright bits of cut, colored glass. In the backyard: vines, beds of little red flowers, and wrought-iron furniture cast in squiggly decorative patterns and painted white. There is also a child's toy, a Big Wheel tricycle.

Nicky wonders who lives there. Whose Big Wheel that is. But the thought passes quickly.

That's not what Nicky came up here for.

He wants to see what Buddy saw.

The backyard ends at a chain-link fence topped with a rim of barbed wire, his father's idea. Beneath the fence, dropping maybe six feet beneath the garden level, was the tenement's alley: rough concrete, gray metal garbage cans, a drain, and more pigeon shit.

As kids, the alley served as a jail for their games of ring-a-lario. Once, when they were playing, Nicky found his brother on the roof. He had never captured Buddy in ring-a-lario, and as Nicky ran to him, it became clear that he never would. Buddy began to laugh, then hopped over the ledge, still laughing, as if Buddy would rather jump off the roof than go to the jail, rather die than get caught by his kid brother in a game of ring-a-lario. Nicky hollered his brother's name as he ran to the ledge. The tears already welling up as he peered over the side, seeing nothing in the alley, wondering if maybe Buddy had super secret powers that enabled him to vanish, hoping, praying that he did, then hearing Buddy's giddy laugh, Buddy crouched against the wall on the rusty fire escape beneath him, Buddy teasing his brother, "You still never got me, Nicky . . ."

And now, Nicky wants to believe Buddy has merely vanished again, that he's laughing on the fire escape somewhere. He looks down into the alley. There is no chalk outline, like in the movies, to mark the spot. Yeah, but it wasn't like Buddy was murdered, they only do that when you get murdered. Nicky figures that all signs of his brother's end—the mess of blood and brains, of guts—were washed away with a garden hose.

Tears stream down his cheek. The alley remains still. Buddy swore he fucked Mary Rocca—Mary Missile Titties, was what everybody called her—in this very same alley. Nicky never knew if Buddy was telling the truth. But now he can imagine it, Buddy fucking Mary Missile Titties, as he begins to pop a boner himself, visualizing Buddy pushing her up against the brick wall underneath the fence, his arms curling under her thighs like muscular serpents, gathering himself, lifting Mary Missile Titties, her feet now free of the ground, exhaling as he enters her, then Buddy humping away, quickly, as if he were stealing something.

That's how it must have been.

A long time ago.

Before Buddy got sick.

Before he dove off the roof.

Nicky was out playing ball when it happened.

His father was waiting on the stoop when he got back from Thompson Street Park.

His father said, "It's better this way. Your brother wasn't right."

Frank Battaglia held his son close, his grip tightening, preventing Nicky from running into the alley. Frank Battaglia mumbled to himself he was only protecting the kid. Nicky could smell the Aqua Velva.

"You can't go in there," his father said. "Give your father a kiss. Give me a kiss . . . for Buddy."

He hadn't heard his father speak the name, Buddy, in a while. Most of the time, Frank Battaglia referred to his eldest son as "that fucking zombie."

On the stoop, Nicky did as he was told.

Gave his father a kiss. Nicky wanted to make him proud.

Buddy had been living like a zombie, living dead ever since he came home from the jail, the real one at Rikers Island.

But Nicky could feel everything change right there on the stoop.

Buddy dying made it official. His failed obligations—as firstborn, as the father's namesake—now fell to Nicky. It was very clear.

That's what all this boxing shit was all about, being a man and all that. His father would bother him about it, saying, "You're gonna learn how to fight. I'm putting you in the Gloves."

Frank Battaglia ran those lines all the time. Swore up and down that the very next day he was gonna take the kid to Costello's gym, toughen him up, put him in the Gloves.

The thing was, those very next days never seemed to arrive. Frank was always busy: at the club, the union, maybe with one of his girlfriends. The thought would leave as quickly as it came, which was just fine with Nicky.

But in these days since Buddy went off the roof, Frank Battaglia has become insistent: "You gotta go in the ring now, Nicky. I gotta make a man outta you."

Nicky knows he's running out of very next days.

And all he can think of is getting hit, how he doesn't want to get smacked. Fuck that. His old man smacks him enough.

Boxing builds character, his father would say.

That's how you build character, huh, by getting smacked?

Buddy never smacked him. Not once.

Buddy was his protector.

In his memory, the concrete alley becomes a big blue pool. Nicky can smell the suntan lotion. He can recall perfectly now . . .

The family is at the pool of the Diplomat Hotel in Florida. Frank Battaglia likes to come here for vacation, says it has class, that all these garmento Jews can't be wrong. Nicky's five years old and afraid of the water. His mother holds him in the pool, her arms around his belly. Nicky flutters about in the water. His eyes are closed, his head turned to the side, his face a sour spasm, as if he's been forced to suck a lemon.

Frank Battaglia approaches, belly out, a swing in his shoulders, carrying an umbrella-garnished cocktail. "Let 'im go, Theresa," he yells at his wife, laying the drink on the cabana table. "I'm gonna teach him how to swim."

"He's doin' fine, Frankie. Really."

"C'mere." Frank pulls Nicky from the pool. "You're gonna swim, Nicky. I'm gonna show you how."

Frank Battaglia carries his son alongside the pool, toward the deeper water. "I'm gonna show ya."

Nicky can hear his mother. She can whine and holler at the same time. "Fraaaannn-kkeeee."

"Don't you lissen a her," says Frank, stroking his son's wet hair. "You gonna swim great."

Next thing he knows, Nicky is flying through the air like a sack of laundry, crashing ass-first into the deep water. The water fills his lungs, scorches his nostrils. An eternity of panic passed before Nicky arrives by frantic doggie paddle at the pool's rough lip. There, he begins to spit up water, to shudder and hiccup. Nicky wipes the snot from his face and begins to cry.

"See," says Frank, sipping from his umbrella drink. "See what I mean, Theresa? The kid could swim the whole time. He ain't ascared no more."

In the foreground, Nicky sees his brother, who is ten years old, begin his charge, howling as he comes. Nicky recognizes the look on Buddy's face: the pure, quick rage, oblivious to consequence, the look that frightens Nicky, whose intuition tells him that Buddy is challenging the natural order of things, that his charge is inexorable, and that it leads toward something very bad.

Buddy hurtles on, lowering his head and shoulders, exploding against the fleshy sidewall underneath Frank Battaglia's ribs, catching him from behind, surprising him, driving him into the water . . .

And up on the roof, as his remembrance ends, the spider crawls up Nicky's back again. Just like that. Just like it did in the church.

"Buddy," he screams. Desperate. Like that day they were playing ring-a-lario. He wonders if his brother hopped over the ledge.

"Buddy."

Or if he made a swan dive.

"Buddy."

If he was laughing.

"Buddy!"

No laughter now. Just the echo of his own howl. Nicky rests his cheek against the tile, a crybaby, weeping again, weeping until he is empty of tears, until they are nothing but a thin, crusty film, until he is at rest, suspended along the back of his neck, in tingles and traces, like the spider. But not the spider.

Something equal, but opposite.

With a voice.

"Are you all right?"

Samantha's fingertip lingers at the nape of his neck, then pulls back suddenly as Nicky begins to rustle. She's alarmed with herself, as if she had put her finger in a live socket.

"Are you all right?" Her tone is colder now.

It takes him a long moment to wake, and several more to get his bearings, to remember where he is and what he was doing. Embarrassment sets in. He feels like he's been caught.

The girl, Sam-Samantha, is standing over him, still wearing the Rum Raisin shirt. It seems as if her legs begin somewhere just below her throat. Nicky struggles to his feet and brushes himself off.

"I was . . . I was just resting."

She can see he's been crying, at least that's what it looks like. "Do you always rest on the roof?"

"I don't know. Sometimes, I guess . . . Why are you here?"

"Just curious. I wanted to see what it looks like."

"The roof?"

"No, the view. The area."

That's what she calls the neighborhood, the area. "It's very pretty, really," she says.

Five stories above the street, New York loses some of its dirt, its anger, its menace. The sun is setting behind her, hanging over the Hudson River, a ball of pink and red set against a cool, cloudy sky. The sunset throws a glimmer over the warehouses and the water towers, over her, too.

"Where are you from?" he asks, still a bit too dreamy to be shy.

"From here. From Manhattan."

Nicky's never heard anyone say they're from Manhattan, at least not the way she says it, the way she makes it sound, like you need a passport to get there.

"What do you do?" he asks.

"What do I do?" She finds the question vaguely amusing, and explains that she works in a gallery, even if it's not much of a gallery, but still, it pays the bills. "The Lawrence Riefenstal Gallery, on Spring Street? Do you know where it is?"

Nicky has an idea, probably one of those places near

Ben's Pizza, but he shakes his head, no. He's never been in an art gallery, and he doesn't want to sound stupid.

"Well, anyway, that's where I met Sal," she says. "He came in to ask about a certain piece. Poor dear looked so lost. It was kind of cute, really, I mean, everybody knows we don't handle that kind of thing."

Nicky doesn't quite understand. "Who's Sal?"

"Mr. Colosimo."

"The Fatman?" Nicky can't figure this at all.

"Is that what you call him?"

"That's what my father calls him."

"Really?"

"Sometimes . . . he means it in a nice way, you know, like a nickname."

"I see. It's kind of cute, actually. The Fatman. Sort of film *noir*, don't you think?"

"He means it like they're friends."

Samantha finds his coltish quality to her liking. Already, she knows enough to know that he's nothing at all like the father, flexing his muscles on the stoop, and nothing like the men she has known. Her thoughts flash first to those boys from Collegiate and Dalton and Trinity, spoiled children with long hair and arrogant, upturned noses, with rumpled button-down shirts and rep ties, walking about with Frisbees or lacrosse sticks, and later, those young men in the clubs, CBGB's and Max's, all of them the same, as same in their way as the preps were in theirs: thin, bone white, using more mascara than toothpaste, dressed in black. Rockers with needles: here have some, this'll take the edge off, helping her, probing with the spike, finding the vein, shooting the smack into her arm, then later her ankle, the chamber filling with blood, then letting go of the gluey rubber hose, letting go with her teeth, nodding. Then they would touch her. The boys in the band. Vampires.

She shakes off the memory and finds herself staring at Nicky. "And what do you do?"

"I don't know. I play ball . . . basketball."

"At school?"

"Yea, I go to Xavier." He wonders if that will impress her as it impresses the girls in the neighborhood.

"Is that like Loyola? I think I once knew a boy who went to Loyola."

"Loyola? Yeah, that's uptown, right?"

She nods, still studying him.

"I think I played there one time," he says. "I play all over really. Uptown, downtown, East Side, Brooklyn. Over West Fourth Street."

Nicky wonders if the curl at the corner of her lips is the beginning of a smile. Or if she's just trying not to laugh.

"West Fourth, you know where that is?" he asks nervously, trying to avoid any awkward gaps in the conversation. "By the subway stop, across from the Waverly."

"I think so. A lot of people come to watch, no?"

"Yeah. I'll be there tomorrow," he says. "In the morning."

"I see. Is that all you do, play basketball?"

"I'm gonna box," he says quietly. "Gonna learn, I mean."

"What on earth for?"

"My father. My father wants me to."

"Your father, Frank?"

"Yeah, he says it builds character." Another stupid line, though Nicky finds its humor and begins to smirk at the silly-serious way it sounds. "Yeah, he says it'll make me a man."

"You needn't be in such a hurry."

"It's not me," he says, wondering how much he can trust her. "It's my father."

"Well, tell your father not to be in such a hurry."

"I wish I could. But it's not really like that. I mean, he's not like the kind of guy you can tell him no. Besides, you know, he's doing it for my own good and all."

"You don't look like a boxer," she says, punching him playfully on the arm.

"It's not something you look like," says Nicky.

"Yes it is," she says. "And you're much too cute."

Nicky starts to blush.

Samantha turns to him, the last sliver of sun throwing a shimmer over her hair. "Why were you crying?" she asks.

Can he trust her?

Does he want to? How much does he want someone to tell?

"My brother died."

"Oh," she says. "I'm sorry. I didn't mean . . ."

"He jumped off the roof. This one."

She steps closer, moving toward him as if by instinct.

"His name was Buddy."

Samantha Broderick runs her hands around to the nape of his neck, making him again feel that which is equal and opposite to the spider, making him look at her, repeating something told to her long after the last syringe was taken from her arm, telling him "you can't suffer for anyone else," but wishing she could, if only for a moment, wishing for some of his pain, just a taste, finding herself resisting an absurd urge, long dormant, unbeknownst even to her, feeling like a vampire herself now, and wishing to start at the traces of his tears, believing they taste of sugar, not salt.

CHAPTER

7

THE NEXT MORNING finds Nicky Battaglia on the basketball court at West Fourth and Sixth Avenue, the
blacktop already gooey from the sun. Nicky is here to
celebrate the sweet season's dawn. He has his reasons.
Basketball was one of Buddy's gifts to him.

He followed his brother like a puppy, as Buddy
introduced him to municipal matrices of concrete and
asphalt. The school yards and playgrounds imbued him
with a sense of geography, of boundary—St. Columba's,
the Green Court over in the Chelsea projects, the parks
on Houston, Horatio, and Thompson streets. And the
dusty gyms: St. Anthony's, Leroy Street, the gym in the
church basement, dank, with old wooden backboards and
tile floors. But he likes asphalt better. He remembers how
it was, him and Buddy, how they used to line the fence
at West Fourth Street, watching the games.

Buddy's been gone little more than a week, and Nicky
still hears him, still hears his brother saying . . .

". . . You think you're a ballplayer running games up
Leroy gym or over on Thompson Street. But that's little
baby shit. You ain't nothin' till you can rock with the
brothers at West Fourth. You gotta come off in one of

these real summer games. When all the people come by to see, when the real ballplayers are out . . ."

A day like today, Nicky thinks.

They've come from all over: Brooklyn, Bronx, Queens, Manhattan, pronounced "Mahattin." Nicky knows a lot of them, even the older guys. He knows them from the parks, others from high school games, and still others from summer leagues of years past. Some of them he knows from up the gym, on Leroy Street, and even from the youth center in the church basement. It's not like it used to be; they let the brothers in those places.

West Fourth is a venue of some renown, and the audience is four-deep at the chain-link fence. The whole world, it seems to him, is in attendance. By geography, many of them live in the Village. But they are not part of the neighborhood, not the way he has been raised by his father to think of it.

Nicky sees the has-been black guys sipping from their forties, forty-ounce bottles of Olde English or Colt 45 or Schlitz Bull. He sees the kid crack gangsters, precocious criminals with Five-Percenter names like Justice and Prince. They wear baseball caps, University of Miami and Chicago Bulls, Timberland boots, babysitting Jeeps and Nissans with black-tinted windows, their precious chariots of the street, double-parked on Sixth, engines shut, windows down, stereos blasting WBLS, choreographing the fantastic pageant.

At the fence, there are Christopher Street swishers and their graffiti artist callboys with names like Tito and Hector, Wall Street preppies passing the time in their lives between Dartmouth and Darien, freaky white girls with black boots, black jeans, black T-shirts, reams of distressed black hair and rings through their noses, leftover hippies, able-bodied beggars in wheelchairs collecting change in soggy soda cups from Blimpie's, spoiled Jewish kids from Long Island, from Roslyn or Woodmere, they come with haircuts like British pop stars to study business administration at NYU, an obese bald man in a lawn chair whose T-shirt reads, "I'm not losing my hair, this is a solar panel for a sex machine," would-be rap stars, black chicks with biker shorts, bangle earrings, and babies, they are the cuties with booties, the LayDeez of the Eighties, Jesus freaks, sinsemilla salesmen, incense prophets, and a couple of guys from the neighborhood, one of whom is Tommy Sick.

Tommy Sick is showing off his new brindle pit bull. He raises them. Like a hobby. Mary Rocca is with him, Mary Missile Titties, the precious, green-eyed, gum-chewing daughter of a small-time racket guy, Mary with hair as lustrous and dark as a reflecting pool, who would no doubt bleed cherry-chocolate syrup, whose lean frame harnesses a pair of magnificently poised titties aimed at the upper reaches of the atmosphere. Buddy fucked her in the alley. And so, in an imaginary sense, has Nicky. In his most marvelous mirage, Nicky has loved her like a movie star.

But nothing so marvelous as Sam-Samantha. She too comes into focus now. She must be passing through and decided to stop for a look. Their eyes meet. No, he told her he'd be here. She came to see him. She's smiling at him now. At least he thinks she is.

An indecent shiver runs through Nicky.

And the whole world is four-deep at the chain-link fence.

I'm Nicky Nice, he thinks. Nicky Nice. What he feels is not unlike the debutante at the cotillion. There is great delight in his step. He's got his floppy socks, adjusted Pistol Pete style, the way Buddy taught him, got his shorts hanging around the knees, hi-top black sneakers. He is schoolyard splendid. His T-shirt: "Our Lady of the Most Precious Blood Youth Center."

He can hear one of the black chicks say, "Oooh, Shaquilla, looka him. Look, he so cute. He bo'legged."

Nicky can move. He feels good. He feels pure. A kid he knows from a long-ago game at the Boys Brotherhood Republic, name of Asberry or Raspberry or some crazy black shit like that, comes at him. Nicky sticks one in his face. Pow. Right there. Like Pistol motherfucking Pete. Pow.

"You ain't shit," sneers the black kid. "Pussy mother-fucker."

Next trip down, Nicky gets the ball again. He steps right, then crosses over left with the ball, leaving that silly kid behind, burnt like toast. Nicky floats into the lane, crowded with bodies, up and into the middle of an airborne scrum from which his left arm reaches out and away from his own momentum. I'm big and bad, he thinks, I'm Nicky Battaglia from Bedford Street, float-ing, floating, feels so nice, he knows the ball is in, he feels it touch the net softly, a teardrop, how right this is, better than pussy, better than Mary Missile Titties, better than all the pussies in the world except maybe what is her name . . . Sam-Samantha. He hears the black chicks going, "Oooohhh," and someone says, "Yeah, you know him, from the neighborhood, yeah, that's his kid."

Coming down now, Nicky is more than satisfied with himself; he is vain beyond reason. Buddy flashes into his mind. Buddy, he wishes Buddy could see him now. It's gonna turn out all right, Buddy, I miss you, I love you, but it's gonna be fine, I'm doin' O.K., bro. He believes that Sam-Samantha is watching and that she will let him love her, and he wants Buddy to know about that, too, and then he hears something that calls him like a curse.

"Hey, whattaya think you're doing, huh?"

His father.

His moment of great glory ends prematurely. "The fuck is this?" Frank Battaglia is wearing white leather Keds, pants from a Sergio Tacchini warmup suit, and that familiar guinea tuxedo, a sleeveless undershirt. He has walked onto the court by himself, as confident as he is ignorant, entirely unaware of what he has ruined. Frank Battaglia sees only his son. This place, these people, they do not exist for him. There are no faggots and freaks, no niggers and nut-jobs in his neighborhood.

Nicky sits on the asphalt, his humiliation on public display, his father scolding like they're at the dinner table. "You ain't 'posed to be here. You ain't 'posed to disrespect me like this."

For disrespect, Nicky gets two smacks. His head rolls

with each as he tries to locate Sam-Samantha among the crowd. But the only familiar face staring at him belongs to Tommy Sick, who smiles as he pulls the pit bull's leash taut. Mary Rocca giggles and covers her eyes, nestling her cheek against Tommy Sick's chest.

"I'm trying to make you a goddamn man, give you some, some character and I find you here playing this, this, this African handball with the *moolinyans*. What the fuck is this?"

One of the black guys takes exception to Frank's disruption of the game, but an older fellow, everyone calls him Pops, catches him with a look: Don't, don't you dare, you ain't got no idea who this guy is, you don't belong in his private business.

Frank picks Nicky up by the shirt, gives him another smack, and drags him to the waiting car, a black Chrysler New Yorker triple parked on Sixth. He tosses Nicky into the backseat and walks around to let himself in. To sit beside his son.

From the driver's seat, Cheech adjusts the rearview mirror to get a better look at the kid. "Hey, Nicky, how you doin'?"

"Hey, Cheech."

"Cheech, can you imagine the nerve of this kid?" says Frank. "Nicky, I thought we had a deal. I thought we were gonna spend whattayoucallit. Whattayoucallit, Cheech?"

"Quality time."

"That's right. Quality time." Frank likes the sound of it.

Nicky does not.

Tough shit. Frank has it all arranged. "Boxing builds character," he says. "We're gonna put you in the Gloves, the Golden Gloves. I been thinking about this. Been thinkin' 'bout it for a long time. This is how it's gotta be. You're my son. It's my, my, how do you say, it's my jurisdiction. We can't put this off no longer, we gotta make a man outta you."

For Nicky, that very next day has finally arrived. He can sense the imperative notes in his father's voice, that in some very unknown and important way his father is trying to make things right, and that it has something to do with Buddy, always Buddy, Buddy who used to tell him, "Fuck all that boxing shit, look what it did to Pop." Nicky never understood why Buddy was always saying that. He just figured it was nothing he needed to know.

Cheech put the car in gear and heads up Sixth. "You wanna make your kid a man, Frank? Get 'im a piece a ass. Heh, heh, heh. How 'bout Rocca's kid? Mary Melons. I see you, Nicky. I see you looking at Mary Melon's tits."

"You wanna drive the car, Cheech? I'm trying to talk to my kid."

"Cheech," says Nicky, snorting a chuckle, "it's Mary Missile Titties."

"Imagine a skinny little thing like that got such big breasts. Hey, Frank, you think the old man knows everybody in the neighborhood wants to bang his . . ."

"Everybody shut the fuck up," Frank screams. "I'm trying to do something here. Nicky, you're not gonna learn anything with those *moolinyans* at the park."

"But I like playing ball. You shoulda seen me. I'm good."

"Cheech, what I gotta do with this kid? I want to spend quality time with my son. Is that a crime? Can they put me in Leavenworth for that? Every rat, motherfucking, scoundrel, pointy head, FBI faggot bastid is out there, working twenty-four hours a day to put me away and all I wanna do is spend time with my boy. My boy. But he don't got time for me. No. He wants to hang out with niggers in the park."

The car veers left on Greenwich, past the P.S. 41 school yard. Nicky leans over to check out who's playing.

"Nicky, what are you gonna learn out there? How to smoke dope and drink that Olde English?" Now Frank's tone softens. "I do this out of love. I wanted this for Buddy. But now it's you. You're all I got left."

Nicky mouths the words to the speech he already knows, keeping silent time with his father.

"One day you're gonna thank me."

Cheech gives the kid a look from the rearview mirror, his wink tells Nicky to relax. Humor the old man, humor yourself, it's not like he's not gonna change.

"Didja see the other one?" asks Cheech. "The one that moved into your building? I seen her. Cute. Cute girl. But no titties."

Nicky says nothing. His old man must have told Cheech about Sam-Samantha. Assholes. He hopes she didn't see his father smack him.

"Nicky, am I your father?"

"What?"

"Am I your father? Do you trust me?"

"Yeah."

"Then listen to what I say."

"Yeah."

"Son, lemme tell you something."

"What?"

"Boxing builds character."

CHAPTER

8

THE BIG, BLACK Chrysler glides to a halt on a side street off Eighth Avenue. The garment district is built high and dense, forming dirty, rectangular caverns against the skyline. Sunlight slices down onto the street at severe angles. Men push rambling racks of furs over the sidewalk. Nicky wonders why his father and Cheech insist on calling them Jewish airplanes. Jews don't do the pushing anymore. Even Nicky understands that that city, that city of Friday night fights, of benign bookies, of Broadway, that mythological city of white people, is over. Even if his old man insists otherwise.

Cheech goes to the trunk without having to be told and returns with a gym bag.

"This is a gift," says Frank. "Me to you. Remember that."

Nicky peruses the contents—a cup and leather supporter, cloth hand wraps, jump rope, boxing shoes, gloves, one pair for the heavy bag and another set of fourteen-ounce red ones for sparring. He understands that each of the items are married to a theory and a purpose, though precisely what, he does not know. The bag gives off a pleasant, leathery scent, like an unbroken baseball mitt. Nicky's stomach is queasy with his father's generosity.

"Go in there, you ask for a guy name Toodie Gleason. I straightened all this out already. The guy's expectin' you. I been tellin' him 'bout you. He's gonna look out for you, train you. But the first day, I want you to go in there yourself. I ain't training today. I don't want people talking, saying, 'There goes his kid.' *Capisce?*"

"Sure."

Frank presses a small key in his palm.

"Use my locker. It's the first one by the door . . . O.K.?"

Nicky would like to say something. But the words don't come.

"I'll see ya up the house later. I wanna know how everything went. Don't fuck around. This is an honor. Now go."

Nicky would like to say: "Gee, Pop, I really don't feel like being a fighter. I'm not a tough guy. I'm not like you. Buddy was the fighter. Me? I'd rather be playing ball with the yoms at the park."

But he knows better than to refuse his father's favors. He knows that Frank Battaglia considers this a ceremony, a great one, a shining moment of his patrimony.

What, then, does it matter that he wants to play ball? His secret aversion to fighting, to getting hit—his fear—none of that counts in his father's estimation. As Frank Battaglia sees it, boxing shall be mandatory in the curriculum, more valuable than books, more practical than numbers.

And even more than that. So much more. Nicky can sense as much. Boxing is part of his father's confused covenant with the past. And this place, Costello's, is a landmark of that memory.

Nicky pushes through the big steel door, feeling like the biggest fraud in the world.

He has entered another place: secret and stoic, a ghastly museum, the antithesis of the basketball court. The buzzer startles him, makes him jump. The buzzer is a strange watch. It goes off at three-minute intervals, and then a minute later, signifying round and rest. Nicky will never quite get used to the sound. The buzzer makes time repeat without moving forward. But in that sense, time is irrelevant at Costello's, where broken old men ride piggyback on the vain dreams of young men, where there is always a last best chance, where past and present mingle like strangers in a Turkish bath.

Nicky looks around now, trying to gather himself. There are no clocks. No calendars. No windows. Only a faint, fluorescent flicker. The air is moist and heavy, a sweaty-stale gas.

The spectators' bleachers are set in an alcove to the side of the steel door. The spectators are quite old, most of them, perched on the benches like a college of damaged, degenerate cardinals: pensioners, retired cut-men and managers, ex-fighters, old-time jazz club junkies. Their New York is ending with the modest decimals of a Social Security check. They come every day. To remember. To feed and be fed, to nourish the head. To bear witness. And pass the time.

Nicky takes note: this one wears a plaid jacket and puffs Luckies, that one a fedora, another guy with a translucent plastic hospital bracelet.

He feels their eyes upon him. They have been watching him since he opened the door. He pivots, now face-to-face with the one with white hair and whiskers, a thatch of unruly strands protruding from his nose. His pale shirt is soup-stained. He sits still as a lizard.

"Toodie Gleason?" The way Nicky asks, it sounds like an apology. "I'm looking for Toodie Gleason."

The old man looks him up and down, moving only his eyes before finally pointing toward the ring. "There," he whistles through an incomplete row of teeth. His mouth is a wet, black cave. The stink of sweet wine rides out on his breath. "Toodie's over there."

Toodie Gleason is cutting the gauze and adhesive from a fighter's hands. Nicky figured the trainer would be bigger. And older. Toodie Gleason is about thirty, pale and slender, the body of an ex-welterweight. He begins to rub the fighter's hands. The fighter is striking, a heavyweight, but still wiry, still young. His ruddy face is the color of a bad penny. The fighter wears bleached dreadlocks, his mop approaching a shade of orange.

From a distance, Toodie appears almost clean-cut. But the impression is ruined as Nicky moves closer, noticing the scar that runs from temple to jaw. It is the kind of wound for which an explanation would never quite suffice. Nicky tells himself never to stare.

"I'm Nick. My father . . ."

"Yeah." Toodie nods. "I figured."

"I got my . . ."

"The locker's back there. Alls you need today is the wraps. Okay? Gimme a minute with this guy and come back with the wraps." The dreadlock fighter looks through Nicky.

Nicky works his way deeper into the gym, running his hand along the wall, as if it could provide him with balance and direction. The wall's old coat of hospital paint is cracked like dry mud and marked with the tiny traces of ballpoint ink—phone numbers, connections, the calculations of incomplete, larcenous, payday ledgers. The concrete floor is painted a slick, slate gray. Puddles of perspiration shine like shellac.

Nicky slips in the sweaty slick, goes right on his ass. No one's thrown a punch yet, and already he feels down for the count. Nicky wishes he were invisible, unseen.

But looking down at him from the ring is a visage unlike any, a face supernatural in its evil, silent, but smiling, mining pleasure from his pain, comprehending everything from an opposite place. Nicky can feel his heart beat as he discerns the features: almost albino, a short, spiked shock of white hair, Roman nose, flared nostrils, a tattoo over the left eye, a dagger dripping blood.

It is more than a glance that they share; it is an intuition of fear, Nicky's.

He gathers himself quickly and moves on, passing the third ring where fighters are now sparring. Nicky takes it all in, trying not to compare himself with any of the combatants. That would crush him. Globules of sweat and mineral jelly fly from their stricken faces like diamond teardrops. Behind the rings, they pound heavy bags wound with silver tape. They time the crazy, temperamental path of leather balls suspended by an elastic cord. They shadowbox. Spitty whispers punctuate pantomime combinations: ssshhh-ssshhh-ssshhh-ssshhh. Ssshhh-ssshhh-ssshhh.

He sees boys from the Barrio and Bed-Stuy, no older than he, greased like eels, sweating through their dreams. Shamrock white hopes with wrecked faces, lumpy layers of eyebrow scar and skeleton pug noses. Wall Street guys with something to prove.

Their noise fades some as Nicky closes the door behind him.

His father's locker is crowded: lifetime supply of Aqua Velva, boxing gear, thongs, soap dish, bathrobe, selection of brushes, hair dryer, too. The wise guys his father's age are funny like that, like they all want to be Joe Pepitone.

Taped inside the locker door is a brittle yellowed newspaper clipping, not a whole article, just some words beneath a photograph. The image is preserved in a cardboard frame: two fighters, one on the canvas, the other still lunging, a ferocious strain rippling through sinew and muscle, across his arms, his shoulders, his lats, his stomach. At first, Nicky does not recognize him. His father has long since outgrown that young man's body. But the expression, that look in his eyes, gives him up. That look has never changed: lusty in its rage, greedy, beyond reason, desperate and hungry, eyes ablaze. His father must have been born with that look.

Nicky cannot make out the month and day from the smudged clipping. But the year was 1965.

He reads:

Elwood City, Pa.—They call him the Bedford Brawler, and last night at the Armory Frank Battaglia of Bedford Street in Greenwich Village showed why. Battaglia needed only two rounds to do away with Johnny Mancuso of Altoona. A left uppercut-straight right combination put Mancuso on queer street, while Battaglia raised his record to 13—0. Next month, the kid powerhouse from the Village is slated to make his New York debut on a Garden undercard. A good-looking Italian kid from the city, they're saying the sky's the limit for Frankie Batts.

Nicky studies the clipping, just beginning to understand.

His father is still collecting entries for his scrapbook, searching for an addendum, an antidote, a correction, that which he must have to fix a secret regret.

What that is, Nicky does not know.

He is frightened. But more than that, much more, he wants to please his father.

Make him proud.

TOODIE GLEASON WAVES Nicky through the ropes. "C'mon," he says abruptly.

Nicky snakes through awkwardly. Once in the ring, he can feel the eyes from the bleachers upon him again.

Toodie grabs his left hand, holds it up to Nicky's face. "We're always gonna start with the left. Everything begins with the left," says Toodie, impatiently reciting a speech. "We're gonna do things correctly, O.K.? Now watch what I do."

He weaves the cloth wrap into a soft cast, wrist first, crisscrossing over the meat of the hand, once around the thumb, to the knuckles, four times around, back over the meat of the hand to finish again at the wrist. Ties it off real neat, finishing a routine that seems indulgent and strangely tender. Nicky interprets is as an acknowledgment of what will come, and how bad it will be.

He considers his wrapped hand as if for the first time, touching it like a blind man, wiggling his fingers.

"Remember what that feels like," says Toodie. "It's gotta feel like that every time."

"I understand."

"Left hand first."

"I understand."

"We're gonna do things right."

"Yeah."

"Nick, is it?"

"What?"

"Nick, something I gotta axe you, and I don't wanna say it the wrong way but . . . do you wanna be here?"

Nicky shrugs, his honesty as unwitting as his gaze, which has settled on Toodie's scar.

"I didn't think so."

"Hey, you kidding? No. Yeah. I want to. Course I wanna."

"It's O.K." Toodie speaks softly now. "It's O.K. if you don't."

"I want to . . . really," Nicky pleads, his voice approaching a whine. There would be hell to pay if Toodie ratted him out, told his father that he didn't want to fight.

"Look, maybe you got an interest in this," says Toodie. "And maybe you don't. Maybe you learn something. Maybe you end up doing this for yourself. But I know why you're here."

Toodie would like to discourage the kid. He doesn't have the time. A kid like this doesn't belong here. Spoiled kid, Toodie thinks. Probably not his fault, but spoiled anyways. Most of them are like that. Toodie searches Nicky's face. The boy trying not to give himself up.

"You're here same as me," he says. "Your old man asked us to be here. But we both know your old man don't really ask, does he?"

Nicky nods slowly.

"I don't mean nothin' personal," says Toodie, "if you understand what I mean."

Toodie checks for a reaction. Nicky is staring at his scar.

"I got it a long time ago," he says. "And every day since, I been trying to convince myself that I won."

Nicky acts like he doesn't hear.

"A shank, piece of a bedpost."

Right then, Nicky decides to grant Toodie a measure of trust. "Must have hurt like a bastard, huh?"

"Never felt a thing. Not until after, a long time after.

Today I look in the mirror and it scares the shit out of me. Hurts even to think about it."

"I'm not scared. Really."

"Only two kinds of people say they ain't scared. You ain't crazy. So you gotta be lying."

Nicky shrugs.

"Now lissen," says Toodie, "if I'm gonna train you, I have the right to ask certain things from you."

"What?"

"I'm gonna ask you to go against your instincts. I'm gonna ask you to go against your imagination. I'm gonna ask you to control your fear. I don't know what you're like in the street"—Toodie looks him over again—"but here you can't cheat. Everybody in this room is full of shit, like everywheres else. Guys trying to make a score, trying to run cons, trying to prove something, make up for something, all kinds of crazy reasons. But this ring, this ring is no fix. Y'understan' what I'm saying? This ring is the most honest place in the world. You can't hit no one with a bat. Can't get your boys. Can't talk your way out of it." He hesitates for a moment, deciding against better judgment to test again. "Pally," he says, "in this ring, you can't call your old man."

No one has ever said that to Nicky. Not to his face.

"Alls I'm saying is you gotta trust me. You trust me, I'm gonna trust you. Otherwise someone gets hurt. And I ain't someone. Now put up your hands."

Toodie Gleason shows Nicky how to stand, distributing his one-hundred-and-sixty-odd pounds on the balls of his feet, shoulder width apart.

Already, Toodie knows enough to tell that the kid is naturally graceful, a good athlete. But not a fighter. Not by a long shot.

He teaches Nicky to jab. Elbows in. Flick it out. Snap the wrist near the end. Pull it back. Hit my hand. Chin down. Protect the chin. The nerves meet at the chin. Look at the other guy's head and shoulders. That's all you gotta see. That's all that's real. The rest is bullshit.

Power comes from the shoulders, he tells the boy. No. No. Don't load up. They load up punches in the movies.

John Wayne loads up. Sylvester Stallone loads up. Nicky Battaglia jabs. You jab. Good. Again. Good. That's it, pally. Again.

They fall into a rhythm and fatigue begins to bore its way through Nicky's shoulder.

Again. Again. Again.

With each blow, Toodie's hand needs less room to give.

Nicky thinks of Toodie's hand as a computer, like those pitching machines at the church feast, the ones that tell you how fast you can throw a baseball when you're drunk. Nicky imagines Toodie's hand supplies instantaneous readouts, charting the declining force behind his pussy jab.

What Nicky is wondering: Can he gauge my heart from my jab?

His gaze drifts to the next ring, where the creepy guy with the dagger tattoo over his eye is pummeling his opponent. Dagger-eye keeps coming. Even after the opponent drops.

"What the hell are you looking at?"

Nicky is mesmerized and does not answer. Now guys are storming the ring, trying to pull Dagger-eye off the opponent. But Dagger-eye does not go gently. He is like a werewolf interrupted in mid-feeding, his chest heaving with rage. But that twinkle of delight rushes across his face, his glance again meeting with Nicky's as the opponent is dragged away. Nicky hears someone laugh: Hey, least he didn't bite nobody this time. Oh, but the opponent was mauled. Nicky can see the man's face, like bloody oatmeal.

"Hey," says Toodie, yanking at the boy's arm. "I'm talking to you. That has nothing to do with you."

It takes Nicky a moment just to get his bearings. Remember where he was, where he is.

"Keep jabbing," Toodie barks. "Again. Again. Again. Each action has a responsibility. You're not getting it back. You don't get it back. You get hit. Again. Get it back. Again."

No use. The kid's concentration has gone slack.

Toodie throws an open-hand right, landing flush against Nicky's cheek.

Smack.

"Again."

Again, Nicky gets smacked in the mouth.

Toodie had meant to tap his ear. The kid saw it coming. But he closed his eyes, flinched, turned into the blow.

Stunned, Nicky paws at his mouth, examines his glove. His lip feels like it's giving birth. Nicky thinks of his father, wondering: Would he kill me or would he kill Toodie?

A thin film of blood spreads across his teeth.

It's not that Toodie was out of line. He just forgot.

Who this kid is.

"I'm sorry," he says, feeling rotten, but also thinking that he shouldn't really have to apologize. "It's just that guys will punch you in the face. They will lay you right the fuck out. This shit is for real, pally."

Toodie orders him to keep punching. Nicky does as he is told, but his blows are weak and without much effort. Ordinarily, Toodie would be offended and tell the kid not to come back. But he won't. For a lot of reasons he won't. Toodie Gleason can't help but wonder about this kid, the tired look in his eyes, the way he surrenders so easily, as if Nicky Battaglia is too used to taking a beating.

CHAPTER

9

HAVING JUST DEVOURED the right side of the menu, Salvatore Colosimo now digests with tall glasses of brandy and soda, one after another. The restaurant, once a Sutton Place carriage house, is lit with many candles, each of which occurs to him as a murmur in the dark, a memory, a memorial. The meal has made him maudlin. Salvatore Colosimo cannot help but wonder if anyone will light a candle for him, the thought interrupted as he tries to stifle a burp, pressing his fat fist to his chest. His bulldog jowls are like a fleshy bib as he eyes Samantha Broderick across the table.

She's a good girl, he thinks, but not for him. Not like that. Not even when he could do something about it. Very beautiful, but not his type. Her coloring and her frame are too light. Back in his day, Salvatore Colosimo enjoyed dark plump women with hips and asses and slightly immodest rolls about their bellies. Warm women, and he doubts if she could be that way. She draws on her cigarette and he focuses on the lean, hard muscles in her arm, detecting qualities both wounded and wolf-like. It is a pity to think of her in pain. She says she used to drink too much. He only wishes he could get her to eat, something more than lettuce at least, a veal chop perhaps.

Samantha takes a final, hard drag on her Marlboro, kills it in the ashtray, and pats his hand.

"Sal," she says, "you shouldn't eat like that."

The Fatman nods at her ashtray, which is taken away and promptly replaced by the owner himself. The owner, eager to please "Don Salvatore," as he calls him, is Latin handsome with a ponytail.

Salvatore Colosimo says, "The smokes'll kill you first. One puff is worse than ten T-bones. You gotta cut that out. Pretty girl like you, the smokes is what age you quick. Don't worry about the food. It makes me happy. One thing I learned, you take what you can get. And the way things are, I can get a good table in a good joint. I just can't get laid no more." He winks at her. "Not with my figure," he says.

She giggles. She appreciates him: his croak, his humor, his generosity, his power, even his girth. It has been a while since Samantha Broderick felt this way about anyone. She likes him. And most of all what she likes is that he has never tried to lay a hand on her. Samantha Broderick leans over the table and plants a kiss on his forehead.

"You wanna cut it out," he says. "People gonna get the wrong idea. I got a reputation to uphold."

"Thank you, Sal."

"You're very welcome, kiddo. What are you thanking me for?"

"I don't know. A lot of things. The apartment, I guess."

"I just didn't want you staying in a place you weren't happy is all."

Samantha had been living at the Chelsea Hotel since her release from the Betty Ford Clinic. She didn't like the Chelsea, what with all the confused kids with smack and Southern Comfort, pilgrims from Parsippany to Paris, asking for the room where Sid Vicious killed his girl. She had been there too long. Staying at the Chelsea was like renting at the scene of the crime.

Samantha Broderick comes from a fine WASP family

on the Upper East Side. She graduated from Le Lycée Français and later from Bryn Mawr. And with her degree in art history, she went slumming in the East Village, assuming the identity of "Barbarella," lead singer for Bambi's Banshees, a knockoff Blondie band which toured the late seventies and early eighties in places like CBGB's, Max's Kansas City, the Mudd Club. Samantha bought her outfits at Manic Panic on St. Mark's Place. She took to the stage wearing leathers and a boa, bleached her hair white with a purple streak. By the time Bambi's Banshees pressed their hit underground single, "Bambi Sucks," Samantha Broderick had already fallen deeply into her sad sleep, her addiction.

"The guy at the apartment, he give you any trouble?"

"Me? No. You mean Mr. Battaglia? He seems perfectly harmless. Why would you say that?"

"'Cause the guy's a *gavon*."

"And what's a *gavon*, Sal?"

"A caveman. Like an ape."

"Well, he seems perfectly nice." She lights another Marlboro. "Why do you dislike him so?"

"Reminds me of too many guys I used to know. Thinks he's playing a part in some gangster movie, only the movie's a rerun. I remember I seen him fight this one time. He wasn't a tough guy. Not then, not now. Alls he is is another one wants to be a movie star."

"What do you mean, you saw Mr. Battaglia fight?"

"Box. I saw him box. It was many years ago at the Garden. People came to me, they say this guy Frank is this and that, a real killer. So I go watch him, they got him against this colored kid. And it's not that he loses. I don't mind that. You take what you can get. It's that he falls apart." He searches her eyes. "You understand what I'm saying."

"I don't think so. I don't get the point of it, boxing."

"Doesn't matter, neither do I. But he bothers you, you let me know."

"Oh, please."

"You let me know."

"Sal, he's not going to bother me. I've been around

much worse, believe me. Besides, how bad can he be? His son seems so nice." She's smiling now, trying to restore his good cheer. "He's kind of cute."

"Better you should smoke Luckies."

Now Samantha winks. "I just take what I can get," she says.

"It ain't funny, being that guy's kid I mean. He had another son. That one went crazy, you know, like nuts. He was just like the father, thought he was a tough guy. Got thrown in the joint, came out, starting doing crazy things around the neighborhood. I felt bad for the kid, though. My nephew was friends with him. Until a few weeks ago. Frank's kid, he kilt himself. Threw himself off a roof."

"I'm so sorry," she says. ". . . He's probably in a lot of pain."

"Who?"

She thinks of Nicky, but says, "The father."

"The way I figure, the father probably killed the son. In a manner of speakin'."

"That's silly, Sal. And you know it."

"Maybe. Hell, what do I know? I don't even got kids. Alls I got is that same nephew, and that stupid prick became a priest. Matter a fact, not only do I pay for him to go to the seminary, but I hadda pull strings to get him back in the neighborhood. He tells me he wants to work over there in the church on Carmine Street. Now I ask you, does that make sense? To go back to where you're from? I love that silly kid, but I wanted him to better himself. You know, bad enough he became a priest, but at least get the hell out of the neighborhood."

"A priest? Is that worse than a gangster?"

"Sure."

Salvatore Colosimo gestures for the owner to bring more brandy.

"I got you a present," she says.

"We're gonna be engaged?"

"Stop. You're much too handsome for me, anyway."

He waits for her to light another cigarette. "You gonna tell me what it is?"

"Why should I?"

"'Cause I'm too damn old to guess."

"I got the painting, Sal. Well, it's not the original of course. It's a copy. A friend from the gallery does reproductions. He's very good, actually. It looks just like the original."

"You're a good kid, you know that?" he says. "I knew you're a good kid when I met you."

She remembers the day they met. Samantha had been at the gallery about a year, since her release from Betty Ford. Sal walked in with Fritzy two paces behind wearing a black suit. You couldn't help but notice them; all Fritzy needed was a violin case. And Sal was so big, so obviously the boss, telling his bodyguard not to snicker, that this was art, Sal trying to seem serious, like a collector, trying to make sense of the paintings and their price tags, which must have been awfully difficult.

The Lawrence Riefenstal Gallery, the most venerable in Soho, was in the midst of a show inspired by subway graffiti. Mr. Riefenstal himself was breathless with talk of salvaging a subway car from the Transit Authority, and having it "redone by an authentic vandal" and reselling it for millions. Make a terrific cover story in *New York* magazine, he said: the New Graffiti Aesthetic. It was terrible stuff. Fritzy was right to giggle.

Finally, Sal approached, an endearing uncertainty in his eyes, as if he were going to ask for dirty magazines behind the counter. Instead, he put a postcard on the table.

"I'd like to find that," he said, touching it. "The real one, if I could."

She picked up the card, read the back: Salvador Dali's *Discovery of America by Christopher Columbus*.

And now, in the restaurant, Samantha Broderick tells him that she couldn't get the real one.

"Hey, I take what I can get," he says. "Besides, nobody ever got me a present. I mean, no strings attached."

"No problem, kiddo." A broad smile spreads across her face. "It's in the car. I left it with Fritzy."

The Eurotrash owner comes by with the bill, practically bowing, asking if everything was to Mr. Colosimo's liking. The Fatman peels the Ben Franklins from his roll, but pays the owner no mind. His gaze is riveted on Samantha, who is about to explain, as she explains during each of their after-dinner conversations, the history and the theory of the painting.

She produces a text from her handbag and begins: the *Discovery of America* dates to 1959, which, by coincidence, is the year of her birth. The vision was born of Dali's paranoid dream, inspired by a metaphysical alchemist from Catalonia, the rocks of cabo crues form geological signs above the standard of the immaculate conception which is planted in the soil of the new land, and Columbus, a Catalan Jew, is welcomed by St. Narcissus, the patron saint of Gerona, and flies.

Samantha's voice speaks of a money much different from his: older money, the thievery of her ancestors now long forgotten, without mention in the history books. WASP's, the greatest gangsters of all, he thinks, they had to be, to dream up a country like this. The notes in her well-bred voice, the careful consonants, make him remember when Italians like him weren't even considered white people, when they were all *gavons*, which somehow trips into his recollection of Albert Anastasia in the barber chair, how he, Salvatore Colosimo, a fat little punk kid they used to call Tiny—a name these silly newspaper reporters still use—how he lifted the steaming towel to get a peak at that miserable fuck's face, how Albert sighed like a sweetheart. Like Tiny was another guy who showed up to give him a hand-job. And remembering, Tiny Colosimo still has this image of the towel after he was done, after he pressed the revolver against the soft, damp cloth, after he had made his bones: a black planet inside a red fire, surrounded by pink gases. How would Salvador Dali have painted Albert's last shave?

Tiny wonders if he will be forgiven. Sure, Albert was a miserable motherfuck who got what was coming. But he wants to tell her, this girl named Samantha, about

Anastasia, about a lot of things. In a way, he wants her to hear his confession. All of a sudden he feels old, watching this girl smoke cigarettes.

Take what you can get, he tells himself.

"Tell me again, Sal," she says. "Tell me why you wanted the painting."

"When I was a kid," he says. "I used to go to church. Right over there on Carmine Street. They had paintings on the ceiling, very beautiful, very blue, a lot of light in the color. And now that I'm sort of retired, I have some time to myself, I'm looking through this book, a book of pictures, and I see it. Now maybe I don't know what I'm talking about, things like this, but it seemed like something I saw as a boy. In the church, I mean. The *Discovery of America by Christopher Columbus*. I don't know why, but it seems like it should have been on the ceiling of the church."

SALVATORE COLOSIMO CANNOT help but admire the bounce in her gait as she steps from the restaurant into the warm breezy evening. It makes him feel good to see her move like that, happily, though he wishes again that he could have made her more plump.

The Mercedes is parked under a street lamp, with Fritzy waiting at the wheel. Samantha taps at his window. The smoked glass comes down, then the trunk pops. Samantha fetches the painting, tearing impatiently at the heavy brown paper, and presents the canvas, not yet framed, under the street lamp.

"Do you like it?" she asks.

Colosimo nods gravely, focusing on the standard of the immaculate conception and St. Narcissus. She was right. It does look like the real thing, at least as he imagined the real one should look.

"Gorgeous."

"I never gave anyone a present before," she says. ". . . I mean, no strings attached." Samantha leans over to peck him on the cheek. But as she pulls back, she sees something frantic, even frightening, flash in his eyes. He can't get the words out. Finally, he grabs her, a massive hand over each of her shoulders. He could break her; he can sense that from her tremble, and it makes him feel like a *gavon*.

"No, no," he says. "I just want you to make me a promise."

He feels her slack surrender, too frightened to move. He didn't mean for that to happen.

"One day," says Salvatore Colosimo, "I want you to light a candle for me."

CHAPTER
10

SAMANTHA BRODERICK RESTS comfortably in the back-seat, the interior of the Mercedes limousine like a soundproof capsule. The darkness soothes her. Only the rare stream of light gets through the smoked glass, and the rear window is blackened by the open trunk. That's where Sal is, showing his present to Fritzy.

How pleased he was with the painting. And how silly she was to think he would pull anything. He's just a nice man, she tells herself. She can barely feel the engine idle as she turns on the stereo. Maria Callas is in the middle of *Tosca*. Sal put in the tape on their way to the restaurant. "That's kul-cha, kiddo," he'd said. Sal's diction makes her smile, but she's not in the mood for Callas, or for kul-cha, and replaces them both with the radio, turning the dial in search of that station, what did Sal call it? The Perry Como station. That's it, yes, Frank Sinatra is singing "It Was a Very Good Year." That's more like it. Samantha Broderick turns up the volume and eases into the leather seat, closing her eyes, falling almost instantly into a light, tingly, dreamy consciousness, her mind running to Sal's picture, and St. Narcissus, and how Nicky Battaglia seemed every bit as cute.

● ● ●

ACROSS THE STREET, Frank and Cheech watch from between parked cars. Crouching in the gutter makes Cheech feel like a kid again, like they're playing a grown-up game of ring-a-lario. "Ring-a-lario one, two, three, ring-a-lario one, two, three, ring-a-lario one, two, three," he whispers, and then, smiling, making a pistol with his fingers—"Boom."

Frank scolds him to be quiet. But Cheech wants to go. He knows: you gotta do it now, do 'em all, the girl in the backseat, too.

Wait, says Frank. He wants another moment to study Colosimo.

What's that fat bastard doing?

Like he's explaining something to Fritzy. What the fuck is it they're putting in the trunk? What did they steal? A picture? A fucking picture? Frank watches Fritzy give the canvas a once-over and nod in approval. "Nice," he says. "Real nice." Frank can see him mouth the words. Fuckin' guy, Frank thinks, the Fatman could show him a bag a shit and Fritzy would say, "Nice, boss. Want me to eat it?"

Cheech gives Frank a nudge. Can't wait any longer. Cheech springs from his crouch and begins to walk briskly toward the Mercedes, reaching into his waistband for a silver .25 automatic, something for a real pro, sounds like a popgun, such a quiet piece, especially when you get real close, when you put it right up against the guy, let his body muffle the sound. Cheech holds the gun barrel up, behind his ear. He looks like in the movies, Frank thinks, like he knows what he's doing. Frank follows in hurry-up style, not nearly as smooth, or as calm.

The plan is for Cheech to clip Fritzy and leave Fatman for Frank. "I want that cocksucker for myself," Frank had said.

Cheech performs his instructions exactly, rolling up from behind, unnoticed even as he steps into the cone of light emanating from the street lamp. He wraps his left arm around Fritzy's throat, pulling him close, then, using the gun barrel, locates a spot under his ribs. So silent, so smooth, a ballet without music. All you can hear is Fritzy's groan. Cheech spins him around by the shoulder, a final pirouette, the line going slack as his grip slides down Fritzy's arm, then, two in the heart. Cheech lets go of the wrist, dropping Fritzy peacefully, perfectly in the gutter.

And here comes Frank, a little too slow, his surprise ruined. Salvatore Colosimo rests the painting in the trunk. He is without any tremor at all as he turns to meet Frank. It's as if he understands how this is to end.

Frank is a couple of steps too far from the Fatman when he sets his feet to aim. Frank has a Browning 9-millimeter automatic, a big gun. A stupid gun, Cheech had told him, sounds like fucking cannon, plus it jams all the time.

But I wanna blow his goddamn head off, said Frank.

Now, Cheech holds his breath waiting for the cannon to sound, but all he can hear is the flinty click, metal on metal. Fucking guy, he thinks, I told him.

Salvatore Colosimo trains his eyes on Frank's. A low growl comes from his belly.

"You wanna fight, Frank?" he croaks. "C'mere. Let's fight. C'mon, put the gun down, you fucking ape. We'll do it in the street. Right here. Sure, like we was kids in the street. C'mon, I seen you fight, Frank. I know you. I know what you are."

Frank has already missed his cue. Cheech knows: Never let a guy look in your eyes. Never let him talk to you. Don't think about it. That's what's got Frank all fucked up, thinking about it. The Fatman's talking to him, reeling him in.

"You're the tough guy, Frank. You're the fighter. Big fighter, right, Frank? Remember? Your mother's cunt, big fighter. What, you need your boys for me? The Bedord Brawler, right? Remember? You need a gun, a gun for a fat old bastard like me? C'mon. C'mere, Frank. I know you. I know you, you coward mohterf—"

It seems that the Fatman collapses even before the report of the little .25 automatic. Cheech catches him in the side, then straight on, in the heart. He had to. It was getting out of hand.

"Why'dja do that?" yells Frank. "I tole you lemme do that."

Frank Battaglia hurries to the Fatman, slumped in the sticky summertime gutter. Across all these years he can hear the Fatman telling him, *I got a piece a work that'll suit you just fine.* It is something only Frank can hear. He stomps the Fatman's corpse, kicking the huge torso. "See what you did," screams Frank. "See what you fucking did?" He does not hear Cheech yelling for him to stop. He can't hear anything but the Fatman, who is still telling him: *A piece a work that'll suit you just fine.* Like Frank was some piece of shit. He stands over the corpse, firing, firing, until his big gun is empty, until there is no sound but that metal click.

"Let's go," says Cheech. "Let's go."

"I had him," says Frank. "Why'dja do it?"

Cheech shows him a sympathetic look and breaks into a sprint, knowing that Frank will follow. Cheech runs down the street, toward the river, talking to himself:

Ring-a-lario one, two, three. Ring-a-lario one, two, three, Ring-a-lario onetwothree.

Like stupid kids.

They forgot about the girl.

CHAPTER

11

NICKY WAKES IN the dark. A gentle roar rises from the street. Reflections of bright-colored lights scamper across the pressed-tin ceiling. The feast. The Feast of Our Lady of the Most Precious Blood.

Yeah. It was summer again.

Nicky runs his tongue across his inner lip, locating the sloppy gash imprint of his tooth. There are flecks of dried blood at the rim of his nostrils, and a rusty taste at the back of his throat. The peak of his left shoulder is achy and stiff.

He has been asleep since returning from the gym. Still woozy and weary, he gets up and opens the window. The roar grows louder. A yellow glow comes from Carmine Street. Nicky spits out a big red lugy.

The bloody nose, at least that wasn't Toodie's fault. Not like when the guy smacked him in the mouth. That he meant to do. Nicky could tell. Toodie meant to teach him a lesson. Everybody's trying to teach him a lesson.

By smacking him.

Nicky hates getting hit, but he thinks about it a lot: about Toodie smacking him, about his father smacking him, about that kid from the gym, that big yom with the bleached dreadlocks. What would happen if that big bastard smacked him?

But he didn't get the bloody nose from a smack. Just from being tired, really. Toodie was teaching him how to stand and jab. It seemed simple. But Nicky got so tired, more tired than he ever got playing ball. Playing ball was a snap. He could run forever. This was a different kind of tired. First, his arms got heavy, then his legs, then, with Toodie reminding him not to lose his stance, to stay balanced, he got awkward, his legs crossing up like pretzels as he tried to throw punches. And through the entire routine, which seemed to last forever, he'd be worrying about Toodie, whether he was about to crack him in the mouth again. The way it happened, Nicky became so exhausted he just kind of tripped face-first into Toodie's shoulder and came away with a bloody nose. Real embarrassing, especially there in the gym. Nicky's nose wouldn't stop bleeding. Finally, Toodie said to get a paper towel from the locker room. Nicky skulked away, head down, shoulders hunched, hands cupped under his nose. Dagger-eye leered at him as he went. Nicky didn't look back, but he could hear Toodie call over to Dagger-eye.

"What the fuck are you looking at?"

Nicky wished Toodie wouldn't have said anything. Hollering at Dagger-eye just made him more real.

Toodie. What to make of that guy?

And that scar.

Funny thing is, Nicky kind of likes him. Even if he is trying to teach him a lesson.

Nicky blows out another lugy, shuts the window, and turns on the radio. The old Emerson hi-fi is set to WBLS, with deejay Vaughn Harper talking his soft baritone on the "Quiet Storm" show, spinning "In the Rain" by the Dramatics. The mopey bass singer comes at him through the speakers: "I'm gonna go outside . . ."

And Nicky backs him up with his own treble: ". . . in the rain . . ."

"You know it may sound crazy."

Nicky: ". . . ya know it may sound crazy . . . body-ump-ba-ba-ba-num-pa . . ."

"In the rain."

By the age of nine, Nicky had mastered a scratchy, sweet wine soprano. He could get up high like Russell Thompkins, Jr., of the Stylistics. He could do a tenor that sounded like Eddie Kendricks without balls. Nicky knows all the words, clichés of the sweet soul music, the cry music, Buddy's music: "foolish pride," "mighty, mighty love Jones," "supernatural thing," "natural high." Rock on with your bad self, Nicky Battaglia.

Buddy was his tutor and his bodyguard. He demanded but one thing in return: a backup singer.

At night, they would listen to Vaughn Harper's "Quiet Storm," singing along with Buddy handling the leads, the deep voices, and even the choreography. Nicky, the backup singer, took the softer parts.

And on nights their father happened to be home, Frank would yell from across the hall: "Keep it down with that nigger music . . . or youse'll eat that fucking stereo."

Nicky would freeze, wanting to dive under the bed. But Buddy would grab his crotch, give it a sarcastic shake. "Like we should listen to Jimmy Roselli tunes, like him," he would say. "Pop's got no appreciation for music."

Now, Nicky thumbs through his brother's records, kept right where Buddy left them, in shoe boxes alongside the old hi-fi. Buddy ordered the music—the 45's, the LP's, and the leftover eight-tracks—by categories of his own invention, inscribing each box in graffiti handwriting, in letters made by a fat Magic Marker and trimmed with metallic gold streaks from a painter's pen.

Chef Disco Buddy: Gloria Gaynor, Cheryl Lynn, Chic, Shalamar, Sister Sledge, and Santa Esmeralda. "Push, Push in the Bush." "Ring My Bell."

Play Dat Funky Music, Buddy: Parliament, Bootsy, Average White Band, Ohio Players, War, Manu Dibango doing "Soul Makossa," Kool & and Gang before they became a wedding band: Jungle Boogie, Open Sesame.

The Theme from Buddy: Isaac Hayes doing *Shaft*. Four

Tops, *Shaft in Africa*. Curtis Mayfield, *Superfly*. "Across 110th Street." The theme from *S.W.A.T.* The theme from *Mahogany*.

Buddy Sex Machine: Black chicks groaning in the background. Sylvia coming on with that soft Puerto Rican fuck-me talk at the end of "Pillow Talk." Major Harris, "Love Won't Let Me Wait." "Sexy Mama," by the Moments. Barry White's "Love Serenade"—"and take off that brassiere, my dear . . ." Donna Summer, moaning.

Buddy Love Music: the Stylistics, the Chi-Lites, the Manhattans, Main Ingredient, the Delfonics, Al Green, Billy Paul, Blue Magic, Marvin Gaye, and Tavares before the *Saturday Night Fever* soundtrack. Buddy broke down the Love Music even further, forming a roster of the twelve baddest 45's of all time.

He once told Nicky, "If you can't get over with the Best of the Buddy Love Music, then you got no rap at all. Put on 'Kiss and Say Goodbye,' you're in like Flynn. And if not—if the Manhattans don't you get you none—then you better hurry your ass to the doctor. 'Cause you need a checkup."

The Manhattans. The Delfonics. The Moments. The Dramatics. Those syrupy slow-jams, that's what he liked the best. Buddy was the scholar of the sweet soul music.

Now Nicky turns up the stereo, "Love TKO" by Teddy Pendergrass: "Think I betta let it go . . ."

". . . let it go, let it go . . ."

". . . 'Cause it looks like another love TKO . . ."

Nicky accompanies Teddy Pendergrass as he used to accompany Buddy, until Teddy's voice becomes Buddy's, until the song is over and the brothers are arguing over who's better: the Delfonics or the Stylistics, Nicky telling his brother that Russell Thompkins, Jr., isn't a fag just 'cause he gets up so high, until Buddy starts to tease him, singing Nicky's still a virgin, Nicky's still a virgin, until Nicky is talking out loud, yelling: "Fuck you, Buddy. I almost got it from Stephanie DeMarco in the church basement . . . but the Irish priest walked in."

Until Nicky realizes he's talking to a ghost.

I gotta get out of here, he thinks. I gotta go some-where.

Nicky shuffles across the hall. The old hexagon tiles, bits of green and black and white, are cold and gritty under his feet. The bare lightbulb in the landing makes him squint.

But it's dark again when he opens the door.

"Ma?"

No answer.

He walks in, past the foyer.

"Ma?"

Nothing.

Her bedroom flickers with light from the T.V. The rerun is something in black and white, but exactly what he cannot tell. Does it make a difference?

Theresa Battaglia sits in a hard-backed chair, her back to her son. Rosary beads twisted around her wrist dangle off the arm of the chair.

Nicky picks up his voice. "Where's Pop?"

He has to repeat the question.

"Out," she says finally. Her voice has no melody, no tone. Just a breathy whisper.

Nicky stands there for a while, intent on her silhouette, unable to figure out if she is weeping. He'd feel better if at least she would move.

"He went to the club with Cheech," she says.

"Do you need anything? You all right, Ma?"

Louder? "Ma, do you need anything?"

This is fucked up, he thinks. This is a horror movie. I gotta get out of here.

Nicky passes the club on his way to the feast. The Rod and Reel is shuttered, a heavy chain on the door. There's no name or sign or anything out front. Just a small American flag decal in the corner of the window. Been there forever.

It doesn't seem right that the Rod and Reel should be closed on a night of the feast. When Nicky was little, his father and Uncle Philly and Cheech would park them-selves in lawn chairs on the sidewalk in front of the club, just bullshitting into the night like regular street-corner sultans. Those nights Nicky remained at his father's side. It made Nicky feel important, that he was different from other kids. Those nights, Nicky could stay up as late as he wanted, until the feast had closed for the night and Carmine Street was being swept.

Tomorrow, if he sees his father, Nicky will ask him where he was.

Frank will give him a look and say, "Business."

Business.

Business my ass, Pop.

The feast is a too-familiar carnival. The hawkers yell at guys to do the right thing by their dates, win something for the ladies, fellas. Shoot a water pistol through a clown's mouth, be first to burst the balloon. Shoot baskets. Shoot an air gun.

Shoot this, Nicky thinks. The feast is some tired-ass shit. At least it smells good, though, the greasy vapor of frying sausages and peppers and braciole and calzones and zeppoles.

Nicky remembers the story about Tommy Sick throwing a nigger from Chelsea into a vat of zeppole oil.

Wonders if it's a true story.

He wanders. No destination.

Rummaging through a rack of oldies at one of the record stands, he searches for a new copy of "Me and Mrs. Jones" by Billy Paul. Buddy's 45 got too scratchy.

Across the rack, a guy in a pink button-down pulls out a record and starts doing some corny twist. "Ooooohhh, Motown," he says. "Sugar pie, honey bunch. That's the Four Tops." His girl in the plaid shirt breaks into a thin smile. What do they do, Nicky wonders, work at a bank?

Jerkoffs, he thinks.

Nicky hates that song, "Sugar Pie Honey Bunch." Doesn't anyone know that the Four Tops did "Ain't No Woman"? "Keeper of the Castle"? How about the theme from *Shaft in Africa*?

> Are you man enough,
> Big and bad enough,
> Are you gonna let 'em shoot you down?

When the evil flies,
And your brother cries,
Are you gonna be around . . .

Buddy took him to the movie years ago. It was double-billed with *Five Fingers of Death* at a once-grand movie palace up on Forty and Deuce. Buddy would bring him there all the time to watch Bruce Lee and Sonny Chiba dispatch armies of Chinks. But that day, Buddy let him get a toke off the joint in the theater.

They walked all the way home in the snow, play-fighting, assuming all the Kung Fu poses. Nicky said his Kung Fu was Shaolin monkey style, the baddest Kung Fu there was.

"Ahh-so," said Buddy. "Yowa style is vewy good, Mista Lee. And so owa yo' technique. But no match for my Tiger Death Lock. You cannot kiw me, Mista Nicky Lee. I will avenge my family's honor."

Nicky flashes Sugar Pie and Honey Bunch a look they don't even see. He wonders where they went to college. Sometimes he thinks his father is right. What the fuck are they doing in the neighborhood, these cunty kids?

Fuck them. And fuck college.

Nicky walks toward the end of the feast, a boundary marked by the baby Ferris wheel where Carmine meets Seventh Avenue. There, he bumps into Gerard Romano.

"Wassup."

"Whattaya doin'?"

"Nothing."

"You wanna smoke a joint?"

"Why not," says Nicky. "Where?"

"How 'bout the park?"

"Wait." Nicky reaches into a plastic garbage can and pulls out two iced bottles of beer with each hand. He nods a thank you at the beer man. Nicky Battaglia doesn't have to pay. Never did.

The boys cross Seventh Avenue toward Leroy Park. The bottles open like foam fountains. In unison, Nicky and Gerard wipe their hands on their pants.

"Oh shit," Gerard mumbles.

"It's only beer."

"No, I mean, oh shit." Gerard raises his bottle ever so slightly. "This fuckin' guy."

Tommy Sick.

"What's up, fellas?" Tommy Sick puts an arm around each of them.

"What's up, Tommy?"

"Was over at Peggy Sue's."

"Anybody there?"

"Just some bitches," says Tommy Sick. "You know how it is."

Nicky thinks of how his day began: on the basketball blacktop, with Tommy Sick and Mary Missile Titties watching from behind the fence, how easily she went into his arms. Both of them, laughing at him. He wonders if Mary Rocca lets Tommy Sick fuck her in the ass. Of course, he understands that no one really "lets" Tommy do anything. That's the wrong way to think about it. Still, Tommy Sick's always talking it, how he fucks broads in the ass.

Nicky watches him closely, how he moves. Tommy Sick is already bouncing to a twisted, manic rhythm in his head.

Bad sign, Nicky thinks.

Gerard sucks on his beer. He sees what's coming, a guy decked out like Captain Fantastic of the fag SS: leather officer's cap, leather pants, leather jacket with chain hanging from the epaulets, motorcycle boots. The whole bit.

Tommy Sick's mouth pulls back into a sly smile. He takes a bullet-shaped cocaine dispenser from his pocket and snorts, quick, greedy hits up each nostril. "Watch this," he says.

The fag has a close-cropped white beard and pink skin. Late thirties, early forties. It's hard to tell with the Third Reich getup.

"Hi Hitla," says Tommy Sick. This is very funny to him.

Nicky and Gerard catch each other's glance. Gerard takes another long swallow.

The fag keeps walking, with his eyes on the pavement.

"Hey, General," says Tommy. "I'm talking to you. Where you goin', honey?"

The fag tries to walk faster, but Tommy catches up, swishing all the way. Puts his arm around the fag. They stop at the corner. The fag doesn't know what to make of Tommy. Nicky can see how frightened this guy is. But he also sees something else.

Tommy Sick whispers into the fag's ear, and they go off together. Tommy Sick looks back, winking at Nicky and Gerard.

The guy's what? Twenty-five, twenty-six, the up-and-coming neighborhood wise guy, and he's still rolling fags?

"C'mon," says Gerard. "Let's get the fuck out of here."

The boys find their way to the park benches that face the lighted handball courts. Gerard spills the contents of his baggie on the concrete checkerboard and begins separating the seeds from the shake with a 970-TITS matchbook.

"Gonna make a big, fuckin' spleef," he says. "For us. For old times." Gerard forces a grin. He feels for Nicky, what with everything that's happened, his brother and all. Look at him, Gerard thinks, just sitting there, staring at the painted wall.

The middle handball court has been colorized into a standard graffiti-style mural. Kids are throwing up similar pieces all over the city, in school yards, lots, alleys, tenement walls, especially in the Spanish neighborhoods, Bushwick, Lower East Side, places like that. Typically, the caricatures are inspired by animation produced before the vandal artists were even born: girls derived from Betty Boop, boys who look like Speed Racer with a dark tan. Most of the pieces feature teardrops and bubbles of blood made to twinkle with parallel crosses of silver and black. Subtlety is not a shade in the palette of spray paint artists. The murals usually feature tombstones of battleship gray bearing the legend: "RIP."

RIP Lucho.

RIP DannyBoy

RIP Wanda.

U Wuz Da Best.

And a heart cracked down the middle, like a block of stone.

This one is a little different, though. This one depicts Father Vincent Ruggiero in full clerical dress, striking a thumbs-up "Keep on Trucking" pose, a cigarette dangling from the side of his mouth and a big red heart— squiggly marks to convey its exuberant beat—pounding out of his chest.

"To Father Vincent—A Kid At Heart!!!"

Father Vincent used to be Buddy's best friend. But that was before he became a priest. That was back in the day when he was just Vinny from Sullivan Street. Vinny was about to graduate from NYU when Buddy got jammed up, arrested for what happened that night in Washington Square Park. Seems like so long ago, thinks Nicky, the spring of '82. Right after that, Vinny split for that seminary somewhere in Jersey.

But each summer, he would come home to run a basketball league, the Blood Invitational he called it, up at Leroy gym. The league was a big hit. Kids came from all over to play, which pissed off the hard-core neighborhood guys, like Nicky's father, who'd complain that Vinny was letting the niggers in the gym.

They could bitch all they wanted.

But they couldn't stop him.

Vinny had connections. The Fatman himself had cradled Vinny at the baptism font. Fatman was his godfather, and loved Vinny like the son he never had. In the neighborhood, Vincent Ruggiero could do as he pleased.

After his first year at the seminary, he scammed a check from the city earmarked for "at-risk youth" and opened Our Lady of the Most Precious Blood Youth Center in the church basement. All of a sudden, there's pregnant Puerto Rican girls and teenage hustlers from the Port Authority coming to Carmine Street to see Father Vincent, who's not even an ordained priest yet, for a job or a lawyer or a doctor, for a place to stay, or mostly, for someone to talk to.

The old-timers in the neighborhood start calling Vinny a social worker asshole, then a hippie priest, and later, half a fag. "He's handing out rubbers to the niggers," they complain. "They're writin' on the walls."

Painting murals on the handball court.

Gerard runs his tongue along the rolling paper, sealing the joint. He looks up at the mural and nods.

"You heard?" he asks. "He's coming back. Vinny. Now he's Father Vincent."

"Sure," says Nicky. "He comes back every summer."

"No. He got a full-time gig at the church. He's a real priest now. He graduated."

"I thought you gotta go somewhere like Iowa after the priest school."

"Nah, he's coming back for good. He got some kind of job, like, Priest of Kids, youth ministry. Some shit like that."

"Yeah?"

"That's what I been trying to tell you."

"How you think he worked that out?" asked Nicky.

"How you think? His uncle Sal. I mean, the Fatman just about built the church, what with all the money he gave. I heard the Fatman even met with the Pope."

"I heard that was bullshit."

"Well, all I know is, Vinny got some crazy pull." Gerard tips his beer, making a toast. "But you, you must know how that is, having pull."

"I never really thought about it like that."

Gerard lights the joint and passes it to Nicky. "It's crazy, huh?" he says.

"What is?"

"Father Vincent. I mean, the guy can never get laid. His whole life, he's not allowed."

"Maybe he'll get some in heaven," says Nicky.

"Yeah, but like what the fuck would make you want to do that? Be a priest, I mean?"

Nicky holds the smoke in his lungs and hands the joint back without answering.

"Guess everyone's got their own reason," says Gerard, slightly embarrassed, staring at the concrete checkerboard. "I'm real sorry 'bout your brother, Nick."

"Yeah." Nicky seems far away, watching the kiddie Ferris wheel, the revolution of colored lights.

"I mean, he was a good guy, you know. Solid."

"Yeah."

"If you need anything, like, you know . . . like . . . I don't know . . ."

"Thanks."

Nicky opens his other beer and begins to size up his friend, wondering if he can kick Gerard's ass. There's nothing personal in this, no animosity. Just Nicky thinking: If I had to . . .

"Who was better," he asks, "Reggie or Thurman?"

Gerard smiles wistfully. "Thurman," he says.

"Fuck you, Thurman," Nicky laughs. "Just 'cause the guy died don't make him better."

Thurman Munson, catcher for the New York Yankees, died in a plane crash, August 1979. Gerard was broken up for quite a while. He was a big Thurman fan. And in the first week of fourth grade at Blood grammar school, he asked Nicky to admit, finally and for the sake of justice, that Thurman was the best. Nicky would do a lot for his friend. But he could not renounce Reggie. Their debate escalated into a brawl. The nuns pried Nicky from battle with red eyes and ringing ears.

During their detention, Gerard told him that Sister Elizabeth was a dyke. Nicky didn't know what a dyke was. But he got a kick out of Gerard's explanation.

His shiner was in bloom by the time he got home. Nicky told his father that he had been fighting.

"You win?"

Nicky nodded, yes.

"Good," said Frank. "But you shoulda kicked 'im in the balls. There's no protection for that. Whenever you're in trouble, kick 'em in the balls."

But now, sitting on the bench, smoking the joint, Nicky cannot imagine kicking Gerard in the balls. Not now or then.

Gerard Romano was his last fight.

He hadn't been in one since. He hadn't the need. No one messed with Nicky Battaglia. He was protected from the world by his father, and protected from his father by Buddy. Just having Buddy around had been enough. Even if he wasn't right.

"Buddy and Reggie," he says.

"Here, finish this," says Gerard, handing Nicky the roach. "You'll feel better."

Gerard is preparing another joint when Nicky taps urgently at his shoulder.

Tommy Sick. He's back. He's wired. He's talking loud.

"I thought youse'd be here," he says, stepping between Gerard and the stash. "Yo, lemme see that." Tommy Sick pulls the coke bullet from his windbreaker and taps out a generous frosting for the joint.

"C'mon, Tommy," says Gerard. "That shit makes me jumpy."

"Do I look jumpy to you?" Tommy Sick begins to chuckle. "The fag general wanted me to fuck 'im in the ass. Started crying. Beggin'. Really. The general was crying." His cackle intensifies. "Hi Hitla."

Nicky and Gerard share a glance. They don't want to hear this.

". . . So what did I do?"

"Poke 'im in the culo?" Gerald giggles.

Stupid, Nicky thinks, real stupid. You can't be funny with this guy. You can't test him.

Tommy Sick swivels around, grabs Gerard by the front of his shirt, pulls him real close. A sweet, nauseating fume hangs on Tommy's breath.

"You want me to poke you in your culo?"

"Nah, Tommy. Nah. I was only messin' . . ."

"You want me to fuck you in the ass?"

"No. No. C'mon."

Tommy Sick shakes him by the collar, Gerard's head bouncing berserk like an unhinged hood ornament.

"Tommy. No."

"Say yes."

"No."

"Say yes."

"No."

"Say yes you want me to fuck you in the ass like the little punk you are."

"No."

"Say yes, motherfucker."

". . . yes . . ."

Finally, Tommy Sick throws him to the ground. "Don't make me do shit I don't want to do," he says. "I'm too old for this anyways. Too old to be hangin' out wich youse."

Tommy Sick lights the joint and begins to smoke.

"So like I was saying," he says, "I laid that cocksucker out. Boom, he goes down. One shot. Boom." Tommy Sick exhales and passes to Nicky. "Then I took his shit," he says.

Nicky draws hard on the joint, holding the smoke as long as he can, until an ape-like noise comes from the back of his throat. He wants to get whacked. Really fucked up. He takes another quick hit.

Tommy Sick stares at him. "Yo, Nicky, don't niggerlip the joint."

Nicky passes to Gerard, who's dusting himself off. Gerard looks like he could use a hit.

The smoke forms a blue-gray cloud. The tip of the joint spinning like a firefly against the backdrop of night. The seeds crackle and pop.

"Cheap shit," says Tommy. "What, youse get your smoke from the yoms in the park?"

Tommy begins to empty his pockets: change, keys, bills, wallet, tiny glass ampules, balloon, whippet canisters, plastic ID card. The items make a scraping noise against the checker table.

Nicky picks up the ID card. The faggot general is a professor of classical literature at NYU. His name is Frederick Feingold. He's wearing a jacket and tie in his ID picture.

Tommy's in a frenzy now, sampling everything on the table. He cracks the ampules in the bandanna, holding it under his nose. Smells like rotten apples, if you could spray rotten apples from an aerosol can.

Nicky recalls what his father likes to say about Tommy Sick: "Kid's got a future. Gonna be a good earner."

Tommy Sick hits each nostril twice. His face flushes as he begins to wheeze with laughter.

Does he know, Nicky wonders, how much I hate him? Now Tommy's on to the whippets.

"When was the last time you saw these shits?" he says, fitting the balloon over the canister, giving it a twist, sucking the nitrous gas out of the inflated balloon.

Tommy Sick finishes with a couple more snorts from his coke bullet.

When he comes down, just enough to see again, Tommy Sick catches Gerard staring at him. At least he thinks so.

"Whatta you looking at?"

"Me? Nothing."

"I didn't think so."

Gerard nods at Nicky. "I gotta go," he says. "Later."

"Fuckin' guy," says Tommy. "It's not like I was smoking that crack. Like some homeless nigger wind-shield washer."

Tommy Sick throws back two white pills. Nicky doesn't even want to ask.

He just wants to finish the joint.

"Heard you started fightin'," says Tommy Sick. "Train-in' for the Gloves."

Just finish the joint, Nicky tells himself. Get whacked, and get out of here.

"Hey, I'm saying something. I heard you been fightin'."

"What'd you hear?"

"Nothin'. Just that, you know, it'd be good for you."

Nicky wonders if Tommy Sick is about to teach him a lesson, too.

Tommy winks at him. "Things is gonna change," he says. "For guys like us."

The joint is dead. So are the lights on the Ferris wheel. "I gotta go, Tommy."

"I'm hearing some things, Nicky."

"Gotta go."

"Hey, I'm sorry about Buddy."

"Yeah."

"I guess it's better this way, huh? That was no way for your brother to live."

"Later."

Walking away, he can hear Tommy yelling: "Hey, where you goin'? I'm talking to you . . ."

Fuck him. Up Carmine Street, the sweepers are out with their big, bristled brooms. The feast is locked up for the night. But the more distance he puts between himself and Tommy Sick, the better he feels. Nicky wonders if he's stoned. Whatever, it don't feel so bad. He starts to pretend he's Larry from the Floaters.

> Cancer, and my name is Larry . . .
> Take my hand,
> Let me take you to love land,
> Let me show you how sweet it could be,
> Sharing your love with Larr-ee
> Float, float on,
> You better float with me, girl, float on,
>   float on, float, float on . . .

Nicky makes slick steps all the way home.

She's there when he gets to the door.

The girl.

What is her name? Sam? Samantha?

Her back is turned. She doesn't see him. Nicky considers Sam-Samantha, for a long time it seems. He imagines how her hair would feel in his hand, like a bolt of cool silk. The notion makes him shiver. So does her ass. The slacks that billow about her legs gather at two perfect, marbleized spheres. Her ass, Nicky decides, is a fucking miracle.

He is stoned.

Yesterday her fingers danced on his neck, sending the spider away. Yes, and she smells like pastry. Nicky recalls this whacked-out book Father Vincent gave him last summer. It was written by a crazy Irish guy, and

Nicky read only what he could determine to be the dirty parts. The guy in the book said pussy smelled like lobster and mayonnaise. And Nicky wonders if this Sam-Samantha, who seems made of sugar and wheat, would produce that spoor as well. If that were even possible.

"Howya doin'?" he asks, ebullient, confident, ready to throw down his most mighty, mighty love Jones rap. Maybe something like: Aquarius, and my name is Nicky . . .

She turns slightly, stopping before their eyes meet.

It has taken him this long to realize that she's weeping. Sooty rivulets of mascara run down her flecked cheeks.

He has never wanted to fuck anyone so much.

Though it occurs to him that may not even be the right word. Fuck.

But now, as their eyes meet, her expression changes: from grief to alarm to fear, wide-eyed fear. Samantha fumbles frantically for her keys, unlocking the door, then shutting it quickly behind her, disappearing.

Nicky stammers at the door. "Can, can, can I get you anything?" he asks. But there's no answer, only the echo of his own voice ringing in his ears.

CHAPTER

12

IT IS AFTER midnight on a Saturday and the newsroom is
dark, except for the cool green glow that comes off the
computer screens and the tiny red numerals flashing
across the police scanner. The editors are gone. The
copyboys are gone. Mushy Flynn is alone. He works
the lobster shift, midnight to eight, which is fine by him.
He can't stand to be around these little pricks who run the
paper. They wouldn't know a story if it bit 'em on the
tuchus.

Mushy listens to the scanner. The scratchy voices that
accompany those red codes are like an oral log of the
city's nightside troubles:

"EDP . . ." Emotionally disturbed person.

"Ten-thirteen, officer needs assistance . . ." Usually
means a cop has stubbed his toe and may now file to
leave the job with a three-quarters disability pension.

"Ten eighty-three." Fresh body. Some ne'er-do-well
junkie.

"Ten thirty-four." Domestic dispute in progress.

Once in a while, say, with a fire in Bushwick or
Brownsville or some godforsaken place, Mushy can hear
the sirens and the howls of children in the night. It all
comes over the radio.

But there's nothing much that'll get him in the paper. It is Mushy's custom to write a memo at dawn, list the dead bodies, the more spectacular car wrecks and fires, and leave it on the editor's desk. Let the rewrite guy handle it in the morning. Fuck 'em, Mushy thinks. He's too old—seventy-six years, with sixty of them in the newspaper business—to be writing cop briefs. Paragraph murders.

Mushy talks to the police scanner. "C'mon, you sonofabitch, gimme something to write." Make it a white girl, he thinks. From a good family. A coed. Jesus, when was the last time we got a coed in the paper? "A front page before I die," Mushy tells the scanner. "Is that too much to ask?"

Mushy Flynn deserves a good story. After all the crap he's put up with, it would only be fair. Even things out. Five nights a week Mushy listens to the police scanner and thinks of the concessions, sacrifices, really, he has made to age. He has given up Luckies for Carltons— low-tar, low-nicotine. It's like trying to smoke a tampon, Mushy thinks. Still, he must do something to appease his doctor. His kidneys are blocked up. He cannot pee. He runs to the bathroom, his dick burning like a fire, and when he gets there, what? Only a little dribble comes out. It's a form of torture. Like this lobster shift. What is that?

Is that any way for Mushy Flynn, who could have been a great newspaperman, to go out? He knows the editors laugh behind his back. They think of him as a fossil. Only his membership in good standing in the Newspaper Guild keeps him from getting fired for some cutie out of Columbia.

He begs the scanner for that single gift: "Blonde Coed." Mushy would show the little pricks what a newspaper story is. He imagines the headline: SEX SLAVE SLAIN, FRIENDS SAY COED WAS GIRL NEXT DOOR.

But all he gets is the litany of EDP's, the shots fired at Livonia and Stone, on Neptune Avenue, on Featherbed Lane in the Bronx, domestic disputes in housing projects. Over the radio, Mushy hears a woman holler in Puerto Rican Spanish.

No newspaper stories out there. Just more shit.

But now, over the scanner, comes a snippet that causes Mushy Flynn to rustle: the voice of a young cop, frantically identifying himself as belonging to a cushy Upper East Side precinct. Rookie patrolman, Mushy thinks. Probably from Suffolk County. Probably on the job because his old man was on the job and the old man's old man before him. The rookie has forgotten about protocol, speaking with excitement, and even some delight.

"This could be something," he says. "It's like a movie. You know the guy, you seen him on TV. You gotta see how fat this old bastard is. In real life, I mean."

Mushy waits for the rookie to provide a location, then jots down the address—Sutton Place. Good address. Fine venue for a murder. And not far from the paper, either.

Ordinarily, Mushy's policy is never to leave the paper during the lobster shift. He used to go out on jobs, sure. Fires. Shootings. Two-bit murders. Mostly pieces of shit. But Mushy would go because he still thought of himself as a newspaperman. He'd hang around a job until he was good and frozen, come back to the office, tap out a helluva piece, and the editors would spike it, or bring it down to a paragraph brief on a wire page, or if the story was big enough, fold Mushy's words into a main bar on the story and act like it was a big deal Mushy's byline was among the several on top of the story.

"Mushy," the editor would say, "we can't use all this stuff."

"If you'll excuse me," Mushy would say, "why not? It's a fucking poem."

"It's old. By the time people pick up the paper tomorrow, it's old. They've already seen it on TV."

"I hate TV."

"It's old, Mushy."

"I'm old, you little prick."

What was the sense, freezing his ass off for the thankless little pricks? If he had to work, he'd work the phone, improve the quotes from the victim's family, and leave a memo. Fuck 'em.

Why bother? The little pricks would just ruin it anyway. Not too long ago he'd slipped the word "gunsel" into his copy. One of the little pricks, a kid hired to be a newspaper editor because he had a Master of Business Administration degree, took the word out. "No one knows what that means," he said.

Mushy Flynn had worked with the best of them: Runyon, Winchell, Cannon. He always figured he had what it took, what those guys had. It's just that Mushy had bad timing. The business had changed on him. The city had changed on him. That's why things didn't work out for Mushy Flynn. That's what he would tell himself, standing over the urinal, alone, trying, forcing himself, to pee.

But tonight, tonight he feels different. He feels lucky. Sutton Place, this could be something. This doesn't look like a piece of shit.

MUSHY FLYNN IS the first reporter at the scene. A disgrace, he thinks, that a man of his advanced years should arrive first, especially since he spent five minutes explaining to the turban-headed cabbie that Sutton Place wasn't in Brooklyn.

His is a smug satisfaction. Mushy Flynn knows that getting there first endows him with a natural advantage. He pays the cabbie, adjusts the brim of his fedora—the last reporter in town to wear one—and brushes at the imaginary dust on the lapel of his overcoat collar. His clothes are old, but neat. Every night, before he goes to work, Mushy irons on the bare Formica table in the studio apartment at the Chelsea Hotel where he lives alone. Mushy Flynn still likes to think of himself as something of a rake.

He lights a Carlton, shoves his hands in his pockets, and walks confidently toward the crime scene, which is already bustling. Detectives mill about, barking orders at each other, trying to figure out who's in charge, while the drones in blue define a crude circumference around a limousine with orange ribbon. Patrolmen are herding the gaggle of onlookers behind the barriers.

"Back behind the line," they holler. "It's two in the goddamn morning, why don't youse all go home?"

Behind him, Mushy hears someone yell, "But I'm with the press."

"No press," says the cop. "They'll have a statement for youse later."

Mushy doesn't look back, doesn't slow his gait. A young kid in uniform, uncertain for a moment, catches his eye. Mushy looks right through him, like the kid's a speck of dust. The young cop lets him pass. Silly kid thinks Mushy's a boss.

Now that whiny voice again, "But I'm with the press . . ." These pishers, he thinks, they go to Columbia to learn that crap? I'm with the press.

The dead body is already covered in a sheet behind the limousine. But Mushy's view is obscured by the chorus of police inspectors and FBI agents crowded inside the crime scene. Maybe Mushy knows one of them. Or maybe he knows one of their fathers. There's gotta be someone around here who'll give him the dope.

It doesn't take long for Mushy to spot the familiar face. Guy's name is Gallagher. Used to be a cop, a good detective who did his twenty and got out. Now he works some kind of organized crime squad for the feds, out of the Southern District U.S. Attorney's office.

Mushy pushes on without even trying to get his attention. Gallagher will be able to straighten him out later. But not now. You don't ruin a good thing, and that's what this is, a good thing.

The crime scene's address is that of a fashionable bistro. There's nothing on the awning, just the name— "April"—in ceramic tile at the cornerstone of what was once a carriage house. There's another young cop at the door.

Mushy gives him the evil eye, too. The cop looks down at his heavy black shoes as Mushy walks into the joint, which is nicely done: tile, mirrors, and candlelight.

Mushy figures dinner for two, good wine, sets you back three hundred dollars. Definitely not a piece of shit.

He asks for the owner, and a Mexican busboy points back toward a dark corner of the restaurant.

Mushy helps himself to a seat at the owner's small marble-topped table. The owner is dressed entirely in black, mid-thirties, Latin. Brazilian, Mushy figures, maybe Argentinian. His hair is swept back in a ponytail.

"You a cop?" the owner asks.

"Worse than that."

"FBI, right?"

"Why don't you let me ask the questions. Or if you want, how about I call INS and they send all your busboys home on the next banana barge. Maybe you, too. Just listen to me. You know the guy that got killed?"

The owner nods grudgingly, measuring Mushy's resolve before he speaks. "Comes in all the time."

Good, Mushy thinks. But he still wants to double check. In the interest of fairness. "You sure you know him?"

"Just from the restaurant."

Now Mushy answers with a silence that makes the owner feel compelled to say something more, as if he must justify himself. "I don't do no business with him or nothing. But I like him, Don Salvatore, the one they call Fat Tiny in the papers. Comes in with a beautiful girl. Fat Tiny was a good customer."

Oh, this will be his fine night, Mushy thinks, better than a whole sorority house of coed sex slaves. "Tiny?" he asks.

"Yeah. Tiny. What, you don't read the papers, cop?"

"Believe me, I read the papers. Now you said Fat Tiny?"

"I already answered these questions."

"Lemme tell you something, señor. I don't give a good goddamn what you answered before. I'm the most important guy here. And tonight, tonight is the most important night of your life. *Capisce?*"

The owner says nothing.

"Tell you what, though, this is a nice place you got here."

"You like?"

"Very much."

"The tile, we had it imported from Firenze."

"Very nice. Now tell me, you said this Fat Tiny came in with a girl?"

"Yeah, nice girl, too."

"Blonde?"

The owner nods vigorously.

"Jesus Christ, that's great . . . she looked like, what?"

"She look—I don't know—she look American. Like, what do you call? WASP. How old, I don't know. She skinny, though. Could be twenties, could be thirties. But nice. Not like a *puta*. They talk about art, her and Fat Tiny."

"Art?"

"He talk to me too about art. I'm an artist you know."

Mushy waves a slow hand, acknowledging the restaurant's decor. "I can see."

"I hear Tiny talks to her about Dali."

"What?"

"Salvador Dali. Maybe a cop never heard of him. But Mr. Colosimo, he knew. He was talking to the girl about a painting he just got. What's the name, I don't know. But it's a Dali painting. I hear when I serve the after-dinner drink. Customers like when the owner serve the after-dinner himself."

"I didn't know Tiny was such an aesthete."

"What, you know him?"

"We go back a ways."

The owner gives him the once-over.

"Don't give me that look, señor. I'm not here asking you for a table by the window. By the way, how much does a guy like Mr. Tiny drop for a meal at a joint like this?"

"Five, six hundred for him and the girl."

Mushy looks impressed.

"More if the scary guy eats, too. But I guess he ain't coming in no more either."

Mushy has to think quickly. What was Tiny's guy's name? "Fritzy?" he says weakly.

"I think. Big guy. Always wear a black suit. He go wherever the boss go."

"Fritzy."

"I don't ask. He don't come in tonight. He wait in the car. But I guess they get him, too."

Mushy tries not to look surprised. "What happened to the girl?"

"Me, I don't know. I hope they didn't get her. Nice girl."

"But you said Fritzy got whacked?"

"I thought you was the cop?"

Stupid, Mushy thinks.

"Tell me," he says, changing the subject, "it might be helpful if you could tell me what Tiny ate." Mushy's thinking in bold type. "His last supper, so to speak."

"The other cops didn't ask me that."

"I'm not like them."

The owner calls to the busboy, who brings a menu, which is calligraphy on parchment, no prices. Ponytail folds the menu in half, runs his hand over the right side of the menu.

"This is what he ate."

"Half the menu?"

The owner shrugs. "He like to eat."

"The girl?"

"*Tricolore* salad with goat cheese and pignoli nuts. She drink Coca-Cola."

"Tiny drink?"

"Brandy in between courses, a bottle Château Lafite. For dessert, a nice Riesling. Grappa with his coffee. He finishes with brandy and soda. For his digestion."

Mushy stuffs the menu into his breast pocket. "Thank you, señor."

"Who you work for?"

"The *Mirror*."

"Oh, shit."

"Lemme tell you something, señor. Don't act like a little prick. You just did the best thing you could have done. You talked to Mushy Flynn. Remember that name, son. 'Cause now you got the hottest joint in town. Believe me. You're gonna be booked solid through April of the next century."

OUTSIDE, THE STREET is jammed now. More cops have arrived. The street is aglow in the harsh light of television cameras. A surly battalion of reporters is caught behind the police barricade, asking to be let through, asking to be where Mushy is.

Mushy takes a deep breath. He can taste it, smell it, the breeze like sweet summer perfume.

"Mushy. How the fuck did you get here?" It's Gallagher. The veins in his bull neck are taut.

"But, Jack," Mushy says innocently, "it's my job."

"What about my fucking job? Get behind the barricade like the other assholes."

"After all I did for your father."

"Mushy, you never did shit for my father. My old man worked sanitation."

"After all I did for you. When you were starting out." Mushy's gaze wanders back toward the barricade, where the police commissioner and an FBI boss are presenting the official disinformation to the herd of reporters. "I got something for you, Jack."

"What?"

"Mystery blonde."

"Nice try. We know about her."

"I got more. How about Tiny Colosimo's hot art?"

"That's what that picture in the trunk is?"

"That picture, as you put it, is by the great surrealist master Salvador Dali."

"Who?"

"It ain't dogs playing pool, O.K., you dumb mick."

"Kike."

"Kike? You're dating yourself, Jack. Besides, I'm not a kike. I'm Mushy Flynn. And I am beyond race. I am beyond ethnicity. I am merely old."

"Fuck you, Mushy." Gallagher jots down "Dolly" on his pad.

"So," asks Mushy. "What do you got?"

"Didn't hear this from me."

"It's always better that way, Jack."

"Tiny was three hundred fifty pounds, right? But the thing is, the old bastard got too big for his dick. Something was wrong with it. The circulation or something. Fat bastard couldn't get a hard-on, couldn't piss right. His plumbing was screwed up. So anyways, he has a fake dick installed. Bend it upright—boom!—you got a hard-on. Just like that. Like a fucking flagpole. The EMS guys found it when they were checking the body."

"You needn't delight so much in the poor man's misfortune," Mushy says gravely. "What about Fritzy?"

"Fritzy had to make the trip with his own dick."

"So what happened, Jack?"

"Who knows? Tiny and Fritzy sure as shit don't. Guess it was just their time."

"I'm gonna miss Tiny."

"Mushy, stop being a senile newspaper asshole. He was a miserable guinea gangster."

"Yeah, but he was our gangster."

Gallagher thinks a moment, then shrugs. "I guess I know what you mean."

"You gotta keep me right on this, Jack."

"I'll do what I can. You know how big this one's gonna get."

"Jack. Please. After all I did for your father?"

"Good night, Mushy."

"Good night, detective."

Mushy walks toward the river, away from the low-flying cloud of hot light designating the reporters' position. Little pricks, all of them. The evening's final edition had already passed through the presses. That's how it is these days. Can't get anything in the paper. Used to be, the presses ran all the night. But tomorrow, only the harmlessly handsome television imbeciles will have the story. Just as well. Let these kids from Columbia rewrite the wire service copy on Monday. Mushy's got this one played just right. He'll show them all what a newspaper story really is.

The street is lined with former carriage houses and brownstones. The trees are decorated with a spray of white lights. Like Christmas in June. Very nice, Mushy thinks. He crosses the street and walks to the end of a landing. Below, the East River shimmers in the night. Mushy can see the ruins of a municipal hospital on Roosevelt Island. He can see the magnificent Pepsi-Cola sign, a neon monument across the river in Long Island City. He sniffs at the air again. The city never ceases to be beautiful. That always surprises him. He thinks of Tiny Colosimo, the first time he saw him. Was it an arraignment? He was young then. Yes, everybody was young.

Bless Tiny for his fake dick. Mushy wishes he had a fake dick of his own. He hopes that Tiny didn't suffer, that he never saw it coming. An odd sentiment, accompanied by a still odder one; Mushy begins to recite the Kaddish. He does this for Tiny. *"Yisgaddal, v'yiskaddash, sh'meh rabbo."* Those are all the words he knows, all that he can remember. It has been many, many years, too many to count, since he had been in a shul. He repeats the words three times.

The prayer is not with him long, though. Mushy has a great, good fortune to consider: Tiny Colosimo, last of the godfathers, struck down gangland-style. Splendid, New York needs this. You can't fill the pages of a newspaper with colored kids shooting each other in housing projects over . . . what is that stuff called, crack. Yes, crack. Imagine that, mere children playing out gangster pictures with live rounds. There's no charm in that. Only gets people depressed. No, you need a story like this.

A story with a little class.

Mushy pats himself down, finds the crumpled pack of Carltons and tosses them away. What he is looking for is in the hip pocket of his overcoat. His last Lucky. He had been saving it. He had hoped there would be a night like this.

The Lucky tastes stale, but good. After all, there's a principle involved.

Moishe Finkelstein from Dumont Avenue in Brownsville unzips his fly, slips his old man's dick between the bars of the fence, offers it to the wind, and lets out a healthy stream of piss toward the East River.

CHAPTER

13

HE LOVES HER this way.

When it gets hot, with only a sheet between her and the evening.

She had fallen asleep with the TV on, but thought to keep the volume real low. That was what you call considerate. Carmen was good like that. She knew he needed peace and quiet to think, what with all she had told him.

They sleep with the window open. It's the only way this time of year. City sounds float into the room like an ether: sirens and traffic in the distance, then, closer, more immediate, the voices of kids hanging out downstairs.

Kids.

They always seem to find him.

Getting into bed, he wonders why that is.

Kids sure as hell don't pay the bills.

He looks around the room, taking inventory: the blistering plaster, the rusty stains that have spread from the ceiling to the walls. The big metal floor fan sounds like the back end of an exhaust vent. Sure be nice to have air conditioning. And a color TV.

This is no way to live, he thinks. She deserves better. Especially now.

He slips in beside her, his soft prick pressing against the fleshy bulb of her ass, and sneaks an arm around her midsection. There is a warmth to her that is apart from the season.

"Come to Popi."

She makes a face, groans without opening her mouth. She sounds like the mummy.

He loves her like this.

He wishes he did better by her.

He just needs some money is all.

Needs to make a score.

At least he got a plan. Something he's been thinking about a long time: his own place. He'll start small, start with some of the kids. The old man was right, the kid with the crazy hair would have a future. Well, at least he should have one anyways. You never can tell. Nothing's a lock. There's always risks.

Whatever. He'll be there as it grows, as the kids grow into fighters and the fighters grow into champions. And if there's no champions, just kids, then so what? It'll be great just the same. It'll be his place.

And he just found the guy who can help him. The guy's got some problems, sure. Matter of fact, long as he's being honest with himself, he has to admit he doesn't even like Frank. But sometimes, you have to overlook certain things. You have to make exceptions.

It's like the tough guys were always saying, you gotta do what you gotta do.

To provide.

Now the mummy stirs. Carmen turns on her side, pulling the sheet with her.

Just wait'll he opens the place, his gym. He's gonna take real good care of Carmen. He's gonna even up the score, take as good care of her as she did of him. Take care of her brother, too. Angel was getting a little wacky with all that Puerto Rican voodoo. That's okay. Angel's just a little sad is all. After he opens the gym, he'll straighten Angel out just fine.

He reaches over to kiss the mummy's belly.

But before he can, a girder of agony runs up his spine.

The pain makes him shudder, then leaves, as swift and stealthy as it came. Always happens like that. All these years, he thinks, and it's still there, never far. Hits you when you're not looking. The pain works like memory.

He wonders if the old man can see what's going on. What would he say? Who knows? One thing's for sure, Paddy Blood wouldn't approve of this arrangement with Frank.

What the fuck. It wasn't the old man's problem. The old man was dead.

That's just the way it is. He needs Frank.

And Frank's kid. What to make of him?

He can see the boy's face now: that puzzled look, the bloody nose. What's his name? Nicky? Yeah, that's it. He feels bad for Nicky. It's something they both know. Nicky doesn't belong in the gym.

Yeah, but you gotta make exceptions, he tells himself. Do what you gotta do.

The TV cuts away from the reruns to a news bulletin. Must be a big story to bust in on "The Odd Couple" like that.

The reporter, the one with the name like a male porno star, is yelling something about "Gangland Slaying." There's a dead guy in the background. At least it looks like a dead guy. Who else they gonna drape in a white sheet?

Getting up from the bed, he cannot help but laugh to himself. These fucking guys.

The poor bastard in the white sheet disintegrates into a blip as he turns off the TV.

Feeling blessed, he kneels beside her. He kisses her openmouthed, sucking gently on her stomach.

Frank's kid comes into his mind again. He does not know why. Only that he sees the kid's face, the way he looked stumbling into him: defeated. Doesn't have what it takes. Paddy Blood used to say, show me a fighter, I'll show you a kid who's been torn down. The old man used to say a kid can't really fight until he's lost something, until he realizes he's alone, until he knows there ain't nobody—not the manager, the cutman, sure as shit not the trainer—who can fight for him.

And maybe that explains Nicky Battaglia, this kid who surrenders so easily. The boy was still looking for someone to fight for him.

Didn't make him a bad kid. But it might make him trouble.

He hopes the boy doesn't get him jammed up with Frank, doesn't rat him out.

You never can tell.

Those kind of kids are spoiled.

There's always risks.

Now, ignoring his wife's grunting protest, he plants a kiss on her splendid, swelling belly.

Toodie Gleason hopes it's a girl.

CHAPTER

14

IN THE DAYS following Salvatore Colosimo's death, Frank would barge into Nicky's room at six-thirty in the morning. It is his idea that they should do their roadwork together. He wears a plastic suit underneath gray cotton sweats to induce profuse perspiration.

"Let's go," he says, "we ain't got much time."

All of a sudden, everything seems very precious to him. Time. Money. A glass of grappa after dinner. Even his family. There are odd moments when Frank becomes downright tender, interrupting Theresa at the stove with a kiss and some flowers. "Put these somewheres," he tells her, a little boy's smile at his lips. And for Nicky there is a medallion of the lady saint. Frank presents it to his son with a declaration. "I got this for you, Nicky," he says, stumbling just a bit with the words. "You know how much, you know, how I love you, kid." Frank smothers the boy in his arms, buries Nicky's face in his chest. Frank looks to have been up all night. He is already sweating and the odor of his Aqua Velva is stale. He pulls Nicky closer. "I don't wanna fight no more, Nicky. Be good boy to your father." He kisses the top of Nicky's head. It seems a long time before he lets Nicky go. Nothing panics Nicky so much as his father's bouts with good feeling and charity.

"C'mon, get dressed," Frank repeats. "There ain't much time."

They trot down Bedford, to Carmine, moving west past Leroy Park. Nicky listens to his father, the short, greedy gasps of his breath.

Running alongside the river, Nicky realizes that his sense of space has been distorted. His world is too small, too hard, too dense. He has lived his entire life in the neighborhood. But here, along the water, everything opens up in one disorienting instant. All of a sudden, there is Jersey, then the giant money buildings down around Wall Street. The world has become startlingly big—the docks, the occasional ocean liner, the barges, the sky. It feels as if he is at the edge of the earth, as if the world begins, or ends, at Pier 40.

"That's where your grampa worked," Frank snorts. "Broke his ass . . . and for what?"

Frank Battaglia rarely speaks of his father. Or his mother for that matter. Nicky thinks it odd to consider him as ever having been somebody's son. His grandparents, Nicholas and Evangeline Battaglia, had died before he was born. He knows very little of them. He imagines his grandmother as being pretty much like the other widows in the neighborhood, all those ladies who whisper the rosary with such diligence.

Of the grandfather for whom he is named, Nicky knows just a bit more. He knows that the man died with lungs blackened by a three-pack-a-day habit of Lucky Strikes. He knows his grandpa was a stevedore, unloading the cargoes of great ships. He understands that it must have been a marginally honest living, collecting the odd items that happened to fall from the cargo pallets. Small-time stuff.

"A sucker's score," says Frank. He does not hide his distaste for his parents' Old World ways. They came from Sicily, immigrants, doomed to think like peasants, content with a railroad flat, grateful for union wages, lacking, by Frank Battaglia's standards, the ambitions, the cravings, the lusty, star-spangled desires.

Frank shakes his head. "For what?"

Nicky runs harder now, down West Street, toward the big buildings, the Trade Center, breaking free. But as he finds his full stride, Frank grabs his T-shirt from behind and yanks him back.

"Where you think you're going, kid?"

CHAPTER
15

MUSHY DOES NOT play his hand at once. He works the story, builds it, gives it legs, as they used to say.

"You'll get my copy at six o'clock," he tells the little pricks. "Don't bother me till then."

For a week after Tiny Colosimo's death, Mushy Flynn lives on the front page. Each day, he feeds the city a little more. He abandons standard newspaper style and writes as a columnist. "Fuck 'em if they don't like it," he mutters. "Let 'em put me back on the lobster."

In Monday's editions, he writes "Tiny's Last Supper," claiming that he has obtained, exclusively, early results of the autopsy from which he "reconstructs" the late, great, five-foot, seven-inch, three-hundred-and-fifty-pound gangster's final feast: brandy, snails, goose liver pâté, hearts of palm and goat cheese glazed with raspberry vinaigrette, wild boar carpaccio, more brandy, the best of bottles from the Rothschild Château, steak frites, more brandy, this time with seltzer, roast duck with Bing cherry sauce, candied sweet potato pudding, and buttered asparagus spears. For dessert, Fritzy the bodyguard was dispatched to fetch a pint of Häagen-Dazs peanut butter double fudge.

The little pricks don't change a word.

The television imbeciles lead the eleven o'clock news with "according to the *Mirror* . . ." calling Tiny the "gastronomic godfather."

At that moment, there is a three-hour wait for a table at April.

On Tuesday, Mushy scores big with "Mystery Blonde." He imagines a woman of considerable breeding. Probably Vassar. Possibly Wellesley. "FBI investigators have a composite sketch of our damsel. She's said to be a contemporary version of the Grace Kelly type."

He is liberal in his use of the words "moll" and "gunsel."

Wednesday, Mushy does the fake penis story, his biggest score of all. He argues that the headline, in deference to Tiny, should read "Prisoner of Love."

"Hey," he tells the little pricks, "a lot of guys' faucets don't run."

But the editors go with "Tiny's Love Thing." In his heart, Mushy knows they are right. After all, it's not *The Wall Street Journal.*

Thursday, he breaks more news, announcing that federal authorities found a "poached painting" at the scene of the crime, a masterpiece by Salvador Dali—*The Discovery of America by Christopher Columbus*. Mushy writes that Tiny's taste in art, albeit stolen, was a sign of the gangster's advanced character, proof of how much Tiny had grown in the job.

"The feds are trying to verify the painting's authenticity," he writes. "But Mushy says: verify shmerify. Tiny Colosimo didn't steal schlock. And truth be told, he deserves some credit. Most wise guys have a notion that never evolves beyond 'Dogs Playing Pool,' plastic slipcovers, and a crucifix."

The little pricks tell him to lose the crucifix line. They say it's offensive. Mushy says if they change a word, his next exclusive will appear in the *Post.*

Nobody touches his copy.

That evening, he appears on a network news segment— "The Last Godfather." Mushy tells the booking lady from the network he is so deep into the story that he must protect himself, safeguard his identity.

The chief crime correspondent for the *New York Mirror*, as he has specified his position, appears before the nation shrouded in shadows. Mushy wears his fedora.

He is living his glory now. Making up for everything. He's up to a pack of Luckies a day. He pisses and it's like a waterfall.

On Friday Mushy goes to the morgue, the newspaper's library of clippings. There he finds a 1952 clip mentioning Salvatore Colosimo as one of several men from the West Village arrested and arraigned on gambling charges.

Mushy is sure that he was there that day. He went to so many of those shit arraignments. He was what, working for the *Post* back then, or was it the *News?* Whatever, he must have been there.

Beginning with the arraignment, Mushy writes a piece, "Tiny and Me." It is full of half-truths, misplaced gossip, and ambitious imaginings, most of which Mushy convinces himself are absolutely true:

He came out of the now-defunct Fathers Club on Sullivan Street, but acquired the requisite experience with gun and garrote working in the service of Albert Anastasia, the Lord High Executioner of Murder Inc.

Albert's brother was a priest. But this Father Anastasia had a weakness for women, one of whom carried the Lord High Executioner's nephew in her womb. Albert decided his brother must die. Murder was one thing, but a broken vow of celibacy another entirely. It would embarrass his mother.

"Tiny," Albert called, "I have a job for you."

"Lord High Executioner," beseeched Tiny, "do not do this thing, for your brother will not die in a state of grace."

Anastasia, concerned with his standing among the angels, accepted Tiny's impudent advice. But things were never the same between the boss and his plump apprentice.

Mushy has always credited—on superlative authorities—Tiny Colosimo as the guy who actually blew away Anastasia as he sat in a barber's chair, in what is now the dreadful Omni Park Hotel.

Toward the end, Tiny was partial to snifters of pale Armagnac and skinny blondes of respectable lineage. "I like the ones whose daddies drink at the Union Club," he would say.

Tiny Colosimo was no two-bit hijacker, no hot head with a union card. He was nothing like these little @#$&s running things today.

One evening, over black coffee and grappa, he told me how he had purchased a pirated oil painting by the Catalonian surrealist Salvador Dali.

"I like the craziness," said Tiny, "the way this guy manipulates it."

Mushy presses the key that zaps the story to the city desk and fires up another Lucky. "It's all sportswriting," he declares aloud.

Sure. Mushy learned that as a kid, back in the days of hot type, when working for the paper was like working for the Irish civil service. The dumb mick editors, ignorant of his talent, had him cover the Golden Gloves prelims. The assignment was beneath him: a bunch of kids pummeling each other in church basements and banquet halls and rec centers. Even then, Mushy knew he was meant for bigger things. He'd come back from those dingy little fights and tell the editor, "Nothing happened."

"Something always happens. Maybe you just didn't see it."

"No."

"Was there any blood?"

"They stopped it too soon."

"Then make up the blood."

Mushy had to think about that one.

"Gotta give the people what they want," said the editor. "Real simple. It's sportswriting is all it is: a good guy, a bad guy, and a little blood. And if you don't get that, make it up."

Wasn't bad advice.

The next morning, Mushy looked in the paper for his story. The dumb mick had changed his byline, from Moishe Finkelstein to Mushy Flynn.

Been that way ever since.

Now, the little prick with the MBA comes by Mushy's desk. He says he wants to chat. Mushy puffs furiously on his Lucky.

The MBA loathes smoke. He considers his decree that made the newsroom a "Smoke Free Zone" as a major accomplishment in contemporary journalism. But he pretends not to notice the gray cloud that hovers over Mushy. He has seen a blip in the circulation figures.

"How's it hanging, Mr. Flynn?"

Little prick. Mushy barely looks up from his computer terminal.

"Listen, Mushy, we've been thinking. This Mafia stuff. This is good stuff. People like this stuff."

Mushy eyeballs him. This kid needs a goddamn chart to know that?

"Anyway, we've been kicking this around. We want you to write a column. Full-time. You know, a diary of the mob. Gangland stuff. No crack killers in the projects. People get sick of that. Too depressing. We need more, you know, real gangsters."

Mushy says nothing. Just smokes.

The MBA says, "You know, make it what you want."

At least the little prick has finally come to his senses.

"I was thinking maybe we should call it"—the MBA makes a frame with his hands for effect—"'Mushy's Mob.'"

Mushy takes a thoughtful drag on his Lucky, then blows a batch of his own personal smog into the little prick's face.

"Yeah," he says. "Yeah, that'll do."

CHAPTER

16

NICKY SITS ON the stoop, reading the *Mirror*.

And wondering who the fuck this guy in the paper thinks he is.

The column logo has Mushy Flynn depicted as a cartoon, like something out of a Dick Tracy strip, with a dark black fedora tilted over his eyes. Beneath the caricature it says: "Mushy's Mob by Mushy Flynn." The way Nicky reads it, Mushy Flynn writes like Dick Young, that old sportswriter in the *Post*, but with bigger words.

The column begins: "In the wake of Tiny Colosimo's untimely demise, Phillip (Philly) Testa and Frank (Frankie Batts) Battaglia have been christened the new boss and underboss of the Corallo crime family, Mushy's Mob has learned exclusively."

What does that make me? Nicky wonders.

He continues: "The upstart hoodlums have shifted their locus of operations from the Ninth Ward Rod and Reel Club on Bedford Street, no longer real fishermen. The new don and his leg-breaker have made themselves lord and viceroy of the Cicero Club, from here on renamed by Mushy as the Bath and Tennis Society of Mulberry Street.

"Lawmen know little about these *gavons* from Greenwich Village. Testa has no record, and had even been considered a loyal friend to Don Colosimo, according to the G-men. A bit more is known about Frankie Batts. He is treasurer of Local 6 of the dockworkers. In 1976, he did nine months of a three-year sentence for labor racketeering. Before that, it seems, he was a prizefighter known as the Bedford Brawler, a *nomme de guerre* said to be as apropos now as it was then. No doubt his pug's training left him eminently qualified for service as a soldier in the labor movement.

"But authorities are much more interested in whether Mssrs. Testa and Battaglia had a prior 'relationship' with the Mystery Blonde. In case you missed it, Mushy's Mob reported exclusively last week that lawmen are looking for a striking, flaxen-haired damsel who accompanied Tiny Colosimo to his Last Supper . . ."

"What the fuck you reading?"

Frank Battaglia steps onto the stoop wearing a black double-breasted, a white-on-white shirt with the big collar, matching pocket square and tie.

"Lemme see that." Frank snatches the paper. He mumbles the words he reads.

"Where's this old bastard gettin' this shit?" says Frank.

"Where you going?" asks Nicky.

"Downtown," says Frank.

"What for?"

"Business. What are you a cop?" Frank goes back to the column. "Bath and Tennis. Fuck is that about? Me and Philly, we don't even play tennis."

Frank wonders if the guy in the paper is trying to call him a pussy. "Don't never let me catch you reading this shit again."

"I'm only reading the sports."

Frank, still reading: "He calls me a *gavon*. This broken fuck calls me *that?* Lies."

Cheech pulls up in the Chrysler, letting it idle at the hydrant across the street, yelling out the window: "Get ready for Freddy."

Frank hollers back, "What, now you're in a hurry?

Fuckin' retard. I'll be there in a second." Then, tucking the paper under his arm, turning to his kid: "I'm telling ya, Nicky. Don't let me catch you reading this shit."

"I told you I only got it for the scores."

Now Philly Testa pokes his head out of the car. "Frank, I'm tired of waiting for your ass."

Frank shouts back, "Hey, I'm talking to my kid, you mind?" He flashes his cousin a dirty look as he starts walking toward the car, walking into a trap.

Suddenly, he's surrounded by them. Like they came out of nowhere with their cameras and microphones and tape recorders and notepads. The Chinese lady is out in front. She wears more makeup in real life than she does on TV.

She's got the microphone in his face.

But Frank doesn't look so upset about it, telling the Chinese lady: "Me? I'm just a neighborhood guy."

"Are you really a boxer?" she asks.

Frank smiles with mock innocence. "Yeah, I still put on the gloves. Now and then."

And Salvatore Colosimo?

"I kind of liked him, the Fatman . . . He wasn't skinny, though." Frank Battaglia's getting laughs from the reporters. They love him.

"So I knew him, so what?" he says. "That don't make me Scarface."

Who?

"Scarface," he says. "Nineteen thirty-two. Starring Paul Muni and George Raft." Frank winks at the Chinese lady. "You ought to see it sometime."

Nicky watches his father get in the back of the Chrysler, Uncle Philly not saying anything, just glaring, thinking what Nicky's thinking, thinking: Jesus Christ, the guy's enjoying this shit.

The Chrysler screeches away. The reporters pack up and go. But Nicky remains on the stoop long after the show is over. Everything is changing so fast, so irreversibly.

Every day his world moves deeper into something bad.

He just doesn't know what.

Nicky considers the condo across the street, a doorman building, built with pale orange cinderblocks, conspicuous in its newness, alone among the row of dirty railroad flats. Sometimes he tries to peek inside, to spy, to see how these people live. His father calls them "snotty WASP's" and "cunty kids." Nicky thinks of words they use, things he doesn't really know: "personal computers," "vertical blinds," "The Arts and Leisure Section," "butcher block," "brunch."

What the fuck was a brunch?

He wonders, Do they smack each other? Do they scream? Do they screw?

Did they know who he was?

The son of the big-time Mafia gangster who lived next door.

The underboss of the Corallo crime family.

The leg-breaker who did a bit.

These reporters, he thinks, they're so full of shit.

Viceroy of the Cicero.

Mystery Blonde.

So full of shit.

Mystery Blonde. Flaxen-haired damsel. The Fatman.

Mystery Blonde . . .

Nah, couldn't be. Not her.

CHAPTER

17

MUSHY FLYNN PUTS a quarter in the pay phone, dials the number, and waits, watching as a pale kid with greasy acne and a green Mohawk walks through the lobby of the Chelsea Hotel. The kid stops at the front desk to ask for the Sid Vicious room. Jesus Christ, thinks Mushy, I can't take this madhouse anymore.

"Organized Crime."

"Jack? That you, Jack?"

"That's me, Mushy. What the fuck are you doing? Lying your ass off in the paper, making heroes of these douche bags."

"What the fuck am I doing? What the fuck are you doing? Don't you have a case to solve? A very big case, I might add."

"A bad guy got whacked, Mushy. Happens every day."

"I'm old so let me get this straight: a Mafia don, the last of this city's great gangsters, was assassinated gangland style outside what is now, thanks to yours truly, the hottest joint in town. He was dining with a young lady of fine pedigree, a mysterious blonde, who I might add, Jack, remains a goddamn mystery to all you civil servants. As a result of said assassination, organized crime is now in the clutches of a gang of vicious upstarts, and you got the balls to tell me it happens every day?"

"What do you want, Mushy?"

"I want it all, but I'll start with the girl."

"Still nothing. Don't know who she is, where she came from."

"What about the painting?"

"The guys in the lab are still trying to authenticate. The thing could be a phony . . . not that you give a shit."

"You got anyone at the scene? Witnesses?"

"Not yet."

"Not yet is not good, Jack."

"We're working day and night. I'm breaking my ass. Why don't you solve the big case, you're the goddamn expert. By the way, that Mushy Mob getup, you look like something out of Dick Tracy."

"Not good at all, Jack. But tell me, 'cause you know I love you, and you know I think you're a helluva cop, even if you are Irish, but tell me, what are you doing with the taxpayers' money while the killers of Tiny Colosimo go free?"

"You know something, Mushy? I liked you better when you were a busted old valise."

"After all I did for your father, you talk to me like that. Just tell me, how do you think the bosses are gonna like it when Mushy's Mob reports that the United States Attorney and the Federal Bureau of Investigation and the New York City Police Department don't know their ass from their elbow in the biggest organized crime case since 1957?"

"What was fifty-seven?"

"Anastasia."

"Forgot. You know, I don't go back as far as you, Mushy."

"So tell me how the bosses would like a story like that? Nice front page, huh? The Federal Bureau of Idiots."

"I'm too tired for this shit, Mushy."

"Tell me, who are Testa and Battaglia?"

"I *told* you, they're jerkoffs. They got a club on Bedford Street, Ninth Ward Rod and Reel or some typical guinea shit like that, and they sit around scratching their balls and drinking coffee and talking about what big men they are, what great fucking outdoorsmen, and you can't hear shit 'cause they got this Perry Como music playing all the time. So stop breaking balls."

"What do you mean, you can't hear anything?"

"Mushy . . ."

"What do you mean, Perry Como music?"

"Mushy Flynn, the world's dumbest Jew."

"You got a wire in there?"

"World's dumbest Jew. It's been in there a year already. Ever since the politician U.S. Attorney decided he wants to be mayor. They run the ILA and the meatpackers out of there. The only problem is, you can't hear a thing. Like I said, alls you can hear is Perry Como music."

"You were holding out on me, Jack."

"Mushy, so help me God, if there's a word about that wire in the paper—a word—I will hunt you down like the old dog you are."

"Jack, I'm offended. I would never, ever. We're friends, Jack. I knew your father. The only question now is, how are you gonna make it up to me?"

"Make it up to you? Lissen, I already told you more than I should, enough for me to lose my job. Mushy, you gave your word, now I gotta go back to work. I got a guy I'm speaking to."

"A rat?"

"That's not the word we use."

"An informant?"

"Maybe."

"Just tell me one thing, this guy, this alleged informant, he ever been in that Rod and Reel Club?"

". . . maybe."

"How many times?"

"How the fuck do I know? . . . Let's just say he's in there regularly. Okay? Don't let me see 'regularly' in the paper."

"Wouldn't dream of it. This guy, your guy you're talking to, he knows what's going on?"

"I sure as shit hope so."

"Trying to hold out on me, huh?"

"Mushy, me? Nah. By the way, how's the plumbing these days? You pissin' good?"

"Like a waterfall, Jack."

JACK GALLAGHER HAS a big, broad grin as he hangs up the phone, thinking: Mushy-fucking-Flynn. How long has he known that guy? He was what, a rookie in the Seven-Three over in Brownsville. He had beaten the shit out of some heroin pushers working a school yard, right outside P.S. 66 on New Lots. The next day a teacher from the school calls the *Mirror*, probably to complain about police brutality, and Mushy Flynn shows up at the precinct. He does a story, writing all this shit about the scourge of drugs, the rookie cop who cares, the wide-eyed children who look up to him, the whole bit. The next week, the *Daily News* does a story: "Jack Gallagher, Hero of the Month." It wasn't long after that the bosses made him a detective. He spent the next nineteen years of his life in Brooklyn North, shaking down dirt bags for confessions, telling them: I'm your best friend, pally, and this, this is the most important day of your life. Either you tell me what happened, or you can tell the brothers in Rikers, 'cause I'm sure they'll think you're pretty.

Jack Gallagher can't help but chuckle thinking of the funny shit some of the skells used to say: I didn't see no shooting, offisah. I was busy *sodomizing* my car . . . I didn't see what happened. I was lookin' at the time, checkin' my *Rolodex* . . . Nah, I ain't got no priors on my sheet, just a summons for lewd and *lavicious* . . . I tell you, Gallagher, but it's between us. It's gotta be *unanimous.*

Funny bastards. Jack almost misses them.

He got out of the P.D., right after he did his twenty. Last case he worked was a little kid from the projects, Antonio Witherspoon, eight years old, shot in a crossfire on Dumont Avenue. Jack stayed up all night in Kings

County Hospital, waiting for the doctors to finish with the kid so he could get a statement. But by the time they let him into the ER, Antonio Witherspoon was already on his way out. The boy lay there, all those fucking tubes coming out of his arm and his nose. Jack couldn't do a goddamn thing but watch as Antonio Witherspoon became a ghost.

When the sun came up, Jack put in his papers. Fuck it. He had no wife, no kids, no one to answer to. Just an outstanding offer from the U.S. Attorney's office to work the Organized Crime squad.

To work with a better class of skell.

The kind they make movies about. The kind that Mushy Flynn loves.

The notion makes him snicker again: the way he played Mushy. Using Mushy as much as Mushy used him.

Jack Gallagher gets up and lets himself into the next room where his guy is waiting. His big informant is an old Italian guy named Alphonse Garguilo. He runs some deli in the neighborhood and a restaurant called Garguilo's of Thompson Street. Twice a week, he brings food to the wise guys at the club. They say his kid got whacked.

"You got anything to tell me?" Gallagher asks him.

"I no tell you anything."

"O.K."

"What kine man you think I am?"

"I said O.K.," says Gallagher. "That's fine. You're free to go."

CHAPTER

18

NICKY PORES THROUGH a book called Rockin' Steady, *about a basketball player named Walt "Clyde" Frazier. Clyde doesn't even play for the Knicks anymore. But that doesn't matter. It's important, like the music, mostly because Buddy says it is. Buddy's a little wacky like that.*

The paperback is billed as a "Guide to Cool." And as Nicky wants so very much to be cool, like Buddy and like Clyde, he studies the photograph of the "Clyde Super Bed," which looks like a small spaceship with mirrors. He memorizes the indexed catalog; "Clyde's Wardrobe Stats": five applejack caps, a baby blue lambskin suit, a black coat made of elephant hide, jeans with a UFO patch, and two orgy belts, the ones with sexual positions corresponding to each astrological sign. Nicky wonders when he'll be old enough to wear an orgy belt.

"I bet Clyde gets a lot pussy."

"Shhhh. Shattup." Buddy points at the Emerson hi-fi. "Yo, turn it up." Vaughn Harper is spinning "Have You Seen Her" on the "Quiet Storm."

"That's what I'm talking about," says Buddy. "The Chi-Lites. The girl likes to feel a little sad, like she wants to feel your heart break a little."

Nicky doesn't quite understand. "What's it like," he asks, "to fuck?"

"Feels like you got rocket ships in your ass."

"How's it smell?"

Buddy shoves a stubby middle finger under his brother's nose. "Here," he says. "That's Mary Rocca's."

There is a rim of dirt under Buddy's fingernail. But the only scents Nicky can detect come from roach clips and Trojan grease. He knows because he has stolen one of his father's rubbers and examined it.

"Buddy, it don't smell like fish."

"It ain't supposed to, stupid."

"Would you fuck a black girl?"

Buddy assumes an almost professional posture to consider the question. "Sure," he says. "Lots of 'em: Cleopatra Jones, Foxy Brown, Christie Love. You gotta like any woman got their own theme music." Buddy points an imaginary pistol at his kid brother. "Freeze, sugar."

Now a hot white light, the sun streaking across Nicky's eyes.

He's been dreaming, again, another real life dream, exactly as it happened. That's how it's been lately, that imagination of his which runs so wild in the day has become dormant in his sleep. His dreams are no longer dreams so much as remembrances populated by ghosts.

Nicky squints, turning from the light. An array of sharp shadows have gathered high on the wall. Nicky reads them like a sundial. It must be late, he thinks. Shit.

He groans. He stirs, feeling the soreness that he brings home from the gym. Two weeks at the gym and still the aches linger: at the peak of his left shoulder, under his armpits, across the muscled bands of his stomach, even in his lungs. It all feels like dread.

All of him, except his dick.

He starts to pull on it.

He's been jerking-off a lot.

He's never fucked a girl, but he has an idea. Buddy told him. Yeah, Buddy said it was like rocket ships in your ass.

His mind runs to Mary Rocca. He imagines her doing

things. Specific things. Dirty things. Cleopatra Jones, he can imagine having her, too.

And the girl. Sam-Samantha. He hasn't seen her around but he wishes to God he had. He remembers her crying. Shutting her door. She's his Mystery Blonde. Try as he may, he cannot recall her face, only disembodied pieces of it, her nose, the curl in her lip, but not the whole face. He wants to envision her well, accurately, perfectly. He wants to imagine her doing things, too. But his mind's eye is blurry and Sam-Samantha does not come into focus. That's just how it happens. He finds himself jerking-off to the idea of her.

Struggling furiously with his hard-on.

He's about to come when his mother knocks at the door.

"Your father wants to speak to you."

Panic. ". . . I'm sleeping, Ma."

"Nick-eee."

"Ma."

"Nicky, your father wants you in the kitchen . . . Now."

FRANK BATTAGLIA SITS at the table with all the Sunday papers: the *Post*, the *News*, the *Mirror*, even the *Times*, which Nicky thinks odd since the *Times* doesn't publish the lines and the sports pages suck. Frank wears his morning uniform: a guinea-tee and boxers. Nicky can see he's already pissed off, probably something in the papers.

"Here," Frank says finally. "I almost forgot. These came for you." He slides a batch of torn envelopes across the table. The letters are addressed to Nicky, but Frank had already taken the liberty of examining their contents, as he is paranoid about anything that arrives with the sanction of the federal government.

The letters bear all sorts of fancy emblems and crests. Most of them were postmarked months ago, sent from the athletic departments of various colleges: Monmouth, St. Francis in Brooklyn, Holy Cross, Fordham. There was even one from Yale.

Each envelope note reads much the same: "Dear Nicho-

las . . . looking for fine young men like you . . . playing basketball . . . scholarship . . . opportunities . . . beautiful campus . . . look forward to seeing you."

College, Nicky thinks, college coaches writing to him,
talking about a full boat ride. And his old man never even
said anything. Nicky flips through the brochures in a
daze, shuffling through photographs of students reading
in lawn chairs under big shady trees, gathered in semi-
nars and laboratories, and buildings with massive, white,
Corinthian-style columns. Nicky could go to college.
He's always been smart. He's known that since he was a
little kid, since his mother taught him to read, arranging
those magnetized alphabet letters across the refrigerator.

The brochure from Yale celebrates a sprawling lawn,
libraries that look like great gray cathedrals, dormitories
with courtyards called quadrangles. Nicky thinks of the
girl, Sam-Samantha. She would be impressed if he told
her he was going to Yale.

Frank snatches the glossy booklet from his son. "Hey,
Nicky," he asks, "what's a quadrangle? That a gay bar?"

"Real funny, Pop."

"Nicky, I wanna talk to you. There's some things we
gotta discuss."

"What's the matter?"

Frank holds up the Sunday *Mirror*. The paper is
already folded back to page three, which is a big Mushy
Flynn story. The word "E-X-C-L-U-S-I-V-E" forms a
pale banner of red ink, set diagonally across pages four
and five, underneath reams of black type. The two-
page spread is graced by a large display photograph of
Uncle Phillip and Frank Battaglia bullshitting in front of
the Rod and Reel. They wear floral polyester shirts with
collars cut like the wings of an airplane. Their slacks—
they were called "double knits" back then—ride high
over their waists, with wraparound belts encasing their
love handles. Philly Testa is adjusting a pair of dark
shades. Frank Battaglia, his mouth wide open, is patting
his chest, an urban Tarzan. It's an old photograph, mid- to
late seventies, Nicky figures. The lensman was an FBI

agent working surveillance. The bold-type caption in the newspaper begins: *"Thing one and thing two."*

Frank sets the paper down in front of his son. "G'wan," he says. "Read it."

Nicky looks quizzically at his father. Perhaps this is a test. That's not beyond him. Nicky is now forbidden to read even the sports pages, much less that "half-assed old Jew-mick cocksucker," as Mushy Flynn is now referred to in the Battaglia household.

"But I thought . . ."

"Read the fuckin' thing out loud. Read it so your mother can hear, too. 'Cause I don't wanna answer no questions from youse later."

Nicky searches for an answer in his mother's eyes, but Theresa Battaglia's attention remains riveted on the breakfast to be. It's easier for her that way.

"G'head, read it."

Nicky begins hesitantly, stumbling over the words: "'Philly Testa, the last of the Village hoodlums, is in a fix: another victim of rat poison . . .'"

"'. . . Mushy's Mob has learned, and learned exclusively we might add, that the feds are about to drop the big one on the caretakers of the Bath and Tennis Society of Mulberry Street—the debonair and ruthless Philly Testa, and his sidekick, Frankie (Frankie Batts) Battaglia, the ex-pug . . .'"

Nicky looks up, begging for mercy. "But . . ."

"Read it," Frank yells. "G'wan."

"'Our favorite Republicans at the Department of Justice say this one's gonna be a big-time RICO indictment, pinning the murder of Salvatore "Tiny" Colosimo squarely on the broad shoulders of the dapper Testa and Frankie Batts.

"'At this writing, the feds have a little-bitty rat nibbling away at some cheese. Said rodent is out there right now, closer to the nouveau godfathers than ever they would have suspected.

"'Mushy himself would like to thank the United States Government and the rat, whoever he may turn out to be. Now the readers know Mushy's ethical position on rats. But this time, Mushy condones everything on utilitarian grounds. Mushy wants very much for the killers of Tiny Colosimo to roast in the seventh rung of Lucifer's Lockdown.

" 'They are young, stupid, and brutal, but worse than that, they possess little imagination. They are merely hoodlums whose success speaks volumes for the lack of talent out there.

" 'The feds say they got this one cold. There's a rat out there . . .' "

"Enough," Frank bellows. "I ever catch you reading this shit, I will personally . . ."

"But you said . . ."

"I know. I know. That little half Jew–half mick motherfuck. *Ming*. I shoulda known he woulda liked that cheap cocksucker the Fatman." Frank slaps away his coffee cup, which explodes on the floor like porcelain shrapnel.

"Clean that shit up, Theresa."

Theresa Battaglia scurries to the scene, mopping up the spilled coffee with a damp dishrag. For a moment, she looks as if she wants to say something.

She doesn't say much anymore. But her mere glance is enough to startle Nicky. His mother was once a splendid-looking woman—dark and lush, with full lips and a slender delicate nose. But her beauties have dissipated. She seems to be aging poorly, if that's what it is. Theresa Battaglia has become bony and brittle. She had been particular and deft with her makeup. But now her skin, once smooth as marble, is layered with a rough, greasy cosmetic cake. Her rouge is thick, almost clownish. Her eyebrow pencil leaves a vulgar trace. A smear of lipstick runs off the corner of her mouth. She wears an electric shade of eye shadow.

Nicky watches her, on her knees, collecting the broken bits of china, even as he tries to explain himself to his father. "You know I never read that stuff in the papers," he says.

"You're a good kid, Nicky. I just don't want you to have to hear it on the street. I just want you to know that there's people out there who want to hurt me and Philly. And I want you to know this is all bullshit. I didn't kill that fat fuck. But I swear to God I'm gonna find this rat bastid and suck his motherfucking heart out."

"Suck his heart out," Nicky says quietly. "Yeah."

"This whole thing of ours is falling apart," says Frank. "The neighborhood's a piece a shit. I'm falling over faggots and fuckheads in the street. There's beggars all over. This used to be a good place to live. You know what I'm saying, son? Now, I don't even know no one in this neighborhood anymore. Fuckin' gooks running fruit stores, they make like they don't understand the insurance policies. Chinese restaurants, ever try to shake down a Chink? Carmine Street, they got comic book stores and fag hairdressers. Fucking Cheech goes to the fag hairdresser to explain he gotta pay in, the guy wants to give him a blow job. I'm telling you, the fags are out of hand. Used to be, certain guys of ours ran the fag joints. Hey, it was a nice score. But it was also—how do you say?—a public service. We kept 'em down by the piers, out of the way of the fuckin' civilized people, so's the fags couldn't corrupt nobody's children. But now, *now* they got their own politicians. They say they're coming out of the closet, spreading their curse, that AIDS shit. The *closet*? What the fuck is that? I feel like I'm in a closet living here in my own neighborhood. You can't even get up enough regular guys for a Vegas night no more. And how 'bout those yoms with the, you know, those octopus heads?"

"The Rastas?"

"Yeah. Looks like they got a head of snakes. That's what I'm saying, Nicky. This whole thing's goin' to shit. And the government, the government don't play fair no more, neither. They'd put a bug up your ass if they could. Rats and bugs, that's what they're about. Can't catch you like a man. Tell you what, I'd like to indict those WASP whore motherfuckers. I got no civil rights. You read all those books, you know what I'm talking about. Even the lawyer, Vanderpool, he says it's to the point where me and Philly got no constitutional protections. He says

Thomas Jefferson didn't write up the law so's some rat bastid could crawl out from under a rock. There's only one civil right left: what they call the client-lawyer privilege. That means what I say to him, to Vanderpool, is off limits. And vice versa. But that's only to protect the thieving lawyers so's they get paid no matter what."

"It's not right," says Nicky.

"Of course it ain't right. I mean, the only ones got civil rights is niggers and rats. Fuckin' rats. The government is a piece of shit. Nicky, you know how much taxes I pay? And for what? So the government could pay for some snitch scumbag to live in Arizona? *Ming*, it's the most dishonorable thing you could do, being a rat. I mean that. Nothing is worse than that . . . except maybe raping your mother, your sister, taking it in the ass, crazy shit like that."

Frank's gaze narrows. "Nicky, I want you to tell me if you see anything, you know, maybe you hear things."

"I don't hear things like that. I'm not around like that. You know."

"Well, start. Start being around. You gotta grow up sometime."

"Yeah. I understand."

"Now tell me, yesterday with Toodie, how'd it go?"

"I dunno. Two weeks, he's still teaching me to jab."

"Good. Good. He gotta teach you the right way. Lemme see."

"C'mon, Dad. I just woke up."

"C'mere." Frank gets off his chair and puts up his hands. "Lemme see."

"Ma," Nicky whines, "do I gotta?"

Theresa mumbles her answer without looking up from her frying pans. "Do like your father wants," she says. "It's easier that way."

"Who axed you?" hollers Frank. "What do you mean, 'It's easier that way'? Cook breakfast and leave me with my son."

"Ma . . ."

"Ma . . . do I gotta?" says Frank, mimicking his son's bleating whine. "Now show me what he taught ya."

Nicky begins to jab as per his father's command—harder, more, faster, double up.

"Good, he's teaching you good," says Frank. "You don't know what it took to get a guy like that. A guy like Toodie."

"Whatta you mean?"

"A guy like that, he don't train just anyone. He's a major guy. He's got shit for brains, business-wise I mean. But he's got, whattayoucall, he's got integrity. A guy like that, he understands what it takes to make a fighter."

"How come you know so much about him?"

"'Cause when I was a kid, when I was fighting, I was trained by Paddy Blood."

"So who's that?"

"Who's that? Paddy Blood was the guy taught Toodie everything. Taught him the old way, the right way, everything like it should be. And that's how he's gonna teach you."

"I kind of want to talk to you about that."

"What?"

"I thought this summer I could be playing some ball. You know, even those letters say I could get a scholarship."

"Go to college if you want, fine. But don't start with all this scholarship nonsense, Nicky. I don't need that. I'll pay for you myself. I'm warning you, don't start shit. You wanna play ball, do it on your own time. First, you're gonna learn to be a fighter. That's your job now. We're gonna put you in the Gloves."

"I'm not starting shit. It's just that . . ."

"Don't disappoint me, Nicky."

"I don't want to disappoint you."

"It would break my heart."

"I just . . ."

"Lemme tell you something, you don't appreciate what I'm giving you. I shoulda done this for your brother—rest in peace. *Ming,* I think about it all the time. I shoulda done this for Buddy. Maybe what happened wouldn't a happened if he was, you know, if he was stronger. Maybe the bad things wouldn't a happened."

Buddy, Nicky thinks, it always comes back to Buddy.

"Your brother, he wasn't strong enough."

"Let Buddy rest in peace." Nicky's words are a test, even at a whisper.

"What?"

"I didn't say nothing."

"Don't think you're slick with me. Now tell me again what you . . ."

"I said, let him be." Nicky's voice is strong and clear now, his eyes locked on his father's. "He's dead, Pop. He was a fucking wacko and now he's dead. He can't touch you no more. So let him be."

For a fine moment, Nicky stands in awe of his own idiot courage. Then he realizes; he's in a world of shit.

Frank Battaglia circles his son, nodding, grinning, glaring, until Nicky's steadfast expression fractures with fear. "You know, sometimes I think to myself that you're not my son. Could be, who's to say? Maybe you're somebody else's kid. But my boy wouldn't talk to his father like that. I love you, I give you anything, but then you go and say something like that. You say that to me? That I should leave Buddy alone? You little cunt. You tell me that? Nicky, I axe you to be a man and now you gonna show me. You're gonna show me again what he taught you."

Frank puts up his hands and Nicky lashes at them on command. He can feel his heart thumping. He knows just how badly this can end.

"Pull back the jab," says Frank.

"I am."

"Don't let it sit out there."

"I'm pullin' it . . ."

Boom. Even openhanded, Frank's slap feels like a brick against Nicky's temple. "C'mon, motherfucker," he says. "You talk, you back it up."

Nicky continues to punch dutifully. Frank bangs him again, on the other side this time. "C'mon, tough guy," he says.

What comes next, Nicky doesn't even want to know where it's from, something he had kept inside, for so long and for such a moment, a missile armed with all his angers. Frank is asking for another jab and Nicky loads up a right hand, cocks it all the way back, all the way from his hips, aiming for the pressed-in gristle in his father's nose. For a moment, he believes in the punch, that it will liberate him.

Frank catches the fist in his hand, which closes like a great jaw. Nicky thrashes, but his father's grasp only tightens. Frank begins to growl as he beats on his son, pushing Nicky backward by the trapped fist, toppling him over a chair.

"Don't you ever cross that line," he yells. "I tried so hard for Buddy. You hear me?" Frank grits his teeth, growling again, all of this playing out on instinct now. He kicks Nicky in the ribs, once, twice.

"Take care of your little fuckin' baby son, Theresa. You done a number on this one, too."

Nicky does not open his eyes until he hears the door slam. Then he sees his mother, moving in her slow sleepy way, setting a plate of sausage and eggs by his place at the table. "Nicky, hurry up. We're gonna be late for church." Their eyes meet again, each of them suspended in states of disbelief. "Nicky," she says, "are you gonna be wanting ketchup?"

CHAPTER
19

NICKY STUDIES THE constellation of the apocalypse, as seen through the fleur-de-lis trellis of the confessional booth. The end of the world is depicted in the mural on the vaulted apse, an opera set against flood and flame, and the lady saint, dimpled and pink and baby fat, is handing out rosaries. Kind of funny, he thinks. Buddy would snicker at the magnificent ceiling, saying that if the world was really ending no one would be saying rosaries, everybody'd be out getting laid, humping like bunnies.

Our Lady of the Most Precious Blood was founded a century before Nicky Battaglia's New York, and remains the ancient edifice in his world. It was built with nickels and dimes collected by the Society for the Protection of Italian Immigrants, people who believed in gilt and gold and suffering statues. Nicky understands that his ancestors could not afford subtlety. He also understands that the poor worship well, that somehow they find it easier to believe in God and the saints, to fathom superstitions, blessings, magic and miracles, whether they are asked for from the bleachers at the Stadium or the grandstand at Belmont or the pews of this church.

A sweet, musty fragrance permeates the mahogany

box, sin's humidor. When Nicky was a kid, the confessional frightened him. But not anymore.

"Bless me, Father, for I have sinned. It's been . . ."

"You sinned? That's a surprise."

"Isn't that what you're supposed to say?"

"Yeah, that's what you're supposed to say. Then I'm supposed to say, 'Tell me your sins,' and coax you into telling me that you jerk-off. Right? Isn't that it? You're gonna tell me you had 'impure thoughts,' I love it. If God gets pissed off about impure thoughts we're all gonna roast. Anyway, you say you got impure thoughts, and I'm supposed to ask, 'Did you touch, feel, or rub in any way?' You confess. I tell you, 'Those are very serious sins, son.' I put the numbers in my computer, let the Almighty guide me in the math, work out a penitent equivalence for your sins—couple Hail Marys, maybe an Our Father—and we're all even. We're good. If you've done something ain't covered in the book, I press the switch for the trapdoor. You go straight to hell, to spend eternity with Satan's angels, all of whom look like Sister Margaret. Isn't that how it's supposed to go?"

Nicky snickers. "Damn, Father Vincent."

"There will be no damning in here. And no name calling, either. There's such a thing called the Seal of the Confessional, remember? I'd like to do this by the book, sort of."

"Okay."

"I'm real sorry about your uncle Sal. I know how you felt about him."

"Thank you. I loved him very much. He was very good to me. But what happened to him was a consequence of the way he lived. There's no sense lying about it. Not in here at least.

"I'm glad you're back, Vinny. I heard you were coming. You know, it's kind of hard confessing to the Irish priest."

Each Sunday since Buddy's death, Theresa Battaglia puts on her black funeral ensemble and drags her Nicky to the church. She is morbidly punctual. Nicky proceeds to the confessional while Theresa Battaglia lights a candle in front of St. Anne or St. Rita, then prays with the rest of the mournful sorority, those old women, widows whose husbands were stevedores and short-order cooks and truckers and sanitation men and butchers and meat packers and maybe even, a couple of them, gangsters. They sit in the pews and mouth the words to the rosary in unison. Like a silent movie, Nicky thinks. It makes him uncomfortable to see his mother among their ranks. The old women are so close to beyond; they are intimate with death. But there she is, Ma, where it now seems she will always be, professional sufferer, dutiful griever, praying for miracles but witnessing none, then praying some more. Nicky watches his mother through the fleur-de-lis trellis. Prayer gives her pain a cadence, and perhaps, some relief.

"Will she ever be the same?" Nicky asks.

"No. None of us will."

"I think she's getting worse, Father Vinny."

"She is."

"Scares me. Scares the shit out of me."

"Maybe she should frighten you. I don't mean to sound cruel. She's been through a lot. But you want to save somebody, save yourself first."

"I'm O.K.," says Nicky, touching his ribs, still tender where his father kicked him.

"You're full of shit. You're not O.K."

Still watching his mother, Nicky asks, "You think Buddy, you know, you think Buddy got it from her? You know, like a disease."

"It doesn't happen like that. Not really. It happens for a lot of reasons, and I know what you're asking, but no, it's not like a curse of the blood."

"I heard someplace maybe it is."

"Hereditary? Nah. Get that out of your mind. She got her problems. He had his. And you, you got yours."

"I really do miss him, Father. Remember he taught me how to play ball. Remember? You and him. You were the guys taught me to play ball."

"I remember. Horatio Park. Thompson Street. The church basement."

"Yeah, and remember you and Buddy got the yoms from Chelsea to come down?"

"Do you have to say 'yom'?"

"Sorry, Father."

"He loved to play, Buddy. But I tell you what, he had no game."

"C'mon, Father, a little respect for the dead. Buddy could play a little . . ."

"Look, I loved him like a brother, too. And I miss him something awful. But let's be honest. He couldn't play for shit."

"Yeah, I guess you're right."

"Nicky?"

"What?"

"You gonna tell me about your old man or not?"

He knows, Nicky thinks. He always knows.

"Same old, same old. Only now, he don't want me to play ball this summer. He wants me to be a fighter, a boxer. He's got this idea, like I should be a tough guy. This morning, I tell him I'm not crazy about this boxing stuff and he goes off his nut. First he says some things. Then I say some things. He was out of line. I was out of line. You know how that goes; he winds up smacking me pretty good. I guess I don't even blame him no more. I think he's more sick over Buddy than he lets on. Plus, you'd think I'd know better by now. Like, why aggravate him to begin with? Especially today. You see the paper?"

"Rat poison? Yeah, I saw it."

"He was real upset. Cursing the government and all that. But he's right; they are out to get him. Really. They gotta make it like he's some kind of big Mafia guy. He got a right to be upset. I guess I should have shut my mouth. Here I am, I should be confessing to disrespect or whatever it is. They're pricks, the government. They wanna make my father out to be some kind of Dillinger, like he was in a movie or something."

"Nicky, that's the way it is. Sure, he's your father, sure, but he's another guy, too."

"Yeah, I know, but he didn't kill your uncle Sal. He wouldn't do that."

"I hope you're right."

"I know I'm right," says Nicky. "What's not right is the government. What's not right is someone's ratting out my father and Philly. Someone with them. That's the lowest thing."

"It's pretty low. I give you that."

"It's bullshit is what it is, excuse me, Father. Some Joe Bottabing, probably somebody we know—from the neighborhood—is ratting out my father."

"What, you really believe there's honor among these guys? Don't be a silly kid."

"Look, my father and Philly do what they do. Just like your uncle Sal did what he did. I'm not stupid. But at least they don't hurt nobody, you know, on the outside. And at least they don't rat."

"No, I guess they don't. And you're right; that part sucks."

Nicky pauses. "You think Buddy woulda turned out like them," he asks, "like a gangster?"

"Lord knows he was crazy enough. He was a tough kid, too. But I could never see him living that life. And hey, I should know, I was born to it, too. Don't think you're the only one. But if you ask me, I have to say, no. I never saw that in your brother. Matter of fact, I could never even imagine Buddy grown up. I can't envision him being anything other than what he was—a kid, a sweet, crazy kid."

Nicky chuckles. "Remember Clyde's 'Guide to Cool'?"

"Sure. How many orgy belts did Clyde have?"

"Two," says Nicky. "You think he's watching?"

"Clyde?"

"No, Buddy."

"I'd like to think so."

"Father?"

"What?"

"How come you didn't say the mass? When he died, how come you didn't say the mass?"

CHAPTER

20

CHEECH DEFRANCO PULLS up in the New Yorker and waits on Bedford Street. He does this most mornings—sipping coffee, smoking Parliaments, and scratching his balls. Sometimes he thumbs through the copy of *Juggs* magazine he keeps under the seat. There's always a little time to kill, waiting at the curb until Frank and his kid are ready to go to the gym.

Cheech grew up two blocks away, and still lives with his mother in the walk-up on Morton Street. He had been an awkward, acned kid. But he's done well for himself. Cheech is the most reliable killer in the crew. He doesn't need to be high on rage or booze to do a piece of work. Never did. Guys trust him; after all, he's just a goof, a fucking retard, a smiling, knock-around wise guy who lives with his mother and sends roses to hookers. Guys let him get close. And once you're close, forget about it. A real pro, that's what Cheech is. And that's what's been bothering him, wondering if the Fatman's blonde broad got a look at him.

It wasn't a neat job. Frank let the Fatman look in his eyes, let the old bastard start talking. Got Frank thinking to himself. Yeah, Frank fucked up. But it wasn't like you could tell him.

Then again, a girl like that probably wouldn't know what it was she was seeing even if she saw something. Nah, Cheech tells himself, she didn't see nothing.

Cheech doesn't like people to get the wrong impression about him. He doesn't think of himself as a killer or a strong-arm guy. What he really is, is a big guy in the labor movement, a regular Samuel Gompers. On income tax forms he lists his occupation as business agent for Local 6, the International Longshoremen's Association. You need a suit for a job like that.

If I'm such a retard, he thinks, how come I'm wearing such a nice suit?

He used to get them made-to-order at Delisi's, like all the wise guys. But lately, he's been shopping at Barney's. He'll walk in and order up a rack of Hugo Boss or Perry Ellis, like he's getting a cheeseburger and fries. The fag salesman tells him he has a good body for clothes. Cheech gets a kick out of that. Barney's is more classier than Delisi's.

But the truth is, no matter what he wears, no matter how much money he spends, Cheech always looks as if he had just returned from a sleepless week spent throwing dice. Cheech goes six-three, with long arms, narrow chest, pot belly. His tie always seems askew, and the collars of those white-on-white shirts always bunch up, as his neck is too small for his belly. His clothes are stained with his mother's soups and sauces.

Cheech inspects himself in the rearview mirror, adjusting his tie, patterned after a bleeding orange sunset, kind of like the wallpaper in one of those Vegas motels. The mirror catches the twinkle from the almond-sized jewel in his pinky ring. It catches something else, too.

The girl.

She can't see him, but he's watching everything she does, studying her through the smoked glass as she steps into the morning wearing a sundress, a nice white number with pale blue flowers. Cheech decides she would smell like soap. Nice legs, too. But no titties.

And here comes Frank and the kid, returning from their run. Frank looks tired as shit. Nicky walks ahead. The girl, she's walking straight for him. She's smiling. No, not like that, she's really smiling. Like she knows the kid. Like she likes him. Holy shit, what's that all about? Little Nicky, he don't know what the fuck to do. Kid's looking at her like she shits crushed fruit. Now here comes Frank, making like a big man, like he ain't tired at all, putting an arm around Nicky, asking her how she likes the neighborhood, if there's anything he can do for her, it'd be a pleasure. Frank's going through the whole routine, but all the while he's looking her dead in the eyes, this skinny little girl, wondering how much she saw, how much she knows. Fucking Frank, he comes on too strong. Look at him—winking at the girl. She don't even know what to say.

DRIVING FRANK AROUND, every day's the same. Frank asks, "You been smoking in the car?"

"Who me?"

"You been smoking in the car?"

"Who?"

"Are you retarded?"

"Who's retarded?"

"I thought I smelt smoke. Don't be smoking in the car, Cheech. I told you, the air don't circulate. I'm training. The kid's training."

Cheech looks back at Nicky in the rearview.

"You training, killer?"

No answer. The kid doesn't look so thrilled. Cheech can't help but feel for Nicky. You'd think Frank would lighten up on him. The guy should understand his son don't give a flying fuck for fighting.

"Hey, Nicky," he says, "maybe you should get laid. Why don't you go with that girl, what's her name, Bazooka Bosoms?"

Nicky cracks a smile. He always smiles for his Uncle Cheech, ever since he was little.

"You mean Mary Missile Titties."

"Yeah, that's right. But I guess that's out of the question, killer. I mean, since you're in training and all."

"Cheech," says Frank, "do me a favor and just drive the fucking car."

"O.K., Batman."

"Fuckin' retard."

"Frank, I seen you talking to that girl. We got a problem?"

"I don't know."

"Well, the way I figure, we got a problem if you think we got a problem. Maybe I should talk to her, you know, feel her out."

"Lemme think."

"I'd feel her up," says Cheech, winking at Nicky in the mirror, "but she got no titties."

"Please," says Frank. "Just drive."

"Nice girl, though. Huh? I seen killer over here checking her out. Ain't that right, killer? You love her. I seen it in your eyes. I was watching both a youse."

Nicky flushes. She said hello to me, he tells himself. She smiled, too. And that wasn't just any smile. That was a nice one, like she meant it. How cool was that?

He was afraid she'd never speak to him again. He hasn't seen her since that night in front of her apartment. That was the night she ran into the house crying, yeah, and he was so stoned.

That was the night the Fatman got his . . .

So what the fuck did Cheech mean, "We got a problem"? They got a problem with Samantha?

She knew the Fatman, sure. But Nicky wants to tell them, they got it all wrong. They got her all wrong. She's no Mystery Blonde, at least not how they're thinking about it. She's not like that. She smiled at him.

Yeah, he thinks, I should tell them, just to clear things up. Just so there's no misunderstandings.

Just not now. It's not a good time.

His old man's turned white as a ghost. Beads of sweat have gathered on his forehead. He's begun to twitch, a rage surging through him. Frank Battaglia tries to remain still, to calm himself with deep breaths. But it's no use. His chest feels as if it's caught in a vise. And the vise only tightens, until his deepest breath becomes a gasp, until he can't take it anymore, until he starts pounding on the dashboard with his fist.

"Who's the rat?" he screams. "Who's the fuckin' rat?"

CHAPTER

21

FRANK RECOVERS QUICKLY. Walking into the gym, he carries himself like a pharaoh. Guys turn their heads, like a movie star just came in. Nicky follows behind, wishing as he wishes each time he walks through those doors that he was invisible. Cheech lugs all the gear, but stops to shake hands with everyone from the little Spanish flyweights to the big black heavyweights to the old guys perched on the bleachers. Like he knew them all from way back.

"How ya doin'?"

"How's the hand? Feel good?"

"Nah, don't you believe what you read in the papers. They ain't got nothing on us." Cheech grabs his crotch. "*This* is what they got."

Frank walks on, gritting his teeth, acknowledging no one until they're in the locker room. Then he turns to Nicky.

"When you gonna start sparrin'?"

Nicky can feel his heart jump. "I don't know."

"Hey, the kid's gotta learn what he's doing first," says Cheech. "It ain't like you can rush it. Takes a while, even you said."

Frank gives him a look, then asks again. "Toodie, he say when you're gonna start fighting?"

"He didn't say nothing about it."

"Well, that's gonna change. I ain't paying him for my health."

FRANK WATCHES CLOSELY as his son trains.

Nicky assumes the postures and the form with ease. It's a simple pantomime: jab, hook, straight right, upper-cut, slipping, weaving. Nicky has an intuition for move-ment, all the easy, natural grace his father lacks.

Something about that pisses Frank off. It's like the kid got something he didn't deserve.

Nicky is smooth at all the stations. Just a few weeks into his training and he can tap out a quick, light rhythm on the heavy bag. He can skip rope like a Double Dutch girl. He prances around the crazy ball, a leather globe suspended by elastic cords, bobbing and weaving, jab-bing, anticipating the absurd, temperamental angle of its rebound without becoming awkward. He even looks good shadowboxing, rehearsing combinations, trying to throw a sequence of punches that makes sense. He has learned to choreograph his own slick ballet without any imagined opponents, admiring himself in the mirror, his movements melding improvisation and narcissism.

Nicky looks good. But as soon as Toodie gets him in the ring, he comes undone.

There, the simplest moves fluster him. He is quickly out of sync and out of breath. Toodie's wearing pads, like flattened catcher's mitts, waving them to suggest punches. It's only a rehearsal, but something about the ring makes the fear palpable.

"Slip it," says Toodie.

The trick is to avoid the punch slightly, to become intimate with the danger, to feel its wind and its sweat, but not its power. The problem is, Nicky doesn't have the nerve. Or the discipline. He dives under Toodie's out-stretched arm, closing his eyes, holding his breath, like a child would dive under a wave. Nicky's reflexes are cowardly. He has learned to cover up, run away, close his eyes, and hold his breath until Frank's foul moods have passed.

"C'mon, Nick, you can do better."

But Nicky can't help himself. Every time Toodie throws one of those fake jabs, he flinches. Or blinks. Or backs away.

A waste of time, thinks Toodie. He's embarrassed, being seen in the ring with this kid. Embarrassed for the kid, too. Maybe it's better just to tell his old man the truth, that he can't teach his kid to fight. "Nicky," he asks quietly, "what the fuck are you doin'?"

"I'm trying to do what you say." Nicky's gaze drifts toward the next ring, where his father is laughing at something Dagger-eye said. Look at them: like asshole buddies, leaning against the ring post. Already, Nicky has seen Dagger-eye hurt a few guys in the gym. And while that seems to impress Frank, it scares the shit out of Nicky. It seems that Dagger-eye is always there, lurking, watching him, that evil empty leer inciting the worst in Nicky's imagination.

"Look at me when I'm talking to you," says Toodie. "Now relax, kid. Relax."

They try again. But it's no use.

Nicky feels like apologizing. He can see his father from the corner of his eye, shaking his head in disgust, thinking: My kid's a pussy.

Finally, Toodie throws down the pads in disgust and calls over to the bleachers.

Now Jackie Farrell comes off the wooden bench like a gargoyle summoned to life. Nicky recognizes him from the first day at the gym—the old toothless guy, the wino.

Frank nods at him as he climbs through the ropes. But Jackie Farrell gives no sign of acknowledgment. His expression does not change, that look of weary contempt on his lined face.

What's that all about, Nicky wonders, like they already know each other.

"Help me with this," says Toodie.

Jackie gets behind Nicky, close as he can get, and sticks his big red nose just under the kid's ear. "Relax, pally," he whispers, his breath making a whistling sound. For a moment, Nicky thinks he will gag on the sweet rotten fumes of Wild Irish Rose. He tries to squirm away, but Jackie reaches into his shorts, grabs the elastic waistband, and pulls Nicky closer. "You ain't goin' nowheres, pally. You're staying right here wit' me."

"You can't pull away no more," says Toodie.

Again, he begins to throw with the pads, slowly at first, so Nicky can time him, get some confidence and some rhythm. When Nicky tries to pull away, Jackie Farrell presses into the small of his spine. When he lurches forward, Jackie yanks him back by his underwear.

Gradually, Toodie quickens the pace. But Nicky's still too skittish. A moment of panic causes him to get smacked, nothing much, but smacked just the same.

"See," says Toodie, "thinking about it hurts more than the real thing."

CHAPTER

22

ANGEL KIND OF likes the gangster's kid. He's a nice boy. And maybe he can't fight for shit, but he listens real good. Sitting in the bleachers, digesting a meal of Yodels and NuGrape, Angel tells him how earlier this very morning he had been shit-canned from his job at the Strawberry Fields Health Spa on Great Jones Street. For twenty bucks an hour, half of which went to the spa's lesbian proprietor, Angel would teach white women to box. Actually, it ain't boxing, just how to hit the bag, skip the rope. Aerobics, that's what they call it. Angel's students include lady stockbrokers, receptionists, literary agents, aspiring actresses, and an associate professor of comparative literature who's always trying to get him to read the poems of Hilda Doolittle. He was humping them all.

The way it worked was, he'd tell them that a real fighter always got a rubdown. Then he would take them to the room with the rubbing table. Angel would work them over slowly, probing with gentle hands, eventually locating those places of pressure and heat. Next thing you knew, they were doing the real aerobics, the sanitary paper crinkling underneath them. But Angel was always a gentleman, always he told them they were beautiful and that they made him feel like a man. That's what they tipped him for—service, consideration, reliability. Each morning, he lit a purple Chango Macho candle to ensure his virility.

But today, the boss, this dyke lady with a crew cut, tells him he's fired. It must have been the professor, says Angel. She would get real loud when they were doing it, and the boss must have heard. "There's liability issues," she said. Didn't even give him the week's pay. She didn't have to. Angel was off the books. That's O.K., though, Angel's got something for her. He'll go to the botanica and get a twelve-ounce aerosol can of the Sacred Heart of Jesus spray and some Go Away Evil incense. Put a whammy on that bitch.

"She just mad 'cause I's getting more pussy than she is," says Angel. "Fuckit. I get me another job. I been working all my life."

His first job was a child's labor, fighting with his brothers on the corner of Avenue D and Tenth Street. Men would pitch pennies and nickels into a hat for as long as the Cruz brothers kept clobbering each other. "The drunker the old mens got," says Angel, "the less harder we hadda hit each other. The best was when the old mens had already been playin' celo. By the time they finished with the dice, they was so drunk, they got no idea what they was seeing. So me and my bros, we do the pitty-pat. We make it look real good, though. One time, we even use the fake blood. You know, take a ketchup pack from McDonald's, put it in your mouth, and pow! Bite the ketchup, make like you got hit. The shit gets all over your face, and you just laying there, like you been shot in the movies, and the old mens start yelling. They go crazy when they see the blood. One guy, he puts a twenty spot in the hat. How you like that, kid, a twenty spot for some ketchups?"

Now Dagger-eye walks past the bleachers, winking at Nicky on his way out the door. Angel pretends not to notice.

"I ever tell you about me and Duran?" he asks.

It was the best night of his life. It was at the Garden. Angel Cruz and Roberto Duran were then lightweights.

And Duran, whose hands were stone, was in his ferocious prime.

Angel says, "Duran, he walking aroun' like he so big and bad, you know, like, I don't know, like he gotta go bathroom a somethin'. Then he looks a me, he says, 'You ain't shit.' He says in Spanish 'cause dat uneducate mofucka cannot espeak no English."

"Yeah, so?"

"So I tells him, *'Tu madre es un puta.'* Yo momi's a ho. You shoulda seen his face. He get crazy. Steam come out his head like he gonna esplode. Then I tell Duran, 'I did you momi in the culo.' I wink a him like he's my sweetheart. So, he come at me, say he gonna kill me. All those white guys at the Garden, they gotta separate him. Now I know: I can't break a egg, but I got his ass. He chase me around that night. He wanna kill me so bad he could not breathe. Only one time, he hit me. Broke my rib in the fourf roun'. But I no say nothing. I no even tell the doc after the fight 'cause I no want nobody to know."

"You won?"

"Hell no. I got robbed. Spli' decision. But that's O.K."

Nicky doesn't understand.

"Don't you see? I was never so escared in my life. Duran was the toughest mofucker there was. Before the fight, I throw up just thinking about him. But that night, he couldn't touch me. And maybe I'm a little messed up now, but no one can take that from me."

Angel Cruz drains his NuGrape soda and lets out a belch. "Hey, kid," he says, "don't be tellin' nobody he broke my rib, all right?"

"You know I wouldn't say nothing."

"I know. You good kid. You can't fight for shit, but you good kid. Maybe you could tell your popi take it easy on me?"

THE BUZZER SOUNDS, and Nicky moves closer to get a better view. Frank chasing Angel around the ring reminds him of Bluto and Olive Oyl in the cartoons. Despite his father's obvious bad intentions, there is a comedy to their act. Frank has one eager, grunting, straight-ahead gear of pursuit. But Angel is by various turns an artist of escape, a contortionist, a slick clown, a jellyfish, a snake.

Only when Frank begins to pant does Angel allow himself to be grabbed. Frank leans on him until he catches his breath, then tries to sneak in a few to the body. But Angel slithers away, leaving Frank in an awkward embrace with the thin air.

But he keeps after him, locating his target and turning to charge. Frank lunges with uppercuts and meathouse right hands. Angel will pop him back, a couple of soft jabs, but just to temper Frank's rage, to tranquillize him some. Angel makes sure the blows look more vicious than they are. Frank didn't want to think anyone was going easy on him.

Angel even allows himself to be hit. Sort of. Frank would unleash an angry fusillade of punches, but he can't hit him good. There is always a roll, a slip, a smother, to muffle the blow.

Finally, Frank catches him with a shot to the liver. Angel thought he had caught most of it on his forearm, but he goes down anyway: takes a knee, head down, solemn, like a football player thanking end-zone Jesus.

Frank swaggers back to his corner, spits up his mouthpiece, and offers his arms to Toodie. The trainer responds dutifully, cutting the tape and removing the gloves. But the look Nicky sees on his face, it's like he's got a headache.

"You the man, Frank, you the man." Cheech is jumping up and down, hands clasped over his head.

"Pay the kid," says Frank.

Cheech walks out into the ring and peels two Ben Franklins from his roll. "Y'O.K., kid?" he asks.

"Yeah, I be O.K. Jus' a little out of shape. The boss, he hit hard, huh?"

Cheech works the Bennies into the thumb crook of Angel's glove. "Don't get 'im mad."

"I'm tellin' you."

Angel remains on one knee even after Cheech walks off. Then he turns to Nicky, a sly smile on his lips, and winks.

CHAPTER
23

"BLESS ME, FATHER, for I have sinned."

"Tell me your sins, my son."

"Tell me what happened."

"What happened when?"

"The night at the gym, starting that night."

"I thought this was your confession."

"There's just some things I wanna be clear on."

"Nicky, you're talking about something that happened a long time ago."

"I know. I was twelve."

"Well, then you gotta remember how it was. Me and Buddy used to play every night in the gym in the church basement. At first it was just neighborhood guys. Then we got some of the black kids from Chelsea to come down, you know, better comp."

The more the priest explains, the more he becomes like the boy he used to be—Vinny from Sullivan Street. "All the old-timers and the wise guys got upset. I mean, it's not like they're crazy about the brothers in the first place. Now they're pissed off about kids from the projects setting foot on hallowed ground, saying, 'What, we're running some kind of settlement house in the church?' Telling me and Buddy, they get all they need in

Attica, why youse gotta bring 'em down here? Then, what happens is, you know Mrs. Lombardi?"

"From Cornelia Street."

"Right. Mrs. Lombardi from Cornelia Street gets her purse snatched. Next thing you know, the whole neighborhood is screaming, 'The niggers from Chelsea did it. Yeah, it's those kids Buddy and Vinny brought around.' Like it was a fact just 'cause they said so, 'cause that's how they wanted it to be. So a few nights later, we're in the gym, playing ball, and Tommy Sick busts in with some of the wannabes, you know who I'm talking about."

"Yeah, the guys who seen too many *Godfather* movies."

"Exactly. And of course, they all got bats. Tommy Sick's already got this bad sweaty look on his face. Like he's hopped up on something."

"I know what you're talking about," says Nicky. "I seen that look."

"Then Tommy Sick says, 'All niggers out of the gym.' And the game just stops. The black kids realize they're surrounded. And they start looking at me and Buddy like, 'What's going on? You guys gotta straighten this out.'

"Buddy says, 'C'mon, Tommy, we're playing a game. These ain't bad kids. I'm vouching for them. Besides, we only got a few points to go.'

"And Tommy starts into how 'These fuckin' niggers from Chelsea knocked over an old lady. This is a neighborhood thing. You should know better. Mind your business, Buddy.'

"So Buddy says, 'Mind your business, asshole. We're just playing ball . . .'

"Now the wannabes with the bats start moving in, like nobody's getting out alive.

"Then Buddy calls Tommy out. Buddy says, 'Me and you, let's go.' Right there in the gym. Right in front of all Tommy's boys. And you know a guy like Tommy Sick can't be embarrassed in front of his boys. I'll never forget, he makes this sound, from his gut, a grunt, like he was an animal . . . which I guess he is. Tommy Sick picks up a bat and takes a swing. You could hear the bat go through the air—whoosh. And even when I think about it, I see it like it was in a comic book, you know, like the bat leaves a trail, a streak. But your brother was the best. You ever see Sonny Chiba in *The Streetfighter*?"

"Buddy took me to see it," Nicky says. "On Forty and Deuce."

"Well, Buddy was like Sonny Chiba, only better. He ducks under the bat and throws himself at Tommy Sick. Everything gets quiet. I remember the sound the bat made when it hit the tile floor, like an echo. Buddy and Tommy Sick, they got each other by the throat now. They were like that for a long time, locked together, like who was gonna break first?"

Nicky can imagine the scene. Buddy and Tommy Sick at each other's throats, clasped at arm's length. A gurgling stalemate.

"Then Tommy Sick's tough guys surround them, waiting for a clean shot at Buddy. So I step in: 'Get away. Let 'em straighten it out themselves.' One of the junior wise guys pokes me in the stomach with the bat. Boom—I go down. Meanwhile, Tommy Sick can't hold off Buddy no more. Buddy starts pounding on him, throwing him a good beating, and at first I want to cheer. But then I get scared. Buddy's banging Tommy's head on the floor, and I start thinking he's gonna kill Tommy Sick, right there in the basement of the church. I'm yelling, 'Stop, Buddy, stop, you're gonna kill this guy.' Finally, the wannabes start pulling him off, and the last thing Buddy does, he hits Tommy Sick a short right hand. Bing. Tommy's mouth just explodes. Blood everywhere. They gotta carry him away. His eyes were fluttering, all white on the inside."

Nicky has a vision of Tommy Sick's mouth: the lip split, the wound blooming, becoming as deep and dark and complicated as a rose, leaving a trail of scarlet droplets on the tile floor.

"And as they're taking Tommy Sick away, one of the wise guys says, 'Youse don't know what youse did.' Now I'm thinking, 'Hey, we gotta get the black kids out the

gym before these jerkoffs come back.' But Buddy—
Buddy picks up the basketball, starts pounding it on the
floor. His eyes are still bulging, his chest's heaving.
'C'mon,' he says, 'we gonna finish the game or what?' "

"You finished the game?"

"Nah. You kidding? We hustled the kids out through
the church."

"And then?"

"Then?" says Father Vincent. "Then we found a world
of shit."

CHAPTER
24

FRANK PRESIDES AT the head of the table, with Nicky and Cheech at his either side. Toodie sits opposite Frank, introducing the black kid with the orange dreadlocks as Khe Sahn Witherspoon. Khe Sahn keeps his eyes to himself and lets Toodie do all the talking.

Toodie's voice is heavy with the proper, respectful sentiment. "I just wanna tell you, Frank," he says, "how much we appreciate all you done. I mean, all you're doing . . ."

Frank Battaglia puts up his hands, the gesture meant to be magnanimous, but also to tell Toodie to shut up. If anyone's giving a speech, it's gonna be Frank. "No need," he says. "It's my pleasure. But let's eat first. Eat first, talk later."

Frank opens his menu, a cue for everyone else to do likewise, then mumbles through the appetizers, shaking his head. Each dish seems an insult to him. It's not supposed to be like this, he thinks. Garguilo's of Thompson Street isn't supposed to have menus. Not for a guy like him, anyway.

He told Garguilo not to fuck with the restaurant.

For years, Garguilo's was a reliable red sauce joint. The waiters spoke Italian. The walls featured crude fluorescent murals—scenes of Venice, gondolas and moonlight, a slice of moon outlined by tiny lightbulbs. And no menus.

Frank gave Garguilo the shylock money to take the place "upscale." But he didn't know "upscale" meant out-of-work actors and fags for waiters. Or that midnight in Venice would be replaced by tile and marble finished with a fake patina. He didn't know upscale meant menus.

"Shitty mushrooms?" says Frank.

"Can't you read?" says Cheech. "Shiitake mushroom."

"Yeah, but what the fuck is it?"

"I think that gives you AIDS."

"Pretty soon this whole neighborhood is gonna have AIDS."

The waiter is blond and handsome. Cheech figures he could play a doctor in a soap opera . . . until he opens his mouth, pronouncing the specials in an effeminate lilt, going on and on about shiitake mushrooms, and balsamic vinegar and polenta, which Cheech describes as a fancy version of that shit they serve you in the army, grits.

Frank cuts him short. "I want veal Oscar," he says.

"I don't think we do that anymore," says the waiter.

Frank doesn't know what pisses him off more, that the waiter's a fag, or that he doesn't know who Frank is. What, don't queers read the papers?

"Tell the guy in the kitchen. Tell 'im it's for Frank Batts. And tell him if he puts any shitty mushrooms on the veal Oscar I will personally go back there and suck his heart out."

"Mmmm. That sounds good."

Frank grinds his teeth, it's all he can do to keep from making a scene. "Bring four veal Oscars and two a those big plates of fish salad."

"Fish salad?"

"Are you deaf? . . . Tell the guy none a that fake crab shit, that Jap shit."

"Anything else . . . sir?"

"Yeah." Frank nods at Khe Sahn. "Whatta ya want?"

"Spaghetti?" Khe Sahn looks at Toodie to see if it's O.K.

"Yeah, bring him a big bowl," says Frank. "And a Coca-Cola. Cokes for each a the kids, house red for us."

"The one that comes in the straw basket?" Now the waiter strikes a bitchy drag queen pose, rolling his eyes, arching his back, putting a hand behind his hip. "Anything else?"

"Yeah, one thing," says Frank. "You ever get shit on your dick?"

"Pardon?"

"You ever get shit on your dick?"

The waiter stares back at Frank, his front foot tapping nervously. "Only with tough guys," he says.

Cheech doubles over with laughter, repeating the line—"Only with tough guys"—until all that comes out is a gassy wheeze. Pretty soon, Frank is laughing, too. Sometimes, Frank forgets what a funny bastard he really is.

When the wine arrives, Frank proposes a toast. "To Toodie's new joint."

OVER THE MEAL, Toodie becomes effusive, explaining that he wants to train young fighters, maybe, with a little luck, even a few contenders. Toodie thinks he has something to teach the kids.

He's saying he's wanted to do this for a long time, open his own place.

Saying that he trusts Frank.

But hearing the old man's ghost whisper in his ear: You're the one's gotta live with himself.

Forget Paddy Blood, he thinks, do what you gotta do. "Appreciate it, Frank. All you done."

"Whatever," says Frank. "Whatever it is, Toodie, you got it. Money ain't a problem no more."

"It was the only way I could see clear to do it," says Toodie. "Coming to you."

"Hey, it ain't like you gotta apologize. Besides, I always wanted to do something, you know . . . do something for the kids."

"And the papers make it like we ain't got no feelings," says Cheech. "Can you imagine?"

"I'm glad youse came tonight," says Frank, nodding at Khe Sahn. "I wanted to check on my investment."

Toodie doesn't quite like how that sounds, calling the kid an investment. "Khe Sahn's good," he says. "What I mean is, I think he has some character. I say that here because you should know, not because I want to embarrass him. But the thing is, it takes time. A lot of time."

"Sure," says Frank. "That's what I want. Takes time to build champions."

"It's too soon to even talk like that, Frank."

"Well, I know you wouldn't steer me wrong. I know you not wasting time with a bum."

Frank turns to Khe Sahn, gestures at his bleached dreadlocks, making a curlicue outline with his index finger. "Tell me something," he asks, "why you got the hair like that, all crazy and everything?"

"Me?" asks Khe Sahn, not quite sure if this Mafia gangster from the papers is actually speaking to him. Toodie gives him a nudge.

"I don't know," says Khe Sahn. "It's just a thing . . ."

"You're not one a those rajamen, are you?" he asks. "The ones smoking that shit all day long?"

Khe Sahn shrugs. He holds his fork like a club.

Frank looks at Toodie. "Is he?"

"He's a kid, Frank."

"He's the next heavyweight champ."

"Fuckin'-A," says Cheech.

"I just can't get over that octopus hair."

"I told you, Frank, he's a kid. The girls today, they like that look."

Frank eyeballs the waiter. "I think *this* girl likes it."

"We gonna have to go soon," says Toodie. "I gotta get Khe back to Brooklyn."

"Sure," says Frank. "Just tell me one thing. How you think Nicky here is gonna do in the Gloves?"

"I don't know. It's early."

"Yeah, I know all that, too early to tell. But humor me. How's he gonna do?"

The poor kid, Toodie thinks, he looks sick. He's turning white.

"Tell me," Frank insists. "Is there something I should know? Kid's been in the gym a month already, when's he gonna start sparring?"

Probably never. That's what Toodie wants to say. He wants to tell the guy, why don't you leave your kid alone? But he doesn't. "There's just a few things we gotta straighten out first," he says.

"Like what?"

"It's just some . . ."

"You wanna tell me? I mean, I'm the guy puttin' up the money. I just wanna know is all. I don't want you to be treatin' my kid like half a fag."

"It's nothing major. Just some technical things." Toodie feels like a real rat scumbag, knowing full well by now that the kid doesn't belong in the ring, but playing along anyway, knowing also that Frank's boy is his meal ticket. Toodie can actually see the fear inch up Nicky Battaglia's back as Paddy Blood's ghost whispers in his ear, *"You the one's gotta live with himself."*

"Don't worry, Frank," he says, excusing himself from the table. "Nicky'll be fine."

FRANK LEAVES A Ben Franklin on the tip dish. The meal was shit. The service was worse. But pride forbids anything less. Plus, you can never tell with the papers. They could write up a whole story on how much you tip. You wouldn't want that Mushy Mob guy calling you a cheap bastard in the papers.

The waiter snatches the hundred without so much as a thank you. Just a sneer. Only with tough guys.

I'll show you who's a tough guy, Frank thinks.

"Wait here."

"Where you going?" asks Cheech. "Don't do nothing stupid."

Too late. Frank has already intercepted the waiter in the short corridor leading to Garguilo's kitchen. Nicky and Cheech can do nothing but watch as Frank gets even more heated. The waiter's giving him back talk. Frank Battaglia holds the waiter responsible for all that is wrong with his world, for things he cannot even name, for the watercress and tofu and the fags and the cunty college kids and those guys with the octopus heads, and the RICO statute and Bella Abzug and her army of Bolshevik PTA mothers who had taken politics from the good DeSapio bosses and for the bums who never pay their vig on time and the homeless and the crackhead niggers and all the assholes who ruined his neighborhood.

Frank had it all planned, his time, his time as a big racket boss, but the neighborhood went sour on him. The city went sour on him. Boss of what? Frank turns back toward his table, then abruptly, with great, disgraceful surprise, reaches back and cracks the waiter across the bridge of the nose with the back of his hand. The waiter drops to his knee, clutching his nose. Blood seeps between his fingers, trickling onto the floor.

What's he gonna do? What's anybody gonna do? It wasn't like old man Garguilo could beef to him about smacking the help. Frank told Garguilo not to fuck with the restaurant.

He walks from the table mumbling, "Leave that fag a hundred bucks, he don't even say 'Thank you.' Like I'm a jerkoff.

"Shitty mushrooms my ass."

CHAPTER
25

JIMMY ROSELLI IS singing "Mala Femmina" on the Perry Como station as Philly Testa stirs a lemon rind into his thick black coffee. "Tell me again," he says. "'Cause I figure it's better than reading it in the paper. Tell me again how youse did it."

Cheech begins to explain eagerly. "Well, we was waiting between the cars, right? Like we was kids, like we was playing ring-a-lario. And the Fatman, he . . ."

"No," says Philly. "Not you. You tell me, Frank."

"What's to tell? We rolled up on 'em, Cheech did Fritzy. I did Fatman. That's what we agreed on."

"You did Colosimo?"

"Yeah . . . well." Frank is watching Cheech from the corner of his eye now.

"All by yourself?" Philly asks. "Just like that, blew his head off, huh?"

"That how we had it planned, but . . ."

"You're one tough guy, Frank. Always were."

"Philly, don't start that."

"Don't start what, Frank? Did you do him yourself? Or did this Rhodes Scholar here have to pull the trigger 'cause you shit yourself?"

"Hey, Phil. Don't start. I tole you. We agreed ta . . ."

"Youse agreed upon it, right?"

"Right."

"And when youse made this so-called agreement, where the fuck was I?"

"You were . . ."

"Where was I? On the fucking moon, Frank?"

"I thought . . ."

"You didn't think for shit, you dumb ape."

"*Ming*. I don't gotta be insulted, Philly. We didn't want to bother you. I thought you gave it your blessing. Between the lines, I mean."

"My blessing? When was that?"

"That day."

"What day?"

"The day Cheech brought in Scarface and Cagney."

"Oh, *that* day. How could I forget?" Philly sips his black coffee, his eyes right on Frank's.

Cheech says, "It was just like the movies."

"Of course it was," says Philly. "And now Frank here is a fucking movie star. Isn't that right, Frank?"

"Why you gotta break balls?"

"I'm just saying. You read the papers, you know how it is. You're a big man now. You like it, ain't that right, Frank? I seen you talking to that Chinese lady from the TV. I even hear you're in the boxing business now. Got your own nigger fighter. You don't tell me, though, I gotta hear it in the street. Hear you gonna put him on a card in Atlantic City. That's great, Frank. You're a star. So tell me, who's gonna play you in the movie?"

"He was thinking maybe De Niro," says Cheech. "But I figure that guy from *The Godfather*, you know the one who says, 'May your first child be a masculine child.' For me, I want that actor, what's his name? Good-looking guy . . . Armand Assante, that's him. Broads love that guy."

"You wanna shut the fuck up?" says Frank. "This is a serious thing."

"Leave him alone, Frank. Alls he is is speaking the truth. What's wrong with that? We're supposed to be friends."

"We was just messing around," says Cheech.

"If you ask me," says Philly, "I would get Peter Lorre to play Frank."

"Peter Lorre? He don't look nothing like Frank."

"Yeah. But he always played the weasel."

"You callin' me a weasel, Phil?"

"If that's how you wanna read it, between the lines."

"You're gonna tell me you ain't glad Fatman's dead? You're gonna tell me you didn't want to be the boss. You're gonna tell me you told me *not* to do it?"

"No, Frank, I ain't gonna tell you none of that. The thing is, say whatever you want about the Fatman, but how you think he got to be old as he was? Before you pulled this number you barely ever saw his name in the papers. You didn't see him running that act for the Chinese lady on TV. You didn't see none a that. Because the Fatman knew; once you're a movie star, you go. One way or another, they get you. See, nobody minds if you do business. They just don't want you to rub it in, embarrass them. But now you made it so we're all overnight sensations. Public enemies and all that shit. Now they're gonna come after us. And I don't know about you, matter of fact, I don't know if I really give a shit no more, but I'd like to live at least as long as Colosimo. And I don't wanna be bunking with Leroy fucking Washington the rest of my life, neither, some black bastard trying to make me his wife."

"It ain't like that for us, Phil."

"Oh no? What, you think it's like the old days, pay the hacks and they let you run the prison pork store?"

"What I did, I did for you, too, Philly."

"That's true," says Cheech. "He even said, 'We gotta do this for Philly.'"

"He said that? That's too bad. 'Cause that makes you a bullshit artist, Frank. Maybe even a liar. What you did, you did for you."

"I swear on my kid," says Frank.

"Please, your kid got enough problems without you swearing on him," says Philly. "Alls I wanna know now is, who knew. Who else knew youse were gonna do this?"

"Just us," says Cheech.

An uneasy silence passes through the club before Frank says, "C'mon, that's crazy. That's so sick that's like saying you could be the rat, Phil."

"I'll pretend I never heard you say that. What I'm talking about is, maybe they don't even got a rat. Maybe they're just bluffing. You ever consider that?"

Frank shakes his head.

"Of course not. You're too much of a tough guy. Then again, we can't be too careful with this. What about this girl?"

Frank and Cheech shrug, giving each other a look.

"We don't think she saw nothing," says Cheech.

"Whattaya mean, you don't think? I read this little Dick Tracy guy in the paper, he keeps talking about the fucking Mystery Blonde. But youse don't think she saw nothing?"

"Even if she did," says Frank, "she ain't the type who'd wanna get involved."

"You know something I don't?"

"Nah," says Frank. "Just, you know, checking her out. You want me to take care of it?"

"You've taken care of enough, thank you. Cheech, why don't you pay her a visit. See what she really knows. Be a gentleman, though. Don't get out of line. Last thing we need is a problem with a white girl."

"Sure," says Cheech.

"I'm telling you, Frank. Stay away from her. We got enough problems."

"There's no need for you to treat me like this, Philly."

"Tell me something, Frank, this black kid of yours, this fighter, he as tough as you were?"

"They say he got a future."

"Like they used to say about you?"

"Whatta you mean by that?"

"You know what I mean, Frank."

"No, why don't you tell me?"

The cousins now find themselves locked in a stare-down contest, each trying to bore through the other's eyes.

"That fat old bastard he must a shit himself, huh?"

"I guess."

"Sure. He must've been scared, going to meet his maker and all. I mean, how could he not be?"

Frank turns away, conceding the loss.

"How could he not be?" says Philly Testa. "Coming face-to-face with Frankie Batts, the Bedford Brawler."

CHAPTER
26

TOODIE'S BIG SCORE smells of axle grease. The Empire Gym, as he has decided to call it, is being hastily constructed on the second story of an abandoned garage sandwiched between a bodega and a botanica on Tenth Street off Avenue C. Back in the Alphabet City, not too far from where the old Imperial Boxing Club used to be.

The Imperial. That was Avenue A and Fourteenth Street. And that was so many years ago. Angel brought him in off the street. He had been fighting again. Toodie doesn't recall much about his opponent, merely that he was from the Jacob Riis projects, and that he had those big, blue suede Pro-Keds, those sneakers fat with rubber and all the rage. Toodie wanted a pair; so he popped the kid in the mouth. Then Angel came running from across the street, yanked him off the other kid, and said if he was gonna fight, not to waste his time sly-rapping guys in the street like a little punk. "You comin' with me, kid," Angel said. Toodie didn't protest much. Everybody in the neighborhood knew Angel, the guy who almost beat Duran. Toodie had always wanted Angel to notice him.

It was the first time Toodie can remember anyone giving a shit about him. He had always thought of himself as an orphan. His father was a tenement super on the Lower East Side, real mean when he was drunk, which was most of the time. His mother, well, she was never really right. She heard voices. So did Toodie. Only the voices he heard said, Get the fuck out.

So he did. The last scene Toodie remembers was his parents in the kitchen, his old man drunk, standing over her, holding and hitting, then emptying a garbage can on her head. The worst thing Toodie ever saw was the sludgy streak over her lip. By the age of sixteen, Toodie Gleason was living on the street, where Angel found him. He was the bully of Avenue B, but unable to exhaust his rage.

Until Angel brought him to the Imperial Boxing Club.

Toodie watched in fascination as fighters played rat-a-tat-tat on the speed bags, wondering if he could do that, too, if there was a magic in that rhythm, and if in some way the magic could protect him. Angel called over to Paddy Blood and said, "I found me a tough guy. The bully of the block."

The old man wore big brown shoes, a tattered cardigan, and a flannel shirt buttoned to the top. Toodie could smell him as he came closer, like a damp camphor cloud. All of a sudden he felt ashamed. Paddy Blood looked him up and down, saying nothing, but somehow knowing what a mean, miserable little prick this boy was, but also how damaged.

"You scared, kid?" asked Paddy Blood.

"I ain't scared a nothin', mister."

"Then get the hell outta here. Just what I need, Angel. A bully and a liar, too. Why do you bring me these kids?"

And now, in this place of his own, Toodie can hear the old man all over again. The voice brings a wistful smile to his lips.

Why do you bring me these kids?

There's nobody here, except for him and Jackie Farrell, who's nursing a pint of wine. And it's not much of a gym yet, just the speed bag, a mirrored wall, a rough concrete floor, and a fixture for the heavy bag, which is on the way. "Don't worry about nothing," Frank had said, "just put it all on the bill." Carpenters are coming to build a ring next week, and Toodie can't wait. He can't wait until it sounds like a real gym—with that speed bag serenade, those magic rhythms. He wants to hear the urgent respiration of the fighters, his fighters, the creak and jangle of the chains as they pound the heavy bag. Toodie can imagine the day, years from now, when these bare brick walls are covered with bright yellow bills announcing the bouts, each signifying a sacred, minor history, the placards like postcards addressed to posterity. Sure, Toodie wants to make a score, but he also wants something else, something that will make everything right, square all his debts.

Why do you bring me these kids?

One day, Toodie vows, this gym's gonna be full of these kids.

He turns to Jackie Farrell and asks, "Whatta you think the old man woulda said?"

"He woulda said it's nice."

"Nah, you know what I mean."

"He woulda said, you're the one's gotta live with yourself."

"Yeah. I know."

"He would'na liked you taking money from this Frank. I told you about him. I told you about that night. I don't think Paddy ever forgave himself for gettin' involved with him."

"But you don't understand. You . . ."

"It ain't what I understand. You asked me what he woulda thought. I'm just telling you."

"He wouldn't of understood anyway."

"No, that ain't true. You're just saying that so's you feel right about everything."

Toodie tries to look hurt.

Jackie takes a swig of the Wild Irish. "Don't get mad at me."

"I ain't mad, Jackie. Just that that's bullshit. He wouldn't of understood."

"If you say so."

"No. Not 'cause I say so. 'Cause it's the truth." Of late, Toodie knows only his own truth, located inside his wife,

Carmen. Her swollen belly fills him with an awe, equal parts terror and bliss. Sometimes, he believes he can actually see nature's course flood her womb with blood and light. The vision tells him to do whatever he's gotta do. "Paddy never had a wife," he says.

"No," says Jackie. "He never had a wife."

"And he never had a kid."

"No," says Jackie. "There was only you. You and the colored kid with the crazy hair, the one you're lettin' this gangster use for his entertainment."

"Christ, Jackie, I don't have a pot to piss in. Soon my old lady's gonna be out to here with a kid, who, so help me, will not grow up in the same shit I grew up in. I got Khe Sahn to think of—and let's be realistic—how do you think I'm ever gonna get some juice for his career? I got Angel, who's we both agree is not in his right mind. And to be honest, I gotta think of you, too. Look at you, drinking that shit."

Jackie's face runs red with rage. "Lissen, ya little punk," he says, "I can take care of myself. And so can Angel. Who are you to take care a him?"

"Look, Jackie, I didn't mean to insult you. But you got a Social Security check and a liver probably looks like Swiss cheese. And Angel? C'mon. The guy thinks he's some kind of voodoo priest."

It was too bad what happened to Angel. He retired from the ring with enough money for a house in Sheepshead Bay. He had a son, five years old. One day the kid and a friend go down to the water, say they're going to look for starfish. Only, Angel's boy never came back. The cops said he slipped off the pier and drowned. Angel had never been the same. He was another one, hearing voices. His only therapy is that Puerto Rican voodoo. What the fuck is that called? Toodie can never remember . . . Santeria, yeah, that's it. That was Angel—Mr. Santeria—lighting candles, talking to saints, trying to get his kid back from the dead.

"You do what you gotta do," Jackie says sourly. "Like the rest of the tough guys. Just tell me one thing: what's gonna happen when you tell this Frank his kid just ain't got it? That he's a coward just like his father?"

"The kid ain't a coward. We don't know that yet. He's a nice kid."

"He's a sweetheart. But he's scared of his shadow."

"We'll take care of that."

"Oh yeah? And how 'bout the colored kid with the hair? You gonna let this Frank ruin him, too?"

"No, he's just talking about putting him on a card in Atlantic City is all."

"Atlantic City?" Jackie asks disgustedly.

"Yeah, Khe Sahn's pro debut. Frank said he could arrange it. He got friends there."

"Of course he does. Now lissen to me, Toodie. That kid could be a good fighter, a helluva fighter. But he ain't ready for no pro debut. And he ain't ready for no Atlantic City."

"I know what I'm doing," says Toodie. "We'd get him somebody he can handle. Build his confidence. Besides, it's just talk."

"You're letting this guinea gangster call the shots. And I'm telling you now, everything he touches turns to shit. You shouldn't even be talking to him. You read the papers. Just talking to him makes you an accessory."

"I ain't a accessory to nothing," says Toodie.

"Keep tellin' yourself that," says Jackie, "after you put the kid in the ring."

"Like you said, I'm just doing what I gotta do."

"So am I." Jackie takes another swig to steady himself. Then he sets down the bottle and starts to walk away.

Toodie calls after him. But Jackie Farrell never looks back, leaving Toodie to sit down and dwell in his own defeated silence until Angel arrives with Nicky and Khe Sahn. The boys are carrying a new heavy bag.

Angel shows them where to hang it, then goes about his other business. Angel gets out a mop and a pail, which he fills from the slop sink. He mixes in holy water and a ruby-colored liquid that looks like shampoo. It's called Dragon's Blood. It costs $1.99 a bottle and is manufactured on Webster Avenue in the Bronx. Angel begins mopping the floor.

"What are you doing?" Toodie asks.

"Bad spirits," he says. "Gotta wash them away. I'm gonna bless the place." Angel looks back toward Nicky and Khe Sahn, who are mounting the heavy bag. "Maybe it give these kids some balls."

After mopping, Angel dips his finger in the pail and runs it along the frame of the door. He mounts a postcard from St. Michael—a boy saint with wings and a sword—above the entranceway. Next, he lights a yellow candle for San Marco de Leon and sets it by the foot of the door. "Go away evil," he says. "Don't come in no more. Go home to yo' mami."

Toodie walks off shaking his head. The heavy bag has been mounted. Khe Sahn grabs an old pair of bag gloves. Doesn't even bother to wrap his hands. Toodie watches as Khe Sahn begins to beat out slow, tentative measures on the hard smooth bag, just now starting to soften its guts. Nicky stands off to the side. The kid looks so lost.

"You all right, pally?"

"Me? Sure."

"That's good," says Toodie, watching as Khe Sahn's punches become harder and faster, as he starts to grunt with their force, as the chains begin to jangle and dance.

Nicky ambles over to the big plate-glass window that looks out over the rubble-strewn lot behind the gym. Looking through the window, the neighborhood seems relentlessly drab, tedious shades broken only by the intermittent psychedelia of graffiti murals.

There's one across the back lot, over this short field of weeds and tires and broken glass. It occupies a tenement's entire rear wall, huge, of epic intention, unlike anything Nicky has ever seen, but also, in some ways familiar. The caricatures are distinctive, melding both bubble gum and primitive styles. There are the faces of Elvis and Marilyn, of Brando in *The Godfather*, Ronald and Nancy Reagan, who is smiling, holding up a syringe, the words in a bubble of blood at the tip: "Just Say Know." There is DiMaggio hitting a home run, and a lady with a black Afro, whom Nicky does not know to be Angela Davis, screaming "Attica." Fritz the Cat in a cleric's collar and the hooded, robed figure of Death, brandishing his sickle, and perched on Death's shoulder, Tweety Bird from the cartoon. Pacino's *Scarface* with a machine gun: "Say Hello to My Wittle Friend." Hippies hoist the Puerto Rican flag at Iwo Jima. Wounded lovers embrace, arrows through their backs. High on the wall are planets ringed with gas, and bald eagles flying between purple-black cliffs. Below, a black forest with mushrooms and unicorns. The mural is fraught with slogans: "Don't Beleeve the Hype," "Justice for Michael Stewart," "Die Yuppie Scum."

And toward the lower corner, the piece becomes more familiar, more ghostly: the artist's signature, which Nicky already knows, and black dogs, saliva dripping from their teeth, run from a hot white coliseum. Rising from the weeds near the base of this symphonic hallucination is a tombstone bearing the legend: "RIP Buddy, U Wuz Da Best."

Nicky begins to remember.

It was the still before sunup.

He was twelve years old . . .

In a train yard somewhere in the Bronx. He can see the white rim of light around Yankee Stadium, a coliseum glowing among the ruins. Buddy has convinced him to come here, along with Vinny from Sullivan Street and his other friend, a coffee-colored kid named Toussaint, the best graffiti bomber on the Lower East Side. They're all very high.

The trains seem like mechanical serpents, assembled in lines that run to forever. Their steel wheels are even with Nicky's chest. Toussaint had said that big dogs roam these yards, that they're trained to bite off your balls. Nicky becomes dizzy, imagining a posse of black wolves with blank red eyes.

Now Buddy throws up an arc of pink paint on the hull of a train. Buddy works fast.

Nicky is mesmerized, watching as the spray dots form a complete, fantastic signature of big, bulbous letters.

"Dogs!" Toussaint shouts. "Yo, the dogs."

The boys stop, straining to hear.

"I'm tellin' y'all, they coming." Toussaint's face

convulses with fear. Vinny reads his expression and begins to sprint for the fence. Nicky turns to his brother. Now Buddy thinks he hears something, a bark. Yes, the dogs. The dogs are coming. Run, Buddy yells, run.

Buddy gives his brother a boost onto the fence. Nicky claws a grip and begins to climb frantically. He jumps off at the top, dropping safely into Vinny's waiting arms.

The fence is still shaking and creaking as Nicky looks back into the yard.

Toussaint is on the ground, clutching his leg. His wail mingles with what Nicky hears as the cruel yelp of the dogs. Now one appears from under the train's mechanical guts. The dog lives only in the shadows, but Nicky is sure that the dog is real.

Buddy is almost at the top of the fence when he lets go, falling back into the darkness of the train yard. The black dog is about to make a mad dash for his friend. And so is Buddy Battaglia.

CHAPTER
27

"BLESS ME, FATHER, for I have sinned."

"Tell me your sins."

"Tell me," says Nicky, "after that night at the gym, what happened then?"

"Well, your brother cracked Tommy around pretty good, and it got all around the neighborhood, which was bad 'cause it embarrassed Tommy Sick, but also because . . ." Father Vincent unsnaps the button that fastens his collar and lets out a sigh. "You want the truth? I mean even if it hurts. You still want to know?"

"You mean you're gonna say something bad about my father," says Nicky. "And you don't want me to take it personal."

"Pretty much."

"Go ahead."

"The bad thing was it embarrassed your father. Turns out it was your old man who sent Tommy Sick and them to the gym, you know, like they were going to avenge Mrs. Lombardi and clean up the neighborhood and all that other crap by beating up the black kids with baseball bats. Only Buddy messed up the whole plan. Now the whole neighborhood knows Buddy went against his own father. Here's your old man and he wants everybody to know what a tough guy he is, a man of respect and all that, and it comes out looking like he can't even control his own kid, which of course was true."

"It was always like that," says Nicky. "Even when we were little." In his mind's eye, Nicky sees his brother staring at dead rabbits in the butcher's window. "It always bothered my old man."

"Your father was furious."

"I heard about that. I remember how crazy mad he was," says Nicky. The morning after Buddy beat up Tommy Sick, Frank barged into Buddy's room. "You think it's fucking funny," he yelled. "You think this is some kinda joke to disrespect me like that." Nicky watched from the hallway as his father pulled Buddy from the bed and smacked him across the face. Buddy spat out a little blood, but he wasn't surprised. He just got up and brushed himself off, real matter of fact. "You can't hurt me, Pop," he said.

Now, in the confessional, Father Vincent says, "Anyway, we hadda go have a sit-down at the Rod and Reel. Your father told us we had to make up for it."

"Make up for what?"

"For screwing up his plan to make the neighborhood safe for white people."

"What did Buddy have to say to that?"

"He just played along with it. We're sitting at the card table in the club, and when your pop's not looking he winks at me. Like he was telling me: 'Don't worry, whatever he says, we ain't gonna do it anyway.' Buddy figured he had some kind of plan."

"So how did my father want you to make things right?"

"Simple, he said we had to go to Washington Square and kick the drug dealers out of the park. Of course, me being Colosimo's favorite nephew, he couldn't make me. But he could make his son do it. And if Buddy had to go, then so did I. I mean, at this point, we're in it together."

"My father wanted you to get rid of the Jamaicans?"

"The whole crew. All the dread brothers selling oregano and nickel bags and Ex-Lax coke. It was like your old man had it all planned, like he had it all thought through. I mean, somebody comes in here tells me they did a bad thing, I tell them to do so many Hail Marys and so many Our Fathers to make up for it. Well, with your father, it was the same deal. You know: 'Youse messed up, you tampered with the order of things, now you're gonna make amends by kicking the niggers out of the park.' Like that would have solved everything."

"The way he looks at things," says Nicky, "it probably would've."

"Of course. Only it didn't work out like that."

The story is headed toward the scene of a crime to which the priest does not want to return. He wants to be finished with Vinny Ruggiero of Sullivan Street. But Nicky won't let him forget.

"So?" he says. "G'wan."

"So we go to the park, me, Buddy, and Tommy Sick, who's coming along to check up on us and report back to your old man, you know, give him the old 'mission accomplished' bit. Me and Buddy, we got baseball bats. But before we hit the park, Tommy gives Buddy a piece. His face is still a mess from the beating and he breaks out into this real shit-eating grin. 'Here,' he says, 'your father wants you to have this in case anything happens.' The gun was black, a revolver, nothing like what these kids have today—nine millimeters, Uzis—all this artillery they walk around with. We both touched it. I never held a gun before. I don't think Buddy ever did either. It was so heavy. He puts it in his waistband, but he's still winking at me, like, 'Just go along with this, Vin, don't worry, everything's gonna be fine.' Tommy Sick stops at the corner, you know where they all play chess? 'Don't youse fuck nothin' up,' he says. Now me and Buddy, we go into the park."

Nicky can envision the scene unfold: the park like a glistening, black forest, its darkness broken by quick lines of light, moonlight, streetlight, shooting through the unkempt vegetation. The chess players remain silent, punching their time clocks as Buddy and Vinny walk over the pockmarked asphalt tiles, slowly, uncertainly, making their way into the park, the bats in their hands.

"We find the dreads in the middle of the park," says the priest. "Near the fountain, you know where I'm talking about?"

Nicky knows, behind the famous white arch, a monument to George Washington.

"The Jamaicans are hanging out counting money, sending guys to get from the stash. Buddy finds the head dread. He says he knows the guy. At least he thinks he does."

"Buddy thought he knew everybody," says Nicky. "Thought everybody hanging out in the street was his friend."

"That's what I'm saying," says Vinny. "Buddy thought he could talk to the guy. He goes up to him, this big Jamaican and says, 'Yo, righteous rastaman, you gotta do me a favor.' Guy looks up like he's seen a ghost. All of a sudden, there's two gindaloons from the neighborhood holding Louisville Sluggers. Buddy puts his bat on the ground, holds up his hands—peace, brother. I do the same as Buddy, but I'm thinking, God, I hope he knows what the fuck he's doing.

"Buddy says to the rasta, 'You know me. I just wanna talk.' And the rasta decides he's seen Buddy around and it's okay. He goes over and puts his arm around your brother, real friendly, and Buddy starts explaining, like, 'We're gonna yell and make a lotta noise and could you and your guys just get lost for an hour? We'll make it up to youse.'"

"So what did dread do?"

"Guy starts to laugh. For some reason, this is the funniest thing he ever heard. Just breaks him up. Then Buddy starts to laugh. Then I start to laugh, too. But the guys sitting on the edge of the fountain, all the dread heads, they don't think it's so funny. I'm watching from the corner of my eye and they're just staring us down, big, dead-eye stares. Now, Buddy bangs his bat against the side of the fountain and he starts screaming so Tommy Sick can hear and think we're doing what we're supposed to do. And the head dread, he's still laughing.

Still think's it's the funniest thing. Buddy starts howling at the moon, just to make sure Tommy can hear, and his windbreaker rides up on his stomach, you know what I mean? Now one of the dreads sees the gun. 'Yo, white boy blood clot strapped.' Next thing I know, they're all running at Buddy. But the head dread, he tells them to back off, that Buddy doesn't mean any harm. There's a standoff for a moment. I'm thinking Buddy was right, everything was gonna be cool. Then, all of a sudden, here comes Tommy Sick running through the park yelling, 'All niggers out the park.' Tommy Sick's got a gun, too. One of his own. The asshole starts firing in the air. Now everybody's scrambling.

"The dreads pick up the bats and pile on Buddy. I jump in the pile, trying to get 'em off. I get in a few good shots, get rocked a couple, too. Buddy's fighting back now. And his gun comes out of his waistband. It's loose on the ground, makes a scraping noise, never forget that. We're all grabbing for the gun. And so help me—the head dread—he's off to the side watching and he's still laughing his ass off. Now Buddy gets up and one of the rastas comes at him from behind. The guy's got a bat. He's got a clean shot, too. Your brother can't see him. But I can. And so can Tommy Sick; he's got the gun in his hand. Everybody was scrambling, we were all . . . everything was going so fast . . ."

Father Vincent pauses to hold back tears. His voice cracks as he resumes the story. "Then there's a blast. Boom. The dreadlock drops the bat, and all of a sudden he looks like a kid again. He doesn't quite understand what's happening. Probably couldn't believe he'd been shot, but all the viciousness, the rage, all the angry poisons just drain right out of his face. Then he just kind of falls on the ground, real slow. But his eyes stay open. I was watching him. We all were, just like everything stopped. I remember thinking that his wrists were so skinny. He was trying to say something."

"What?" Nicky asks.

"Never got the words out. He just stopped. Just like

that. Everything was quiet for a moment, then the sirens. We heard the sirens and took off."

"Where?"

"I don't remember where. Just that I couldn't get that kid out of my mind. Everywhere I ran, all I could see was this kid, trying to make the words."

"That's why you became a priest," says Nicky. "Isn't it?"

"That, and other reasons. But that's when it started. That kid died and I was born. Or reborn . . . whatever the hell you want to call it. It wasn't nothing corny, like they teach you in school. But watching him die, that was the first moment I believed in God. I knew I wanted to be . . . saved."

An eerie quiet comes over the musty box. Nicky has more questions. But not for today. This installment of the confession has ended badly. He remains kneeling, listening through the trellis until the silence is broken, until the priest begins to whimper for the boy he was, Vinny Ruggiero of Sullivan Street, asking again that that boy be forgiven.

Instinct tells Nicky to embrace the priest, to be of some comfort to his brother's friend. But that doesn't seem right, not here in the church. So he rises, mumbles a faint apology, and excuses himself.

The air is damp and cool. It is dusk and remnants of sunshine streak through the stained glass, shading the sanctuary in a deep blue haze. The church is still as a tomb. Nicky's confession ran long and his mother left without him. Even the mourning widows, they are gone, too, replaced by a solitary, female form. Nicky's footsteps make lonely little echoes as he approaches. Nah, he thinks, it can't be. Not her.

Oh, but it is.

Samantha Broderick is presiding over her own private ceremony, lost in her own therapeutic trance, whispering as she lights a candle, one of so many along a three-tiered row, each flicker another ghost, another good, grieving wish, dissolving into molten teardrops, then cooling, remembrance and regret coming together, frozen as wax stalactites dripping off a black iron ledge.

Nicky stops a pace behind her, still unnoticed, wondering what prayer it is that she mumbles, what language, what religion. Why is she here? And for whom?

"I could walk you home," he says. "I mean, if you don't mind."

IT DOES NOT seem possible to Nicky that Mrs. Doyle ever lived here. Or even that he lives here, in this building, his father's tenement. The apartment's walls are now lined with shelves of imposing volumes. Nicky peruses the titles: *The Brandywine Tradition, Matisse: The Paper Cutouts, Political Graphics: Art as a Weapon, Pop Art Redefined, The Duality of Vision, The Surrealists,* big books about people named Motherwell, Pollock, Rembrandt, Frank Schoonover, Edward Hopper, Delacroix, and Degas. Two still-lifes hang in between the picture frame windows—a small painting of split pears resting on a clean white tablecloth, and another, larger, more misty piece depicting white roses and lemons. Nicky inspects them, amazed that both shadow and light can be reduced to mere gobs of paint.

"I've had those forever," she says. "They were my mother's."

"Nice," says Nicky, trying not to notice the trace of her perfume that lingers in the apartment. "Real nice." He points toward the bookshelves, not knowing quite what to say. "All those books, I mean."

Samantha fumbles for a Marlboro. She's pale as porcelain. Faint, smoky circles have gathered under her eyes. She doesn't seem anything like the last time Nicky saw her, the day she smiled at him in front of the building. She probably doesn't even remember that. "You O.K.?" he asks.

Samantha forces a fragile cheer to her face. "Oh, it's nothing. I just feel a little rundown."

They share an awkward moment now, avoiding each other's eyes as she lights the cigarette. "Do you go to church often?" she asks.

"Confession."

"Oh," she says. "And do you have much to confess?"

"I don't know," he shrugs. "It's not really like that. I

mean, that's not why I go. You see, the priest, he used to hang out with my brother. They were like best friends."

"Your brother . . . Buddy?"

"Buddy, right," he says. "It's not really confession. I just go there and he sort of explains what happened to Buddy. I mean, how my brother got sick like he did."

Samantha nods. Her silence makes him nervous. Nicky searches for a conversation. "What are you?" he asks.

She doesn't understand.

". . . like what religion?"

Samantha has to think about that one for a moment. "Episcopal," she says, the declaration bringing a thin, ironic smile to her lips. "I guess . . . Would you mind if I put on some music?"

Nicky watches over her shoulder as Samantha goes through her records. The collection begins with Miles Davis, Thelonious Monk, Chet Baker—then falls off into a chronological arrangement. Nicky can imagine each album as corresponding to a season in her life, considering each vinyl disc as a clue to who and where she has been: Elton John, Peter Frampton, Jethro Tull's "Aqualung," Zeppelin, Blondie, Television, the Flying Lizards, the Slits, X Ray Specs, Tones on Tail, Sisters of Mercy, and the 45 pressed by Bambi's Banshees, from which Nicky does not recognize the photograph featuring Samantha decked out like Mad Max.

He swallows hard, confounded by her egregious bad taste. Maybe she had an unhappy childhood.

"Do you have a preference?" she asks.

"Nah, whatever you want."

Samantha selects Chet Baker's rendition of "My Funny Valentine," which Nicky is surprised to find that he actually likes, the velvet melody.

"Who were you lighting a candle for?"

"Sal. Mr. Colosimo."

"Did you . . ." he asks, ". . . did you love him?"

"No, I liked him very much, but not like you're thinking. It's really quite sad what happened, though. Just before he died, he asked if I would light a candle for him. It was as if he knew."

Nicky detects the little bit of tremble in her voice.

"I'm sorry," she says. "I haven't been sleeping well."

Nicky finds her an ashtray. Samantha rests her Marlboro on the back of a ceramic mermaid. She seems almost alone now, pursing her lips approvingly at the softest tones.

"You're the Mystery Blonde, aren't you?"

She considers him for a long moment before answering. "I guess."

"What happened?"

"I don't really . . ."

"Please. I gotta know."

"I fell asleep in the limousine. The stereo was on, you see, I had put the music up rather high, and I couldn't see . . ." Samantha stops herself, realizing how improbable this all sounds, and stamps out her cigarette. "There were some loud noises, almost like a truck backfiring. I woke up, I saw two bodies in the street, and I ran away."

"Are you just saying that?"

"A man is killed. Two men in fact. One of whom had been very good to me, and you ask if I'm just saying that?"

"I'm sorry, it's just that the papers are saying . . ."

"I don't read the papers," she says curtly.

"Everybody reads the papers."

"I don't."

"Then how come you know you were the Mystery Blonde?"

"Don't be a child," she says.

"Did you go to the cops?"

Samantha shakes her head and lights another cigarette.

"Did the cops come to you?"

"No. I didn't want to get involved. I never saw that before. I mean, I never saw anyone dead. Murdered, I should say. But what can the police do? They can't bring Sal back. I have nothing to tell them. I didn't see anything happen. If I did, if I thought it would help, I might have—how do they say it?—I might have come forward."

"Did you see my father there?"

"Why, should I have seen your father? . . . Did your father kill Sal?"

"No. That's the papers saying that. My father didn't like the Fatman, but he didn't kill no one."

"Are you just saying that?"

"No."

"Then, why do you ask if I saw him?"

"'Cause they say there's guys that're gonna dime him out, make up a story like he did it. You know, rats."

"Rats?"

"Snitches, the lowest kind of people. Guys who'd turn on their own friends to save themselves."

"I see. Nicky, tell me, if your father were a killer, would you still love him?"

Nicky does not answer.

She asks again. "Would you?"

"He's my father," Nicky says. "Of course."

"Will you tell him that I was there? In the car?"

"I don't think so."

"Why?"

"'Cause I wouldn't want to rat you out."

Samantha finds herself moving closer now, in a strange rapture. Something about Chet Baker's horn has soothed her. And something about the way this boy says it again, slowly, "I'd never rat you out." Suddenly, she is incapable of shame, thinking, well, thinking like a man, like men she has known, in that preening, alley cat, rub up against it sort of way, looking into his eyes, pressing her advantage, feeling him, helpless and hard, much to his chagrin, she kisses him. She's light-headed at first, then, it's as if she were high, drunk, stoned, nodding, all of that, and more, and she is in her own fantastic melodrama, wondering if this boy, Nicky, had in some strange way been sent to her.

Or, if it's just that she hasn't gotten laid in ages.

Hasn't even been touched.

Hasn't allowed anyone.

She catches herself. Panic, embarrassment, confusion all conspire to drive away her bliss as quickly as it came. She pushes him off. "I'm sorry," she says. "I can't."

Nicky doesn't understand. "Can't what?"

She takes him by the hand and hurries him out the door. "You don't understand," she says. "You have to go."

CHAPTER
28

"HE A GANGSTA, right? Like in the movies?"

"Who?" Toodie asks.

"That man Frank," says Khe Sahn.

"What's it to you?"

"Nothing. I seen it in the papers."

"Don't be so impressed."

The buzzer sounds and they go back to work. Toodie puts on the pads. Khe Sahn pushes in his mouthpiece. They've been at it all morning, calibrating the fighter's moves by ever finer margins. Toodie begins to crowd his fighter. "Don't throw the jab too close, 'cause you don't see his right hand," says Toodie. "Remember, the only knockout punch is the one you don't see."

Khe Sahn nods, trying to say something through the mouthpiece.

The kid only has to be told once, and that amazes Toodie, how well he listens. Working with Khe Sahn is a pleasure, but also an obligation. Kind of like an inheritance, bestowed on the day of Paddy Blood's last will and testament.

They were at the Imperial. It was hot, middle of the summer, but Toodie didn't know anything was the matter until Paddy Blood undid the top button of his shirt.

"You wanna sit down?"

Paddy Blood pawed at the air in annoyance, even as Toodie propped him up on a wooden stool in the corner. How light the old man had become—as if his dissipation had been self-inflicted, purposeful and premeditated, part of a plan he had kept from Toodie. He told Khe Sahn to go to the pay phone and call for an ambulance. Khe Sahn froze. Toodie had to yell at him, hurry, goddammit, call 911.

Then Paddy Blood spoke up in a hoarse, gurgling whisper. "Anything happens to me," he said, "you look after the kid."

"Don't be silly," said Toodie, "nothing's gonna happen to you. Can't catch your breath is all."

"Promise me," said Paddy Blood.

"You don't even gotta axe me that."

"Promise."

"I swear," said Toodie. "Just don't say nothing. Save your strength."

Paddy said, "Tell that kid he don't even need to get a haircut."

"Sure, Paddy."

"Be careful with him. Take him along slow."

"Don't talk."

"That kid could be a champ."

"Save your strength."

"I love that kid."

Then Paddy Blood closed his eyes. Toodie began to rub the old man's hands, trying to preserve a warmth, to prevent the ghastly pallor from spreading. Already his skin seemed translucent, a purplish undertow gathering beneath its surface. Toodie found the little yellow pill the old man kept in the breast pocket of his shirt. He placed it on Paddy Blood's tongue and tried to inch it down the old man's throat. But it was no use. The pill became a messy dot of paste.

Finally, Toodie brought Paddy Blood's hand to his cheek and began to weep. It was the first time he could recall his own tears, and their taste, thin and salty, made him feel almost normal, like everyone else . . . like somebody's kid. And there was not only grief in those tones, but spite, too. I know you love Khe Sahn, he whispered, but what about me? Say you love me. Let me hear you say I was as good as a son.

At the funeral, Khe Sahn swore he would become a champ. He swore he'd bring the championship belts to Paddy Blood's grave.

Don't swear so much, said Toodie, just keep working.

And now, in the Empire Gym, Toodie jabs at Khe Sahn, teaching him that most noble skill, how to duck. "That's it," he says, "like you're kneeling in church. Only less. Now slide in with the front foot. That's it. Now you come up into him."

Khe Sahn hits the pads—pop, pop, pop. Perfect. The kid understands the subtle geometries as well as the grappling crafts. Paddy Blood was right; he's a natural. It's no wonder Khe Sahn's never been down. Toodie can teach him all he needs to know, except one thing. You can't teach anyone to take a punch. That you're born with. Sometimes you find it in yourself. Sometimes you don't.

Toodie runs Khe Sahn through the workout until he spots Cheech DeFranco standing at the door, examining the Santeria candle. "Keep going like I told you," he tells his fighter.

Cheech holds up a brown paper bag as Toodie approaches.

"The money," he says. "This is the first five."

"I thought Frank said ten to start."

"There was a line at the bank. Look, I wouldn't worry. Frank'll take care of everything. I just came up here 'cause he don't like to touch the money no more. Also, I wanna warn you, he's on his way up, and he's already in one of those moods. Been reading the papers. So please don't go aggravating him."

"Sure, but what's he want up here?"

"Says he wants to speak to you."

"What about?"

Cheech points toward the ring, where Khe Sahn is

snorting furiously at make-believe opponents. "Him, I think."

Now Frank walks in, bigger and louder than ever, going through the whole routine, the "Howya been, kid?" the kissing on the cheeks.

"Why you hadda pick a neighborhood like this?" he asks. "It's like a fucking Tarzan movie. Only Puerto Rican."

"I grew up around here, Frank."

Frank is looking around, inspecting.

"What's the candles for, good luck?"

"Something like that."

"Hey, whattaya need luck for? You got the package I sent?"

"Yeah," says Toodie. "Thanks a lot."

"That's what I like to see," says Frank, appraising Khe Sahn with his eyes. "A young man learning his trade."

"He's gonna be fine."

"That's what I wanna talk with you about. Moving him along." Frank jerks his thumb, and Cheech takes his cue to leave.

"I'll be in the car you need me," says Cheech. "Gotta make sure the hubcaps is still there."

"Fucking guy," says Frank, shaking his head. "He take care of you?"

"I told you, yeah."

"Good. You need anything?"

"Well, we still owe for the ring. Plus the landlord says he needs security."

"Security? Tell him there ain't no security in this neighborhood. Nah. Better yet, don't you even worry about it. I'll have Cheech speak to the guy."

"So what do you want to talk to me about?"

"What, you're in a rush?"

"No. It ain't that."

"You don't like me or something?"

"Nah. Really."

"We're friends, right?" Frank asks. "You ever hear people talking about me?"

"No," says Toodie. "Not how you mean."

"How do you know what I mean?"

"I see the papers."

"But if you heard people saying things, you'd let me know?"

Toodie doesn't really know what to make of a question like that. "I would never stand for anyone ratting anyone out . . ." he says, ". . . if that's what you mean."

"That's exactly what I mean," says Frank. "And that's why I like you. Why I'm helping you out here."

"I thought it was 'cause of Paddy Blood."

"That too," says Frank. "But now you gotta help me out."

Toodie sees right through Frank. He sees his justification. He imagines a child, his, his baby daughter, stumbling toward him. First steps. She's wearing those square white baby boots. Sunlight in her curls.

"You listening?"

"Sure."

"Good. 'Cause I know this guy in Philly, see. A friend of ours, well, a friend of mine actually. He can work everything out. Make a good match for us. You know, get the kid started. Turn 'im pro in Atlantic City. Like I said, the guy's from Philly, and things being how they are, he wants to get on my good side. Guy wants to show me something, you know, an act of good faith."

Now Toodie is watching the fighter. Khe Sahn's doing his five hundred sit-ups. Truth is, he's ready for a pro debut.

"Do I have any say in this?" asks Toodie.

"This time? Not really. I just wanna see what we got here."

"I don't want anything to happen, Frank. I wanna build him up slow."

"Same as me. What, you think I wanna devalue my investment?"

"To you, he's a fighter. To me, he's more than that. I don't want anything to happen."

"I swear on my kid nothing can happen," says Frank. "Like I said, we're dealing with a friend of mine. Only the ring is square."

CHAPTER
29

CHEECH DEFRANCO DRAINS his third amaretto and cream and studies the girl on stage, trying to figure out what she used to be. One thing about the girls at the Tip Top Lounge, they all used to be something else. It's not like they were born to be professional tittie dancers, the kind Frank likes, the ones that come off an operating table with a rack looks like a pair of nuclear warheads. Those fake things are cold and hard, it's like trying to feel up a statue.

Cheech prefers a woman like this one, on the stage, leaning over with her hands on the mirrored wall and shaking her ass. She's no headliner, that's for sure. No headliners at the Tip Top Lounge. Cheech likes it like that. Means the girls are more—how do you say?—more down to earth. Not as stuck up.

She pushes off the mirror, leaving the latest in a series of smudgy fingerprints, and spins into a sloppy pirouette, something she must have picked up watching "Dance Fever." Poor girl almost falls over, what with those big heels, and the smile leaves her face briefly. Cheech hopes no one saw her graceless moment, at least not any of these jerkoffs. Look at them, sitting at the bar: office managers and postal workers and salesmen and even an off-duty cop down the end, fucking guy in a ninety-nine-dollar suit trying to look like he ain't looking. What the fuck. Nobody knows him. That's why he comes here.

The girl stumbles back into the rhythm of the music, the "Lido Shuffle" by Boz Scaggs. There's a lot to like about her, he thinks. She's dark, probably Puerto Rican, and she has nipples like Hershey's kisses. Also, she don't have no tattoos. Cheech can't stand that, broads with tattoos. Some of these dancers got little spiders and snakes. They put 'em on their thighs, their shoulders, their ankles. Terrible, looks like black and blue marks. Someone should tell these girls.

The other thing he likes about this girl is the stretch marks. Stretch marks are okay by Cheech. Means the broad got a kid. In his way of thinking, the stretch marks endow the tittie dancer with warm, worldly qualities, an intimate knowledge of love and loss. It means she knows a whole hell of a lot more than some platinum headliner who just wants to go through your wallet. No, she ain't stuck up. She used to be somebody else. Somebody's mother.

There was this one broad used to dance here, a little pale for his tastes, but wonderful anyway. She was Irish. Not Irish from New York, Irish from Ireland. Could barely understand her, the way she talked. Sinead, that was her name. Cheech never heard a name like that before. Once in a while Sinead would work as a substitute teacher at St. Brendan's Grammar School in the Bronx. She lived off Gun Hill Road with her five-year-old boy. His name was Colin. Cheech loved that kid. He'd show up every Saturday and take Colin for the day. They went to Van Cortlandt Park, the Botanical Gardens, Yankee games, the Bronx Zoo. One time, Cheech took him to Coney Island, to the aquarium. One of the whales had just had a kid, a little gray one, about the size of a bathtub. Cheech named him Benji the Baby Whale. Colin got a kick out of that. What a laugh the kid had. His two front teeth had fallen out, and Cheech, playing the tooth fairy, gave him a Ben Franklin for each.

After Coney Island, they went to Randazzo's in Sheeps-head Bay. Colin ate two bowls of macaroni.

A few days later, Sinead called, said she got a job as a nurse at Montefiore Hospital. Said she was very sorry, but that she had to get on with her life.

It wasn't the kind of thing Cheech could get mad about. He couldn't really blame her. He understood what it meant, that he'd be going back to nightcaps of amaretto and cream at the Tip Top Lounge. He'd miss the girl, and miss the kid even more. But all things considered, it wasn't the worst thing that could have happened. At least hanging out here at the Tip Top, he catches a break. Here, no one knows who he is. And there's no Frank Battaglia around to drive him crazy. Fucking Frank is getting on his nerves, taking it out on everybody, but mostly him, and Nicky, too. And that's too bad. Nicky's a sweet kid and he deserves better than Frank all the time screaming about how this one could be a rat and that one, too, and how he's gonna suck all their hearts out.

Cheech points to his glass. The bartender, a spent biker chick with a spider tattooed above her left tit, pours him another amaretto and cream. "The guy down there's paying," she says.

"What guy?"

"Guy at the end of the bar," she says. "The cop."

JACK GALLAGHER KNOWS from the NYSIS computer and the bullshit FBI intelligence jacket that Cheech De-Franco was born July 4, 1943. His old man split when he was eight years old. He flunked out of two high schools, first LaSalle, then one of the old 600 schools, the ones for kids who had earned J.D. cards. As an adult, DeFranco's sheet lists three offenses, two for assault, another for soliciting prostitution. The cases were dropped before they got to trial. Cheech DeFranco has had one address his entire life, 53 Morton Street, where he still lives with his mother. No wife. No kids. He pulls down $165,000 on the books as a business agent for the ILA, and still Jack knows he's gotta be paying for it. This Cheech is not what you'd call handsome.

That's not the worst of it, though. Gallagher's been clocking Cheech for a week now and it's got to the point where he almost feels bad for the guy. Imagine having to work for Frankie Batts. What a shit life that must be.

Frank uses him as his bagman—around the Westside meat market, on the docks, in the garment center. He's been with Frank all this time, since they were kids, and Frank still calls him "the retard." Talks to him like an errand boy: Drive me here, wait in the car, shut the fuck up, take my kid to the gym, pay the man. The tapes aren't clear, matter of fact the sound quality sucks, but you can sure make out Frank Battaglia getting on Cheech De-Franco's case. "Hey, Cheech, why you always gotta be such a fucking retard, can't you see we're talking 'bout something important?"

That's got to wear on a guy.

Now Jack makes his move across the bar. When he gets there, Cheech is drinking something that looks like you'd get it in a Chinese restaurant—an aquamarine liquid topped with a foamy meringue-like head and an orange paper umbrella. The drink Gallagher bought, the amaretto and cream, rests untouched in the well of the bar.

"I thought you was just a cop," says Cheech.

"Used to be."

"What, you got a promotion?"

"Retired. Now I'm with your fan club. The Southern District."

"Shoulda known," says Cheech, nodding at Gallagher's feet. Wing-tips. Ugliest shoes ever. Every federal agent he ever saw had a pair.

"Oh, you mean these?" says Gallagher. "When I signed on, they tell me every agent gets a discount with the Bostonian wing-tip company. I figured what the fuck. I got a lifetime supply."

Cheech draws hard on the straw of his drink and goes back to watching the girl. She looks great under the mirrored ball, dancing to "Boogie Nights."

"If you don't got nothing to say, then get the fuck out 'cause I was having a good time before you came."

Gallagher finishes his beer and motions the biker chick for another. Then he pulls a pen from his breast-pocket and begins to write on a cocktail napkin. When he's finished, Jack Gallagher places the napkin by Cheech's drink.

The napkin jottings are phone numbers—for Cheech, Frank, and Philly Testa, the numbers at the ILA, the number at the Rod and Reel. "We been up on all the lines," says Gallagher. "Plus there's a bug in the club."

"So what. That's what they got lawyers for."

"And we got a witness," says Gallagher. "In the shooting."

"I don't know what the fuck you're talking about."

"You know. The Fatman."

"I don't know no Fatman." Cheech scoops an orange slice from the bottom of the glass and sucks the fruit from the rind. "What, some blond broad I read about in the papers?"

"I can't tell you that."

"I can't tell you to fucking blow me you're so full of shit."

"Suit yourself," says Gallagher. "By the way, long as we're on the subject, your boss, Frank? I gotta tell ya, guy must be one royal pain in the ass to work for."

Cheech can't help himself, and begins to grin. "He got his moments."

"I mean, drive me here, drive me there, take my kid here, be ready at such and such a time, do this, do that."

"Hey, you know how it is. All bosses is pricks," says Cheech. "At least with my boss, we know where the other's been, you know. We known each other since we were kids."

"Sure," says Gallagher. "I understand. You guys go back together. What's that name he calls you?"

"What?"

"The retard," says Gallagher, looking in his eyes. "That's it. The retard."

Cheech flinches, trying to control a sudden rage. Gallagher can see his anger is not something to trifle with, but wants to test this guy anyway. See how far he can push. "Yeah," he says, "we were laughing about that in the office, me and the guys. No offense, of course. I mean, it's just funny how he says it, you know, the retard."

Cheech takes a fresh drink from the bar and pivots on the red vinyl stool. Cheech should've known better than to let this guy look him in the eyes. Should never of even talked to this cop.

"Heard Frank used to be a fighter, huh? . . . The Bedford Brawler?"

Cheech refuses to go for the bait. His eyes remain riveted on the girl's dimpled dancing ass. His concentration earns Gallagher's grudging admiration.

"Tell me something. The Bedford Brawler, does he always go around smacking fag waiters?"

Cheech just shrugs, trying not to listen, trying to think of the tooth fairy and baby whales.

"Look, I'm sorry," Gallagher says quietly. "You don't have to say nothing. Just listen. I won't bullshit you no more. You're going down. We got the unions. We're gonna get you for the Fatman. It's only a matter of time, but it's gonna happen, and sooner rather than later. You're gonna do a ton of time, Cheech." Here, Jack Gallagher pauses to consider some of the old lines he'd run on the skells: "Your parole officer ain't been born yet." Or "By the time you get out, they'll have pussy in a can." He thinks about running those lines on Cheech, then decides to take a pass. Why bother? After all, this Cheech was a better class of skell.

"I seen your sheet," Gallagher tells him. "Seen you never did any time. This is gonna be federal time, but it's gonna be hard—Leavenworth, Marion. You see, the problem's your guy Frank. Frank is making all youse famous. My people hate that. Makes 'em look stupider than they already are."

Now the cop waits for some kind of response. But Cheech remains mute, silently enthralled by remembrances of the little kid Colin with his missing front teeth and his mother's warm white ass.

"The point is," Gallagher continues, "you don't have

to do all that time. Shit, you don't have to do any if you don't want. We know you don't make decisions. We know it wasn't your idea to do the Fatman. All you gotta do is flip. The FBI guys, they got a name for it. They say, tell Cheech alls he gotta do is 'join the team.' How you like that? 'Join the team.' I know, bunch of hard-ons those guys. You should see 'em, fucking guys from Iowa, Idaho, got one I think he's from a goddamn Indian reservation. Join the team, they say. And I know what you're thinking. You're thinking you been doing this all your life, living a certain way, and now I come along and tell you you should be a punk. Not only that, but I gotta convince you that all of a sudden being a punk is like walking with God. Personally, I can't tell you that. I can tell you the guys you work for, especially that Frank, are shit. I can tell you that you might as well save yourself, that it makes sense. I can even tell you that we can get you all the tittie bars and umbrella drinks you want, that they can put you somewheres nice—you ever think a Arizona?—and that if this case gets any hotter, gets any more press, you should hold out till they throw a Ford Taurus in the deal. But I can't tell you you won't be a punk. The thing is, Mr. DeFranco, this is the most important day of your life. This is the day you get to be smart."

Cheech gives the dancer a final, admiring look, then swivels on his stool, a thin, wistful smile on his lips. He throws up his hands, acknowledging the cop's con but also, his logic. "I can't do that," he says.

"Why not?"

Cheech slaps a generous stack of bills on the bar and gets up to leave. "'Cause I'm the retard," he says.

GALLAGHER FINISHES HIS beer alone, then goes to the pay phone, thinking how impressed he was with Cheech DeFranco, how the guy tried so hard to keep under control, even when he gave him that song and dance about the Mystery Blonde. Guy's got every reason in the world to rat—except one. Now Gallagher wonders, if things were reversed whether he'd have the same stones as Cheech? Or if all they got in common is that they both gotta pay for it. Gallagher punches in the number for the front desk at the Chelsea Hotel.

"Mushy Flynn, please."

"Who?" asks the concierge.

"You see the old guy with the fedora waiting in the lobby. That's him. Tell him the Hero of the Month is calling."

It's gotten to the point where Jack Gallagher's feeling a little lousy about doing what he's got to do.

CHAPTER
30

NICKY GAZES OUT the window as the Chrysler rolls over the Jersey Turnpike. It seems to him that the Garden State is nothing more than the repetition of smokestacks belching noxious clouds, some huge, corroding chemistry experiment. But his father is always talking about how he's moving the family to Jersey, saying, 'You can't see the niggers and the taxes are less.' Something about both taxes and black people is profoundly disturbing to Frank Battaglia. Then again, these days, everything bugs Nicky's old man.

He'd been nutty all morning, long before they hit the Holland Tunnel.

There had been another Mushy Flynn column in the paper:

> A capo in the Corallo crime family has apparently turned down an offer to rat out his boss, Frank (Frankie Batts) Battaglia, Mushy's Mob has learned.
>
> Agents approached one Angelo (Cheech) DeFranco at the Tip Top Lounge, a go-go joint at 640 Sixth Avenue, where he was admiring the talent and taking a well-deserved respite from his unappreciated task as Battaglia's valet.

It seems that Frankie Batts has abused his so-called pal since they were kids, addressing him with the quaint salutation: "You @#$%ing retard!" You can hear it on all the wiretaps.

G-men appealed to whatever resentment and common sense this hoodlum may have. They harped on DeFranco's status as Gangland's Stepin Fetchit and the inevitability of long, hard time for crimes committed on orders that most certainly were not his.

But DeFranco declined the offer without so much as a second thought. In doing so, he proved that he is a stand-up guy, but also that his nickname is entirely apropos . . .

Now, as Cheech takes the exit for the Garden State Parkway, Frank says, "You go to the tittie bar to get away from me?"

"Whatsa matter I can't have no quality time? . . . Tell you the truth, you been getting on my nerves. Been riding me pretty hard."

"How come you didn't tell me?"

"What's to tell? I been going there for years. I need permission?"

"So this joint, it's like a secret you got. Something I'm not supposed to know about."

"This is what I mean. You're breaking my balls again."

A contemptuous glare comes to Frank's face. "How come you didn't tell me about the feds?"

"I thought we went through this already," says Cheech. "First of all, it wasn't like it says in the paper. It was only one guy, some guy you could tell used to be a cop, a real busted-down valise. And I didn't tell you 'cause I didn't want you to get all crazy like you are right now."

"How'd the paper know everything?"

"I tole you. 'Cause that rat bastid agent musta dimed me out."

"What do you mean the agent was a rat, the agent dimed you out? What, youse are partners?"

"Jesus Christ, Frank. I can't fucking believe you."

"Believe me. How is it they know how we talk?"

"What, that you call me a retard?"

"Yeah, like that."

"How do you think? Probably knocked the earphones off their heads when they were listening. You're so goddamn loud."

"How do I know you're telling the truth?"

"Please, Frank, I'm asking you—out of respect 'cause I know you're under a lot of pressure—but don't play this shit with me, all right? We still got a long drive."

"Bullshit, we got a long drive. How do I know you and this agent didn't make a deal?"

"How do I know you don't take it up the ass?"

"How do you know I don't? What I'm saying is, maybe nobody really knows nothing about anybody."

"Well, if that's the way you think. I guess you got your answer."

"Fuck you. What was the guy's name?"

"Who? The guy who poked you in the can?"

"Don't be a smart guy. The cop. The agent, I mean."

"I didn't ask."

"That's real convenient, Cheech. You don't know his name, so I can't even check him out. I don't like how this feels."

"How this feels? How the fuck you think I feel? The guy calling me a retard in the paper." Cheech hopes none of his girls from the Tip Top Lounge read the *Mirror*.

"Tell me again," says Frank. "What did he say about the girl?"

"Can't you see what they're doing? They're running a game, the cop and the newspaper guy. Trying to get us scared so's one of us, somebody, folds up. They don't got nothing except their talk. If you don't get scared, you ain't got nothing to worry about. You even said so yourself: number one, Vanderpool the lawyer says whatever they come up with he can get thrown out of court, number two, we never say much on the phones and they probably can't hear shit except for you calling me names even if we did, and number three, the girl ain't a problem."

"That's what you say."

"That's what I know. I follow her and find her on line in the cheese store. She's buying mozzarella and prosciutto, you know, rolled together. Now remember, this blonde girl never seen me before unless she seen me that night with the Fatman. So I make like I'm on line in the store, too, and I tell her not to get it like that, all rolled up. I tell her it's better to get the mozzarella, then go next door and get the prosciutto. Better to get them separate. You get it all rolled together, the cheese gets hard. You don't want it like that, I tell her. That's for people from out of town. Also, I told her to get some of the ricotta. You gotta admit, the ricotta they got over there is fucking wonderful, Frank. Besides, I say, you're too skinny anyways. She smiles when I say that. She says thank you, thank you so much, and she's smiling and I'm smiling and everybody loves everybody. I mean, she don't think nothing of it, she don't even blink. Now, lemme axe you, if she saw me blow Fritzy's heart out of his chest, you think she'd be talking to me like I'm her fucking uncle? I'm telling you: it was a limo, she was in the backseat, which you can't see shit out the back anyway, plus the trunk was up. Plus it's fucking midnight."

Frank thinks it through for a moment and says, "So maybe she didn't see you. That don't mean she didn't see me."

"The girl didn't see nothing, Frank, so please don't make us a problem where we ain't got none. Please, I'm asking a favor."

"Maybe they put it in her mind," says Frank. "Maybe they put it in her mind that I was there and killed the Fatman."

"They? Who's they?"

"I don't know. The cops. The feds. The fucking guy from the paper. Who knows? Maybe she reads the paper and that puts it in her mind, you know, like, psychology." Frank starts sucking on his teeth and scratching the back of his fist.

Suddenly, Nicky pipes up from the backseat. "Cheech is right," he says. "She didn't see anything."

Cheech almost swerves off the Garden State. Frank takes note of his son for the first time since they left the neighborhood. "How do you know?"

"I spoke to her. Samantha, that's her name. I spoke to her."

"You spoke to her. Oh, and where the fuck did you meet up with this girl?"

"In church."

CHAPTER
31

ROCCO DECAVALCANTE CLIPS the end off his El Presidente and waves it at the workman, one of the crew erecting a prizefight ring in the Iberia Ballroom of the Conquistador Hotel. The worker interprets the order and scurries away in the direction made clear by Rocco's massive Cuban cigar.

So much to take care of, thinks Rocco, so many responsibilities. Though the papers refer to him as the sadistic upstart heir to the fortunes of Philadelphia's Gagliardi crime family, Rocco DeCavalcante prefers to think of himself as the man who brought civilization back to the Conquistador Hotel, which is on the boardwalk in Atlantic City. It was Rocco who restored the place to grandeur, who arranged for the bathrooms to stock not one, but two soaps, including a perfumed bar wrapped in crinkly red cellophane and sealed with an adhesive-backed image of a dark Latin woman with a flower in her hair peeking from behind a fan. It was Rocco who thought to put the doormen in Spanish armor and ordered those gambling chips that look like lost coins from a sunken galleon. It was Rocco who envisioned the waitresses dressed in flamenco getups. It was Rocco DeCavalcante who brought back the headliners—

Jerry Vallee and Don Nickles and Buddy Greco. Everybody but Nick Ramone. Nick Ramone was married to that black broad, what's her name? Whatever, it don't matter. Rocco doesn't approve of that kind of thing. It's not that he's prejudiced or nothing. Fuck no. Matter of fact, he wants to get Lou Rawls to play this very same ballroom.

Rocco plucks the Cuban from his mouth and starts to sing: "You'll never find, dum-dum-da-da-da-dum, another love like mine . . ." His imitation of Lou Rawls's velvet baritone comes out a high-pitched wheeze, like a kazoo. He isn't built for those notes. Rocco DeCavalcante is the size of a jockey, four feet eleven in lifts.

Nick Ramone this, he thinks. Who needs Nick Ramone when you could get Lou Rawls in your joint? Or Bobby Greco.

And that's just the beginning. Soon the Conquistador will be known for more than the finest names in contemporary entertainment. Soon the Conquistador will be known for something else.

Rocco DeCavalcante's bringing in boxing. Boxing his way. Gonna be the hottest venue east of Vegas. Gonna get it on TV: live from the Conquistador Hotel.

Watching these off-the-books workmen set up the ring fills Rocco with an immense happiness. Everything's coming into place, he thinks. Smoke billows from his cigar like a fog machine as he spots Frank Battaglia entering the Iberia Ballroom.

"Frankie Batts," he says. As if they were asshole buddies. "I hear you're famous in New York."

Frank answers with a gesture, a street-corner version of "Aw, shucks."

Rocco clasps Frank by the ears, kisses him twice, then steps back and starts to wave the Cuban around, making a big show of his gindaloon greeting, of his hotel, his ballroom, his ring.

Nicky, who walks in behind Cheech, can sense his father's envy. They look kind of funny together, he thinks, his old man and this Rocco, who is ruddy-faced, but also soft and toy-sized, almost a dwarf. Rocco looks as if he buys his clothes in the children's department. And his voice—how strange—as rough as his complexion, but rapid and gassy and high.

Rocco and Frank are still fawning over each other as Cheech turns to Nicky. "Him," he whispers, "him your father trusts."

There's a story about this Rocco. Frank and Cheech were talking about it in the car on the way down, after they finished bitching at each other. Some union guy was giving him a hard time, and Rocco cut off his pinky with a cigar snipper. They held the union guy down, according to Frank's version, and Rocco went snip, just like that. Then he fed it to a German shepherd named Augie.

Cheech said he'd seen that in a Robert Mitchum movie. A dog what ate a guy's finger? asked Frank. No, said Cheech, it was a movie about Jap mob guys, they go around cutting off their pinkies. That's to show the boss they're stand-up.

Maybe I should try that, said Frank, lemme see your hand.

Now, in the ballroom, Rocco DeCavalcante says, "Let's get it over with."

Khe Sahn comes out first, silent and sullen, with Toodie leading the way. The ringside physician is next. The doctor says he works for the New Jersey State Athletic Control Board. He has orthopedic shoes on his feet and a cigar butt planted in his mouth. The lapels of his orange-brown plaid jacket are sprinkled with ash. Unruly white hairs protrude from his ears and nose.

The doctor taps Khe Sahn's knee with a rubber mallet. He sticks a penlight in his ear. He asks Khe Sahn to follow the path of his index finger. Then he looks back at Rocco and says everything's okay. Khe Sahn looks over at Toodie, wondering if there's anything more. Toodie walks him up to the scale and adjusts the sliding weights himself.

"Two-oh-five," says Rocco DeCavalcante, imitating a ring announcer. Khe Sahn skulks off. "I love it," Rocco calls to Frank. "Where'd you find this kid?" Like a hyperactive elf, Rocco twirls his fingers around his head.

"That hair," he says. "Great. Great fucking gimmick. Where do they get that? Is it like a perm? Can I get it?"

Now comes the opponent. He plods forth in steel-tipped boots and jeans splotched with plaster and paint. A few minutes ago, he was just another guy working here in the Iberia Ballroom. Then Rocco waved his cigar and made him a fighter. He has nappy hair and yellow, bloodshot eyes. He strips down, revealing a small, sloppy belly. His briefs are gray and with holes.

The doctor goes through the routine again. The opponent seems an obedient sort, barely awake.

Toodie rubs Khe Sahn's shoulders, studying the opponent, thinking: At least Frank didn't fuck up the order. It's important to build a kid's confidence at the start. You need a guy like this the first time out, he tells himself, you need a professional bum.

Again, Rocco announces the weight in loud ringside fashion, then winks at Frank. "So's I robbed the grave-yard for ya," he says. "A deal's a deal."

TOODIE IS JOLTED awake at the sound of a smoke alarm. He falls off the couch, where he had fallen asleep watching the Mets game, and stumbles to the bathroom. There he finds his ace cornerman, Angel Cruz, mumbling a magic language. Angel remains as oblivious to Toodie as he is to the electric siren.

Toodie throws back the shower curtain, behind which Khe Sahn Witherspoon stands naked in the tub, a burnt offering at his feet. It looks like a mound of cremated chicken wings. Toodie rips the smoke alarm from the wall. "What the fuck," he says. "You guys."

"I'm only helping him," Angel protests. "When you fall asleep the kid, he got escared. He axe me to take the scare away."

Toodie douses the burnt offering with a glass of tap water. Whatever it was, Toodie would not like to think of it as having been recently alive. At least not during the Mets game.

"You scared?" he asks Khe Sahn.

Khe Sahn shrugs.

Toodie can see; the kid's petrified. "Put some clothes on," he says. "We'll take a walk."

THE BOARDWALK IS packed. There are baby strollers and bikini swimsuits and bleating seagulls. "Like Coney Island for white people," says Khe Sahn.

"Yeah," says Toodie. "Something like that."

"How come Jackie didn't come? I mean, it's my first pro fight and whatnot."

Toodie knows there's no sense trying to bullshit the kid. "Jackie don't like Frank."

"Shit, I could tell that just being in the gym. But why?"

"Goes back a long way. Frank used to fight when he was a kid, at least that's the story. Some wise guys went to Paddy and told him he should train Frank, that he was gonna be some kind of great white hope. They were selling that line even back then. So anyway, Paddy took him on, and basically, Frank was a dog. I mean, I wasn't there, but that's what Jackie says. That's why he can't stand the guy. Plus, Frank's the type of guy wants to let everybody know he's a big man. Jackie hates that more than anything."

"Big man," says Khe Sahn. "You mean a gangster."

"I mean a guy who's playing the tough guy." Toodie winks at the kid. ". . . You should know all about that."

They continue down the boardwalk in silence, each of them lost in the same remembrance. It was only a few years ago, but it feels like forever, the day they met at the Adolescent Reception and Detention Center on Rikers Island. The corrections officers, the CO's, they would call Paddy to give an exhibition, one of those gigs where Paddy would get up in front of the kids, all of them black or Spanish, and tell them, "Boxing builds character."

That day, Paddy asked if there's any volunteers, if there's any in the crowd of little bandits who wanted to get into the ring with the big hack who'd once made it to the semis of the Gloves. Khe Sahn was sitting in the first row. He started giggling, out of nervousness as much as anything.

"What about you?" said Paddy. "You're such a tough guy?"

"Nah," said Khe Sahn, still goofing for his boys, looking around, holding his nuts, trying to laugh it off, like: who's this old white man think he is?

Paddy asked the hack what he was in for. The guard told him the kid's in for a gun. "A gun?" said Paddy, real loud for everybody to hear. "I shoulda known," he said. "Another punk."

Now Khe Sahn had to get off his seat. "I fight that man," he said quietly, figuring he was better off taking the beating than letting old Paddy Blood call him a punk in front of everyone on the floor.

Khe Sahn strutted into the ring. But Toodie could feel him go limp as he laced the gloves. Khe Sahn wouldn't even look at him as he adjusted the strap on the headgear. The kids were howling with delight. The bell rang and the hack began to punish Khe Sahn methodically: body, body, head, body, no rush, just chopping down a tree. Khe Sahn was up against the ropes, ready to go, his knees already buckling when he reached out with a single, perfect, natural left hook that caught the CO on the point of the chin and knocked him cold.

Paddy whistled softly between his teeth. He'd never seen anything quite like it, that punch, so spontaneous, desperate beyond fear, but naturally perfect, the marriage of form and fury, something the kid never knew he had.

"You ever get out," said Paddy, "give me a call."

A month later, Khe Sahn shows up at the Empire. "Why'd you come?" Paddy asks.

"My brotha," says Khe Sahn. "He was eight years old. He got kilt."

It seemed as good a reason as any. Khe Sahn never mentioned his kid brother again. He's funny like that. Never talks much. Doesn't mean the kid doesn't have feelings, Toodie thinks, just the opposite. For all his talent, Khe Sahn remains emotionally fragile.

They go a good long way on the boardwalk without a word passing between them. It's not until they reach Caesars that Toodie speaks up. "It's okay to be scared,"

he says. "I wouldn't expect nothing different. Everybody's scared. Just do what you been taught, you'll be
fine, believe me."

"What if I lose?"

"You seen the guy. You beat up guys in the gym every
day ten times what this guy is."

"What if something happens?"

"Nothing's gonna happen." Toodie doesn't know what
bothers him more: the tears streaming down Khe Sahn's
cheeks, or his own reflection in the kid's eyes. "Don't
worry," he says. "I'm gonna be there the whole time."

"But if I lose," says Khe Sahn, "ain't nobody gonna
like me no more."

ANGEL KNEADS KHE Sahn's shoulders as Toodie kneels
to wrap his hands. Nicky watches from the other side of
the dressing room. He knows he doesn't belong here.
This is just another place his father told him to be. Keep
an eye on things till I get there, he said. Frank wanted to
stay at the craps table, where he was losing big and
bossing the waitresses around, yelling at them to bring
more Remy Martin, which he kept calling "Billy Martin." Cheech would stand behind him at the table, tipping
the girls.

Now Toodie grabs Khe Sahn fiercely by the back of
the neck. For a second it looks as if he's about to deliver
a head butt, but instead, he stops short, forehead to
forehead, whispering something urgent. Then Khe Sahn
makes a proper fist with his right hand and jams it square
into the palm of his left, then again, snorting.

"Feel okay?" Toodie asks.

Khe Sahn shrugs. "It feel all right," he says. But the
look in his eyes says something else. Nicky knows what
that look means. So does Toodie. He tells the fighter to
get up and start moving.

Khe Sahn starts to throw punches, each blow making
a slapping noise against Toodie's palms, each drawing
another encouraging cheer from Angel.

Until Frank barges in the dressing room.

"That's it," says Frank, swirling the booze in his

snifter. "That's what I like to see." Frank is very loud. He respects no privacies. He tips the snifter at Khe Sahn and Toodie and takes a large gulp of his Billy Martin. "Here's to my investment. I only hope you do better than that fucking Cheech. I hadda leave him at the table. Guy's bad luck, he's losing all my money."

Next, Rocco DeCavalcante lets himself in the dressing room. He doesn't bother to knock, either. Rocco has brought along the old grubby doctor from this afternoon, the wet cigar butt still hanging from his mouth. "Jeez, Frank, I'm glad I found you," says Rocco.

"What's the problem?"

"The problem is this." Rocco holds out a hand into which the doctor places a ream of graph paper. Rocco spreads it against the wall like a map, smoothing away the wrinkles with an arc of his forearm. "The opponent? This is his brain."

"What?" Frank doesn't understand.

"Tell 'im, Doc."

Using his cigar stub as a pointer, the doctor notes the successive cliffs of red ink on the paper. He says they represent the opponent's brain waves. The problem is, they are not sufficiently jagged or high. "We call it amplitude," he says.

"Means the guy's a mummy," says Rocco.

"So?" says Frank.

"So?" says Rocco. "So it's out of my hands."

The doctor looks to Rocco for the glance that grants permission to speak. "As physician for the New Jersey State Athletic Control Board," he says, "I cannot let this bout take place. I'm sorry, gentlemen."

"Frank, I can't apologize enough."

"I thought you said we had a deal."

"Of course we did. How was I to know? You think I knew this kid was a fucking mummy? You think I'm happy about it? This fucks up the whole card. I got investors out there in the audience. I got Bobby Greco out there wants to see the show. There's a lot of people came to see your kid. A lot of people heard." Rocco twirls his fingers about his head, just as he did at the weigh-in. "I mean the hair," he says. "That shit just cracks me up."

"Bobby Greco," says Frank. "He's out there?"

"In the back. It's like, he's a friend so's I gotta give him some privacy."

"I met him once."

"Bobby Greco?"

"Yeah, at the Sands. When I was working for the Fatman . . . when we was all working for the Fatman."

Toodie gets up now, barely able to contain his anger. "Angel, cut the tape off him. He ain't fighting."

"Wait," says Rocco. "That's what I'm trying to tell ya. Wait a second."

"Khe Sahn ain't fighting," says Toodie.

"No, youse got it all wrong," says Rocco. "This ain't a play. We can work something out."

"Not with my fighter."

Rocco looks to Frank for an appeal—like Frank's the voice of reason. "You know me," he says, patting his chest. "We're supposed to be friends."

Angel looks on, dumbfounded, as Toodie snatches the surgical scissors from him. "What, you didn't hear what I said? I do it myself," says Toodie. "My fighter ain't fighting."

"Your fighter?" says Frank.

Rocco says, "Frank, you know I don't mean no harm."

But Frank isn't listening to Rocco. "Your fighter?" he says again.

"Yeah, that's right," says Toodie.

Angel grabs him as he steps toward Frank. But Toodie throws him off. "My fighter," he says. "My fucking fighter."

"Don't," Angel yells. "Don't be stupid with these people."

"Gentlemen," says Rocco. "Please."

Frank tries to play it off like he's amused. He turns to Rocco and says, "See how it is? You give people the world, they still fuck you. Every time happens like that."

"Look, I understand," says Rocco. "Maybe your guy's worried the kid ain't as good as everyone's been saying."

"Maybe you're right," says Frank. "All I know is what this little prick's been telling me."

"Fuck you," Toodie screams. He starts to lunge, but Angel, wanting only to save his friend, tackles Toodie from behind.

Rocco lets out a quick school yard whistle and in comes his muscle. The guy's huge, a guinea Herman Munster in a big, black suit. He stands over Toodie waiting for his instructions.

"Hold up," says Rocco. "Whatever you wanna do, Frank, it's your call. I feel bad. I mean, this is my place. The last thing I wanted is for you to have aggravation."

Now Frank puts his Bally loafer to Toodie's neck. "I give you everything you asked," he says. "And look what you do to me? The only thing keeping you alive is my good manners."

Angel thinks to make a move, but holds off as Herman Munster pulls back his double-breasted, exposing a shiny automatic sticking out of his waistband.

The doctor has seen enough. He begins to apologize, excusing himself from the dressing room. "Hold on, Doc," says Rocco. "You ain't goin' nowhere yet."

Toodie squirms like a fish on a dock, trying to wriggle out from under Frank's loafer. "I should crush you," says Frank.

"Let 'im go," says Nicky.

"Jesus Christ," says Frank. "Not you, too."

"Let him fucking go."

"Can you believe this?" says Frank. "My own kid."

"Please get off 'im," says Khe Sahn. "I fight. Whoever it is, I fight 'im right now."

"You ain't doing shit till I tell you what you're doing." Frank eases up on Toodie's throat as if it were a gas pedal. "Now, Rocco, I gotta know something, I got investments here, too. I gotta know if this is a fucking setup?"

"No, I swear. We got a new opponent. Sure, he's better than the other one. But it'll just make for a more exciting fight. That's alls I'm asking. Give the people something to remember. Other than that, it's a straight-up deal, you got my word."

"So who's the new opponent?"

"Nobody you know," he says. "Just like your kid, another one with a big future. We like him. He's like a late bloomer."

Frank's shoe remains at Toodie's throat. "How do I know," he says, "this one ain't a mummy, too."

Rocco nods at the doctor. "We have this young man's records on file," says the old man. "Based on our evaluation, he seems to be perfectly healthy."

"You got my word, Frank." Rocco DeCavalcante produces an absurdly large Cuban and clips off the end with his engraved sterling Davidoff snippers. He lights the cigar and begins to puff away, pumping the room full of his smoke. "Alls I'm concerned with here is the pleasure of the patrons of the Conquistador Hotel. A good show."

TABLE NUMBER 2 in the Iberia Ballroom: Frank's guzzling Billy Martins while Cheech nurses his amaretto and cream, looking around, asking, "Which one's Bobby Greco?" Nicky's high as a kite, feeling a little better now that he's stoned, less skittish after that bad scene in the dressing room. When they first sat down, Nicky excused himself to go to the men's room, where he reached into the pocket of the double-breasted Cheech had bought him at Barney's. There he found Buddy's old white marble pipe packed with three roaches. Nicky smoked it all quickly while sitting on the pot.

The waitress arrives with a bottle of champagne for the table, compliments of the house. Frank thinks she looks pretty good in her push-up flamenco outfit, her breasts pressed together like halves of a rump, showing a nice smile, a deliberate booty shake, and hair that's a severe shade of blond. Cheech isn't as impressed. He prefers the girls from that other hotel, the one where they dress up in the "I Dream of Jeannie" costumes.

She leans over to fill their glasses. Nicky flushes, breathing in the perfume that comes off her cleavage.

"Leave some room on the table," says Frank. "Bobby Greco's coming."

The cocktail waitress inquires as to the occasion that warrants both Bobby Greco and Dom Perignon.

Frank downs the last of his Billy Martin before pointing toward the ring with his champagne glass. "I got a kid coming up in the next fight," he says.

She seems very impressed.

Soon, Khe Sahn's opponent makes his way into the ring. Frank can't figure out whether the guy's a spic or a nigger, which Cheech reminds them not to say too loud, that it ain't nice in public. The opponent has long hair, layers of tight Jheri curls, copper skin, an aqualine nose, broad lips, and blue eyes. "Blue eyes means he gotta be a white guy," Cheech insists. "I read in a book it's called the 'dominant characteristic.'"

Frank grabs his crotch, then, with the same hand, makes a fist. "This and this," he says, "is your dominant characteristic."

Khe Sahn comes to the ring dry as a bone. His sweat seems to have evaporated under the lights. He has that same stunned look he had in the dressing room. A minute or so into the first round, the opponent catches him with a straight right hand flush on the chin. Khe Sahn acts as if he's been expecting it.

He takes a knee.

And a faint hum of displeasure wafts through the Iberia Ballroom.

"Jesus Christ," Frank says disgustedly.

Khe Sahn is back on his feet by the count of eight. The referee waves him back to the middle of the ring, where he stands in surrender's posture, covering up, hands over his face.

The opponent wastes no time, looking to finish Khe Sahn as quickly as possible, but smart enough to do it without headhunting or lunging. Instead, he punishes Khe Sahn diligently, hard shots to the body, going for those low, indefensible regions that would double him over, break his cowardly posture, and put his chin directly into the line of fire.

Khe Sahn doesn't even bother to throw a punch.

In between rounds, the crowd's disappointed murmur grows into a full chorus of boos. Frank looks like he's about to crush his champagne glass. "Fucking Toodie," he says. "His kid's a punk. This is a goddamn embarrassment."

After the bell, Khe Sahn continues to cover up, seeking an easy way out, a merciful arrangement with his opponent. But the opponent refuses to grant any such accommodation, maintaining his brutal rhythm with punches to the liver, the kidney, the arms, none of them enough to drop Khe Sahn outright. The blows ensure more than pain. Khe Sahn is free to go at any time, but his only exit would be a deliberate knee. The pounding goes on.

And on.

. . . until Khe Sahn Witherspoon finally surrenders, not to the opponent, but to his ferocious instinct, beyond fear. It's his natural talent that comes to him now, again, just as it came to him those years ago, in the Adolescent Reception and Detention Center on Rikers Island.

That perfect left hook.

The Shriners and the hookers and the wise guys and the conventioneers in the Iberia Ballroom grant themselves two silent moments. The first, to comprehend the opponent on his ass. The next, to reverse field and begin cheering for Khe Sahn. Rocco DeCavalcante's newly lit El Presidente drops like a stone from his mouth.

The opponent gets up, and now the fight begins in earnest. Nicky watches very closely from Table Number 2. The patrons of the Conquistador Hotel and Casino become gleeful. They can't get enough, which is exactly what that miniature fucker with the cigar had wanted.

It is a good show, yes, but so much more. Khe Sahn has begun to travel toward savage places, beyond civilization, beyond rules, beyond covenants. There's no return ticket. And his opponent proves a worthy guide.

So evenly matched, the adversaries produce a brutal bout. Each new port in Khe Sahn's journey is marked by another wound: split lip, broken nose, an assortment of mouses all around the eyes, and inward, unseen bruises behind the ribs, in the belly. Each blow preys on Nicky's own imaginings, until he fears he might begin to weep, and tries to steady himself by guzzling the Dom, which tastes like a bitter soda, an unsweet spumante.

Cheech is one of the crowd: cheering wildly, flailing about, spilling his drink. But his father's reaction is more curious. Frank says nothing, brooding with his gaze narrowed on the action. Nicky can tell that something about the fight, the way it has unfolded, bothers him deeply. His father is back to pounding the Billy Martins.

After the fifth, the next to last round, Khe Sahn has trouble finding his corner. Cheech goes to check with the reporters at ringside, where he is told that the kid with the crazy hair had suffered a deep gash to his lip, that the wound ran into his mouth and drained down his throat. Khe Sahn had swallowed a lot of blood. "He's about two quarts low," says one of the reporters, watching Khe Sahn pull himself off the stool by grabbing the ropes. "I don't know how in the fuck this kid's still standing."

At the final bell, Khe Sahn appears dazed and unrecognizable, his face a bloody quilt. Unable to leave his corner, the ref has to raise his victorious arm. Toodie is ashen. He holds out his hand to receive Khe Sahn's mouthpiece, which comes forth in an involuntary convulsion, grisly as an afterbirth.

Nicky hears someone say, "Not bad for a couple a kids."

"Yeah, better than those fag lion tamers they got at the other joint."

"You kiddin' me? This was the fight of the fuckin' year."

In the ring, the doctor waves his cigar stub right to left and back again, asking Khe Sahn to follow its path with his eyes. But the postfight examination ends abruptly with the arrival of two ambulance drivers who shove the doctor aside. The medics work urgently, carrying Khe Sahn to ringside, laying him in a stretcher. One of them punctures Khe Sahn's arm with a syringe while his partner makes the connection to a portable IV bag.

Toodie remains at Khe Sahn's side the whole time, holding his hand, telling the drivers that he is the fighter's legal guardian and that he must ride in the ambulance with them. Khe Sahn's dreamy eyes shut as they begin to wheel him away. Frantically, Angel mumbles mystic prayers. Rocco DeCavalcante tells people to make room, get the fuck away, let 'im get some air. He arrives at Table 2 with a fresh Cuban and a shit-eating grin: "What? You think he's gonna die? You kiddin'? He can't die now. Not in my joint. He's gonna be a fucking star, Frank, I told ya. All ya hadda do is trust me. Tell ya what, though? That Toodie—that his name?—he did some job with the fighter, huh? I mean I figured alls you had was a gimmick, you know, that crazy fucking hair."

Rocco DeCavalcante walks off delighted, twirling his fingers, his gassy little laugh lingering at the table with a plume of his cigar smoke.

Frank nods at Cheech. "Follow them to the hospital," he says. "Make sure that kid gets everything he needs. Anything he wants." A sick chilly sweat has broken out across Frank's brow. He throws back the last of the Billy Martins.

Nicky gets up to leave with Cheech.

Frank calls after his son in a weak voice. "Let that be a lesson to you, son," he says. "That kid had a lotta heart."

Nicky doesn't bother to look back. He finds his way to the casino and begins to wander, checking out the girls in their flamenco outfits, recalling the way his father had ogled that cocktail waitress, and thinking that only now does he understand things about his father Buddy had known long ago, instinctively, perhaps even from birth.

Nicky tours the craps tables, each of them surrounded by a huddled crowd, people craning to see the action, as eager as bystanders at a wreck. The blackjack tables are different. There, it seems as if the players and the dealers already know each other, that they're sharing in an almost guilty routine, the words that pass between them are meager, almost unnecessary, as are the words to all those most familiar rituals. Nicky walks through the rows of slots, pews in this hard-luck church, where old ladies empty cups of quarters into the machines. Their expressionless faith amazes him, one coin after another in hope of a payday that sets off a cacophony of buzzers and bells.

Earlier, his father had given him a handful of chips that are supposed to look like coins from a sunken treasure chest. But Nicky has no interest in gambling. He brings the chips to the cashier. "How do you want it?" asks the lady, a black woman with long red fingernails.

Nicky shrugs, having no idea how much the chips are worth. The lady counts ten crisp, new Ben Franklins and pushes them through the hole in the glass. Nicky wonders what he could buy for Samantha with the money, what would impress her? He looks through the boutiques, through an assortment of items, all of them lamé or leather, and decides against any purchase.

In the Aragonne Lounge, Nicky watches a Tony Bennett lookalike doing Beatles songs. ". . . Something in the way she moves . . ." Samantha would probably laugh at the whole bit: the lounge act, the guy in the hairpiece, the ruffled shirt, the velvet tux. Nicky decides that the world he comes from is just a lot of cheap shit.

He leaves just as the crooner begins a rendition of "Yesterday," and takes the elevator up to the suite. He wants to sleep. He hopes his old man and Cheech are out somewhere.

But they're not. Nicky pauses at the door, eavesdropping. Strange, he thinks. Cheech is actually yelling at his old man. "It ain't right, Frank," he says.

"Whatta you know from right? I don't think he ever did it before. That's not right. Besides, you're the one always saying it'd be good for him."

"Not now, Frank. I'm telling you, not now."

"You're just pissed off I ain't getting nothing for you."

"Don't do it, Frank."

Finally, Nicky knocks and his father comes to the door, no longer wearing his jacket or tie, still sweating, his hair rumpled, like he just got out of bed. Frank's got another bottle of Dom, though, slinging it around carelessly by the glass neck.

They stare at each other for a moment, but it is Cheech who speaks first. "Howya doin', killer?" he says. "We was worried about you."

"You go off don't tell us where you going," says Frank. "I thought we had plans, remember?"

"I gotta get outta here," says Cheech, slamming the door behind him.

Frank takes a seat and pours himself another glass. "Cheech don't like hospitals is all. Ever since we was kids. Hospitals make him all upset." He throws back the champagne like it was a shot. "The fighter's gonna be all right, Nicky. Gonna be just fine. It looked worse than it was."

"How do you know?" There is an edge in Nicky's tone, a challenge too modest for Frank to sense through his boozy bluster.

"What it is," explains Frank, "is the kid's got those big fucking lips. I'm not being funny, neither. They bleed a lot. That's what it was. He gets cut deep in the mouth and it's bleeding like a fucking geyser."

Frank pulls down his own bottom lip to demonstrate. "See?" he says, pointing. "Happened early in the fight. The blood kept going down his own throat. He lost maybe two pints. Cheech talked to the doctor at the hospital."

Frank takes another drink and asks, "Howdya do with the chips I gave ya?"

Nicky shrugs.

"That's O.K. I ain't mad."

"You ain't *mad*?"

Frank still doesn't get it. "Nah. Everybody loses their first time," he says. "I got something better for you anyways."

"You don't mind, I just want to go to sleep."

"Suit yourself."

Nicky goes to his room, shuts the door, and tosses his jacket on the bed where she has been waiting for him. Only now does he understand.

I got something better for you anyways.

The cocktail waitress throws off the covers and approaches, sipping delightedly from her own glass of champagne. She seems a different woman than she did serving drinks in the Iberia Ballroom. Her breasts, now unharnessed, are spongy and raw, what Cheech would call meatloaf titties. The crow's feet at the corner of her eyes look like cracks through dried putty. There's a smudge of lipstick on her front tooth.

She nuzzles close, trying to say something. All Nicky can make out is the word "virgin." Then her voice dissolves into a tipsy giggle.

She plants her open mouth against his. Nicky tastes ashes. Her perfume is faint now. Mostly, she smells of sweat and smoke. She's cold to the touch.

Nicky pulls away. "No," he says.

"That's O.K.," she says, still giggling as she drops to her knees. She unbuckles his belt, unzips his fly, and yanks his jockey briefs down to his knees. The cocktail waitress cups his balls with one hand, as if she is weighing something, a piece of produce. She lets out a sigh and begins to pull on his dick with a practiced, perfunctory finesse.

Nicky wants to fight it.

But can't.

He comes in her mouth. There is a moment of ease. Then, a wave of nausea. Nicky feels like a criminal.

The cocktail waitress takes a few greedy sips of champagne and lets herself out, flicking the light switch off as she closes the door.

Leaving Nicky in the dark.

He can still hear her, though, her tipsy giggle. Now his father begins to chuckle, too. He imagines that she is giving him a full report.

His father sounds so fucking pleased with himself. He can hear him saying, "I ain't gonna kiss ya, though."

CHAPTER
32

OUT ON CARMINE Street, in front of the Blood Youth Center, Father Vincent Ruggiero helps a girl onto a pony, making a bridge with his hands and hoisting her onto the saddle. A gaggle of jealous children look on.

The girl snaps her gum and sticks out her tongue. "You don't need to do that," Father Vincent whispers. He turns to the kids on the church steps. "Everybody's gonna get a chance," he says.

Father Vincent slaps the horse on the rear and winks at Gerard Romano, who begins to lead the pony away, pulling on the reins. Father Vincent tells the kids, "If Gerard tells me anyone got out of line on the horse, they gotta deal with me."

But the kids aren't listening anymore. They're doubled over in laughter at the huge pile of horseshit left on the curb.

Father Vincent watches Gerard lead the girl on the pony down Carmine Street. Her name is Shawnika. Sweet kid, really. She lives in the Lillian Wald Houses, there or Jacob Riis, sometimes he forgets. The girl wears biker shorts and bangle earrings, and walks and talks like she came out of a rap song, which strikes Father Vincent as a kind of Doo Wop on crack. The girl's in the ninth grade at Seward Park. Fourteen years old. Three months' pregnant.

She told him the other day, "My baby father don't want me to have it," she said.

"What do you want to do?" he asked.

"I don't know."

"No. I mean, if you could do anything, what would you do?"

"Anything?"

"Anything . . . you can tell me."

Shawnika had to think about it for a while. Finally she said, "I wanna go for a ride on a pony."

"No problem."

The next day the priest bought a pony from a farm in Pennsylvania. What the hell, he figured, it was a good investment. Father Vincent has this notion that girls are more easily redeemed. Besides, Salvatore Colosimo's last will and testament had proven a windfall for the youth center. Father Vincent had already arranged for the installation of fiberglass backboards and a wooden parquet floor in the gym. Come September, he will expand the after-school program, hiring three additional social workers to handle the load of adolescent agonies— pregnancies, felony arrests, domestic disorders—and establish a tutorial for equivalency diplomas. And that's just the beginning. The other day, he decided to purchase the lease of a defunct leather bar on Christopher Street called Spike. The idea came to him while walking along the piers on West Street. There, he saw all the teenage hustlers rotting like wheat on the docks. Open a youth center for the gay kids, he told himself, get them food and physicals. Wait till the old-timers hear about that, he thought: the Salvatore Colosimo Center for At-Risk Youth. Right there on Christopher Street.

The funny thing is, Uncle Sal wouldn't have minded. Uncle Sal would have said: You think it's the right thing to do, you believe in your heart, then do it . . . and fuck what everybody else says.

That's what Father Vincent's thinking as the old ladies watch him from the windows. They disapprove of him, the hippie priest who puts colored girls on horses, who leaves manure in the street.

Fuck what they say.

Father Vincent goes through the gym in the church basement on his way to the sacristy. There, he changes into his collar.

He has an appointment.

"BLESS ME, FATHER, for I have sinned."

"Tell me your sins."

"Tell me why Buddy went to jail and you didn't."

" 'Cause your brother didn't rat me out. Simple as that. The cops were coming and we got separated. I ran back toward the neighborhood, back how we came. Buddy ran down Sullivan Street, past Googie's."

"Yeah, so?"

"That's where they caught him. Buddy told me about it later. First, they bring him into the precinct, then they start slapping him around. And remember, Buddy was what? Eighteen? Almost as young as you are now. That age, cops slap you around, you're scared. They got a dead body and they got a pretty good idea who was there. They probably already knew it was me and Tommy Sick. The cops tell your brother to give us up or he does a murder rap. Then they give him a paper, a cooperation agreement. They tell him, wise up, all you gotta do is sign that paper, you can walk out of here."

"Buddy wouldn't sign nothing like that."

"Well, he picked up the piece of paper."

". . . yeah . . ."

"And he ate it."

"So that's why he went away, huh?"

"Yeah, that's why."

"And that's why you became a priest."

"That's still only part of it."

CHAPTER
33

IN THE MORNING, Toodie attends Lamaze class with Carmen. First, the instructor, who's like half a nurse, gives a speech about breathing. So far so good. Toodie understands—breathing, relaxation, same principles that a fighter must obey. But then, the lady starts going off on "focus," says you have to find an object to focus on. Bring it with you when you're having the baby. Carmen decides they're gonna focus on Froggy, a purple-and-green stuffed animal she's had since she was a kid. Froggy? Toodie says, you're better off having your brother Angel pick out something with his Puerto Rican voodoo.

Gimme a kiss, Froggy, says Carmen.

After Lamaze, Toodie takes the train all the way out to Brownsville, where Khe Sahn lives in the Tilden projects. Walking through the concrete courtyard, Toodie can almost feel the sights of all the AK's and the Uzis and the nine millimeters trained at his back, thinking the only reason some young boy isn't firing is everybody figures he must be a cop. They're everywhere, these kids, lurking in the hallways, the stairwells, on the benches, in the elevators that smell like piss, all of them slinging this shit called crack. All of a sudden everybody's strapped. Every two-bit punk is a gangster. Every child with a Five-Percenter name thinks he's some kind of Godfather. Now Toodie sees an old lady trying to negotiate a shopping cart over craters in the pavement. He goes to help her, but she looks away as their eyes meet. No one should have to live here, he thinks.

Toodie finds Khe Sahn lying sleepy-eyed across a worn velour sofa. He's watching Kung Fu flicks on a huge new Sony equipped with a matching VCR. Khe Sahn's mother, a tollbooth clerk for the Transit Authority, is away at work.

"I didn't know your purse was that big," says Toodie, pointing at the TV.

"Nah," says Khe Sahn. "Someone got it for me."

"Who?"

"Friend of mine."

"Must be a helluva friend," says Toodie, his suspicion as thick and heavy as the odor of cooking grease that hangs in the apartment.

Khe Sahn eyeballs Toodie, his sentiments just as clear: Don't be telling me about my friends. Don't be telling who I can and can't be taking shit from.

Toodie pretends not to notice, abruptly changing the subject to the wounds around Khe Sahn's eyes. "Lemme see," he says.

It's been two weeks since Atlantic City and Khe Sahn's healing up real nice. But Toodie can't help but wonder if he's already lost the kid. He blames himself, of course. As well he should. Khe Sahn took a terrible beating. Now, Jackie Farrell is gone and Paddy Blood won't leave. The old man's been whispering in his ear since the fight: Goddamn foolish son of a bitch. I didn't tell ya to get the kid all beat to shit his first time out the box. Didn't tell ya to put him on a card for some gangsters in Atlantic City. 'Specially not that guinea bastard. I told ya to take care a the kid, to be careful with him. Was that too much to ask?

Toodie probes the scar tissue with a tender respect. "You're gonna be fine," he says, forcing a smile. "I think you might just heal better than anybody since Ali."

Khe Sahn says nothing. He remains riveted to the action on the screen. Bruce Lee is making noises like a prehistoric bird while defeating armies of extras with his chuka sticks. It occurs to Toodie that he, too, could use a pair of chuka sticks.

To wrap around Frank Battaglia's head.

Geez, the kid took a terrible beating.

"You know," says Toodie, "best thing to do is get back in the gym."

Finally, Khe Sahn gets up to change the VCR. "Yeah," he says, nodding agreeably. "You know I be back."

"You don't need rush into nothing heavy," says Toodie. "No sparring or nothing. Just so's you don't lose your edge."

"I hear you."

Khe Sahn changes the tape, substituting Al Pacino's *Scarface* for *Enter the Dragon*. The movie is already well underway. Pacino is delivering a coked-up speech to white people in a restaurant. Khe Sahn knows the whole bit by heart, the accent, the gestures. He mumbles along with Pacino, oblivious to everything else: "Chew people, chew need somebody like me . . ."

"Yo, Khe," says Toodie, "I gotta be getting back now."

". . . so chew coold say, dere go da bat guy . . ."

"I'll see you in the gym, all right?"

". . . well, take a look, take a goot look . . ."

"I'm real glad you're healing good."

". . . 'cause chew ain't never gonna see . . ."

"You're my boy, Khe. Know that? You my man."

". . . a bad guy like dis again . . ."

IT IS ALREADY past noon when Toodie walks into the Empire. He's always telling the fighters, "In my joint, you're on time or out of line. Gimme excuses, you go back to the street where you came from."

So it doesn't look good, Toodie being late to his own joint.

People notice. The fighters know if you can't walk what you talk.

Shouldn't be no excuses.

Now Toodie catches Nicky's worried glance in the mirror. The kid's funny like that, always looking like he's got the whole world on his shoulders.

Their eyes meet, then Nicky looks away and begins to shadowbox. That's another thing Toodie can't quite figure, how the kid can look so good in front of the mirror, so natural, but can't fight a lick in the ring. What the fuck, he figures, it must run in the blood. Again, he fantasizes about doing a number on Frank with Bruce Lee's chuka sticks, how much he'd like to do that.

Toodie has to remind himself: just 'cause the father is what he is, that don't mean you take it out on the kid.

Nicky's been here at the gym every day since Atlantic City. Everybody knows what happened, how Frank fucked things up, almost got Khe Sahn killed. But Nicky keeps showing up, like he's doing time or something. Nobody talks to him, except for Angel, who tells him, "Fuck all a dem, kid, you with me."

Nicky puts in long hours. Angel even gave him a key to the place. Most days he's already wrapped and working by the time Toodie arrives.

Look at him, Toodie thinks, like he wants to say something.

Problem is, there ain't nothing to say.

Toodie has made a little office for himself in the Empire, wedging an old beat-up desk in the corner by the slop sink. That's where he finds Frank, his feet up on the desk, waiting for him. Now Frank's got the cigar thing working, like he wants you to believe he's had a stogie in his mouth all his life. What an asshole.

"I just wanna tell ya, no hard feelings." Frank gets up and puts out his hand.

Toodie just looks at it.

"You don't gotta be like that," says Frank. "But I still respect you. There's not a lotta guys wouldn't shake my hand."

Toodie nods toward a stocky young fighter with a ridged forehead and a pushed-in face, a born gargoyle. The Tasmanian Devil tattoo on his bicep seems entirely apropos.

"If I was out of line," says Frank, "then I'm sorry."

Toodie refuses to be suckered into conversation. It's not like you can make this Frank understand. Jackie was right. The old man was right. One way or another, these guys make it harder for you to live with yourself.

"The kid's gonna be taken care of good," says Frank. "His family, too."

Toodie pretends not to hear and calls to the Tasmanian Devil. "You're up," he says.

"I made it up to you," Frank continues. "You don't owe nothing on this place no more. Plus, I left a gift in the desk drawer. Let's let bygones be bygones."

These guys, Toodie thinks, they think there's different rules for them than for everybody else. Like they can get out from under anything. He jerks his thumb at the Tasmanian Devil. "In the ring," he says.

Frank is trying his best to be nice, but Toodie's testing his patience. "Hey, let's cut the bullshit," he says. "The kid fought a great fight. I was proud a him. I was proud to call him my fighter. But it ain't like there's a problem. He's gonna be good as new. We checked it out."

Toodie grabs a pair of pads, still oblivious to Frank, whose expression has taken on a suggestion of menace. Frank doesn't like being ignored, especially by some ingrate trainer who ain't himself much more than a snot-nose kid in a T-shirt.

"You wanna be a tough guy, fine," he says. "We could be tough guys here. Just remember one thing, alls I came to you for was to get my kid ready to go in the ring. You gave me your word. But my kid, look at him, you still got 'im in front of a mirror. Like he's some kind of faggot."

"He ain't ready," Toodie said.

"Whattaya mean he ain't ready? I see him with my own eyes. Look at him, he ain't ready my ass."

"You want Nicky in the ring?"

"What are you deaf?"

Toodie puts down the pads and hollers for Nicky to come over.

The boy's face goes slack as he approaches. His wet eyes beg for Toodie to explain.

But all Toodie does is toss a pair of twelve-ounce gloves at him. "Put these on," he says. "It's time."

The gym's sweaty, staccato rhythms and respirations are suddenly suspended; the Empire has gone quiet.

"Who said youse all could stop?" Toodie bellows. "Go back to work or back to the fucking street where you hoodlums came from."

A few of the fighters begin beating tentatively on the bags, still watching to see what will happen. The fighters understand what's going down and most of them are rooting for a little blood. Maybe even justice. It's only fair that Little Lord Fauntleroy take a beating, too.

Nicky presents his gloved hands to Angel to be tied and taped. Angel does as he's asked. He wants to tell the kid something, but can't. He looks for Toodie to appeal the decision.

"I know what I'm doing," says Toodie. "The guy paid to see his kid fight. I ain't gonna not live up to my end."

Santana, the Tasmanian Devil, gives him a questioning look.

"Straight up," Toodie tells him. Meaning: You don't have to worry about the gangster. You don't have to take it easy on his kid, either. Just fight, do what you gotta do.

The boys each go about 160, but their pounds are so differently distributed that Nicky looks overmatched.

Frank sucks approvingly on his cigar watching his kid throw warm-up punches.

The buzzer sounds and Nicky meanders out of his corner.

Ain't gonna be much of a fight, thinks Toodie.

So what, he tells himself, so the kid'll catch a beating. It'll be on his father's head, not mine. Besides, maybe it's about time the kid learned what the deal was. What is that they say? The apple don't fall so far from the tree. Sure, that's it. Nicky's basically the same as his old man. The only difference is, the son don't even pretend he's not a coward.

Look at him. Nicky won't so much as throw a punch.

Toodie looks over at Frank, thinking: Fuck you, Frank. That's you in there, you and yours.

All that time Toodie spent teaching the kid to slip and weave—what a waste. Nicky offers nothing but his hands against the blows.

He does not fight back. He seeks to negotiate that treaty, that acknowledgment, that unspoken covenant with the Tasmanian Devil that the punishment not exceed certain decent, civilized conventions, that he will in no way be violated. There is a place where Nicky Battaglia does not want to go; there are instincts—both his and his opponent's—he does not want to arouse, and prices, permanent ones, he does not want to pay. He does not even want to think of that; for Nicky Battaglia is more terrified of beatings imagined than real.

But the Tasmanian Devil senses only weakness. He is not that good a fighter, certainly not possessed of Nicky's graceful gifts. But at this moment, the Tasmanian Devil is perfectly paired as Nicky Battaglia's opposite. He is mean. He enjoys punishment. There's a glee in his grunt.

Nicky takes a knee. It looks like he went down just to catch his breath.

Then, another flurry. Another surrender. It looks as if submission is his natural posture, as if Nicky had been born on one knee.

Toodie catches the silent exchange between father and son. Nicky shrugs apologetically as he gets up, mouthing the words, "I'm sorry." Frank trembles, gnashing his teeth, the small muscles popping behind his jaw as he struggles to suppress his rage.

On his third pass, Nicky walks right into the blows, going blindly, like a kid wading into the deep water with his eyes closed. Nicky's trying to get knocked out.

He wants to go as quickly as possible.

But the Tasmanian Devil has another idea. He doesn't want to let Nicky off so easy. He stays mostly on the body.

Nicky's taking an awful lot of hits.

Frank jerks back his head, then catches himself.

Toodie begins to wince.

Here, the two men engage each other in a game of

chicken. How much will Nicky take? How far will they let it go?

Nicky's mouthpiece, a mangled horseshoe of faint crimson jelly, lands on the ring apron.

Frank sucks on his cigar with expressionless concentration.

Toodie pauses, watching Frank watching him. Waiting. Waiting. Waiting until he can wait no more. Until he rushes into the ring.

Nicky let it get out of hand, he thinks, that's what happens when you give in too easy.

Toodie holds the boy up by the armpits. He doesn't know how he'll ever be able to live with himself.

Frank has taken something from him, something you can never get back. Toodie struggles to prop Nicky on a stool, then leans over the ropes. "Hey, tough guy," he says, "you happy now?"

CHAPTER
34

JACK GALLAGHER WAITS behind the wheel of a government-issue Dodge Aries parked outside the Empire gym. Stupid car, he thinks. Jack would much prefer a Crown Vic or a Gran Fury, like he used to drive when he worked for the city, the kind of car that'd get all the corner boys off their asses just to announce his arrival. Jack doesn't care who makes him. He'd just like to feel a little like a cop again. The federal guys, they're not cops. This one guy in the office, his name is Lars. He's from Minnesota or someplace. A regular fucking G-man that one. The United States Government takes Lars from Minnesota, puts him in a Dodge Aries on Mulberry Street, and tells him to catch wise guys. Guy's got a better chance catching the clap. Your tax dollars at work. No wonder the feds gotta justify everything by making every shitheel wise guy into another Al Capone.

Like this Frank.

Here he comes.

Look at him, checking the weather. The sky is the color of dirty muslin sacks, about to rupture with summer rain. For some reason, the idea of Frank Battaglia as a television meteorologist moves Gallagher to laugh out loud. He can hear him now: It's gonna fucking pour, what

the fuck you gonna do about it? This is Frank fuckin'
Battaglia, Eyewitness Weather.

Gallagher puts the Aries in a slow roll, staying a few
yards ahead of Frank. Gallagher watches him closely in
the rearview, wondering what the fuck happened up there
in that gym. Look at him, the nervous fuck—white as a
sheet, scratching the back of his fist. Now he's shrugging
his shoulders, like a fighter, flapping his elbows, twitch-
ing his head left to right.

This guy, thinks Gallagher. So full a shit.

He pulls up alongside Frank's Lincoln, sealing it against
the curb. Waiting for Frank to pound on the trunk, which
he does, then come around to the driver's side, which he
does, and issue his stream of curses and threats, which he
does.

"Cocksucker," he screams, banging on the window.
"You don't move this fucking thing, I'm gonna . . ."

Gallagher is smiling as he rolls down the window.
"Oh," he says, feigning surprise. "It's only you. I was
waiting for my other pal. What's his name?"

Frank is confused, slow to realize who's talking to him
like this.

"Cheech," says Gallagher. "That's it. I was waiting for
Cheech. Ain't he driving you today, Frank?"

"I got nothing to say to you."

"I know, Frank. You're a tough guy from way back.
But I gotta tell you, you look like shit. What happened up
there? Somebody throw you a beating?"

Frank is doing his best to look impatient and annoyed.
Guy's like a kid. Gallagher half expects him to start
whining: Can I go now?

"Anyways, I don't wanna give you the wrong impression," he says. "Cheech surprised me. Cheech is a
stand-up guy. I coulda saved him a lot of time, but he's
gotta be hardheaded. You know, it's just like you say,
Frank. The guy's a retard."

"Fuck you."

Good, Gallagher thinks, great. "You're gonna do time,
Frank. A lot."

Frank grabs his crotch, gives it a shake. "Do this a lot," he says.

Gallagher starts to snicker, thinking again about Frank the weatherman: Youse don't like rain in the forecast? Blow me. The guy's supposed to be this big-time wise guy. Look at him, just another skell, the same now as he must have been years ago.

"Go 'head and laugh," says Frank. "That's what you guys got—dick. My lawyer's gonna sue youse all. Youse are violating my civil rights."

The same line of shit Gallagher heard for all those years arresting mouthy black kids. Now Gallagher gets out of the car. He, too, works from remembered behaviors. "You have no civil rights," he says, becoming a cop again, poking Frank in the chest. "And the only thing you might get violated is your asshole."

"I should kill you," says Frank. "You weren't a cop, I . . ."

"I'm sure you could. I mean, you're the tough guy. You're the fighter. Ain't that right?"

"I ain't doing no time."

"Lissen, motherfucker, if I felt like it, I'd throw you in the car right now. For assault one. For hitting the waiter."

Frank looks puzzled. "What . . . ?"

"In Garguilo's."

Now he remembers. "The fag?"

"Yeah, he filed a complaint. You're gonna love the joint, Frank. I mean if you're still beating up fags, you'll be right at home. But you know all about that. You been in before, right?"

No answer.

"Attica, right?"

"Leavenworth."

"Sure. Well, it's not like that anymore, Frank. Remember? All you guinea gangsters getting together like it was some kind of bowling league. What I'm saying is, you can't get veal Oscar sent to your cell. And you can't get Cubans. This is the first time I seen you with a stogie, though. Where'd you get 'em, that midget mutt in Atlantic City?"

"Why don't you tell me? You're the guy following me."

"I haven't been following you, Frank. I think the guy they got following you, his name is Lars. Tell me, not for nothing, but in your whole life, did you ever meet a guy named Lars?"

Frank shakes his head.

"Me neither. Not till I came to work for the feds. It cracks me up, though. They got guys named Lars chasing guys like you and they wonder why nothing ever gets done."

"You mind?" says Frank, looking at the sky. "It's gonna fucking pour."

"I let you go, sure, just gotta gimme a chance to explain myself. See, I used to be a city cop. I was a detective out of Brooklyn North—Brownsville, East New York, Bed-Stuy, all real shitholes. Every day, I see some poor fuck with his brains blown out. Every-fucking-day. And usually, the perp was just some kid trying to be a big man, another jerkoff who'd seen too many movies—*The Godfather, Superfly, The Godfather Meets SuperFly*, all that shit. Anyway, pretty soon, all the perps is the same to you, each one is just another little nigger with a gun. It happens. Don't mean you're any more or less prejudiced than anyone else. Just happens. But that's one of the reasons I left the P.D. I didn't like thinking of everybody as a little nigger."

"I gotta hear this," asks Frank, "or can I go?"

"That's exactly what I'm talking about, Frank: 'Can I go?' You see, I joined up with the feds 'cause it's supposed to be, like, a higher level, like I'm working a better class of bad guys. At least that's what they say. The newspapers, they make you something you're not 'cause I guess it sells. And my bosses, they go for it, too, 'cause the bigger you are, the bigger they feel. These guys like Lars? They love you. But they don't get it. They look at you, they want to build conspiracies and fuck around with wiretaps and unions and lawyers. You know how many lawyers it takes to make a case against you and your boss, Philly? That's a lot of diplomas, a lot of smart people. Me? I think different. I'm more stupid. But still, I know better. I know who you are." Gallagher moves in closer now, getting right in Frank's face. "I seen the Fatman and Fritzy lying in the gutter—don't get me wrong, my heart don't break for them—but I know right then the perp isn't some Al Capone, some Public Enemy Number One. Fuck no! Colosimo is just another poor fuck with his brains running into the gutter. And you, Frank, you're just another little nigger with a gun."

"You finished yet?"

"Almost . . . I thought I was doing good, no?"

A rumble of thunder, an invisible tracer of sound, surges across the sky. Gallagher waits to hear the final crack before continuing. "Anyway, I was thinking to myself, what does that do? Putting you behind bars. That still leaves Philly Testa. And Philly, as you well know, is more than another little jerkoff like you. Shit, the way things work, your boss is a regular criminal mastermind. At least that's what Lars says. I mean, no one thinks for a second it was you gave the order to whack out the Fatman."

Look at him seethe, Gallagher thinks. You can play this guy like a record. "Frank, I tell you the same thing I told Cheech, even though, to be honest, I like him more than you. First one in gets the best deal, maybe the only deal. Lars don't need much, what with all the tapes."

Now Frank tries to stare down the cop. Ain't that just like a stupid kid?

"I know, I know," says Gallagher, "you ain't gonna do it no way. You're a tough guy."

The rain begins to fall.

"Just one thing, Frank. There's this story been around for years. Says that one night you fought at the Garden and got your ass kicked. But the punch line, the thing that gets everyone is, Philly bet against you? Is that true?"

An assortment of angry twitches and tremors run across Frank's face. "Who told you that?"

"Who the fuck do you think?"

"Who?"

Gallagher's enjoying it now, more than he has in a long time, working this asshole, fucking with him. Winking at him. "I guess the Fatman must've told her."

"Told who?"

"The Mystery Blonde."

CHAPTER

35

SAMANTHA BRODERICK CONSIDERS Nicky, this strange way that she feels for him. There's no name for it: not like, more complicated than mere lust, but certainly not love, though symptoms of each run through her powerful peculiar attraction to the boy. She knows that matters of affection, like art, are above and beyond logic. But she tries to rationalize it anyway. First, she understands that the boy cannot hurt her. But more than that, there seems something almost nourishing about him. She tells herself that she is merely thinking like the men she has known, each and every one of them—was Sal really an exception?—having been in one way or another, a lech, lusting for that which is young and sweet, for girls like ripe pieces of fruit, having arrived at that age in which the contours are most perfect and the sugars most intense. And that's just how she explains her craving for Nicky, a sweet tooth.

Still, a boy?

It's been a long time for her since boys. And though most of her recollections are haphazard fragments, she tries to summon one anyway. But instead of boys, what comes to mind begins with a cardboard match disintegrating under a bottle cap, he says you have fabulous ankles, fabulous he says, nobody will know, and then, in the chamber, the exchange of smack syrup for blood, waiting for her ease to arrive she becomes frightened by the dark plasma, her own, more black than red, more bile than blood, thinking that something must be wrong with her, ugly, unholy, yes, that's what she thinks, how she justifies herself as she waits for relief, for the fantastic morphine kaleidoscope.

And perhaps that explains the day on the roof, why the boy aroused in her such dormant, lecherous, bloodsucking instincts. He's a transfusion, blood sugar.

Strange, but true, and funny as hell. She's got a crush on a sixteen-year-old boy, well, more than a crush, really; she wants to devour him. The thought gives her pause for an amused, self-deprecating chuckle. Samantha has traveled an awful long way to hear the sound of her own laughter.

Samantha likes where she is. This morning, for instance, was an absolute pleasure. She had a late Sunday breakfast, hot, sweet espresso, laced with lemon and a touch of anise, a ridged flaky pastry shell with thick rum-flavored cream inside. She walked back from the bakery, delighted by the brilliant morning light, by the improbable sight of a girl on a pony in front of the church.

Finally. She feels good. She feels *healthy*.

She surveys the apartment for items that have made the journey with her, artifacts of her survival. There are the still lifes and the Hogarth etching, a plate from *Marriage à la Mode*, all of which belonged to her mother, the Marlboro cigarettes, the tiny bottle of Chanel perfume, the paper record jacket from Bambi's Banshees' underground hit "Bambi Sucks," featuring a photograph of her wearing the standard-issue studded dog collar, the bleached white hair, the black nail polish.

The flip side of "Bambi Sucks" was "He's So Fine," originally performed by the Chiffons but redone by Bambi's Banshees in a style that replaced all melodies and harmonies with amplified, atonal anarchy.

Again, Samantha Broderick can't help but laugh at

herself, at who she was, anyway. Better to be a lech than a downtown diva.

"He's So Fine." Samantha hums the tune the right way as she goes to answer the knock at her door.

The chain lock is taut for the briefest instant, then snaps, like a broken bracelet thrown across the room.

At first, she doesn't understand.

Even as he strikes her, the back of his hand raising a warm, metallic taste in her mouth.

In a rush, he is on top of her, Frank is, yelling something about "that fat bastard."

Only then, does she begin to understand. This, too, is beyond logic.

His eyes tell her as much. She reads his intention and instinct from his eyes, motivations that make sense only to him, base and beastly as he, a bully.

She prays for relief, the morphine kaleidoscope, perhaps. It would be easier, maybe even endurable that way. Samantha Broderick realizes that she must take leave of herself.

CHAPTER
36

THERESA BATTAGLIA BRINGS Nicky's breakfast in a big black pan.

"Ma, I ain't that hungry this morning."

Deaf to his protest, she begins to spoon scrambled eggs onto his plate. Her blank stare makes him nervous. Nicky doesn't even want to imagine what it is that she sees. He takes a forkful from the mount on his plate. The eggs are burned and hard as putty.

"Real good, Ma," he says. "I just ain't that hungry."

He forces another bite, and another, until it becomes clear that Theresa Battaglia does not care whether he eats.

"Where's Pop?" he asks. Nicky likes to know his father's schedule as his days are now planned in avoidance of him.

"Where's Pop?"

Finally, Theresa Battaglia raises her raspy voice. "He called," she says. "While you were sleeping."

"Yeah . . . so?"

"He's in jail," she says. Nothing crosses her face, no hint of bother, aggravation, alarm.

"What happened?" Nicky grabs her by the arm, trying to shake her from her stupor. "Tell me."

"He told me to call him."

"Call who?"

"Vanderpool," she says. "The lawyer."

Nicky lets her arm drop like a lost cause. His mother's idiot serenity is impenetrable.

"It's time," she says. "Take me to the church."

"BLESS ME, FATHER, for I have sinned . . . They got my old man."

"I heard on the news. They said they got him and Cheech. Last night downtown, outside the Cicero Club."

"My uncle Phil?"

"Don't you worry about him. Phil Testa will take care of himself."

"I feel like I should feel worse than I do."

"Don't sweat it," says Father Vincent. "You don't even know what you feel yet."

"They called Vanderpool."

"He's a good lawyer," the priest says solemnly. "I mean, look what he did for your brother."

"Whatta you mean, what he did for my brother?"

"Well, what I mean is he's a pretty slick lawyer. He's the one who got Buddy off. After Buddy ate the paper, the cops put him through the system, figured if they stuck him in Rikers, he'd reconsider, that eventually he'd give up me and Tommy Sick for what happened in the park. So your old man calls Vanderpool. Vanderpool asks the DA for a new lineup to identify Buddy as the suspect. He makes all kinds of civil rights arguments and it takes him about a week to get one. The cops only had one eyewitness without a rap sheet. The way I heard it, there's nine guys in the lineup and Buddy's number five. The cops were sneaky like that. They put Buddy right in the middle, shine a light on him, and it's kind of like sticking a sign on his head: 'Pick me, I did it. Here I am, guilty as sin.' Anyway, Vanderpool watches real close as the guy identifies Buddy, then he asks for a break. Vanderpool says he wants to do it again—just to make sure—but this time he says the cops gotta move Buddy from the five spot to the three spot. Now the witness comes back five minutes later. The cops ask him all over again: Who'd you see that night in the park? He looks at the cops like they're stupid and right away, he goes: 'That guy, number five.' Get it? Vanderpool just switched the bodies. Now you got the case dismissed. Buddy walks right out of Rikers."

"Sure," says Nicky. "He walked right out. Only problem was, just like my father says: He was already a fucking zombie."

"Look all I'm saying is, your father's in good hands. Vanderpool knows what he's doing. Things will work themselves out."

"Like they did for Buddy?"

"I didn't mean . . ."

"Or like they did for you?"

"I'm sorry . . . I."

"I'm sorry, too," says Nicky, tripping into remembrance . . .

He had tried to visit Buddy in Rikers. He took the city bus from Thirty-fourth Street with all the inmates' wives and girlfriends and their little kids. When he got there, the CO's made him wait on a long line. It took forever. Then, at the Plexiglas barrier, the guards told him Frank Battaglia, Jr., could no longer receive visitors. He had been transferred to the infirmary.

That was a few days before Vanderpool pulled the switch.

But already too late.

Buddy came home, sure. But the way Nicky thinks about it now, he had already died in the jail.

Nicky never actually asked what happened. But it wouldn't have mattered anyway. There were no answers. Buddy barely spoke after he came home. At first, each and every twitch was an event, an unfulfilled optimism, a false, fleeting hope that somehow Buddy would wake, that he would be as he was.

The doctors had a name for the condition, but Nicky can never remember the word.

It took a while for Buddy to wake up. He would endure brief, biting spasms, thrashing for those moments like a fish on a line. Buddy was tethered to a nightmare. Nicky began to think maybe it was better that way; there must have been reasons why those memories were forbidden to his brother's consciousness.

Later on, Buddy would sit in front of the TV. Mostly, he'd watch reruns, game shows, talk shows. He would flip the dial—from "Donahue" to "I Love Lucy"—without so much as blinking.

Nicky would play some of the old tunes—the Stylistics, the Manhattans, Blue Magic. Nicky would sing and move in time with the record, imitating the choreography, the drop steps, sweeps and spins, an arc of the hand, a fingertip flutter to imitate raindrops. Once in a while, Buddy would stir approvingly, as if he were about to wake.

Then there came times when Buddy would come to, more than awake, acting out a scene already in progress, full of rage and rebellion.

Buddy would escape.

He would be gone for a day, or days, maybe as long as a week. Nicky remembers what the doctors called that—"manic episode."

Eventually, the cops would find Buddy roaming somewhere. They would find him wandering around the piers. Once, he hitchhiked upstate, someplace called Ulster County. Another time, they caught him trying to rob a bank. He didn't have a weapon, just a note demanding all the money. Buddy was still writing it when the cops caught him. The note was eight single-spaced legal pages, front and back. That's what the cops said, anyway. They said a lot of things. The cops enjoyed it, bringing the big gangster's kid home. The neighbors would turn on their lights and peer out the windows. At the stoop, Frank would look up, see who was watching.

Like it was a secret.

But everybody knew. The whole neighborhood.

Of course no one said anything to Frank's face. Or to Nicky's. But the whispers hung over them like a noxious ether. People enjoyed the idea that it was Frank's boy who'd been so stricken. *Geez, that Frank's kid became some kinda crazy fag.*

That's the one got turned out in the joint?

Yeah, he musta liked it.

The whole neighborhood knew.

Theresa brought Buddy to more doctors. She called them specialists. Frank called them quacks.

They'd scream at each other every night. Their arguments seemed to echo through the entire building: Theresa pleading that all her son needed was more time, Frank saying that the kid was a fucking zombie, a curse.

"I don't like the way he looks at me," said Frank. "Even before, I never liked how he looked at me."

After each episode, Buddy would be admitted to a mental ward at St. Vincent's. The hospital was like a jail. Nicky wasn't allowed to visit.

And Frank didn't bother. By now, he was trying to pretend that his namesake son no longer existed.

But sometimes Buddy made that impossible.

A few months ago, Nicky came home to find his brother pointing a gun. Go ahead, shoot, said Frank, you can't do it. That was the truth. Buddy couldn't do it. He began to sob. He was broken. But he had broken Frank, too. Not long after that, Buddy was gone for good.

NOW, IN THE confessional, Nicky can still hear Father Vincent telling him not to worry, that the lawyer will take care of everything. But Nicky has nothing more to say to the priest. Through the trellis, he watches his mother mouthing her devout mantra, wishing that he, too, had a belief, any at all, no matter how psychotic, how perverse, how wrong or bankrupt. He needs a faith as strong as hers, any magic, any system of faith or spirits that would grant him protection.

CHAPTER
37

AS PRODUCED BY the newspapers and the six o'clock news, the arraignment of Frank Battaglia and Cheech DeFranco is an ill-mannered epic. The great granite steps of the United States District Courthouse become tiers in an enormous sound stage, jammed with crowds of television cameras and reporters and legions of unpaid extras. Even the courtroom takes on the surly chaos of a big-budget movie set. A federal judge appointed by Lyndon Baines Johnson reads that morning's "Mushy's Mob" column into the record and rules that Frank Battaglia and Cheech DeFranco are "proven dangers to the community." They are sent without bail to the Metropolitan Correctional Center, ninth floor, north wing, where Frank is immersed in a dismal light.

The windows that gird the rec room on Nine North are caked with soot, reducing rays of the most brilliant sunshine to an incoming haze the tone of exhaust fumes. The light does not seem particular to MCC, or Nine North for that matter. Rather, it seems the only thing that fits Frank's recollection of prison.

The dreary Dickensian-style fortress he remembers has been replaced with glazed tile and bright plastic chairs, almost like a new public school. The rec room, where Frank and Cheech play hands of scoop and pinochle, is now called the multipurpose room. It smells of industrial cleaner, and the periodic odor of ghastly, warm hospital-style food. There's also a coffeepot and a Magic Chef microwave.

The multipurpose room is packed with kids, cocaine dealers with graffiti names. Some of them have already grown full body armor, layers of hard-time muscles with initials branded on their arms. Others are nothing more than spindly children. Little niggers and spics, thinks Frank, too young for federal time. They should be out playing with switchblades and jumping turnstiles.

In the old days, the other inmates needed permission just to look at a made guy. But these kids are not respectful so much as awed. To them, Frank is neither good nor bad, not even much feared. He is beyond all that. He is famous. It's as if he's walked right out of the papers, off the TV, and straight into Nine North.

Frank can hear them whisper.

"Yo, he the guy from the paper."

"Nah, that ain't him. That's his boy."

"But I heard he the bad man."

"He ain't shit."

"Nah, he use to be a fighter. My man in the paper, that ole nigger in the hat, he is writing about him."

That scumbag cop was right, thinks Frank.

Things have changed.

ON THEIR THIRD day inside, Frank turns to Cheech and says, "Remember when you could order out for lunch, shit you could get a lobster sent over from the Palm?"

Cheech looks around the room.

"These little kids, you think they ever ate a lobster?"

Frank smirks. "Kidding me? Alls they know is McDonald's."

"And Uzis," says Cheech. "You know, I never even thought about using a piece like that. In real life, I mean."

"What's to know? Pull the trigger, you're a big man," Frank scoffs. "It ain't like you gotta look the guy in the eye."

"I heard they prepay for their own funerals," says Cheech. "Like they know they ain't gonna live long so they make their own arrangements in advance. While they're still living."

Frank has no patience for this kind of talk. "You speak to Philly like I told you?"

"I couldn't get through."

"What the fuck does that mean?"

"Means no one answered the phone. What are you worried about anyway? I thought the lawyer Vanderpool said the case was nothing but shit, smoke and mirrors. Didn't he say you couldn't hear nothing on those wiretaps? And Philly said not to worry neither. Didn't Philly say everything was being worked out?"

"Where the fuck have I heard that before? Philly saying everything had been worked out. Work out this. Wasn't it him that said: 'Don't worry, we fixed it so youse could make bail'?" Frank slaps the Formica table. "And where are we now?"

"Don't get mad at me."

"I ain't mad at you. I'm mad at him. I know what this is about. He's pissed off about the case getting all this press. Well, what the fuck did he expect? I mean, whatever happened, he was the one that wanted to be boss of the whole world."

"He said not to call from here."

"That's what I'm talking about, Cheech. That's what bothers me."

Cheech shrugs, thinking: What's the use?

"What?" says Frank. "You think I'm gonna say something bad, too? Think I'm a jerkoff? You think I don't know how to talk right on the phone?"

"Philly said not to . . ."

"Don't tell me no more what Philly said."

"But . . ."

"Go. Dial him up for me."

Frank nods at the pay phone where one of the bony kids is hollering into the receiver: "Yo, you tell them to change the papers. My name ain't Antonio Simms no more. My name Foundation Seven. Yeah, tell 'im that, hizzoner hisself. And yo, that other thing, the jew'ry? Them receipts was all in your office. You know they can't be doing that shit, taking my gold. That's the attorney-client privilegeship."

Look at this, thinks Frank. Another tough guy, this kid on the phone. Jesus Christ, what's the world coming to? Mr. Foundation Seven weighs maybe a buck and a quarter. Uzi, my ass.

Frank watches with amusement as Cheech taps the kid on the shoulder, then jerks his thumb back at Frank, telling him "Someone's gotta use the phone." The kid begins a whiny protest, but one of the big jailhouse yoms cuts it short with a look. "Step off," the guy mutters. "Better let the man use the phone."

Foundation Seven skulks away. Cheech dials the number and waves Frank to the phone, like he's holding a parking space. He hands Frank the receiver.

It's ringing.

Frank looks over at the big yom with the muscles and grins. "Kids," he says.

But the big yom doesn't say anything.

Still ringing.

Now Frank's getting pissed off thinking of Philly. The guy acts like he shits crushed fruit. Who the fuck is he? Philly says he got it all worked out. Sure. Just like he had it all worked out that night at the Garden.

Frank has a vision of Philly counting money.

"Cocksucker." Frank finally realizes that all of Nine North is watching him, that no one's gonna pick up the phone, and that once again Philly's making him look bad.

Now Foundation Seven comes into his view. Fucking kid. Looks like he's gagging, a hand cupped over his mouth, like he's spitting out a bad clam.

Frank looks down at him. "You? What the fuck do you want?"

Frank blinks before he sees it.

The razor doesn't hurt so bad, not nearly so much as he would have imagined. At first, it feels like somebody pinching his cheek.

His body surges with adrenaline, then goes slack.

Frank is taking leave of himself now, watching the slow-motion action from another place.

The multipurpose room becomes animated, these crazy kids are yelling hilariously. Like some kind of school assembly got out of hand. A pep rally in hell.

"Yo the zipper. He gave my man the zipper."

Cheech breaks the Mr. Coffee pot over Foundation Seven's head.

From that other place, Frank touches his face. Warm and wet.

There will be a scar, something permanent. He understands that. The linoleum floor is a red wash.

But it doesn't hurt so much. He can live with that.

CHAPTER
38

VANDERPOOL CALLS NICKY to his office at the New York University Law School, where he is a celebrated professor of criminal procedure. He has arranged for Nicky to visit Frank at the MCC, also to deliver a message.

"It's not complicated," says the lawyer, "but it's quite important. Please tell your father there are strong appellate issues concerning the denial of bail. In other words, Nicky, we should be able to get the magistrate's decision overturned. Also, remind him that, objectively speaking, the prosecution's case is extremely weak. Or, as your father might say, a complete piece of shit. Finally, tell him I've been in touch with counsel for Philip Testa and that I've passed on my utmost personal assurance that there is absolutely no reason whatsoever for any extraordinary concerns that they might have."

Nicky nods somberly.

"Any questions?"

"Nah." Actually, Nicky would like to ask this Vanderpool about Buddy, about the lineup at the precinct, about what happened. But it doesn't feel right now. Vanderpool, for all his slick smarts, has a hyperactive glance. He doesn't look Nicky in the eye.

The lawyer hands him a roll of quarters. "For the

vending machines," he says. "Snickers, as I understand it, has become the great delicacy of the Family Visitation Room."

Nicky is almost out the door when Vanderpool calls back to him. "I just want to warn you," he says. "Your father's had an accident, got into a bit of a jam. It may appear somewhat unpleasant for now, but he'll be fine. Besides, I've prepared a lawsuit naming the facility, the Federal Bureau of Prisons, and the Southern District. It's not the type of thing I normally handle, personal injury. But I couldn't resist. Please don't forget to tell your father, he should get a kick out of it all." Now Vanderpool winks at the boy. "We'll take the bastards to the cleaners."

THE MORNING SUN is already beating down hard into the Family Visitation Room as Frank reaches across the table for his son. Wanting to provide a measure of comfort and assurance, Frank begins to knead the boy's shoulder. "Don't worry," he whispers. "It ain't nearly as bad as it looks."

The raw track of butterfly stitches commences as a dastardly squiggle above Frank's right eyebrow and continues, after the blinking interruption, at the top of his cheekbone, running to an abrupt, unceremonious halt just below the corner of his lip. The wound glistens, as it has been traced with a jelly-like salve. But the disfiguration is not nearly the most alarming evidence of trauma. Rather, it is something less specific, something in Frank's strange mood—humor, ease, even peace.

"Hey," says Frank, "it's not like I was a movie star anyways."

Nicky can sense the change in physical idioms: the self-deprecating grin, the warm hand now brushing his cheek. The hot, bloated anger is gone. It's as if the razor had cut deeper than the wound itself suggests, as if the blade let out evil gasses and shucked the tense, tiny facial muscles into flaccid states of relaxation, bleeding away what seemed so permanent, that taut scowl.

"What the heck," says Frank, his words light as confetti. He hears himself, how silly he sounds—What the heck—and begins to giggle.

"Are you okay?"

"I'm gonna be," says Frank. "We're all gonna be."

"Fucking niggers," Nicky grouses, as if it's his duty to put the remark on the record.

Frank shakes his head, mildly amused.

"Vanderpool said he's gonna sue the whole fucking jail."

"Is that right?"

"Yeah," says Nicky. "Plus, Vanderpool says not to worry. Objectively, he said, objectively speaking, the case can't stick. Also there's appellate . . ."

Frank is waving off Nicky's prepared remarks. "Don't worry about none of that."

"What?"

Frank has so much to tell him, so much to explain. But where to begin? "I want you to know," he says, "that I love you. And your mother. I love her, too."

Nicky hesitates, takes a deep breath, and resumes the message. "He also said that Uncle Philly's lawyer called and that . . ."

Frank reaches for his son's hand. "I said it's gonna be O.K.," he says. "A lot of things gotta be fixed up. But it's gonna be O.K."

Nicky doesn't get it. "Where's Cheech?" he asks.

"I don't know."

"I got something for him," says Nicky. The boy looks around suspiciously before unbuttoning his shirt and pulling out a copy of *Juggs* magazine.

Frank puts up his hands, palms facing forward, politely indicating that he cannot accept the contraband. His vacant smile frightens his son. Nicky now wonders if his father is entering a state of madness. Like Buddy. Like his mother. Is his father becoming a zombie, too? And will it happen to him?

Nicky produces a half-dozen Snickers bars and pushes them across the table. "These are for you," he says.

Frank just stares at the table, the smooth surface of

which now resembles a sundial, cut sharply by the summer sun into regions of shadow and light. Now he looks up, pointing toward the large windows.

"They clean 'em here," he says. "In the family room."

"What?"

"They wash the windows."

The poor kid still didn't understand, thinks Frank, his expression dissolving into a thin, detached smile. In the ecstatic psychosis of his reformation, Frank Battaglia has become sublime, metaphysical, somehow connecting the shards of light with choral music that he alone hears. He understands now. He has come to comprehend how badly he has behaved. There is so much to rectify: unspeakable, secret evils to be undone. But he can fix it. He can fix it all, restoring a righteous order to his family. So grateful is Frank Battaglia for this chance, he will gladly suffer the most severe penance.

He now considers himself equal but opposite to the man he was.

But Frank Battaglia still does what he has to do. What he can justify.

"We're gonna be a family again," he whispers.

"What's the matter?" Nicky pleads.

"Nothing."

"Tell me."

"I seen the light."

CHAPTER
39

THERESA BATTAGLIA WALKS two paces ahead of her son on their way to the church. "Hurry," she says, "we can't be late."

Hurry for what? Nicky thinks. For a voice she hears in her head? "Don't worry, Ma," he says. "The old ladies'll wait for you."

Irrational urgencies, neuroses both slight and severe, are her constant affliction. Still, on this morning, Nicky cannot help but be surprised by the distinct purpose in his mother's step, her peculiar, private sense of destination.

"Hurry," she says.

"What the fuck," Nicky mumbles, stopping in his tracks, hands on his hips, watching as she walks ahead without him. His mother doesn't even look back.

And doesn't go up the steps to the church, either.

There's a guy holding a car door open for her. Nodding at her. Helping her in. Holding her hand as she smooths over her black skirt.

What the fuck?

Now the guy holding the door is waving him on.

"C'mon," he says. "Get in."

Up close, Nicky can see the guy—a cop.

"Let's go," says the cop.

Nicky freezes, seized by the sudden sensation that his world, his alone, is actually turning, as if he were spinning on a separate axis in another orbit, along a bewildering, vertiginous arc plotted by a calculus that contradicts the laws of gravity.

Now his mother issues an urgent whine from the car. "Nick-eee! Get in."

Nicky follows her voice, feeling as though he just dropped from the sky. The cop closes the door behind him and gets behind the wheel. There's another guy sitting next to him. This one doesn't look like a cop. He looks like the smiling asshole from the Chevy commercials on TV.

"Hi," he says, "I'm Lars. It's a pleasure, Mrs. Battaglia."

"Likewise."

"I'm Jack Gallagher."

Waiting at the red light on Seventh Avenue, the cop eyeballs Nicky through the rearview mirror. "Mrs. Battaglia?" he asks softly.

"Yes?"

"I thought you said you were going to tell your son."

"No," she says, looking out the window.

Jack the cop shakes his head and Lars, the guy from the Chevy commercial, leans over to whisper in his ear. The cop grimaces, peeling out on Seventh, then making a hard left against traffic on Downing Street and another, doubling back to the house.

There's a U-Haul out front. A team of white men in jumpsuits are piling the artifacts of the Battaglia family into the back of the truck: vases and bureaus and chests and drawers, his mother's religious statues.

"Everything's in order, Mrs. Battaglia," says the Chevy guy, Lars, signaling Gallagher to move on.

Nicky spots a guy in a jumpsuit carrying off the shoe box of the Buddy Love Music, featuring Buddy's baddest 45's of all time.

"Wait up," he says. "I want that stuff."

"All personal items will be returned to you at your final destination," says Lars.

"Now."

Theresa Battaglia lets out a sigh. "Nicky, please don't be difficult."

"Then I ain't going."

Gallagher calls to the agent in the jumpsuit, who comes quickly with the shoe box containing the best of the Buddy Love 45's, a dog-eared copy of Clyde Frazier's "Guide to Cool," and another book, a gift from Father Vinny. "This what you want?" Gallagher asks.

"Yeah."

"Let the kid have it."

The Chevy guy bristles in his seat. This is not the protocol. "No time for this, Jack," he says. "Let's get out of here."

NO ONE SAYS a word until they're on the Jersey side of the Holland Tunnel, when Gallagher asks Theresa Battaglia for permission to speak to her son.

"Sure." She seems blissfully occupied just looking out the window watching as her world fades from view.

"Nick, your father wanted to tell you in person. But he couldn't. It wasn't safe."

Nicky glares back at the cop through the rearview.

"Look, your father had a choice, not a great one, but a choice anyway. He made a decision. He believes this is in you and your mother's best interests. And maybe you don't want to hear it from me, but I'm gonna tell you something: he's right. We talked it over, me and your old man. We went over it a lot of times, back and forth, and part of the deal was he made me give my word about something . . . He made me promise to look after you."

Gallagher looks back at the boy, wanting to see how the line plays.

"Fuck you, cop."

"Don't say that, Nicky," whispers Theresa. "He didn't do nothing wrong."

Now Lars the Chevy guy pipes in: "You're going to have to get with the program, kid."

Gallagher gives him a dirty look.

Nicky smolders in silence until the Dodge turns off at the exit for Newark Airport.

"Where we going?"

Gallagher shrugs. "America," he mutters.

"That's funny, Jack," says the Chevy guy. "America."

"Hysterical."

CHAPTER
40

THERESA BATTAGLIA'S BLANK gaze remains fixed on the carpet of clouds that passes beneath the jet's engines. The plane's upward struggle through rough, jostling air does nothing to disturb her. Already, her face has become less taut. Nicky realizes that his mother accepts her unknown fate, that she has from the moment the cop held the door for her.

But he does not. And as the plane tilts through the surging winds, he is beset with a strange vertigo.

When he was four years old his mother brought him to the Museum of Natural History to see the great whale that hung from the ceiling. The whale was too big, its dimensions too absurd for even his imagination. Nicky began to cry, believing that the whale would fall from its hoisted moorings, crushing them both. His mother held him tight until he was all cried out. And it occurs to him now that while Theresa Battaglia was once a different type of woman, he remains that frightened little boy.

Nicky feels as he did that day: disoriented, abandoned by the standard sense of place and proportion. He's just too spent to cry. Faces flash across his mind's eye like slides: his father, of course, but also Buddy and Vinny, Samantha, Cheech, Toodie and Angel and Khe Sahn,

Tommy Sick, Mary Missile Titties. Nicky forces them to dissolve. That is his strategy, to suffocate imagination and remembrance.

He makes up his mind to arrive at his future, however fucked up it may be, with as little as possible. Each of those faces must die to him. He can almost feel the plane become lighter as it lurches toward an easier altitude, as Nicky begins to jettison all his recollected baggage, each of those recurring faces, one by one, until all that remains of the past, all that will survive his journey into the future is the half ounce of Gerard Romano's fine Colombian and the change from his thousand-dollar cash-out in Atlantic City.

The life he knew has run its course. Nicky Battaglia does not grieve. He is merely bewildered.

His father is a rat.

And that can never be undone.

American Flight 0021 touches down in Bluff's Head, South Carolina. Mother and son deplane flanked by the two federal agents, the cop and the Chevy guy.

The cop pats Nicky knowingly on the elbow. "Maybe we could play some golf," he says.

Nicky recoils at the touch. He can't yet shake the dizziness. Stepping into the Southern sunshine, Nicky Battaglia is plagued with the sense that he has entered a bizarre new dimension.

Lars rents a car, another Dodge Aries, and Gallagher drives. They get on a federal highway that takes them over an intracoastal waterway and onto the island. Bluff's Head Island has recently undergone a realtor's renaissance, a coastal town reborn as a series of golf resorts. It is a ten-minute drive from the airport to the Indigo Run Plantation, a weathered condominium complex which predates the island's real estate boom. The two-bedroom apartment is done in worn wicker furniture with sodden pillows in floral patterns. There is the vague odor of mildew.

Theresa checks the kitchen, opening the cupboard made of plasticized wood, complete with faux knots in the veneer. She examines the dented aluminum coffee percolator, the blender, the rubber spatulas. Her assessment is not so much an inventory as an anticipation, nodding knowingly to herself, imagining what it will be like living here.

"Not as nice as Spanish Wells," Lars declares cheerfully, "but we're not like DEA, you know. We don't go over budget."

Gallagher pulls the cord for the vertical blinds, revealing sliding glass doors and a concrete terrace with old beach chairs. There's a magnificent view of the shimmering ocean.

"Sometimes," he says, "real early in the morning, you can see schools of dolphin."

"But don't get too used to it," says Lars. "This is just a temporary location. Until we get you settled permanently."

"Where?" asks Teresa.

"Nobody knows yet," he says. "That decision will be made by the boys in Washington. They're doing a Threat Assessment analysis right now. It's for your own good. In the meantime, your things are being stored in a warehouse, awaiting transfer to the permanent location. That'll be based foremost on your safety, but also the regional employment outlook, your anticipated adaptability with the new environment, a lot of factors."

"And my husband?"

"Mr. Battaglia has been moved to a safe location within the MCC. He might have to do a little time, in protective custody of course. Don't worry, though, it's just for appearances. But realistically, I wouldn't expect him to join you until, oh, I don't know . . ."

"When?" she asks sharply.

"Well, it's difficult to say. He's being debriefed."

"What does that mean, debriefed?"

"Prepared. There's an awful lot of material to go over. The case has blossomed: the unions, this matter with Mr. Colosimo, the conspiracy by Mr. Philip Testa . . . but I guess you know all about that."

"I don't know anything about that," she says. "I just want to know when he's getting out."

"By New Year's," he says. "Maybe."

Theresa Battaglia goes back to her kitchen.

"It's not as bad as it sounds," says Lars.

"Who said it was so bad?"

"We can arrange phone contact. Just let us know."

"Sure," says Theresa, examining a spotty glass in the light, deciding that everything must be cleaned and cleaned again. She begins stacking glasses and plates into the dishwasher. "I don't know where any of this stuff has been," she says.

"Feel free," says Lars. "I have to head back to the big city. But you'll be in good hands here. Agent Gallagher will remain here with you."

Theresa looks up from her dishes. "What?"

"Preliminary indications from Threat Assessment are that it's safer if he stays. Not that there's any danger. But just in case. Besides, we find that it's always less conspicuous—especially during the initial stages of the program—to maintain the illusion of a family unit."

Theresa gives Gallagher the once-over. "I don't know where you think you're sleeping in my house."

"The couch, I guess," Gallagher says apologetically. "Look, Mrs. Battaglia, that Threat Assessment bit isn't really the whole story. I told you before, your husband and I spent an awful lot of time together, hashing this all out. You develop a mutual trust, it sounds funny, me saying this to you, but you become sort of close. That doesn't mean we're friends, I don't want to insult you. But we asked certain things of him, and he asked certain things of us. One of those things was that I look after you and your son. Personally."

"Is that what he told you?" she asks. "Is that what he said when he became a rat?"

Gallagher let out a deep breath. "Your husband, he understood what he was doing."

"Understood what?" she asks, pressing for the first time in a long while.

"The day he made his decision, he understood that that was the most important day in his life."

"Figures," she says, going back to her dishes.

"We have a present for you," says Lars, nodding cheerfully at Gallagher, who then empties the contents of a manila envelope on the kitchen counter. Like a dealer throwing out hands from a bad deck of cards, Gallagher sorts the documents into two piles—one for Theresa, another for her son.

Nicky is dumbfounded, trying to sound out the words to his new American name. He stares in disbelief at the officially sanctioned frauds: birth certificate, Social Security card, driver's license, complete with pirated photograph from his Xavier High School ID.

"I don't even drive," he sneers.

"Says right there you can," says Gallagher.

Finally, Gallagher throws out the last card in his deck, that old, creased wallet photograph of Frank posing with his dukes up. "Your old man wants you to have that," he says.

Nicky won't even pick it up off the table.

"We hope you understand the need for prudence," says Lars. "This has become quite a big case. There's been a lot of attention in the media."

Gallagher whispers an aside to Nicky. Maybe he can make it easier—for both of them. "Guy's from Minnesota," he explains.

But Nicky turns away with a scowl, looking out the window, vowing never to speak his new name. Jack Gallagher walks awkwardly into the kitchenette, where he waits to present Theresa her documents. But Theresa remains at the sink, scrubbing the pots and pans by hand now. Steam rises from the soapy water.

"Put it over there," she says. "On the counter."

Jack Gallagher shrugs. "I'm sorry," he says.

"It ain't your fault," she says. "Besides, a deal's a deal."

THE VERTIGO REMAINS with Nicky for each and every moment of his exile on Bluff's Head Island. The terrain seems alien. He is lost without the familiar density of New York, the city's anarchy, its dirt, its accustomed sights and sounds—fire hydrants and chainlink fences and subway grates and manhole covers, angry horns and rumbling subways. Bluff's Head Island overwhelms his bearings, like a magnet held to a compass.

The island is overrun with new developments, which, as he discovers, are inhabited by the superior class of white people, there being two out here: those who golf and those who drive pickups. Most of the developments are called "Plantations." They feature eighteen holes, a guard booth out front, recently planted palm trees fortified with wire and wooden stakes, speed bumps, and thatched Tiki bars by the pool.

The developments seem odd, but no more than the churches, which are unlike any he has ever seen: clean and new, with tan bricks and lines like the slope of a pitched tent. The roads are strange, too, with turning lanes and cool grassy traffic islands for the ordered, sensibly engineered flow of mid-size sedans and yellow school buses and camouflaged convoy trucks from the nearby Marine base. As far as Nicky can tell, this new place is a paved plain scented with exhaust fumes, repeating itself with Little League fields, strip malls, outlet stores, Dairy Queens, 7-Elevens, where they sell *Penthouse* magazine sheathed in protective plastic, Taco Bells, Piggly Wiggly supermarkets, Pizza Huts.

Nicky wonders what it is that Pizza Hut tastes like, compared to Golden's on Carmine, or Ben's on Spring Street. But the notion is fleeting, as Nicky recalls the vow of his new discipline—to forget.

He tries very hard to forget.

Remembrance is a sickness he must sweat away like a fever. Nicky runs for miles on the beach, the wet sand beneath his feet packed like a slab of setting concrete. He watches secretly for the dolphins, imagining them as unicorns of the sea, as if their sight would somehow liberate him. But the dolphins never come. He could run the beach forever, but all he is left with is the small comfort of fatigue.

He plays ball with the local brothers in a park by what is called "the middle school." He talks to no one. Says nothing. Just plays. But there, too, his bearings prove lost. The baskets hang off concrete arcs arranged in equidistant rows, like the ribs of some extinct, gargantuan beast. The backboards are small and dead, rounded-off pieces of white metal. Nicky can't shoot against such an empty background, no buildings, no walls, nothing but sky.

He buys a leather Everlast jump rope at the sporting goods store, and begins to skip in time on the terrace, facing the ocean.

He's cheating now, going against his own vow. It was Toodie who explained to him the secret of jumping rope, that the rope develops a confident, coordinated cadence, the conservation of movement, that the rope, properly used, is a minor medicine for fluster. Nicky has a vague notion of its rhythm as therapy, as he taps out a beat, the leather slapping and scraping against the bare landing. It's as if he were tuned and timid liked a gyroscope, as if he could recalibrate his internal motors to achieve a new state of balance, the rope going faster and faster now around its ball-bearing axis, defining a whirring, blurry circumference and a passive trance against his loneliness.

Nicky can go for hours, facing the ocean, waiting for the dolphins, his back turned to this infuriating cop and his mother.

EXILE IS FAR kinder to Theresa Battaglia. Each day, she recovers something more of herself, until, it seems to Nicky, that she has become more than she was.

Her body, dormant so long, now proves its resiliency. It happens in stages. She gets rid of the gray hair, then lightens the rich brown color with strands of auburn. She makes frequent trips to the nail salon in the mall for manicures and pedicures.

"Where are you going now, Ma?" he asks.

"I have an appointment," she says. "Waxing."

Nicky doesn't even want to know.

She says cheerful hellos to the neighbors, all of whom have names like Chuck Steak.

"Hi, I'm Chuck Steak."

Jerkoffs, Nicky thinks.

Some days, his mother lies on the beach, reading books. Nicky checks the titles: *Hollywood Wives* by Jackie Collins, *The Handbook to Higher Consciousness, The Road Less Traveled.*

Nicky reads the first sentence—"Life is difficult"—thinking, No shit, Sherlock.

Her TV shows begin to infuriate him: "Oprah," "Donahue." Then, later, public television, documentaries on the holocaust of baby seals.

"Isn't that terrible, Nicky?"

What the fuck.

She plants boxes of geraniums on the terrace.

One day she says, "I think I'm going to get a cockatiel. For the house."

"A what?" he asks.

"A bird, like a little parrot."

"Not in my house," he says.

She buys a plaid skirt at the Brooks Brothers outlet store instead. Gallagher drives her there. Gallagher drives her everywhere, like some rent-a-cop chaperon. Nicky wants to tell him: Why don't you go back and do what you're paid for, catch some criminals, go get the niggers on the subways.

One day he's gonna tell him that.

Nicky watches his mother check herself out in the mirror, so pleased, smoothing over the plaid skirt. Her belly and legs have taken on a womanly weight. Yes, Nicky thinks, she is more than she was, but also, perhaps, more than she has a right to be.

The kitchen, her kitchen, is madness.

She stocks it with Hamburger Helper, Oscar Mayer bologna, Kraft Singles, Cheez Whiz, Wonder bread. The pork store, the supermarket, the greengrocer, the bakery, all of them have been replaced by Piggly Wiggly.

Every night, it's the same. Nicky says, "I ain't eating that."

"Don't be difficult, honey."

"What is it?"

"They had a sale at Piggly Wiggly."

"Yeah, but what is it?"

"A casserole."

And that cop, Gallagher, starts with the mmmm-mmmm good bit. Like he likes it.

What a full of shit con man he is. Look at him, talking about why he retired from the cops, some sob story about watching a kid dying in a hospital in Brooklyn.

And his mom? She goes for that sorry-ass line, agreeing with this douche bag, sympathizing, saying, "I heard that. I mean, I read it. I read that being a cop—a police officer—is one of the most stressful occupations."

Who made her an expert?

"Don't look so tough to me," says Nicky. "Not the gig he's got."

"That'll be enough," she says.

The cop pretends like he's not part of the argument. Nicky senses his unease, and seizes on it.

He tells Jack Gallagher what he's been meaning to tell him: Why don't you go back to Brooklyn, with all the niggers, and be a real cop, go catch real criminals, instead of this bullshit. He screams something about civil rights.

"Nicky!" she hollers.

"I ain't hungry no more," he says, pushing away his plate, leaving the table, slamming the door behind him.

Gallagher finds him half an hour later. Nicky is sitting on the beach in the darkness smoking a joint.

"What?" he says. "You gonna put me in jail?"

Gallagher takes a seat beside him.

"You want some?" snickers Nicky.

"I could probably use it," says Gallagher.

Nicky can sense his power over the cop, that he wants Nicky to like him. They sit there, listening to the surf for a while, their silence more awkward for the cop than the kid. Gallagher wants to say something, something nice, reassuring. He just doesn't know what.

Finally he mumbles, "Looks like the Mets are gonna win it all."

Nicky turns his head slowly, taking a short toke, careful to show his contempt. "I like the Yankees," he says. Then, thinking better of it, wanting to rub in the defeat, he adds, "Except for Strawberry. The only one I like is Darryl."

"Yeah," says Gallagher. "I kind of like him, too, crazy fuck."

"Don't lie," says Nicky. "How could a cop like Darryl? You like that other guy, the catcher."

"Gary Carter?"

"Yeah."

"Why'd you say that?"

"'Cause he talks like your boy, that smiling asshole."

"Who?"

Nicky rolls out the answer in an effeminate drone. "Hi, I'm Laaaarrrrs," he says.

"I see what you're saying," says Gallagher. "He can be a little irritating."

They talk some more, Gallagher trying to be friends, Nicky trying to break balls. Gallagher says he used to play some ball, too. Back in the old days.

"Where?" Nicky asks.

"Power."

"You play with Jabbar?"

"Alcindor back then. I was a few years ahead of him."

Nicky has a vision of Jack Gallagher in horn-rimmed glasses, white Converse, black socks, too-tight satin shorts. The guy must've been a scrub. From way back.

"You ever hear of Roger Brown?"

Nicky shakes his head.

"Connie Hawkins?"

"Him, yeah. My brother told me."

"Yeah? Well, I played with those guys up in the Rucker Tournament."

"Get the fuck outta here."

"No. Really. I set picks for them," says Gallagher. "That was my job. The thing was, those guys were so good, they didn't need nobody to set picks."

Nicky puts out the joint in the cool sand and begins to fumble for his Baggie and papers, wanting to roll another joint. He doesn't want to smoke it so much as he wants to piss off the cop.

Gallagher shakes his head. "I'm sorry about your brother," he says.

Nicky looks out, marveling at the moonlight, the phosphorescent spine it lays across the ocean. "So am I," he says, his voice weak and drifting. Nicky's high as a kite, so high he forgets his discipline. Something's still bothering him, something he wants to know. "My father," he asks, "why did he . . . you know?"

"Colosimo?"

Nicky nods.

"Phil Testa gave the order," Gallagher says gravely. "Your uncle, it was his idea."

"And Cheech?"

"It's too bad, really. I kind of liked hanging out with him. He was O.K."

Nicky finds himself studying Gallagher—his guilt, his regret, his decent good manners—all as tangible as the yellow, moonlit glow set against his silhouette.

"It's my job," says Gallagher.

Nicky has a good idea what the cop means by that. It's his way of conceding, of asking Nicky to respect his right to privacy, the privileged prohibition against self-incrimination. In other words: Don't ask me what I really think of your old man, for my sake, sure, but also for yours.

EVENTUALLY, THEY DO things together, Nicky and the cop. And while Nicky is careful to avoid anything that could result in a measure of affection or empathy between them, he does agree to one-on-one. The games are a terrible mismatch. The kid moves so well, and so tirelessly. The cop is relentless, but plodding and slow with his age. Nicky leaves him wheezing on the court. Gallagher never complains, though. It's as if this were part of his expected punishment.

Fuck him anyway, Nicky thinks.

One day, Gallagher convinces him to shoot a round of golf. Gallagher shows up all happy, dressed like Magnum, P.I. "I been looking forward to getting you out here," he says.

Nicky discovers that he cannot hit the tiny white ball, not in his dizzy daytime condition.

He remains in the golf cart, trying to ruin Gallagher's day with a teenager's version of passive resistance.

"You O.K.?" Gallagher asks.

"Me? I'm fine. Just don't feel like playing."

When they get back to Indigo Run Plantation, Nicky learns that his mother has finally purchased the cockatiel.

It's a cross between a cockatoo and a parakeet, she explains, outlining the features: a small gray bird with flushes of yellow and orange around the cheeks. "I'm going to call her Brenda," she says.

"That's a nice name," says Gallagher. "Brenda."

The bird doesn't even mimic conversation, just whistles. All the goddamn time. It has but three notes—incessant, infuriating, idiotic—each of them mocking Nicky's predicament.

Theresa takes Brenda out of the cage to perch on her shoulder as she cooks her casseroles.

What the fuck.

THE SCHOOL YEAR begins.

Nicky's the only new student in the senior class.

And the only one who can't drive. Gallagher keeps asking if he wants to learn, if he wants to take the Dodge Aries for a spin. But Nicky is steadfast in his refusal. Each morning, a yellow bus arrives to take him to the high school.

Enrollment is overwhelmingly black, kids who speak in a low country dialect which Nicky does not bother to understand. Most of the white kids in Cumberland County, sons and daughters of the military and golfing classes, attend Christian academies. Those who attend the public schools belong to the pickup-truck class.

They listen to Van Halen and call Nicky Fonzie behind his back.

Dumb niggers and dumb white trash, he thinks, the banter in his mind becoming unwittingly like his father's. Fuck 'em all.

Teachers call on him in class. But Nicky does not

respond. He does not recognize his new name, the one on his driver's license.

Nicky begins to play a game: How long can he go without saying anything to anyone? He has stepped into a severe solitary, a dizzy dimension of loneliness, unconnected to anything or anyone.

The Mets win the World Series. Nicky could give a shit.

He runs on the beach, plays ball, skips rope. And talks to nobody.

At night, he masturbates, breaking his vow, trying to imagine the girl Samantha. Wanting her to whisper something in his ear. But not knowing what.

The loneliness has him in a clench.

The summer lingers down south. And so does the daylight. It's as if time does not pass. The mornings remain hot deep into October. Too hot to give a shit. Fuck it, he thinks, fuck it all. Nicky passes on the school bus and runs his miles on the beach, reaching the total exhaustion necessary for a mild relief. There is nowhere left to go.

He lets himself in the apartment quietly, as he'd rather not get caught skipping school.

It takes him a few moments to comprehend the ecstatic murmur coming from behind his mother's closed door. He freezes as her moan builds from a soft, grateful whimper.

To a crescendo of angry, cursing tongues. Obscenities.

Nicky cannot help but listen. He finds himself getting a hard-on.

Now, from behind the door, comes a trickle of laughter, his mother's, followed by a deep, muted voice, a man's voice.

The cop.

Nicky falls to his knees, faint, and hobbles to the terrace. Nicky pulls himself up by the railing, knocking over his mother's geraniums. He wonders if this is the moment when the vertigo finally overtakes him. He can hear the bird making her imbecile sounds as he leans over the side, vomiting.

It's a shame, Nicky thinks. He never got to see the dolphins.

CHAPTER
41

"BLESS ME, FATHER, for I have sinned."

"You O.K.?"

"I guess."

"How'd you get here?"

"Airplane. Got a ticket with the money I had left over from my big score in Atlantic City."

"Anyone see you coming in?"

"Yeah, I think."

"Who?"

"Mary Missile Titties. It was dark, but she saw me. Coming out of the subway on West Fourth. I didn't know what to say. She just looked at me, like, dirty looks, you know what I mean? I kept walking."

"Damn."

"I saw the paper."

"It's been like that every day. They can't get enough. One day, the papers got him a hero, you know: the Man Who Broke the Mob. Like he's man of the year. Next day, they're calling him a rat, the rat of all time. The worst is that old maniac from the *Mirror*."

"I know," says Nicky.

There was another Mushy Flynn exclusive waiting for him in the newspaper rack when he got off at La Guardia.

Nice big headline, too: KING RAT!!! WHAT FRANKIE BATTS TOLD THE FEDS, a front-page splash featuring a cartoon of an immense, gray rodent, standing on its hindquarters, nibbling a piece of cheese. Only the rat's face was Frank Battaglia's mug shot. By the time Nicky got back to the neighborhood, it seemed that copies of the *Mirror*'s front page were plastered on every wall from the subway to the church.

"I was trying to tell you on the phone," says Father Vincent. "This is no place to be. Isn't there anywhere else? Anybody you know?"

"Nope. I guess you're the only one I got. The only one left."

"Jesus, Nicky. What are we gonna do with you?"

"Well, you could do your job. I mean, I got a lot of impure thoughts. You could take my confession . . ."

Father Vincent shuts his eyes. When he finally answers, his voice is weak. "Maybe you should take mine."

"You mean priests jerk off, too?"

"No, I'm serious, I . . ."

"You wanna tell me about Buddy, right? The rest of the story?"

"Yes. In a way."

"Look, I was only messing around. You don't have to do that no more. C'mon, Father Vinny. We don't have time for this. It's getting late."

"Hear my confession, Nicky."

The quiver in the priest's voice quickens Nicky's blood. "Maybe it's something you don't need to tell me," he says. "You know, better unsaid."

"No," says the priest. "I have to tell someone and it's gotta be you. You see, I think I can straighten this out with God . . . eventually, I mean. But I gotta straighten it out with you, too . . . I need your forgiveness."

"Whatever it is, Father Vinny, I forgive you."

"It's not that simple. You have to hear it first, decide for yourself. Is that O.K.?"

"I guess."

"The night we went into the park? The night that kid got killed."

"Go on."

"It was me."

"What do you mean?"

"I killed him, Nicky. It was me. I pulled the trigger. I watched him die."

The confession is not nearly as shocking as the priest would have thought.

"I figured it might be something like that," says Nicky. "I mean, it was a possibility. In my mind, when you said it should have been you instead of Buddy . . . But you were only helping my brother. Right?"

Father Vincent doesn't answer.

"You were only doing it for Buddy, right?"

"Don't you understand?"

Nicky shakes his head. "No."

"I liked it. Part of me. A part of me liked it." Now Vinny Ruggiero of Sullivan Street breaks down, surrendering to an exquisite, long-anticipated grief. He puts his head in his hands, weeping, wailing, his chest heaving to the rhythm of his sobs.

A wind whistles through the great church doors. Something has come in off the street. Something that howls.

Tommy Sick.

Nicky pounds on the screen, trying to roust the priest. But Vinny is now beyond anything so mundane as a warning. He remains in a trance of his own making, ranting in an altered language, sorrowful, hysterical, ancient, unintelligible dialects with origins Nicky can only imagine: Sicilian, Roman, Latin, Hebrew, a mantra, a spell, a poem and a prayer, for absolution.

Nicky picks up his gym bag and runs from the booth, somehow believing that the priest has given him his blessing to leave the scene. Turning down the aisle, he catches a glimpse of Tommy Sick raising the gun, pointing it straight up, toward the arch of the cupola, but not firing, and not giving chase.

There is no way Tommy Sick can catch him, not now, not as he runs past the sacristy, down into the maze of stairs, through the catacomb bowels of the church, to he knows not where.

•   •   •

"MOVE."

Father Vincent accepts the directions silently, his hands up, stumbling forward with each poke of the gun at the small of his back.

"Where is he?" yells Tommy Sick. "Where the fuck did he go?" Vinny the priest is really pissing him off by not answering.

"I shoulda known," he says, nudging Vinny back toward the sacristy. "I shoulda known that little faggot would run to you."

Sweating with anger, Tommy Sick marches him up those most secret steps.

"You're a faggot, too. You ain't even a priest. You're nothing but a little homo. Yeah, that's right. Just like your boy. Just like Buddy. Just another faggot who takes it up the ass."

The priest tries not to listen. He remembers his uncle Sal bringing him to the Statue of Liberty, taking him by the hand as they walked up the steps into the maiden's head. Uncle Sal wasn't so impressed with the view from her crown. "Next week," he said, "I take you to the circus."

Tommy Sick pokes him with the gun barrel again, prodding him from the steps at the bell tower landing. "Move, motherfucker."

They proceed with caution along the creaky wooden planks, around the massive bell. Tommy Sick can't help but look down through the floor's circular cutaway under the bell, into the guts of the church.

Vinny snickers at him.

"What, you think it's funny, faggot?" says Tommy Sick, forcing him to the ledge.

Vinny picks up the coo of a pigeon nestled above, and the sweet, rotten scent that comes off the damp wooden beams. The neighborhood looks good from up here, he thinks. The streets are slick from a gentle rain. The reflections of neon and traffic lights run over the asphalt like faint trails of watercolor.

Tommy Sick breaks a black beauty in half and hits each nostril.

"You better tell me where that little bastard is," he says. "This don't have nothing to do with you no more."

The priest turns around slowly, facing the gunman, sending him into an even higher state of agitation.

"Vinny, this shit's getting out of hand," says Tommy Sick, watching as the priest breaks into an uncanny, contented smile.

"Don't make me do nothing, Vinny."

"Why not?"

"I'll fucking do it."

"So do it."

"I'm telling you . . ."

"Can't?"

"Just tell me where the fuck he is. That's all I wanna know."

"Can't do it? What are you, a fag?"

"Don't."

"That's O.K., Tommy. I know what you are. You don't have to hide from me. It doesn't go anywhere with me. Hell, we go way back, don't we, Tommy . . . It'll be our secret."

Vinny watches Tommy Sick, watches suspicion giving way to surrender.

"I can make you feel better, Tommy."

Vinny reaches for him, his arm snaking around the collar of Tommy Sick's leather jacket, behind his neck, pulling him close, cradling Tommy Sick's head under his chin, feeling him sigh with relief, gratefully, closer still, feeling him begin to heave, until it occurs to him that Tommy Sick is weeping. Vinny leans back, doing the work for them both now, easing into their descent, shivering through ages as they go, each of them bound by an intimate, clandestine history, falling, Vinny sees the spray paint signature left many years ago, by his friend, on a lark, when they were kids, "I want my name in the steeple," he had said. "Yeah," said Vinny, "but who's gonna see it, who's gonna know?" "You're gonna know, you and me," he had said, and yes, that is what Vinny sees now, on his way down, as he becomes lighter, as the battering ram passes through his chest, and Buddy's name gives way to the black sheet of sky.

CHAPTER

42

SAMANTHA BRODERICK SOAKS in the bathtub, the scalding water turning her fair skin splotchy red. She barely feels it, though. She's been numb for a while now. Too long, she thinks. She took leave that day, a season ago, when it was still hot, and only now, soaking in the tub, trying to float, is she beginning to locate herself again.

She remembers everything in an oddly clinical way. The nurses at St. Vincent's took her through the entire protocol, as they referred to it, as if her body itself were various exhibits of evidence. But they seemed like fair, decent women, and she did as they told her, remaining obedient as they drew blood, instructed her to pee in a cup, as they took various pluckings and combings from her pubic hair, as they placed her in the stirrups, swabbing her insides for cultures.

Samantha offered no protest, and wonders now if she was brave or merely broken.

"Who did this to you?" asked the nurse.

"I don't know his name," she said.

The nurse shook her head and sent Samantha home with a bottle of Demerol.

She tried one, then put the bottle away, hid it behind the antacids and the perfumes and cold creams in the recesses of her bathroom cabinet. The medicine felt too much like junk.

She might as well do the real thing.

She thought about it.

She thought about a lot of things. None of which, thank God, she did.

But she has been numb ever since, stricken with a perversion of the metabolism, a weak, anemic stupor, a deadening of the senses, but also, a protection. For he has been near the entire time, the father. Filthy. He is in the newspapers, on the television.

But she never told anyone. She never even cried.

Only now, soaking in the tub, does the numbness begin to ebb. She soaks until the water is lukewarm then pats herself dry with a towel, finding a minor relief, a feeling that she is almost clean. She pulls her hair back, looking into the mirror, and discovers a deep, quirky hunger. Her stomach is growling.

For almost three months, Samantha has sustained herself with a diet of Nutrament and popcorn. Now she craves something altogether different. She goes to the all-night Korean grocer on the corner, filling her plastic basket with bitter greens of every variety: arugula, red leaf lettuce, watercress, radicchio, chicory, frisée, dandelion leaves. She throws in a fresh, ripe tomato for color. And for the dressing a thin-skinned lemon, olive oil, and a bottle of raspberry vinegar.

She hurries home. The streets are lonely and glistening. The rain has left its faint perfume. She's very hungry.

She's jiggling with the door lock as he comes upon her, running at her, it seems, out of breath.

He's screaming something. But she cannot understand the words. Or the desperate look on his face.

Is it terror?

Or rage?

There's no time to consider his intention. She assumes the worst.

He's charging for her. At last that's how it seems . . .

As she leaves herself. Again. And again, it feels as if she's watching it happen from above.

Samantha drops the bag of groceries and clocks him, using the bottle of vinegar like the barrel of a bat. It shatters above his forehead along the right side of his skull.

He collapses with a sad, defeated groan.

She turns the key, pushing the door open with her hip, and, after some deliberation, decides to drag him inside. His trail leaves a red smear across the floor tiles. She mops it up quickly, sweeping gooey bits of black glass into the dustpan.

Samantha wonders if he's dying, or dead. If she has killed him.

She drags him deeper into the living room, propping his head on a pillow, covering him with an old wool blanket. Listening to him gurgle.

But not touching him. Trying to avoid that.

Samantha regards him as a wounded animal, dangerous, predatory, capable of sudden, inexplicable blood-lusts.

Now come the sirens, many, howling, from all directions, breaking through the evening's quiet, even through the numb buzzing in her head. The sirens move closer, then away, around the corner.

Within moments, patrolmen are going door to door, canvassing the neighborhood. They ring her bell. She sidles against the door and waits in the dark, not wanting to so much as breathe, listening to their deep dumb voices:

"Something, huh? A priest and another guy. A regular lovers' quarrel."

"Let's go, already. No one's fucking home. I'll buy."

Only now does she realize: they hadn't come for her.

Maybe for the boy, though.

For Nicky.

Or perhaps, it now occurs, for what he was running from. Something he did.

She can hear him now, his troubled gasps for air.

But what to do with him?

She goes to the kitchen, selecting a Ginsu knife from the drawer.

She will kill him if she has to.

She knows what he is, by what he comes from.

THE FIRST NIGHT, Samantha doesn't sleep. She remains against the wall, her only comfort a corduroy pillow. She keeps her eyes on Nicky, the Ginsu knife at her side.

She watches him through the darkness, almost wanting to help, to keep him alive, but not at the price of touching him.

Finally, his shakes and shivers become unbearable. She crawls to him, holding the knife. Yes, she will if she has to.

Samantha feels the pulse at his neck, lingering there no longer than absolutely necessary. The beat is frighteningly rapid. He's sweaty with fever.

She finds what she needs in her bathroom, then hurries back, picking the bits of glass from his scalp, cleaning the wound with iodine. The gash does not seem so large to have bled so. He cringes as she applies the antiseptic.

The fever has left him soaked in sweat, hostage to all manner of unceasing, involuntary tremors and twitches.

She holds him up, the knife in one hand, and the back of his head in the other. Wake up, she says, wake up, Nicky.

He does not wake, but yet he obeys as she puts the Demerol on his tongue, a glass of water to his mouth, and tells him to drink.

It is not long before Nicky falls into a deep, calmer sleep.

So begins their routine. Every few hours he rustles, feverish and shivering. And Samantha eases him with the Demerol. He seems to like the Demerol.

But his eyes remain closed. He says nothing, not thank you, not even a grateful nod.

As if this were expected. Who is it that she is to him now, she wonders. A girl? His mother? Did he really accept her medicines mistaking her for his mother? And where did he think he was? Tending to his wound, she encounters a strange jealousy, wishing that someone had tended to hers.

By morning, the right side of his face is black with the blood that has settled around his right eye socket. She calls the gallery, saying she's feeling under the weather, her eyes on him the whole time. Alarmed at the persistence of his shivers, she soaks a washcloth in rubbing alcohol and lays it across his forehead. His trembles continue to prey upon her as the day wears on, until she allows his pitiful condition to affect her better judgment. She unbuttons his shirt, and rubs him down with the alcohol. Just to break the fever, she tells herself.

Samantha must keep her mind clear, and the Ginsu knife at her side.

The evening news leads with the "bizarre" story of the hoodlum and the priest, said to be the "long-lost nephew of deceased godfather Salvatore Colosimo." The two men had apparently toppled from the bell tower of Our Lady of the Most Precious Blood. The police were unsure how to classify the dead men. Murder? Suicide? or Murder-slash-suicide? "Those are all options we presently have under investigation right now," said a police inspector. A loaded revolver was recovered at the scene.

It becomes clear to her now, yes, that's what he had been running from. Whatever happened at the church accounted for both the sirens and for that horribly frantic look on his face. Perhaps, she thinks, he's the killer.

But watching Nicky sweat and struggle through his sleep kills only the notion.

At night, she rifles through his gym bag like a thief, finding his toothbrush, an assortment of T-shirts from the Blood Youth Center, tube socks, briefs, a frayed old photograph of a boxer, a brutish-looking man. It takes her a while to realize who. She runs her hand along the inside of the bag, finding the jump rope. And more. There is a *Penthouse* magazine, a frayed biography of a basketball player who sleeps under mirrored ceilings and wears studded leather ponchos and platform shoes, and a copy of *Ironweed* with the inscription: "This is why the

Jesuits teach you to read and write, Nicky. Give it a try one day. Love, Father Vincent." There is also a stack of old 45's: "Sideshow" by Blue Magic; "Kiss and Say Goodbye," the Manhattans; "I'm Still in Love with You," Al Green; "In the Rain," the Dramatics; "Just Don't Want to Be Lonely," the Main Igredient; "Didn't I Blow Your Mind This Time," the Delfonics; "Cowboys to Girls," the Intruders; "Remember What I Told You to Forget," Tavares; "Break Up to Make Up," the Stylistics; "Natural High," Bloodstone; "Be Thankful for What You Got," William DeVaughn; "Float On," the Floaters; "Mighty Love," the Spinners; "Bad, Bold and Beautiful Girl," the Persuaders; "O-O-Oh Child," the Five Stairsteps; "Have You Seen Her," the Chi-Lites; and "Kung Fu Fighting," Carl Douglas.

The titles make her giggle. Bambi's Banshees had once considered pressing a version of "Kung Fu Fighting."

Now the sound of his voice jolts her with adrenaline. She grabs the knife, clutching the plastic handle with both hands, her back to the wall, waiting breathlessly for the wounded animal to wake.

But he remains more unconscious than ever, caught in the throes of a nightmare. Moaning, at first that's what she hears. But listening more closely, she picks up words of agony, words connected to a pain that runs deeper than the recent wound, the Demerol dreams. She would like to know exactly what those words are, and what they mean.

Even as she holds the knife, her conversion has begun.

She would like to ease his pain. Though she cannot yet admit that.

First, she must protect herself.

Samantha keeps her vigil through the night, the morning, and into the next afternoon, as Nicky continues to fight the fevers of his sleep. She feeds him more medicine, and figures out what it is that she must do.

IN HIS DREAMS, Nicky visits with Buddy, who appears with the red eyes of dead rabbits, Buddy, the silent MC of his dreams, trying to say something, but mute. And his father, who walks along Carmine Street with a big black dog straining at the leash. And Samantha. At night, they walk on the Carolina beach, which is illuminated by the great bank of lights at Yankee Stadium. Dolphins dance like ballerinas on the beach, poised on their tailfins. Nicky and Samantha French kiss until she backs off, giggling, as Nicky spits up the rusty Spanish coin she left in the back of his throat. Samantha has become the waitress from the casino, she has been that all the time. His mouth is warm with the taste of his own blood. Father Vinny comes to his dreams, too, in the church, sitting in the pews, holding hands with Tommy Sick, who puts his gun on a red ring pillow for the wedding, the wedding of his mother, who is marrying the cop, Gallagher, whose best man is Mushy Flynn, the guy from the papers. The priest is Angel from the gym, who presides over a Santeria ceremony. Toodie and Khe Sahn are altar boys. But Khe Sahn has no ear. Dagger-eye, he calmly explains, had bitten it off. The endless spray of wiseguy flowers left over from Buddy's funeral has grown into dark vines, creeping through the church, snaking through the trellis of the confessional. Father Vinny calls time-out and serves the host with Cheez Whiz from Piggly Wiggly, which Nicky, kneeling, struggles to refuse, as his father comes from behind, with the black dog in tow, growling in his ear, Cheech starts hollering, "Stop, Frank, it ain't right," but Frank Battaglia goes right on ahead, pinning Nicky's arms to the velvet-covered table, the chalice tumbling over, Frank screaming, "Eat it. Eat it, goddammit, it's good for you. Boxing builds character."

SAMANTHA BRODERICK HAS anticipated this moment, prepared for it, but still, the first troubled notes in Nicky's awakening startle her. Watching him budge grudgingly toward consciousness incites in her conflicting measures of relief and horror.

He opens an eye, blinking in the beams of a low-slung sun. The last brilliance of an early November day slants in over painted wooden shutters that cover the lower half of the window frame.

But Nicky doesn't know yet where he is.

A new dimension of his hallucination, perhaps, one from which there is no waking, one that takes place in the sharpest slash of daylight.

He sees Samantha against the wall, underneath the still life of white roses and lemons. She is watching him, a knife in her hand.

He tries to free himself.

But cannot.

He must strain to decipher her words.

"Are you all right?" she says. "Are you O.K.?"

Consciousness arrives in stages. There's a great pounding all around his head. Ringing in his ears. His vision goes wacky for a moment, like the stuttering end of a film reel, before returning in better focus.

Again, he struggles to free his arms, only to fail and roll over.

The tug at his wrists is proportional with his effort. It dawns on him now that his hands are bound with the leather jump rope.

"Can you hear me?" she says, lighting a Marlboro.

He nods vaguely.

"I'm going to call the hospital," she says. "I think that's best."

Nicky's eyes grow wide. He shakes his head. "No." His voice is a hoarse whisper.

"The police should know what happened."

"No," he says. "Please." Nicky does not recall much yet. He merely knows he has something grievous to hide. Weakly, he offers his arms to be unbound.

"Why?"

"I had to," she says, drawing on her cigarette. She shakes her head. "I'm sorry."

Nicky struggles some more with the bindings. But his battle is palsied and brief. He slumps over on his side, defeated, his pounding head on the pillow. "Hurts," he says.

Samantha gives him more medicine. When she is sure

he is asleep, she runs her fingers through his matted hair.

Nicky sleeps well now.

Untroubled. Through the night.

Even Samantha dozes off. it has been a while since she last rested. But she wakes in the dark with a fright. Nicky has burrowed across the floor—in his sleep?—to find a place, balled up, nestled against her tight, clenched stomach, her small breasts. His fever has broken.

She tries not to move, but after a while falls into the rhythm of his breath, which is rotten and sweet, like a diabetic's. Samantha finds herself wondering what it was that he had wanted to tell her.

In the morning, she pries herself away and showers. When she returns, he is awake. He says he is hungry. She finds a stale box of Count Chocula, something she had around for binges, and feeds him. Nicky gets a kick out of the cereal box. ·

"Do you want to tell me what happened?"

He shakes his head. "I don't even want to think about that."

". . . Would you like to hear some music?"

He shrugs.

She drags over her carton of records, turning over the album covers one by one for his inspection and approval. "Tell me when to stop," she says, "if there's something you'd like to hear."

Nicky grimaces at the selections like unpleasant Rorschach cards. He is woozy, but without inhibition, and suddenly able to muster a delirious wit. "You got me tied up and you don't tell me why. Now you're gonna torture me? Nothing personal, it's just that you don't know anything about music." He nods at his gym bag. "But I got some in there."

"I know."

"You got a thing to play 45's?"

"Yes." She finds a yellow plastic transformer in her "Bambi Sucks" single.

"Go play me 'Natural High,'" he says.

The record repeats on the first scratch. "You gotta kick it on this one."

She taps the stereo, sending up the first crackly twangs, then the drum, keeping time, one-two-three, one-two-three, one-two-three, clearing the way for those high vocals.

"Where did you get this stuff?" she asks.

"This is the Buddy Love Music," he says.

Samantha's smile makes her nose crinkle.

". . . you wanna slow dance?"

She shakes her head, catching herself. "No, that's O.K."

Nicky stands up unsteadily, never so cute or so manipulative as he is now, smiling, offering her his wrists, asking to be untied. "Please," he says.

"No," she says, smiling slyly herself now. Moving toward him. Leading him.

Sort of.

He has a graceful sway in his step, bound or otherwise. She can tell. The tune is pure syrup:

> "Take me in your arms,
>   Thrill me with all of your cha-a-a-rms,
>   And I'll take to the sky on a natural high,
>   Loving you more till the day that I die . . ."

Gently, she pushes him backward, and Nicky follows her lead with that same graceful step. She puts him down on the couch, slowly lifting his arms over his head. It is a moist ache that overcomes her fear, her anger, her shame, even her grief. She sheds a single tear that disappears into the net of hair sweeping tingles across his cheek.

She understands now; he must never know.

"Where were you?" she whispers.

He doesn't want to say.

"Where?"

"Looking for the dolphins."

UNBOUND, THEY BREAK only for food, the menu of bloody steaks and sweets dictated by her psychotic appetite, for exhaustion, pausing long after midnight to watch black-and-white reruns on the TV, for Nicky to change the record, for odd hours of sleep.

They nest like newborns, engulfed in each other's warmth and puzzlement, each studying the other at rest.

They ravage and ravish: making love, screwing, fucking, sucking. The entire street-corner syntax, those verbs and their nouns—cunt, cock, dick, pussy—now seem woefully inadequate to Nicky. The words are too meager to convey the true awe and obscenity.

They are swollen and sore.

Sometimes, it's like they're praying.

And sometimes, they laugh like children.

There are other moments, too, at the edge of a violence.

He bucks, she bites. She leaves marks over his chest and neck and arms. Like a goddamn vampire, he thinks.

She moans, letting go of a secret sorrow.

She weeps.

At first, her tears give him pause. He doesn't want to hurt her. But he learns that after a certain moment, he is not to care.

"Don't stop," she growls.

Afterward, watching him sleep, she wonders if she has aroused a dormant instinct in him, unleashed the predatory nature of his gender, of his blood.

Of his father.

They never speak of him, though.

And Nicky never thinks to leave.

Each morning, she dresses his wound, secretly longing for the scar to survive.

"Tell me about the dolphins," she says.

"Tell me about the other night," he says.

She does, what she's heard and what she knows.

Nicky buckles with sobs. Hiding his face. His tears make her dizzy and wet.

They do it again.

Spent, she swears to be the accomplice in his continued escape.

CHAPTER
43

AT HIS DESK in the newsroom, Mushy Flynn sits beneath a mushroom cloud of cigarette smoke, a phone in his ear. It's some cutie from the Coast.

"We admire your work," she says. "It has a rich tone, a . . . *noir* quality."

"Of course it does," says Mushy.

"We'd like to do a movie, a feature. There's a lot of talent behind the project. People feel very strongly about this—the themes of betrayal and redemption."

"Or course they do," he says. "You know, I met Louis Mayer once."

"I see."

"It was Vegas. I think. Maybe Palm Springs."

"Really."

"What, you think I make these things up?"

"Oh, no. It's just that, well, do you know how we could get in touch with him?"

"Who?"

"Mr. Battaglia," she says. She pronounces the *G*.

"Frankie Batts? I don't know if that's possible," he says. "I'd have to check with my sources. Things are pretty tight now, if you know what I mean."

"Well, we'd like to sign him."

"But *I'm* the writer."

"Yes, but we feel it's better that way . . . For the integrity of the project."

"Integrity," he screams. "What can you tell Mushy Flynn of integrity. You little twinkie, you."

Mushy hangs up, coughing angrily, and stamps his Lucky in the ashtray—"Greetings from Miami Beach"—the only ashtray on the entire seventh floor.

Nobody appreciates. When will they learn? There is no Frank Battaglia without Mushy Flynn.

He surveys the famous front pages that adorn the *Mirror*'s newsroom. He remembers them all, even the ones before his time, before that donkey editor at the *News* changed his first copyboy byline from Moishe Finkelstein to Mushy Flynn. Across all these years, the front-page stories have become intimate, persistent memories. Ruth Snyder, husband killer. Bruno Hauptmann and the Lindbergh Baby. Willie Sutton, the bank robber. The *Hindenburg*. D-Day. The Dodgers ("We Wuz Robbed"). Anastasia in the barber's chair. Red Scares. Ike. Kennedy. Nixon. Ford to City: Up Yours.

And where, Mushy thinks, will the little pricks put his work? After he is gone, where in the pantheon of tabloid glory will one find the name Mushy Flynn?

Mushy's obsession with posterity varies conversely with his health. Everything's been acting up lately. His emphysema. His plumbing. He runs to the bathroom, ready to pee a river, and what comes out? A few drops that burn like a fire. Try living like that.

The urologist can't figure out what it is. Another little prick, that one.

Just like the editors. What, they think this is easy?

Mushy spits the foul phlegm of his emphysema into a handkerchief. Time is a conspiracy, he thinks.

Dan Parker had Frankie Carbo.

Winchell, he had Lepke.

But Mushy Flynn? What's left for him? Who does he have to work with?

Frank fucking Battaglia, that's who.

Nobody appreciates.

And this Jack Gallagher, a two-bit cop, won't even take his calls anymore. After what Mushy did for him. Made him "Hero of the Month."

Used to be, a deal was a deal.

But that's O.K. Mushy knows how to deal with a guy like that.

Just go the other way.

All you gotta know is how.

Like the other day. Guy calls the paper, demanding an audience with "Mushy's Mob." Guy starts hollering into the phone: "Why do you guys always have to make 'em into something they're not. Even when you rip 'im you let 'im take a bow. This guy's a rat bastard coward, always has been. You all shoulda knowed he was gonna turn."

"Yeah, Mack," says Mushy, "and how the hell did you know?"

"I seen him fight."

It's taken Mushy this long to realize this guy's soused. "Sure, Mack," he says. "Sure."

"At the Garden."

"Uh-huh."

"You don't believe me, you bastard. I was his god-damn cutman."

"His what?"

"Ain't you listening? I was in his corner."

"What do you drink, sir?"

"Wild Irish."

"My favorite."

Half an hour later, Mushy is buying drinks at an Eighth Avenue Blarney Stone around the corner from Costello's gym. The wino—his name is Jackie Farrell—is a mess, a character exactly as Mushy figured—not a homeless guy. Not a displaced person. Just an old-fashioned drunk.

"I think I'll have a rye," he tells the bartender.

"Moving up in weight class, huh?" says Mushy.

Jackie gives him a sour look.

"Make it a double," says Mushy.

The drunk gives up the whole story. Frank had the great Paddy Blood in his corner. It was December of '65

at the Garden. Some journeyman from Philly or Newark—
"a colored kid we brought in to lose, just to move a few
rounds with him," is how this Jackie puts it—stand up to
Frank's big punch. Frank panics. He comes apart in the
ring. "No heart," says Jackie. "Even as a kid, this Frank
Batts was a bum."

"What was it you said before?"

"He died like a goddamn dog."

"That's it." Mushy points at Jackie's empty glass.
"Another," he tells the bartender, sliding a twenty spot
under the glass. "Keep 'em coming." Mushy flips up his
collar and turns to leave.

"Where you goin'?" Jackie asks.

"I gotta pee."

NOW, IN THE newsroom, Mushy thinks about Jack
Gallagher, that fucking ingrate. Wait'll he reads this. The
cops don't like it when you make the rats look bad.

That's O.K. Next time, the little prick'll return the call.

And when he does, Mushy will just go back the other
way. Make Frank into a hero: the Man Who Blew the
Whistle and all that. Play up the redemption angle. Even
up the score.

Sure. It's all sportswriting.

That's what Runyon said. Something like that.

Then again, look what Runyon had to work with—
Pretty Amberg. An ugly little monkey that one. Pretty
Amberg bought a laundry business just so he had enough
bags for all the corpses.

Dutch Schultz once told Pretty, "I'm coming in as your
partner in Brooklyn."

"Arthur," said Pretty. "Why don't you put a gun in
your mouth and see how many times you can pull the
trigger."

Then there was the time Pretty spit in Buggsy Gold-
stein's soup. Buggsy didn't say a word. And Buggsy
Goldstein was a tough son of a bitch. One of the old
Murder Inc. crew out of Brownsville.

Mushy lights a fresh Lucky, trying to remember
Brownsville. The circuits of his memory have atrophied.

But that doesn't stop Mushy Flynn. Quite the contrary. In his advanced year, Mushy's remembrances are more inspired than ever. He can now place himself at the scene of famous conversations and crimes. He was there, at Midnight Rose's, Saratoga and Livonia, under the el. He was there. He remembers Dukey Maffetore reading L'il Abner comic books between jobs. He heard Pittsburgh Phil brag about the rope trick, about going after a guy in a movie house with a fire ax, about killing Georgie Rudnick for Lepke. They found Rudnick's corpse with sixty-three stab wounds. Pittsburgh Phil, sure, real name Harry Strauss. Used to go with a girl, cute dish named Evelyn Mittelman. They called her the Kiss of Death Girl.

Mushy remembers them all: Dasher Abbadando, Happy Maione, Puggy Feinstein, Louie Capone, Mendy Weiss, Abie Reles, aka Kid Twist, the wingless canary who flew out of the Half-Moon Hotel while under twenty-four-hour police guard.

What could a man of Mushy's gifts have done with a Kid Twist?

Brownsville, thinks Mushy, gathering another phlegmy cough into his handkerchief. Brownsville, the greatest gangsters in the world. His father could never understand. Mushy's father smelled like pickle brine. All the man could do was work and pray, daven at the shul. He hadn't any imagination. And that was a far greater obstacle than language. The old man could never become an American.

They lived on Dumont Avenue. And what is Dumont Avenue now? What is Brownsville? Housing projects, that's what.

Has ever a good story come out of a housing project? One decent front page? Of course not. A few guys tried making up something a few years back, calling it the Black Mafia. But no one wanted to hear that. It didn't sell.

Mushy holds off the urge to pee. He knows it's just a tease. He must wait, which he does, smoking and coughing while considering his enduring accomplishment, the inky fable he has made of this Frank Battaglia.

I should have gone into the movie business, he thinks.

And here comes the little prick, the boy editor, giving Mushy the thumbs-up sign like some smiling politician.

"Great shit," he says, trying not to notice the smoke.

"What's the head?" Mushy asks.

The editor spreads the page proof over the desk. Tomorrow's front page will read: THE NIGHT FRANKIE BATTS . . . DIED LIKE A DOG.

"Where's my exclusive tag?"

"We'll get it in there."

Again, the little prick gives the thumbs-up sign. What a putz. "Great shit," he says again.

"Great shit?" says Mushy. "These are goddamn poems for the masses. Something for the poor bastards to remember."

"They sure are."

"Put it up on the wall," says Mushy, excusing himself to go pee.

CHAPTER

44

NICKY GETS OUT out of the cab under the cover of night. Samantha's kiss lingers at his lips like an oath, even as he walks up the old decrepit steps to the Empire gym.

He stops for a moment to listen. He can hear Toodie scolding someone . . . Khe Sahn, who responds in a pleading, whiny voice: "Yo, T, man, I just need little more time. You know, get my head together." Nicky feels like the worst kind of intruder. He tries to be silent but the stairs announce him, bending and creaking under his weight.

All conversation ceases as he appears in the doorway, in the flickering light of Angel's Puerto Rican voodoo candle.

Toodie's jaw drops, his eyes settling into a contemptuous glare. Khe Sahn stares at the floor. But Angel turns his Yankee cap brimside backward and breaks into a smile. "Holy shit," he says. "My man come back from the dead."

Nicky waits at the door for permission to enter. But Toodie turns his back and takes a seat on the ring apron, muttering to himself. Nicky watches as Angel huddles over his shoulder, whispering in his ear. Toodie shakes his head stubbornly. But Angel continues to negotiate until Toodie gives a disgusted shrug.

Angel waves him in. "You look good, kid," he says. "You get laid or something?"

"Why'd you come here?" asks Toodie.

"I . . . I . . ."

"Why?"

"I got no place to . . . I needed a place . . ."

"I thought you had a place. In Alaska. Or wherever it is they put youse."

"Didn't work out."

"Didn't work out, huh?"

"I thought . . ."

"You thought what?" Toodie snaps.

"C'mon," says Angel, "cut 'im a break."

Now Toodie glares at both the kids, Nicky and Khe Sahn. "Cut me a fucking break, huh?" he says. "These fucking kids."

Angel nods at Nicky and says, "You owe him, Toodie."

"I owe him?"

"You owe him. And plus, you stupid? He ain't got no place to go."

"Nah, that's all right. I'll find somewhere," says Nicky. ". . . Just tell me one thing?"

It embarrasses Toodie to realize that he's actually trying to stare this kid down. "What?"

"That story in the paper? About my father, him fighting at the Garden?"

"I wasn't there."

"Yeah, but you know. Is it the truth? Would Jackie . . ."

"Lie?"

"Yeah."

"He's a mean old prick and a wino. But no, he ain't a liar." Toodie looks sadly toward Khe Sahn. "Matter of fact, he was right about a lot of things."

"So it happened just like that, like the guy wrote up in the paper."

"First time that newspaper guy was ever right. I mean, that's the story I always heard."

"Who told you?"

"Paddy Blood. He's dead."

"Yeah, but what did he tell you?"

"He said whatever you do, don't get involved with people like youse."

Angel makes a face. "Stoopit," he says.

"People like your old man," says Toodie.

Nicky turns to leave, but Angel Cruz motions at Toodie to call him back. "C'mon, Toodie," he says. "Do the right fucking thing."

Finally, Toodie calls back at the boy. "Hey, pally," he says.

"What?"

"You gonna tell me what happened to you?"

"What?"

"Who cut you?"

". . . my girlfriend."

Toodie lets go with a big burst of laughter. Khe Sahn looks puzzled. Angel says, "Your girl? Damn, Nicky, you too young to be gettin' into freaky shit like that."

Nicky begins to laugh at himself. "Yo, least it ain't ugly as yours, Toodie. Where'd you get that?"

Toodie pulls a dripping, cold sixteen-ounce Budweiser from the metal ice bucket he keeps under the ring.

"So?" says Nicky.

"*So?*" repeats Toodie, taken with the boy's newfound impudence. He pops the can and licks at the foam. "So I got it in Rikers. I was young." He looks over at Angel. "I gotta tell him the whole goddamn story?"

"Who's it gonna hurt?"

"Fuckit. Me and some friends get caught snatching chains in the subway, you know, stupid kid shit. A couple of undercovers grab us. The guy who gets me, he's dressed like a rabbi, comes out of nowhere: black coat, black hat, those Jewish Jheri curls hanging off the side, whole bit. They get me and another guy, I forget his name, except that he used to wear those big blue suede Pro-Keds, and that one time, when we was little, I kicked his ass on the street."

"I remember that," says Angel. "You little punk-ass bully."

"Anyway, the cops are real mad at me 'cause I have one of those Saturday night specials in my belt. I wasn't gonna use it. I just wanted to feel like a tough guy . . . Ain't that right, Khe Sahn?"

"I ain't saying nothing."

It now occurs to Nicky that Khe Sahn was never here to work out, that he's been in street clothes the entire time.

"So they bring us down to the precinct," Toodie continues, "or whatever it is in the subways. Dingy place. They put us in different rooms, and start working us. Hard."

"Whattaya mean?"

"They think we're like part of some ring or something. Like we're all little Dillingers. I don't know, maybe a reporter wrote an article on chain snatching that week. Whatever, the cops were real hard-ons. They get me alone, they start telling me I don't have to do no time. Not if I'm smart. You know, 'Help us, we help you.'"

"I don't get it."

"Ask your old man," Toodie shoots back. "They want me to rat everybody out. They go, 'Here,' and show me this piece of paper. They say, 'Your friend signed.' I say, 'Fuck you.' I don't know why, that's just what I said. So they start slapping me around, banging lockers, just trying to make me scared. You know, saying, 'The brothers at Rikers gonna love a cute little white boy like you.' Now they give me a paper to sign, an agreement, they call it. Say, 'This is your last chance.' Now I'm scared shitless, I gotta admit. I'm thinking about ratting 'cause I'm like what, seventeen, eighteen, 139 pounds, that's what I was in the gym, anyway, and I don't wanna go. I never did no time. I told them, 'Gimme me the pen, I'll sign.'"

Toodie takes a long swig from his beer.

Khe Sahn says, "So?"

"Another one with so," says Toodie. "Why you wanna know so bad? The way you're going, you'll be back there soon enough."

"Yo, Toodie, man. I tole you. It ain't like that."

"Nah, it's never like that, Khe, is it?"

"Whajda do?" asks Nicky.

"What would you do?" Toodie's eyes are all over him, waiting for an answer.

"I don't know," he says quietly. "But I know what I'd want to do."

"Yeah? What's that?"

"Eat the paper."

Toodie breaks into a big grin.

"That's what this nigger did," screams Angel. "Toodie ate the mo'fucking paper. That's a true story."

"And that's how I got cut," he says. "I was going to shit it out."

"Huh?"

"In Rikers. I got jumped going into the bathroom. Guy just cuts me—wwwhhhsssttt—opens right up. But I don't feel nothing. Again, I don't have no idea why. That's just how it happened. Next thing I know, I'm all over him, banging his head on the bowl. Boom. Boom. Boom. He's done, like a rag doll. But I'm not stopping. I'm not gonna stop till I kill this guy."

Toodie pauses, waiting for Nicky to nod cautiously, an uncertain gesture that leaves him wondering if the kid actually understands that his instincts were rational, even ethical, within the context of the jailhouse. Toodie kills his beer and continues.

"Then I feel something from behind. Like a pipe. It's the CO's, they're clubbing me to get off this fuck before I actually do kill him, maybe thinking I already did. And that's when I felt the pain. Shot right through my back. Like, I don't even know what, sort of a comet, if you could imagine that. Then everything goes black."

"Damn."

"I wake up in the hospital. Stay there awhile, then, they put me right back in population, back in the dorm. Fucking terrible place. Like hell, only you're living. This time around, though, no one messes with me. See, the guy I cracked was some kind of bad ass, supposed to be, which is bullshit, too, 'cause everyone there was just another bully. Still, all you can do is wait. For the next time. You know someone's coming for you, you just don't know when. So you think about it until that's all you can think about. Until you're good and crazy. You make yourself a shank, thinking: You're gonna do someone if you have to. You'll kill somebody. It becomes a thought, a real one. At night, you can't sleep. You're hearing sounds you don't even want to know what you're hearing. You wanna put the pillow over your head, but you're scared if you do, you're not gonna see the guy when he comes for you. Finally, I get word to Angel. He comes down to see me."

"I never seen my man so scared," says Angel.

"I tell Angel my case is coming up, but I can't hack it no more. I gotta get out. One way or another."

"You was gonna excape?" asks Khe Sahn.

"You could call it that . . . I guess." Toodie cracks another Budweiser. Ordinarily, he'd never let the kids see him drink. But tonight, telling the story, he feels loose. The beer's cold, tastes great. Toodie's already light-headed.

"My court date comes up," he says, "and I'm thinking, I don't even got a lawyer. I figure they're gonna give me one of those freebies. The guys who look at you and say, 'Why didn't you take the deal, asshole?' Then I go see the judge. He tells me I got another lawyer, a pay lawyer, practically introduces me to the guy. Some big shot, real slick. Now I don't know what the fuck is going on. Judge says, 'Does anyone have anything to add before I pronounce sentence?' And who got something to say?"

"Who?" Nicky asks.

Toodie smiles wistfully, his eyes meeting Angel's. "Paddy fucking Blood. That's who."

"I tole Paddy about my man here eating the paper," says Angel. "The old man, he like that story."

Toodie continues, "So Paddy gets up there, the guy's wearing a suit and his Buster Browns. He's got that real white old man's hair. To me, he's looking like fucking Santa Claus. He tells the judge, 'Your honor, I know this young man and I can vouch for his good character.' This comes out of nowhere. You gotta understand: before I got popped, I go to the gym every day, I work out like a son of a bitch, and Paddy, he never even notices me. I figure he didn't even know my name. But there he is telling the judge, 'Your honor, this boy's made some mistakes, and I promise to kick his ass into tomorrow. But you have to understand, sir, this boy here, he has no parents. I am willing to assume that responsibility, Your Honor. I have arranged for employment for him, and I'm willing to become his legal guardian. Our attorney has the papers all prepared.'"

"The way ole Paddy was talking," says Angel, "I thought the judge was gonna cry."

"Me, too," says Toodie. "But then the judge looks at me, says, 'Is that acceptable, young man?' And I'm shaking my head up and down, like, yes, yes, yes, sir. Like, what the fuck else am I gonna say? Then the judge goes, 'Suspended sentence. Five years' probation. Now will you please get the hell outta my courtroom, you little bastard.' On my way out, Paddy's checking out my scar. Calls it a little beauty mark. Asks me, how come I didn't slip it?"

"Fucking guy," says Angel.

"Then you became a fighter?" Nicky asks. "Right?"

"I never did become a fighter."

"I thought . . ."

"Nah, what happened was, he put me in the ring. But I couldn't fight no more. My back would clamp up on me like a vise. That was from when the CO's hit me. It never really healed. For a while, I couldn't even breathe much less fight."

"You could never fight anyway," says Angel. "You was too fucking angry."

"So Paddy says, 'You still gotta repay me.' 'How'm I gonna do that?' I say. 'I'm gonna teach you how,' he says. 'You're gonna train the fighters.' And that's what I did."

"Then, he marry my sister," says Angel. "If I knew that, I never woulda axed Paddy to help straighten him out. Now, they gonna have a kid—half Puerto Rican, half white boy, or whatever it is that you are. Actually, I think my man come from wolves."

"Irish-Jewish," says Toodie, slurping on the Budweiser.

"Jewish?" says Angel. "Shit, I never knew that."

"My mom. I told you about her. She was crazy."

"Well, you is what you momi is," says Angel. "That's what it say in the Bible. So you crazy. You crazy and Jewish."

"I guess," says Toodie, pulling the last two beers from the bucket, handing them to Nicky and Khe Sahn. "Here," he says. "It's O.K. Cheers."

Angel puts his Yankees cap on Toodie's head.

"What are you doing?"

"You'll see," says Angel. "You gotta have a hat."

"What the fuck," says Toodie. "How's it look, Nicky?"

"O.K."

"You're on the run, huh?"

"I guess."

"You do anything bad I should know about?"

"Nah, like I said, it just didn't work out. So I came back."

"You can't go back to your neighborhood."

"No," says Nicky. "But there's still some things I want to know."

"About your old man?"

"That's part of it."

"What's in the bag?"

"My stuff."

"Well, I hope you got some good stuff in there. You know everybody's gonna be looking for you. The cops, the feds, your own people . . . or whatever they are."

"I know."

"Where you gonna go?"

"Haven't figured that out."

"Can't stay with your girl?"

"Nah. She lives in my building. My old building, I mean."

"Neighborhood girl? You trust her?"

"Yeah, I trust her. It's not like what you think."

"If you say so." Now Toodie pauses, adopting a more formal tone: "I have to tell you that I'm sorry about that day when I put you in the ring. I hope you accept my apology. I was angry. But I don't mean it as an excuse. It was unprofessional. You're not a fighter, Nicky. I shoulda told you that from jump street. That's nothing bad on you, I want you to understand. It's just, you're not cut out for that, to be a figher."

"I never wanted to be one."

"Funny thing was, I always liked how you moved. I mean, the way you move, it's pretty, it's natural. There's just more to being a fighter than how slick you can look when no one's fighting back."

"I understand that. It don't bother me no more."

"Good. I'm glad."

Angel takes the beer can from Toodie's hand. "I'm gonna need that," he says.

Angel is arranging things to an order only he can fathom: the bottle of dragon's blood, his divine aerosol sprays, the beer can, a leftover bottle of Jackie Farrell's Wild Irish. He produces a White Owl cigar and a pocket Bible. "Good," he says. "Ole Testament."

"What the fuck are you doing, Angel?"

"Just keep the hat on your head. You gotta wear the hat."

"What?"

"You a Jew, right?"

"Yeah?"

"So, I'm helping you out. I making you a, whatta they call that? Bar mitzvah. That's it. I'm making you a bar mitzvah, Santeria style."

"Holy shit."

"I be the rabbi," he says. "It's all the same anyway: Catholic, Santeria, voodoo, Jewish, Five-Percenter. I mean, basically, it's all about getting blessed, getting forgiven for when you fuck up."

Toodie, Nicky, and even Khe Sahn fall into giddy hysterics watching Angel prepare his ceremony. But as their laughter winds down, they can hear footsteps.

Someone's coming, the creaky stairs announcing his arrival.

"Who the fuck is that?" says Toodie. "Khe, check it out."

Khe Sahn peers quickly down the staircase. "White man," he says. "Look like a DT."

Now Jack Gallagher bellows from below: "Nicky! Nicky, you up there? . . . I'm too old for this shit, Nicky. I just wanna talk."

Toodie sees the panic on the boy's face. "Khe," he says, pointing toward the back window with the fire escape. "Get him out of here."

"Me?"

"Go. Now."

"C'mon." Khe Sahn leads Nicky away, down the fire escape and into the night. Nicky can hear himself gasping for air as they sprint across the rubble-strewn lot, toward the fantastically absurd graffiti mural, the tribute to his brother. Run, Buddy tells him, faster. But Nicky trips on the rubber remnants of a tire, scraping along the pieces of broken bottle and brick. Khe Sahn helps him to his feet.

"Where we going?" asks Nicky.

"The Ville," says Khe Sahn. "We going to the Ville."

CHAPTER
45

KHE SAHN HOLDS his arms high as they enter the project courtyard.

"What you doin', Khe?"

"So no one bust a cap in your white ass," he says. "It's all right, though. They all work for my boy, anyway."

"Who's your boy?"

"He want to meet with you."

NICKY'S FIRST NIGHT in Brownsville, they watch movies on Khe Sahn's VCR. The first show is *Enter the Dragon*.

"Yowa style is vewy good, Mista Lee."

"Monkey Style," says Khe Sahn. He is very impressed. Nicky knows all the words.

During the chain saw scene in *Scarface*, Khe Sahn says, "This is my boy's favorite. This movie."

"Yeah?"

"He think he *is* Scarface."

"No shit."

"I'm Tonio Montana and I want my chuman rights. That's what he always say."

"Khe, you mind if I ask you something?"

"What?"

"You still fighting?"

"Course I'm still fighting. Why you think I ain't fighting no more? It ain't like that. You think that guy hurt me in Atlantic City? Nah, it ain't even like that. I'm just—what you call it?—I'm just taking me a little vacation."

"Oh."

"But don't tell Toodie I said it like that. He don't understand. He don't wanna understand."

Dawn arrives halfway through *Scarface*, and Khe Sahn decides he is tired. "I goin' a bed. You could sleep here, on the couch. It ain't bad. My mom go to work in the morning. But she won't wake you up."

"Your pop?"

"Nah," he says. "Tomorrow, I let you meet my boy. Take you 'round the way."

THE NEXT AFTERNOON, Khe Sahn shows Nicky the sights. He drives a Suzuki Samurai, on loan from "my boy."

As a landscape, Brownsville is relentless—black and blue and gray, shades of gunmetal. The neighborhood is an inheritance for successive generations of the poor. The staccato Sicilian sounds have been replaced with lilting Caribbean cadences. Bodegas and Baptists replace fruit stands and Jews. The Rockaway Boys and the Amboy Dukes and the New Lots Boys became Tomahawks and Jolly Stompers and Five-Percenters. But Nicky doesn't see that, what has happened through time. Nicky's view is mismatched houses, storefront churches, makeshift body shops, basketball courts, planes of ruptured asphalt, barren lots, one after another. Leaky hydrants run into dirty gutter streams. Small children play among the husks of stolen cars, wheelmen commandeering getaways in the make-believe morning, while their brothers, older but just as ignorant of consequence and time, fire Glocks and Uzis and MAC-10s, giddy with the street's new, standard issue of ammunition, nine millimeters in diameter. Young men, survivors of stomach wounds, walk with their colostomy bags in tow. The streets are patrolled by ghostly legions, lonely as lepers, these new bums, the crackheads, collecting odd artifacts for barter in carts pirated from the supermarket or the post office depot. Treachery is part of the landscape. Yellow crime scene tape remains at odd corners fluttering in the wind like broken party ribbon at hangover time. And over everything, as sturdy and enduring as the pyramids and Sphinx, loom the projects, rising in their unclean colors, giving dimension to the treachery, until they become part of the horizon. After a day or so, Nicky knows their names: Albany, Brownsville, Glenmore Plaza, Howard, Langston Hughes, Sethlow, Tilden, Van Dyke, and toward East New York, Cypress Hills and the Pink Houses.

But Nicky travels through unmolested, his safe passage guaranteed by Khe Sahn's boy.

KHE SAHN PULLS over at Sutter and Stone, barking into the school yard. A man walks toward the Suzuki, strangely familiar to Nicky as somebody who used to be somebody else—sunken eyes, tall, maybe six-five, an agonizing stick figure sucking on an ice pop. His voice slurry and slow as cough syrup.

"What it is, Khe?"

Khe Sahn stares at him hard. "Don't 'What it is' me, know what I'm saying?"

"Yo, I'm gettin' that together, taking care a that right now. I'm expecting some shit coming in real soon."

"Don't let it get out of hand."

"I hear you, Khe."

"You know it ain't up to me. It's my boy you fucking with."

"Yeah, yeah, but, Khe, that's what I'm talking about. See, I gotta get right to get you right. See what I'm saying?"

"Don't play that shit."

"Yo, who the white boy?"

"That ain't none a your business."

"Damn, Khe. I'm just axing. Thought maybe he one a them gangsters you be talking about. That man you said bought the gym, got you that gig in Atlantic City. You know, that man in the paper. Yo, I read about him all the time. That's some cold shit, boy."

"I ain't got time for this. I'm busy," says Khe Sahn. "Just make sure you come up with the bank. I can't be making no excuses for you."

"Yo, Khe, you heard about when they shot me, right?"

Khe Sahn rolls his eyes. He knows better than to get into conversations with pipeheads. "Man, what you bothering me? That was a long time ago."

"Yeah, but now I only got one lung, see." The stick figure pulls up his T-shirt to display his scar, a nasty ridged pit in his back. "But mo'fuckers can't hurt me. I'm indestructible. Shee-it. Take Cagney and his girl, Lacey, to do me. But see, the only thing I need is oxygen. And that's what I'm talking 'bout, Khe. You gotta help me breathe."

"Nah."

"You wouldn't a said that back in the day."

"Well, we ain't back in the day no more."

"Yo, Khe, we was boys. 'Member when you was a kid? You be crying like a little baby at the park. I use to bust niggers' ass for picking on you."

Khe Sahn dislodges something under the dashboard and hands it to the man, whose limbs seem like those of a giant praying mantis. "Yo, I gotta put that on the account. Now leave me alone."

Driving away, Khe Sahn turns to Nicky and asks, "Know who that was?"

"Pipehead, so?"

"Yeah, but who he used to be?"

"I kept thinking I seen him somewhere, but I couldn't figure it out."

"You 'memba Skylab?"

"Get outta here."

"That was him back there."

"That's him? My brother used to tell me about that guy. Said he was the baddest ballplayer in the whole city: more moves than Julius, talked more shit than World. They say he used to paint his name on the bottom of his shoes so dudes would never forget who it was who threw it on 'em."

"I'm tellin' you."

"Damn. Skylab. Now he's a pipehead?"

"A customer. Just not a good one. Remember when they used to talk about Skylab, the real one, the spaceship, like, where was it gonna fall?"

"Yeah?"

"Well, the way I figure, Skylab fell right here," says Khe Sahn. "In the Ville."

Khe Sahn drives on, feeling uneasy with Nicky's eyes on him.

"Yo, Nicky, man. Why you gotta be like that?"

"Be like what?"

"Least I got a job."

"Yeah, what's that?"

"Director of Security, that's what my boy call it."

"Yeah, but what do you call it?"

"Yo, what you 'spect me to do? Flip burgers for the clown? Fuck that shit."

"I thought you was a fighter."

"I am. But fuck that shit, too."

Khe Sahn's beeper goes off. "Yo, it's time to see my boy."

Khe Sahn's boy calls himself Tony Montana, after the movie character played by Al Pacino. And like the celluloid Scarface, Khe Sahn's boy has become very rich, very fast, the quality of his merchandise having acquired a fine reputation among the local pipeheads. On Fridays, after the city checks are cashed, they line up around the block to get some of what he's selling in those little plastic vials.

Tony Montana wears shiny double-breasted suits he buys from A. J. Lesters in Harlem and a gold cap dollar sign over his front tooth. He adores gold. He is partial to a diamond-encrusted medallion with a legend that reads "The World Is Mine," and also, a huge three-pointed star, the Mercedes emblem in solid gold, which he wears when driving around the Ville in his Benz.

A pair of bodyguards follow him everywhere—two

big kids named Unique and Understanding. He calls them "Double U," and buys them "W" medallions to wear around their necks. Tony Montana is good to his employees, a least those who are good to him, treating them to dinners at Red Lobster, and handing out the newest, top-of-the-line Nike sneakers as Christmas bonuses.

Tony Montana talks of purchasing a model home in Dix Hills, Long Island. He needs a place to put his things. Tony Montana's got a lot of things. It is his obsession to order items from the Hammacher Schlemmer catalog: artificial putting greens, sterling silver martini mixers, shoe shine machines, recessed globes, video cameras, egg timers, foot massagers, a set of porcelain mugs, each with the name of a different Ivy League college, electric pants pressers, electric money counters, even a miniature electric-powered replica of his Mercedes-Benz.

"Hadda get that," he says, "for one a my sons."

Tony Montana is a devoted father. Sometimes, he leaves "command central," as he calls the abandoned garage on Lott Avenue, in the charge of Double U to be with one of his babies' mothers.

"Gotta take that bitch to *Lemans* class," he says, excusing himself.

Tony Montana is twenty-one years old. He has never done time.

And he loves having Nicky around, likes to pick his brain. "Yo, Nicky," he says, "you could be like my consultant."

Of course, Tony Montana is very big on the movies. He has all the gangster epics, from Cagney to Pacino, on videocassette. "My li'bery," he calls it.

"Yo, Nicky," he asks, "when they sign you up, you know, initiation, they really do all that, like, they give you a gun and cut your finger, then they burn a paper in your hand?"

"I don't know."

"Reason I axe, is I seen it in *The Valachi Papers*."

Tony Montana also has a great collection of tapes, all

the contemporary rap standards, of course, but also, the definitive collection of theme music from the blaxploitation movies: all the *Shaft* soundtracks, *The Mack, Foxy Brown, Three the Hard Way, Superfly, Trouble Man, Cleopatra Jones, Across 110th Street,* and so on.

"Yo, Nicky," he quizzes, "who did *Foxy Brown?*"

"Willie Hutch."

"Damn. What about 'Love Doctor'?"

"Millie Jackson."

"Yeah, but what movie?"

"Cleo-patra Jones."

"Check this boy out. Yo, Nicky, gimme a few bars, you know: 'Are you man enough, Big and bad enough, Are you gonna let 'em shoot you down . . .'"

Nicky picks it up, "'When the evil flies and your brother cries, are you gonna be-ee a-rou-ou-ou-nd.'"

"That cracks me up, when you do that old corny ass shit. Yo, Nicky, where you learn that?"

In due course, Tony Montana gives Nicky a tour of his operation. The product is cooked and bottled and bagged by sloe-eyed, bare-breasted women during all-night shifts called episodes.

"We got 'em like that so they can't steal," he says. "You could even touch they titties if you want. Just don't mess with the product. You know what the man say, 'Don't get high on your own supply.'"

TONY MONTANA IS an avid fan of Mushy Flynn.

"Yo, Nick, man, you know this dude from the papers? I call him the Dick Tracy Man."

"Nah."

"He like from the old days, you know what I'm sayin'? Like Cagney, he from that time, like, the black-and-white time."

"I guess."

"He be writin' all about your daddy."

"Tell me about it."

"That ain't nothin' bad. If he be writing 'bout so much about yo' daddy, that make you famous, too."

Nicky shrugs.

"I wish I was famous," says Tony Montana.

ONE NIGHT, SKYLAB arrives at command central.

"I tole you not to come here no more," says Tony Montana. "I got a reputation."

"I'm here to straighten everything out," says Skylab, trying to smile through a feverish sweat. "I got my shipment in, brother. But I need some oxygen bad."

"Wha'choo got?"

"Lookit." Skylab unzips his hooded sweatshirt, revealing a bulletproof vest. "And I gots more, too."

Tony Montana takes a seat in his deluxe, leather-quilted, mail-order recliner. He considers the vest until his face turns sour.

"This shit ain't no good," he says. "Too light."

"Stop any kind of bullet," says Skylab. "You could check it out yourself."

"Yeah?"

"Shit, yeah. Guarantee or your money back, jack. I leave it here with you now, just lemme get some shit now so I could get breathing."

Slowly, carefully, with great deliberate glee, Tony Montana pulls a shiny silver .25 from his jacket.

"Yo. That ain't what I meant," says Skylab.

"You said check it out. If it works, you be high for a week."

". . . You ain't really gonna shoot me, is you?"

"Nah, I ain't gonna shoot you," says Tony Montana. A sly smile spreads across his face. He tosses the gun at Khe Sahn. "Khe," he says, running a line of Pacino's from the movie, "choot dis piece a chit."

Khe Sahn holds the gun tenuously, staring sadly at the piece.

"Do it," says Tony Montana.

"Yo, I . . ." Khe Sahn can't take his eyes off the gun.

Skylab is dripping sweat now. "Fuckit," says Skylab. "Shoot. The shit works. Just don't be missing."

Nicky shakes his head. "Don't," he says. "Don't do it, Khe."

"Ain't nothing personal," says Tony Montana. "Just bidness. And it ain't no bidness a yours, Nicky. This shit's between the brothers. So shut the fuck up."

"G'head," yells Skylab. "Shoot."

"W'choo waiting for, Khe?" says Tony Montana. "Fuck it, you can't do it, I get Double U to do it."

"Do it, motherfucker," screams Skylab. "Or I tell everybody what a punk ass nigger you really are."

The gun reports with a wicked echo, leaving Nicky red-faced, with ringing in his ears. He feels as if he's been smacked.

Skylab drops to the floor squealing. Khe Sahn stands there helplessly, still holding the gun, looking apologetically toward Nicky. But Nicky does not acknowledge the glance.

Tony Montana nods at Double U. "Yo, don't be letting that nigger die here."

Unique and Understanding walk over to Skylab, standing over him. "Yo, wake up," they say.

It takes a while. Skylab is good and groggy as Unique and Understanding remove the vest. A purple welt rises on Skylab's chest.

"I tole you it work," he says.

Tony Montana throws a dirty look Khe Sahn's way. "And I tole you, it wasn't no thing," he says. "Now get Skylab some a that shit. And get him the fuck outta here."

CHAPTER

46

THE SOFT EVENING light off Washington Square Park casts a burnished glow over the mahogany furniture in John Vanderpool's office. Adjusting his bow tie in the mirror, John Vanderpool can't help but admire himself: natty cuff links, silk scarf, slicked hair. It's not difficult for him to see why that grandmother of gossip who writes for the *Post* recently referred to him as "the dashing John Vanderpool."

As he thinks of it now, Frank Battaglia has been a very good client. As Frankie Batts, this creature of the tabloids, he's endowed his attorney with a certain cachet, which, truth be told, doesn't hurt. John Vanderpool has been at Frank's beck and call for . . . has it been that long? . . . since graduating from Columbia, trying to build a practice while living on his trust fund. His father had tried to warn him off. His father had wanted him to go to Sullivan & Cromwell. But that seemed so pedestrian to John Vanderpool. There were no Frank Battaglias at Sullivan & Cromwell.

Yes, it's been a while. John Vanderpool knows all about Frank, more than anyone, really. It's all in his files.

He had been wrong to worry so. Actually, Frank had made the best decision. For Frank. But also for John

Vanderpool, professor of criminal procedure. The attention, quite frankly, has been overwhelming. Tomorrow, he'll conduct a symposium at the law school: The Ethics of Informing.

A lawyer cannot make decisions for a client. An attorney is merely bound to provide his best advice and his utmost discretion. That's what John Vanderpool has done, no more no less, for Frank Battaglia. And tomorrow, when the students ask, that's what he'll tell them. Tonight, however, there's other business at hand—the ballet. He'll be escorting a baroness. It's a blind date. No doubt, she'll want him to regale her with true tales of the Mafia.

It takes the dashing John Vanderpool a while to realize that he is not alone.

Someone is watching him.

Smiling at him through the mirror.

"Excuse me," says John Vanderpool. "May I help you?"

It is the type of smile—so mirthful in its menace—that quickens the blood.

"Is something wrong, sir?"

The smiling face comes forth from the shadows, drawing closer, silently, like a mime who makes a comedy of dread. The pleasant light does nothing for him: a jagged shock of blond hair and what seems like a teardrop tattooed about his left eye. He picks at his nails with a stiletto knife.

John Vanderpool has seen many such knives, all of them sealed and marked in glassine envelopes. And now the thought occurs to him that this knife will be marked into evidence, too.

"You'll have to go," he says.

Dagger-eye shakes his head.

Something ghastly tugs at John Vanderpool's bowels. The baroness flashes into his mind.

"I have something for you," says the man, "from Mr. Philly Testa. . . ."

CHAPTER
47

TONY MONTANA LOUNGES on his recliner reading Mushy Flynn.

"Yo, Nicky, man, you know this guy? Yo' daddy's pay lawyer?"

Nicky's trying not to listen. He's not in the mood for Tony Montana. Or Mushy Flynn. He wants to be left alone to daydream of Samantha. He wants to see her so bad. The other day, he spoke to her on the phone. She asked him to touch himself.

"Yo, Nicky, I'm saying something."

"Yeah. I know him. So?"

"Well, he got kilt."

"What?"

"Says here, he got cut up pretty good." Tony Montana holds up the front page: "Message from the mob . . . written in blood."

"Lemme see that." Nicky snatches the paper and reads:

John Vanderpool, longtime lawyer and confidant to star stool pigeon Frank Battaglia, was found in a pool of blood in his office at New York University Law School.

Dead as a doornail.

The grisly discovery was made by a minor countess who came looking for him, thinking that the well-heeled barrister had stood her up for their night at the opera.

Bravissimo.

Once again, the Gods of Irony smile on Mushy Flynn.

Vanderpool was scheduled to preside over a symposium at the law school tonight—the Ethics of Informing. No doubt the lawyer would have given an impassioned lecture, defending Frankie Batts's inalienable Right to Rat.

But the Mob, true to its own treacherous ethics, delivered its own dissertation first—written in blood.

The assassin's crude instrument—a common stiletto knife—was left at the scene . . .

Nicky flings the paper across the room.

"They probably after you, too," says Tony Montana.

"How would they know?" Nicky asks sharply. ". . . Unless somebody here gave me up?"

"Yo, Nicky. Don't be looking at me like that. It's yo' daddy who's the rat."

"Fuck you."

"What you say?"

Unique and Understanding look to Tony Montana for instructions.

"Don't hurt the boy," he says. "He just upset is all."

Now Khe Sahn walks into command central. He must have run over from the Tilden projects, as he seems out of breath.

"Look who showed up," says Tony Montana. "Mr. Stone Killer."

"Nicky, I gotta talk to you," says Khe Sahn. "Toodie beep me. Say he gotta meet with you to talk. Says hurry up."

"Where's he at?"

"At the gym."

"What did he want?"

"I don't know. He wouldn't say. Just that it was like, real important."

"You goin' back to the city, you gone need a piece," says Tony Montana. "Double U, give my boy one a yours."

Understanding holds out a nine millimeter for Nicky. "Nah."

"Yo, Nicky, man, don't be stoopit," says Tony Montana.

"I don't need it," says Nicky. ". . . I ain't a tough guy."

"You want me to go with you?" asks Khe Sahn.

"No. Not if you have to ask."

"Yo, Nicky," says Khe Sahn. "You gotta do me a favor."

"What?"

"Don't be telling Toodie 'bout the other night . . . You know, what I did."

"I ain't gonna tell. Who do you think I am? That's your own fucked-up business."

TOODIE IS LEANING on a parked car when Nicky arrives at the Empire. He has that same ashen look he had that night in Atlantic City, when Khe Sahn collapsed in the corner. "Something's happened," he says.

"Just tell me."

"It's hard to explain. First, I gotta ask you to trust me."

"It's not the kind of thing you can ask."

"I know. But you gotta anyway."

Nicky closes his eyes for a moment, taking a deep breath, gathering himself, willing to take Toodie at his word, until the moment is expired, and his eyes are open again and he can see Jack Gallagher coming into view, coming from across the street, a sour expression on the cop's face as he slurps from a cup of coffee. Nicky moves to bolt, but Toodie pounces on him before he can. Toodie spins him around, pinning him against the parked car.

"You fucking bastard. You ratted me out."

"I would never," Toodie whispers. "Please understand."

THE HOSPITAL IS an old one built in the name of an apostle. And waiting for the elevator, Nicky finds himself studying the statue of Jesus: the flinty plaster, the bright shiny paint, the maudlin rouge pigment in the skin tone. Gallagher has tried to prepare him, explaining all that he could. Certain papers were recovered in Vanderpool's safe, legalisms pertaining to the custody of a terrible secret. Gallagher had tried his best, even Nicky could see that. But mere explanation was insufficient. What he was saying went beyond reason, Nicky thought, and could be accounted for only by a magic most evil.

Nicky steps off the elevator docile and dizzy, with Gallagher a pace ahead. A pair of blank eyes greets them through a window slit on the other side of a green steel door. Gallagher shows his badge and the locks click open.

Inside, all colors dissolve into institutional shades of drab. Lunatics in green smocks shuffle along the linoleum floor, their destinations unknown. Some maintain a vow of silence, while others are ever in the midst of modulated, medicated rants. An old lady plays a piano, repeating the same soft notes that begin a Bach cantata, again and again and again. A man in a flannel shirt concentrates on the clock on the wall, keeping one eye closed as his finger traces an arc in line with the second hand.

They share a common pallor, a sheen made even more ghastly by the fluorescent din. They are ghosts, but ghosts as distinct as the people they used to be.

Gallagher leads Nicky down the corridor, pausing at the door. "Are you sure?" he asks.

Nicky opens the door himself.

Buddy is looking at the sun through stained gauze curtains.

He turns around slowly, revealing that he, too, has been infected with that bloodless complexion. His color is like oysters.

Buddy stares at his brother, his gaze unhinged.

"They said you were coming," he says. "When they gave me the salt."

Nicky retreats into Gallagher's arms.

"The saints," says Buddy. "They told me."

It is all Nicky can do to speak. "Buddy. It's me."

"The dogs," he says. "They have rabbits for puppies."

CHAPTER
48

BACK AT THE gym, Nicky asks if it's okay to stay awhile.

"I got a cot in the back," says Toodie, noticing the blank look in the boy's eyes.

Nicky's eyes seem dead. But his mind is cold and clear, like ice. He knows exactly what he's doing.

"I don't know if we can do that, Nick," says Gallagher. "I think you gotta come with me."

"I think it's a little late for that," says Nicky. "I mean, you can make me. But I'll just cut out again. I didn't sign up for nothing and I didn't break no laws. Besides, how would it look if I ratted you out for what you did? You see, I don't mean to be a smart ass, but I ain't going."

"Well, I can't force you to do anything," says Gallagher. "The government can't, either. But I'm sorry for . . . what you been through. I wish you'd let me . . . you know, if there's anything I can do."

"Of course there is. What, you thought I was gonna let you off the hook?"

"I shoulda known."

"I want something from both of youse. Toodie, I want you to make me a fight. And not a bullshit one. A real one."

"You don't wanna do that."

"It's not what I want to do. It's what I have to do."

"That's nonsense, Nicky. And you know it. You ain't got nothing to prove."

"No, that's where you're wrong. I'm not doing this for you. I'm not doing it for my father. Not even for my brother. This is for me. Don't you understand?"

Toodie shakes his head.

"This isn't about fighting no more," says Nicky. "This is the way I get well."

"You should think about this some more."

"Kidding me? I been thinking about this my whole life. Why you think I can't fight for shit?"

"C'mon, Nick. Who'm I gonna get to fight you?"

"I got a guy in mind."

"You're not a fighter."

"Just one fight."

"One fight," Toodie says weakly.

Now Nicky turns to Gallagher. "You gonna help me out, too?"

"Anything."

"I don't want anything. I want a promise."

"You got it."

"I want you to bring my father."

"Jesus, Nicky."

"I know you ain't gonna break your word. And another thing, that reporter? The guy in the paper?"

"Yeah?"

"Bring him, too."

"Why?"

"I want him to write a story," says Nicky. "A big story."

GALLAGHER GOES THROUGH the whole thing with Toodie. He tells Toodie all about how Frank took his own goddamn son, Frank Jr., the one they called Buddy, and put him away in a hospital ward for lunatics. Paid off all the right people, Frank did, slipped some bills to the patrolman, who probably wasn't about to ask questions anyway, took care of a clerk in the medical examiner's office, a guy from the funeral home, probably even the priest who did the service. "Who was gonna know?" says Gallagher. "Frank went down to the morgue to ID the body himself. Who's gonna tell him it isn't his kid? Who? No problem: the casket was closed, the papers were kept with the lawyer, this scumbag Vanderpool—we found them in his office. That fucking pig, the father, a rat, cocksucker, coward, bully motherfucker.

"I think I almost understand it, though. I mean, how the guy thinks. Him and the son never got along. But something happened, the kid got busted for some kind of fight with some Jamaicans in the park. One of those drug dealers, those guys selling loose joints, you know who I'm talking about? One a them died. And the cops pick up Frank Jr. The charges are dropped—but not before the son goes away to Rikers. It don't take a genius to figure out what happened in the joint. By the time the kid gets out of Rikers, he's all fucked up, wacked in the head. Starts talking about Frank like he's the devil, starts embarrassing Frank in public, carrying on, causing scenes at fag joints, telling Frank he was gonna kill him. I think I understand; the son scared the shit out of Frank. Things got worse and worse. Next thing you know, Frank buries someone else in Junior's casket."

"Who?" Toodie asks.

"We think it was some kid," says Gallagher. "Some neighborhood jerkoff got popped trying to hustle a couple of keys. They thought he was gonna snitch. Imagine that. Word is, his old man ran a pork store. Matter of fact, I spoke to the guy myself, an old-time Sicilian guy, trying to get him to turn on Frank. Guy used to wait hand and foot on him at the club. I don't know if he knew anything, but he wouldn't give up Frank. Just couldn't do it."

"It's gonna come out like that?" asks Toodie. "I mean, in the papers."

"Fuckit," says Gallagher. "Let the experts straighten all that out. The guys from the Bureau, they're great at fixing that kind of shit."

"Yeah?" says Toodie, watching Nicky step into the ring. "And how they gonna fix that?"

Nicky has been training with a fury. But something in the boy's eyes makes Toodie shiver. It's been two weeks, and the eyes remain dead as they were the day Nicky came back from the hospital. He's seen too much.

Up in the ring, Angel blesses Nicky—a sprinkling of tap water and some of that Puerto Rican mumbo jumbo for his soul. But Nicky looks right through him. The kid has something else in mind.

The bell rings, and Nicky takes quite a beating.

That's how it's been since his eyes went dead.

The eyes are a light on the imagination. Yet that has gone dead, too. Before, Nicky let his thoughts run wild, paralyzing him with fear. But now, his imagination has been snuffed like a candle. Having suffered, he understands too well: the punches don't hurt so much.

Nicky takes the punches. And keeps on taking them.

Toodie has seen guys take shots before, trying to show how hard they are. But Nicky, he doesn't even flinch.

It's not natural.

What the fuck, Toodie thinks. It's like the old man used to say: Boxing is psychology, not physics. But who can figure out what's in this kid's head?

Is he trying to prove he can survive? Or does he just want to punish himself?

Now Santana, the Tasmanian Devil, who beat Nicky so badly months ago, steps in behind Toodie. He forces a queasy grin, watching as Nicky tries to ordain himself with a beating. "Yo, my man went off his nut, huh? I hear his brother is bugged, too."

"Mind your business, you," Toodie snaps.

When the bell rings, ending a relentless three-round pounding, Toodie grabs Nicky by the arm and takes him to the lockers. He wipes the blood from Nicky's mouth, nose, and chest with a wet sponge. Then he gives the kid a smack. "I don't know what you think you're doing, what you're trying to prove, but if you keep it up, I can't train you no more."

"They can't hurt me," says Nicky. "None a them."

"They don't have to. You're doing it all by yourself. That's not being a fighter."

"So you said yourself, I ain't a fighter."

"Don't get wise with me. It's a lot tougher to slip the punches, to see them coming, to deal with them, than to pull the shit you're pulling. Nicky, you're acting like the worst kind of dog. You just figure it's easier just to get hit. That don't make you tough. Just another asshole who hates himself."

"Put me in with Santana."

"Why? So he can beat on you some more?"

"No, I'll do it the right way. You got my word. You don't like how it's going, you stop it. Throw in the towel. That's your insurance. You don't think I want it known you threw in the towel for me, do you? Besides, how'm I ever gonna fight the other guy if I can't get by Santana?"

"You ain't fighting that guy. I don't want no part of that. Not him."

"Why don't we talk about it after I spar Santana. Then you could make up your mind."

Toodie knows the kid's trying to manipulate him with a cold logic. But he also feels an obligation, as if he must talk Nicky down off a ledge. "Okay, we'll see," he says. "Just don't get nutty on me, though."

"Don't worry about that, Toodie. You know why?"

"Why?"

"Boxing builds character." Nicky winks.

But those dead eyes, they still make Toodie shiver.

"YO, I AIN'T gotta take it easy on him or nothing, do I?"

Toodie looks Santana up and down, no longer able to mask his contempt. "Nah," he says, "just do what you gotta do."

Nicky waits for Toodie to walk off before approaching his opponent. Now he blows a kiss at Santana. "I did your mommy."

"What you say?"

"You heard me," says Nicky, climbing into the ring. "She was good, too."

"I'm a give you some pain, motherfucker."

And that's what Santana does. Driving Nicky up

against the ropes. Using his elbows, his head, the laces of his gloves. Going for the Adam's apple, the liver, the kidneys. Trying to go low.

Nicky takes it.

Angel and Toodie stand by at ringside. Toodie is clutching the towel. He's seen enough. He's going in to stop it. But Angel yanks him back by the arm. "Don't," he says.

"I ain't letting this go on," says Toodie. "Not in my place."

"But I gave him the magic." Angel holds up a playing card, an ace of hearts. "I put one a dese in his cup," he says. "For courage."

"You stupid fuck."

Toodie makes a move, but Angel tightens his grip.

Up in the ring, Santana throws a wide, vicious hook.

But Nicky doesn't take this one. Instead, he comes up and under, then around, switching places with the Tasmanian Devil.

His right hand is perfect. Toodie's never even seen him throw a right.

"Get the fuck up," Nicky yells.

But Santana's out cold.

"Get up," he screams.

Toodie throws down the towel in disgust.

"See," says Angel. "I tole you."

NICKY SHADOWBOXES FOR three-minute intervals, improvising in front of the mirrored panel.

Angel watches him closely. "I seen what you did the other day," he tells him between rounds. "That shit you pull with Santana. Getting him mad like that."

"But I thought . . ."

"I know what you thought, sounding on his moms to get him all crazy."

"Worked, didn't it?"

"It work with Santana. But that shit ain't gonna work with who you wanna fight."

"I ain't scared no more."

"Who you kiddin'? You more escared than ever."

"But remember that story you told me about you and Duran?"

"That's me and Duran. That's not you and this animal. That ain't gonna work for you, talking 'bout his moms."

"Why not?"

"First, 'cause he's already loco. Second, I don't even think he got a momi."

The buzzer sounds and Nicky resumes his shadow-boxing.

"Still too stiff," says Angel. "Too much white boy."

"I need more magic."

"Don't worry, kid. I brought you some." Angel slides a radio-cassette box across the floor and pushes the play button. "Stop punching," he says, "and check this out."

The tune is tinny but familiar: funky Latin disco percussion under a row of horns led by a driving soprano saxophone and a deep African voice talking shit, somewhere between scat and rap.

"I know the song," says Nicky. "'Soul Makossa.'"

"You know it?"

"Manu Dibango, 1973."

"Damn, Nicky."

"So?"

"So? This is what you need. Some a that funky mojo shit in your step."

"I don't get it . . ."

"Lissen to the song, kid. How he's doing it in the song, that's how you gotta fight. You need some more a this." Angel demonstrates, putting his hands on his hips, shaking his pelvis Hula Hoop style. "You gotta get more easier here, more relaxed."

Angel turns up the volume. "Now try again," he says. "Like you was dancing. And one more thing, get that stupid look out your eyes. You ain't fooling no one with that."

Nicky moves well with the music, throwing an easy sway through his shoulders and his hips.

"That's what I'm talking about," says Angel, nodding in approval. "Play dat funky music, white boy."

Toodie comes over. "What are youse doing? Am I running a gym or a fucking disco?"

"Look how nice I got him moving."

Watching Nicky dance, Toodie puts his fingers to his temples and shakes his head, like he's got a migraine. "What the fuck." He can't argue with results.

Angel does the Hula Hoop bit again. "See, what I mean? The kid gonna need this to fight that guy," he says, pulling down an eyelid with his index finger.

"He still ain't fighting that guy."

"Sure he is, T. Look at him. All he needed was some theme music."

AT NIGHT, SAMANTHA comes to him in the gym. She finds his nervous, fumbling urgency kind of comic, but endearing, too. At first, it is all she can do not to laugh. She strokes his hair. But he's ready again. And again.

They fall into varied rhythms, awkwardly at first, but always building, until they are desperate and wailing for relief.

Those nights, Nicky clings to her hair, tugging at the tangles like a spoiled baby. Wanting her that close. He begins to anticipate her tears, to treasure them, to want and expect them: crystal slivers hardened by her secret grief. Nicky never even thinks to ask. But he is sure; she makes these tears only for him.

He is ashamed of how he saw her that first day on the stoop. That feels like an age ago. She is so much more than he could have known. Each moment uncovers new ecstatic epiphanies. Her perfume, of course, but also when she is stale with sweat and smoke from her cigarettes. There are sly, subtle oils in her spit, in her pussy. He could never have thought to consider the pebbled texture that rises with her nipples, or the taut muscles in the small of her back—for she is rigged tight as the mast of a ship—or the brocade of sinew laced around her forearms, or her oddly thick, blunt fingertips, or the way that her hair feels sweeping across his chest, like a cold silk scarf.

She is a potpourri of ingredients foreign to him, aged

with flavors he could not even know. He does not yet have the palette or the words for them: cinnamons and cedars, pine, wheat, chicory, butterscotch and Brie, sherry, walnuts, caramels and licorice, the salt of a foaming sea, the drift smoke of smoldering leaves in autumn.

Samantha dwells too long on the wounds he has collected in the gym. She anoints them with kisses. Her guilt is secret, too. She wishes for new ones to tend.

Then they are spent, and there is a mother in the way she cradles him. Through the skylight comes the dawn, as sad as a stillborn.

She leaves only to return.

Some nights, Samantha shows him another city. They watch great balloons blown up for the Thanksgiving Day parade. They go to the Empire State Building. It is late and lonely on the observation deck, a fierce wind howling in their ears. He can barely hear her as she hikes up her skirt and tells him what to do.

There is another evening, one that they move through like a waltz, bright lights and big windows turned out for the holidays. Fifth Avenue is filled with the scent that rises off salted trays of hot pretzels. She wears a tartan plaid jacket with a velvet collar. She looks like something stolen from a Christmas tree. Her breath rides out to him on winter chill. It makes him dizzy with want.

"Where are we going?" he asks.

"A party," she says. "An opening."

At the gallery, she introduces him as her brother. The plump owner takes him aside and tells him all about the paintings, the importance of the work, the form, the noble primitivism of this hot young artist.

"Spray paint creates a more impressionistic line than you might imagine," he says.

Nicky walks away without excusing himself. He knows all about the hot new artist and his work. More than this fat fag from the gallery will ever know. Nicky guzzles the white wine like Budweiser and goes to take a piss.

But the bathroom is occupied.

The graffiti artist himself is slumped against the toilet, defeated. The syringe hangs off his arm like a broken stem.

Toussaint looks up from his nod. "I wanted to pray for your brother," he whispers. "I just didn't know how."

IN THE MORNINGS, after Samantha's departure, after his roadwork along the FDR Drive, Nicky visits his brother in the hospital.

Buddy speaks snippets of prophesy and myth and backward memory, but very little sense. He talks about his friends the rabbits and the dogs, which Nicky comes to understand as the imaginary emissaries of their father.

"What time is it?" Buddy asks. "Is it time for the salt?"

The nurses deliver the salt with paper cups of luke-warm water. They have the manners of nuns and arrive at regular intervals. The salt has another name, lithium.

It makes Buddy shiver and shake.

Nicky, too. Watching the tremors that register on Buddy's bluish, bloated face, Nicky can feel the dread emanating from his very marrow.

He considers the lithium for himself. Perhaps, if he ate one, they could again find a common language. But Nicky decides not. There aren't any magic cures. Only places he no longer belongs. He's just beginning to understand that.

Sometimes, Buddy's trembles cross a border, from benign to berserk. "They're coming," he cries.

The dogs.

"They can't hurt you," Nicky whispers. "I'm going to kill them all."

"Ma lit a candle for me. But they blew it out."

Nicky holds Buddy's head against his chest, rocking his brother with a tenderness he learned from Samantha. He can hear the crazy old lady playing her piano out in the hall.

"Where did you go?" Buddy asks.

Nicky tells his brother about the dolphins. Buddy seems to understand. Lucid glimmers come as his shakes subside: fragments of humor and truth and remembrance.

Nicky throws out careful questions, quizzing his brother, wanting to make sure he is not an impostor.

"Mary Missile Titties?"

"I thought there was rocket ships in my ass," says Buddy. "Like I wasn't gonna stop."

"Thurman Munson?"

"Reggie was better."

"Remember when Pop threw me in the pool?"

"I took care of him, didn't I? That was before he killed the rabbits that lived across the street from the pork store."

"What was Clyde Frazier's baddest suit?"

"Baby blue lambskin."

"Who was it he could never check?"

"Pistol Pete."

"What about Skylab?"

"Wrote his name on the bottom of his sneakers."

"Who took the girls to loveland?"

"Larry from the Floaters."

"Who was tougher, Bruce Lee or Richard Roundtree?"

"Sonny Ciba coulda kicked both their asses."

Satisfied with Buddy's answers, Nicky returns the next day with Angel's box and a tape he's made. Nicky considers them agents of the exorcism, his own magic.

Together, they go through all the tunes. Nicky and Buddy sound awful, off-key and out of time. Nicky's voice has grown too deep for the high tenors and street-corner sopranos, while Buddy's has become weak and squeaky. But a faint light comes to his eyes as Nicky retrieves the memories with his crude choreography: the spins, the slides, the two-steps. Nicky commands rainbows and raindrops with arcs of his hand.

"I'm your backup singer," said Buddy.

The nurse knocks at the door.

Nicky turns off the radio and tells her to go away.

It's time for Buddy's medication, she says.

Buddy is sitting on the bed, balled-up, his arms over his knees, shaking his head. "No," he whispers.

"Go away," Nicky yells.

And she does, the nurse's easy surrender inciting

Buddy toward a giddy state. He can imagine music in his head now, *Shaft in Africa*.

"Are you man enough?"

"Big and bad enough," Nicky answers.

Buddy begins to laugh. "Yo, Nicky," he says. "Boxing builds character."

Nicky pulls back the gauze curtains. The sun is blinding.

"Did you hear what I said?" Buddy asks. "Boxing builds character . . . Get it?"

"Yeah," Nicky mutters.

"What's the matter?"

"I'm gonna fight tomorrow."

"Don't let him hurt you. Please."

"He can't."

"Why?"

"'Cause you already gave me the magic," says Nicky, squinting into the sun.

"When?"

"When you ate the paper."

Buddy stares at him, wanting to see what his kid brother sees. "Nicky, don't talk crazy," he says. "It scares the shit out of me."

CHAPTER
49

THE DODGE ARIES moves up the FDR, over the Willis Avenue Bridge, to the Major Deegan. Gallagher gets off at the Yankee Stadium exit. Toodie directs him from there, through the uphill side streets. He's been here before, many times.

A sharp turn onto Jerome Avenue leaves a wino staggering with his bottle. In the backseat, Angel taps Nicky. "See that?" he says. "My man, he don't spill a drop."

Nicky remains mute.

Toodie flashes Angel a troubled look through the rearview mirror, thinking: How'd he let himself get talked into this one? When he got to the gym this morning, the kid was alone, dry heaving over the slop sink.

"There's nothing says you have to do this," he told him.

"You said you'd never lie to me."

The gym is up a ways on Jerome, in a blackened brick tenement, an abandoned sweatshop on the second floor, even with the elevated tracks of the number six train. Nicky trails Toodie and Angel and Gallagher up the steps, made of steel and concrete. The stairwell is cold

and hollow and carries the vague odor of urine. Nicky
has never felt so lonely, so weary with loneliness. He can
hear the crazy echo coming from behind a steel door at
the top of the stairs.

A potbellied Puerto Rican guy with black greased hair
is waiting for them at the landing. His name is Manny
and he's wearing a stained guayabera shirt and drinking
from a pint of Bicardi. He greets Toodie with an
embrace. *"Comó está*, Toodie. What it is?" He offers a
shot of the booze.

Toodie declines. And Gallagher excuses himself, saying that he has to check on things. But Angel accepts the
hit of Bacardi. It would be bad luck not to, he says,
before slurping the liquor off the plastic cap.

"Where is he?" says Manny.

Toodie jerks his thumb at Nicky.

Manny nods at Toodie, but keeps a suspicious eye on
the boy. "People is talkin," he says.

Toodie gives him a hard look.

"Don't mean nuttin' to me," says Manny. "I just want
for it to be a good show."

"Where we going?"

Manny pulls back a burlap curtain on the other side of
the landing. "Right here," he says. "We put the other guy
in the other room. Keep 'em separate. Is better like that."

The dressing room, a bathroom, is very cold. Nicky
changes, then examines himself in the mirror. His skin is
dry and white. A wave of nausea washes through his gut.
He sits on a battered toilet while Toodie wraps his hands,
very carefully. When Toodie is finished, Angel begins to
knead the muscles in his shoulders and neck. "You gonna
be just fine, kid," he says.

Gallagher pops his head in, wants to see if everything's O.K. But Angel and Toodie wave him off.

Nicky sits still, the color gone from his face.

Toodie tells him to get up and start moving. There are
reasons for these rituals. Toodie knows: Sit too long and
the fear claims you. It begins to tighten like a harness
around your chest.

Nicky starts to move, but draws no sweat. He can hear full-throated cheers coming from the arena.

Angel's mumbling prayers. He gives Nicky an ace of hearts for his cup, and sprays him with a cool mist, holy water from the tap.

"Cut that shit out," says Toodie. "You gonna freeze him to death."

Soon, fat Manny in the stained guayabera shirt comes in with a fresh pint of Bacardi and cups made of frosted, translucent plastic, the color of hospital bracelets. "I gotta check the gloves," he says.

Toodie ties the laces and runs circles of tape around the wrists. "That too tight?" he asks. Nicky shakes his head. Toodie knows that words are worthless now, still, there are things he wants to tell the boy. But Nicky seems far away, staring at the floor, drifting into that docile state again. Finally, Toodie jerks Nicky by the arms. "Hey," he says.

Fat Manny scribbles his initials on the tape. "Gotta make it official," he says.

Then, pouring rum into plastic cups, he announces a toast. "For *cito*, here. For Junior."

The men nod at Nicky before throwing back the rum. The liquor burns.

"We ready," says Manny. "Is time."

Nicky feels something suck the air out of his chest.

Toodie taps him under the chin. "We're going out there now," he says. "Put your hands on my shoulders."

Nicky does as he is told, grievously obedient, following Toodie, who leads the way wearing a rolled-up towel like a collar. Angel falls in behind him. Nicky can smell the liquor on his breath.

Past the burlap curtain, the steel door opens. Angel has to nudge him through. "Don't worry nothing," he whispers, "everybody is escared."

The gym is roaring as little kids, maybe seven or eight, pummel each other in the center of the ring, flailing as their time draws to a close. The little kids delight the crowd: women in tight jeans with baby strollers, rocking the progeny of various fighters, rum-soaked men, gamblers displaying their faith with worn bills. The room smells of butane from portable heaters that look like torpedoes, and of fry grease from the empanadas and green bananas and the hot dogs.

Nicky studies the little kids, the winner hoisted on his father's shoulders, the loser alone, looking for somebody. A tear escapes from the child's eye as he rushes past Nicky toward the landing.

Now, fat Manny gives the signal. Nicky is marched into the ring.

The noise builds to a steady self-sustaining din. Nicky waits in his corner like a condemned man. He watches Gallagher escort a stooped old man to his seat. Mushy Flynn does not carry himself with any of the arrogant humor Nicky had expected. He clutches his fedora as if someone would take it from him. Every few feet, he stops to spit into a handkerchief. His cheeks are hollow. But his eyes are piercing.

The arena shakes as a train rumbles over the el.

When it passes, Nicky hears his name being called. He turns to the voice.

Frank Battaglia is sitting ringside, behind his son's corner. Lars is next to him, waving, munching happily on a hot dog. His father is more pale and more thin than he remembers; the bulky arrogant chest seems to have evaporated. The razor scar has settled across his face like a thin whip of red licorice. "Nicky," he cries. "Nicky."

A cry for mercy. But Nicky gives none. He's bankrupt of mercy; he hasn't any left. For either of them.

Now, the opponent. Nicky knows much more of his opponent than the flared nostrils, the snarl, the teardrop tattoo. He is intimate with his opponent in ways that seem almost ancient, as old as blackened bricks and broken glass, as the stink in the stairwell, as the blood of all minor myths in a city that repeats itself.

The spider crawls up Nicky's back as he takes leave of himself, waiting for the bell to sound.

CHAPTER

50

HE WAKES GROGGY with pain, his feet dragging on the pavement as Toodie and Angel carry him from the Dodge Aries across Bedford Street, up the stoop, to the apartment on the first floor.

Mushy watches from the car. "Will he be all right?"

"Depends what you mean," says Gallagher. " 'All right.' "

A moment passes, with Mushy thinking that Toodie and Angel are too solemn for his tastes.

"Oh shit," says Gallagher. "Almost forgot."

"Forgot what?"

Gallagher gets out of the car and opens the trunk. The painting, Salvador Dali's *Discovery of America by Christopher Columbus*, is waiting there, tagged as evidence with tiny yellow stickers pertaining to its status in the chain of custody. Gallagher takes it and hurries into the building.

Mushy calls to him from the car. "Can I come with you?"

"What the fuck."

Mushy follows, watching everything from the doorway over Gallagher's shoulder.

Toodie and Angel put the boy down in a girl's lap. A

skinny girl, but well bred, that much is obvious. She strokes his hair, a sublime tenderness in the way she touches him, looks at him. She is his antidote, his medicine against the violence. She is the Mystery Blonde.

The moment endows Mushy with an enchanted, incandescent vision. He can see through things, through walls, through flesh, through brain matter. He can see through her belly, two tiny dancers, blood and light.

Gallagher holds up the painting as an offering.

The Mystery Blonde looks up from the boy and shakes her head, no.

"Me and Angel gonna hang around awhile," says Toodie. "Make sure the kid's all right."

"Yeah," says Gallagher. "Listen, if there's ever anything . . ."

"Yeah. Sure. 'Preciate."

And that's how it's left.

Gallagher drives Mushy back to the Chelsea Hotel.

"You live here?" he says, watching an obese black drag queen walk into the lobby. "I never knew."

Mushy shrugs. "I never thought of it as permanent."

Gallagher points at the bronze plaques at the entrance.

"Who are they?" he asks. "They famous or something?"

"Poets," Mushy answers.

"They should put you up there."

Mushy laughs. "Me? I only wrote one good story the whole time."

"What was that?"

" 'Hero of the Month.' " Mushy puts out his hand. "Thanks, Jack. For everything."

"Don't forget the picture."

"Me?"

"Take it, Mushy. Nobody needs it no more. It's a fake."

Now Mushy Flynn moves through the hotel lobby, past those absurd papier-mâché renderings, the drag queen, and the latest fuchsia-maned pilgrim pleading at the front desk for the Sid Vicious room. A leather-clad dominatrix gets off the elevator accompanied by her snake and her slave, an ex-physicist who has lived here in her service since his release from the sanitarium. They say madness seized him while on fellowship in Brussels, that the equations no longer made sense. He had discovered his calculus to be insufficient, a lie. It lacked magic.

Brilliance and bullshit, Mushy thinks.

The comedy is superb.

Light-headed with bliss, Mushy presses his floor and the elevator kicks into a cranky gear. They say the elevator is haunted. *They* say. Hah! Another sportswriter's trick. He leaves the painting in the elevator. Let someone find it. Let 'em make up a story.

What the fuck.

Mushy's room is December dark, save for the faint glow, almost wet, the traces of neon from the sign beyond his window. Mushy goes to the bathroom and tries to pee. But nothing happens, and so he lies down in bed too tired to remove his clothes.

He's down to his last Lucky.

Smoke 'em while you got 'em, he thinks.

Mushy lights up as the pigeons begin to gather outside his window, their tiny claws clamped to the railing of the ornate iron balcony like toy gargoyles. He listens to them coo. Mushy had always expected winged creatures, sure, but birds of greater ceremony. Hawks, condors, doves. That was how it ought to be, he had thought. But pigeons? Dirty little fuckers. The notion is enough to make him laugh aloud, which he does, until his hysteria gives way to the phlegmy cough.

Mushy's fakery has been exquisite—gangsters and rats and Mystery Blondes—it was all sportswriting, and the cure comes late. But he's thankful nonetheless.

The boy has liberated him. Nicky is his name, Nicky Battaglia. He must remember that, for it must travel with him.

Memory's light is liquid, but still more than clear enough. The boy has allowed him to see things as fantastic as they are true. And this truth is so much better than any of his cheap sportswriter's imaginings.

The opponent was as perfect as the kid. The tattoo—

the dagger dripping blood—was a nice touch, but when you come down to it, that, too, was just a bit of bullshit. Mushy could have thought that up on his own. No, the opponent's value lay in his bare, relentless sadism, the manner in which he dispatched with pretense, with boxing, distilling pure violence from sport.

The kid made a go of it, jabbing and dodging, slipping and sliding from punches with a nifty wiggle and shake. Mushy could see that the moves were all part of the cornerman's instruction, a minor comedy demonstrated between each round, this Spanish guy shaking his hips in some sort of mambo time.

Nicky went down early with a crashing right hand. His logic was impeccable, for the instinct, anybody's, is to submit. Nicky went to his knee, looking around, looking for excuses, until he could find none. Until he got up.

He got up again and again and again.

And again, tried to dance and to dodge.

But the physics between Nicky and his opponent were all wrong. There was no cute method for the kid to avoid the Dagger-eye.

He knew all the low tricks, mauling Nicky into the ropes, coming up headfirst, gashing Nicky at the bridge of the nose. He laced the boy, a move Mushy hadn't seen in years, the motion like almost a curve ball, leaving blood in the boy's eye.

But still able to wiggle away. Nicky slipped a few more punches and jabbed back with his own. Dagger-eye kept coming, though, catching Nicky's jab and locking the arm against his left side. Dagger-eye began to pummel in earnest now. A greater, more beastly pummeling than Mushy had ever seen.

There was a cry to stop the fight, a familiar echo, as old as New York. But the boy stood. He was pitiless. Mushy looked to the father, and saw that ghastly pallor spread across his face, the crimson flash of grief in his eyes. It was then that Mushy understood, sharing that glance between father and son. Nicky's endurance had already been proved. But now, he had turned the burden, all of it, upon his father. He had twisted the equation magnificently.

The blows were now being suffered by the father.

And the blows began to repeat themselves with blood.

The blood of our fathers, Mushy thinks: syrup and salt, sugar and brine.

More than Frank Battaglia could ever handle.

He staggered to the ring, to his son's corner.

And threw in the towel.

Now, a pigeon flies into the room, fluttering in and out of the darkness.

But Mushy's too tired to argue. He feels something warm run down his leg.

He must gather his strength for remembrance. The kid in the ring. In this moment, Mushy admires the mass, the Catholic sense of order and hierarchy, of fathers and sons and holy ghosts. Shit, Gallagher told him everything, Frank and Nicky and what was the brother's name, Buddy. Yes, that's it, they called him Buddy but he was named for the father.

The pigeon begins to pray. Is it mass? Or Kaddish? All things considered, he'd rather hear the Kaddish. *Yisgadal, v'yiskaddash sh'meh rabbo* . . . yes, that's it, only Mushy can't place the voice. Tiny Colosimo? Is that you, Tiny? No, no, no. Not him. Not anyone. And not any prayed blessing, either, but brilliance and bullshit, beyond his own feeble imagination, beyond words, beyond even language. Magic.

It is only magic that makes things the way they ought to be.

Like the kid, Nicky, going back through time, straightening things out.

And Frank Battaglia, throwing in the towel.

Would have made a helluva story.

ACKNOWLEDGMENTS

I'd like to thank Teddy Atlas, the most stand-up guy I know.

Also: Joe Sexton, for listening; Phil Ward and Denis Hamill, for the kick in the ass; David Vigliano and David Gernert, for their faith; Barry Weiss and Amy Rosenbloom, for being like family; Mike McAlary, for his optimism; Kevin Whitmer, for the time; Dan Klores and Abbe Goldman, for the place; Bruce Kriegel, Greg Drozdek, Susan Marchiano, Amy Williams, Charlie Sennott, Joe Ponzi, Harry Ahearn, Louis N. Scarcella, and James Nauwens, for technical assistance; and Johnny Pettinato, across all the years, for everything.

"Poignant and hilarious."—*Los Angeles Times*

"Absolutely charming."—*Chattanooga Times*

"Beautifully written."—*Publishers Weekly*

"Sort of a fundamentalist 'Life with Father' told with the loose familiarity of Holden Caulfield."—*Milwaukee Journal*

"Charming."—*Boston Sunday Globe*

"Splendid laugh-out-loud moments."—*Kirkus Reviews*

"Under Mr. Schaeffer's graceful rendering, this is a story of sympathetic characters, a deft feat considering some of their narrow views."—*Washington Times*

"The wonderful thing about this book is that it feels like a vacation."—*Richmond Times-Dispatch*

PORTOFINO
by Frank Schaeffer

__ 0-425-14981-1/$6.99